About the author

The author was born in Scotland and, after serving in the Army, embarked on a career in industry.

He has worked in several different sectors in senior roles and was latterly CEO of a large international data capture company.

He retired for the first time in 1995 to take on a consultancy designed to help new businesses become established.

In 2018, he finally retired from business life to become a full-time author.

John lives in Scotland and Portugal with his wife and they have two grown-up sons.

THE WATCHERS
The fourth DCI Burt murder mystery

JOHN REID

THE WATCHERS
The fourth DCI Burt murder mystery

Vanguard Press

VANGUARD PAPERBACK

© Copyright 2022
John Reid

A CIP catalogue record for this title is
available from the British Library.

ISBN 978 1 80016 316 4

Vanguard Press is an imprint of
Pegasus Elliot MacKenzie Publishers Ltd
www.pegasuspublishers.com

First Published in 2022

Vanguard Press
Sheraton House, Castle Park
Cambridge England

Printed & Bound in Great Britain

Dedication

To my wife for her continued support and assistance in writing this novel and also to my reading forum for their sometimes humorous but always constructive comments.

Acknowledgements

To my son, David, for his assistance with aeronautical details and to Jim Rush for his researches into the weight of gold.

Chapter One

Honorary Inspector Florance Rough was in the process of leaving her flat for work. She'd decided on a leisurely start to the week. Her job as a Forensic Analyst with the Treasury Department and the police's Financial Crimes Unit had been slow of late. She jokingly assumed October must be a month when swindlers and fraudsters hibernated. Whatever the reason she was pleased to have a light workload.

As she went to put on her coat, she stood looking at herself in the large wall-mounted mirror beside her front door. She acknowledged she had never been small and that ten months ago she had topped close to 240 pounds in weight. She'd tried every diet known to man and despite sticking to them religiously, she had never shed more than a few pounds. That was all history now.

Since she'd met Dr Alison Mills some ten months ago and followed her dietary regime, Florance was now approaching the look of a slightly overweight woman weighing 180 pounds, as opposed to a walking marquee weighing 240. She was excited at the prospect of a lunchtime date to go clothes shopping with Alison who had become a friend, and who was now married to her old boss, DCI Steve Burt. It would be the first time she could remember daring to venture into a dress shop in fear they wouldn't have 4X sizes.

She reminisced about her size and how it had played an important part in her life. Being grossly overweight had been responsible for most of the good things and some of the bad things that had happened to her. From an early age, she had wanted to be a policewoman. She had managed to get a place at Hendon Police College and with a little help from a friendly instructor had passed the course, but her career in uniform hadn't been a success.

She smiled as she recalled being promoted to CID only because the Metropolitan Police Force didn't have a uniform big enough to fit her, and because her boss at the time couldn't be bothered to fill in the paperwork that would have seen her dismissed on medical grounds.

She almost laughed out loud as she remembered being told that the reason for the move to plain clothes and CID, was she would be able to wear clothes that fitted her. She knew she wasn't liked, and fellow officers thought her a liability, unsuitable for frontline police work. No one could envisage a 17-stone, five-foot-eight unfit police constable chasing bad people on foot.

She sighed as she thought about some of the hurtful comments other officers had levelled at her. Names like 'roadblock' and 'Mama Cass', had been normal. Eventually, the Met placed her in a new unit called Special Resolutions. This was to be a cosmetic unit originally set up to be disbanded in six months, to show the politicians that the managers of the Met were capable of slimming the force down and maintaining tight budgetary control. There were two other officers in this new unit, and they too were for the chop when the unit closed down. Florance thought of them with fond memories.

With another sigh Florance — or Flo as she preferred to be called — pulled on her coat. "Well, we showed them, girl, didn't we? Who's laughing now?" A broad grin appeared on her face.

As she lifted her car keys, her front doorbell rang. She didn't receive many visitors, especially not at 07.44 a.m. She opened the door to see one of her neighbours, whose name she didn't know, standing in front of her. After a few seconds of awkward silence, Flo asked, "Yes, can I help you?"

The visitor introduced herself as Mrs Bostrom. "I'm sorry to bother you; I know you've only recently moved in, and we haven't met, but my friend Mrs Clark told me you're with the police. Can you help me? My son is missing."

Flo tried to take in everything this stranger had said. Yes, she'd moved into her two-bedroom apartment in this new development exactly seven weeks ago, today being Monday the 17th of October. She'd not met Mrs Bostrom before and didn't know a Mrs Clark. The jungle drums around here must be good as most people had moved in at the same time.

"Well, Mrs Bostrom, I'm not strictly speaking a police officer now. You'd be better calling the police Missing Persons Bureau. They'll help you." Flo was being as gentle as she could.

Mrs Bostrom was clearly upset and not listening because she carried on.

"He's been out all night. It's not like him. He works in the bank and keeps regular hours. He's thirty-one and his fiancée didn't hear from him all day yesterday. I've called the hospitals…" She raised her voice for emphasis "…and the police, but they said he's not been missing long enough for them to do anything."

Flo knew this was standard procedure, and there was nothing else she could do but, to get rid of this woman, she suggested, "Look, Mrs Bostrom, report it again later today, and let me know what they say tonight. I'll be in after seven."

The neighbour visibly brightened up. "Thank you, dear, that's very kind of you." Mrs Bostrom said no more but turned and left.

Flo closed the door and considered this meeting. She told herself it was nothing, but by being helpful, she may have enhanced her standing with her neighbours.

With her car keys in hand, she closed her door and went down to the underground garage where she kept her 25-year-old lime-green Fiat 500. That car could tell a few stories.

As she bludgeoned her way through the early morning London traffic, she had a eureka moment and realised the new slimmer version of herself no longer had to move her whole body to the right in order to engage third and fourth gear. She could now sit in a central driving position for the whole journey. This realisation cheered her up. The diet was working, and she was now ready for the day ahead.

***

As Flo was fighting London traffic, her ex-boss, DCI Steve Burt, was already at his desk reviewing case files. As head of the Special Resolutions Unit, his remit was like no other in the Metropolitan Police. His was a small band that existed to take over serious crime files that other departments either couldn't solve or feared were just too hard.

Steve was proud of his team's record but occasionally regretted not having more permanent manpower. Within his brief, he could call on officers with specialist skills to assist but only for the duration of particular enquiries.

As he finished a file and put it on his read pile, he heard someone arrive in the outer office. He was sure it was DC Andy Miller. Andy was the junior officer on his team but the one who contributed the most original theories. Indeed, Steve mused, Andy had been responsible for solving several high-profile cases of late just by his lateral thinking.

Steve waited for Andy's usual greeting that was always accompanied by a cup of coffee. Nothing happened. There was someone in the office, but it obviously wasn't Andy. He also knew it wasn't the other member of his team, DI Abul Ishmal because Abul, known as The Cap, wasn't famed for his early rising. He struggled to get in by nine on a quiet day.

The DCI rose from his desk and went to investigate.

He found a woman he didn't recognise standing in the middle of the outer office. She was tall, slim and from what Steve knew of such things seemed expensively dressed. She was looking curiously around when Steve approached her. "Can I help you?"

The newcomer looked at the DCI with something of a superior air. "Yes, if you are Detective Chief Inspector Steven Burt?"

"Yes, I am and who are you?"

"I'm the newly appointed Police Solicitor. It's been suggested I should make your acquaintance as you seem to handle most of the more salacious cases and it's likely we'll be working together more often than not."

Steve had no idea a permanent Met solicitor was being appointed and who would have suggested she should visit him before nine. "Well, it's nice to meet you…" He waited for her name.

"It's Amanda, Amanda Layburn; my office is on the tenth floor." She held out her hand but seemed reluctant. Steve shook it and discovered it was cold and she didn't have a strong handshake.

"Yes, Amanda, who suggested you look me up?" Steve was curious.

"Oh, just various people. You have quite a reputation for bending the rules to get results. It's been said you'll keep me busy. Anyway, if you feel the need for legal advice, you now know where to find me." The new solicitor turned and left.

Steve was both bewildered and bemused. This lady didn't look as though she would be much fun but why had she sought him out? Very curious. The DCI was still considering this meeting when he heard DC Andy Miller arrive.

Steve put the meeting with the newcomer out of his mind. Detective Constable Andrew Miller had come into the office with three large cups of coffee on the off-chance The Cap might arrive early. The coffee would soon clear his mind and cheer him up. A new working week had begun.

Chapter Two

At 09.07 on the same Monday, the 17th of October — and a few minutes after DI Abul Ishmal arrived at New Scotland Yard — a man with a very high Mensa IQ sat in his plush London flat plotting a murder. Not just any murder, with his intellect he arrogantly thought he could plan the perfect murder and get away with it.

He had a problem that could only be solved by someone drawing their last breath within the week. He knew who this person was, where he lived, where he worked and his social habits. He knew everything about him. The man was regarded as a friend by his target. It should be easy, but he hadn't yet worked out a perfect plan. Also, his victim had a high public profile, and his murder would spark a lot of public interest. He would have to be careful.

He recalled the target's holier-than-thou attitude when he'd refused to do the favour the man had asked for as a friend. It was something that he could easily have agreed to and allowed the man to make himself a lot of money without any fuss. *Well,* he thought, *so be it. It's not my fault you wouldn't help me as a friend, so now you have to pay the price.* The man actually smiled at this thought.

He was aware that if a killer had no connection to his victim and if he didn't leave any forensic evidence behind then his chances of being caught were slim. The police were, after all, his intellectual inferiors and unless they were lucky and stumbled across an obvious clue, they were fairly useless at solving even the simplest of crimes. The man had a problem, however. He knew his intended victim and was part of his social set. Whilst he'd not necessarily be a suspect, he'd have a high profile with the police. Despite his low opinion of the boys in blue, he knew they occasionally got lucky. He vowed not to leave any clues behind.

No, he thought, he needed a plan that kept him well away from even talking to the police if he could avoid it. A beautiful, fool proof remote killing, but how? He sat back, closed his eyes and ran various scenarios through his over-developed brain. He needed time to think.

***

Once Abul had arrived at Scotland Yard, he joined his two colleagues for their usual Monday morning meeting and debrief. As always, they assembled in the DCI's inner office and started to review their recent brutal caseload. Over the past ten weeks, they'd been handed six serious crimes that the other units within Scotland Yard were having difficulty solving. To the credit of the three officers gathered around DCI Steve Burt's table, all six had been solved. One of the three argued they should be given time off after such great results, but needless to say, The Cap was outnumbered.

Detective Inspector Abul Ishmal had worked with DCI Steve Burt as the third member of the Special Resolutions Unit since its inception. He regarded his DCI as a friend and colleague. The DCI also thought of The Cap in the same way but understood his weaknesses. He liked to arrive just on time and always took his full annual leave entitlement. He knew every shortcut in the book plus he had an eye for a pretty face or a well-presented figure. Steve also knew he was a dedicated officer when things were serious and knew his wife would kill him if he ever strayed.

"Right, we've cleared these files. Andy, are we up to date with the logs for the six files? I don't want the CPS coming back at us." Steve knew how important paper was to the Crown Prosecution Service.

"Not quite, but I will be before close of play today." DC Andy Miller was the keeper of records and had developed into a first-class detective.

Steve remembered when Andy had first joined him. He had been awkward, shy, and looked as though his mother dressed him in his father's old clothes. But Andy had proven himself and was destined for higher rank.

"OK, let's get to it. Cap, you've got the last set of interview notes to write up and…" The internal phone on Steve's desk rang. It was his immediate boss, Police Commander Alfred Brooks.

"Steve, pop up when you can but now would be a good time. I've got the coffee." The line went dead.

The DCI knew it wasn't an invitation but a command to visit his superior now.

Commander Brooks had been a surprise appointment following the sudden departure of the previous incumbent. Alfie was set to retire but had been promoted and his retirement was postponed for three years. Steve had worked for the Commander when he was a Chief Inspector in Serious Crimes and liked the older policeman.

***

Steve entered Alfie's office after knocking and being shouted in. He noticed that the secretary who acted as a doorkeeper for the Commander wasn't at her desk.

The Commander was sitting in one of the two comfortable chairs he used for informal meetings. As Steve approached, he pointed to the second chair.

"Steve, glad you could come." Alfie had a wicked grin on his face. He knew Steve had no choice. The DCI wasn't sure what was coming.

"How's that lovely wife of yours coming along?"

Alfie was referring to an incident during one of Steve's previous cases that saw his then-fiancée Dr Alison Mills being shot and barely surviving. Skilled medical help and her own strong will had seen her survive and now some eight months later, she was back at work, albeit only three days a week.

"She's fine Alfie, still a bit weak, but definitely on the mend."

The two men reminisced about that case. It had been Steve's tenacity in solving it that had been responsible for Alfie Brooks being here today.

As they drank their coffee, Alfie became more serious. "Right Steve my boy, first things first." Alfie produced a brown envelope from his rear trouser pocket. "This is for you. It's DC Andrew Miller's promotion to Detective Sergeant."

Steve was overjoyed. Andy deserved this and he'd be over the moon, but Steve saw a look in his boss' eyes suggesting it wasn't all joy.

"He's a good lad and after his part organising the task force earlier this year, he's in demand. I've had trouble holding back Chief Superintendent Charles from Human Resources. He says he's had more than a few department heads asking for your DC to be transferred to them. That's not the problem, I can handle HR." Alfie paused. "But the National Crime Agency want him, now he's got sergeant rank; I have it here." Alfie pulled a folded A4 sheet from his side trouser pocket this time. "They say he'd work on their most serious investigations and would be fast-tracked to Inspector within six months subject to his performance."

The Commander looked with sad eyes at Steve. "It's a great opportunity for the lad, Steve. I know you rate him, and the decision has to be his. I suppose I just wanted to say please don't pressurise him to stay with you unless he wants to but show him the request from the NCA."

Steve was both happy and sad at the same time. "There's no way I'd stand in his way Alfie, you know that."

The Commander nodded and shrugged his shoulders.

"I'll be sorry to lose him. He's a cracking bloke but you're right. He'd be daft to turn down the NCA. I'll talk to him." Steve gave a huge sigh. The world was changing and his ugly duckling of a year ago had now fully matured.

The Commander ordered more coffee by shouting towards the closed office door. His secretary was obviously back. This meant Commander Alfie Brooks wasn't finished.

"Now Steve, what about you? You know you've impressed a lot of people on the twelfth floor and let me tell you that's not easy to do." Alfie smiled. "You've got your MBE coming and your clear-up rate is exceptional. There's a Superintendent's job coming up in Vice. I'd like to put you forward and so would the people upstairs." Alfie looked at Steve. "What do you think?"

The DCI didn't know what to think. As a Superintendent, he'd earn more money and could reasonably expect more promotions having broken out of the Chief Inspector ranks. He knew there appeared to be an invisible bar such that if you didn't make Superintendent you'd stick as a Chief Inspector for the remainder of your career but those who got to Superintendent rank usually progressed to better things. His initial reaction was to say yes but he hesitated. "Thanks, Alfie, I appreciate it, but can I think about it? I'm not sure I want Vice and being a Super means more paperwork and being office-bound. I'm happy on the front line."

"Yes, agreed, but remember once you've made Superintendent, Chief Superintendent's only round the corner nine times out of ten." Although the Commander was sincere, he realised his colleague was not a paper-pusher.

The coffee was finished, and Steve got up to leave. As he walked to the door with Alfie's arm on his shoulder he stopped. "I had a visit from an odd lady this morning, an Amanda Layburn. I don't suppose you know anything about her?"

"Ah well…" The Commander stood beside Steve. "She's new. No one knows too much about her. We hear her husband's some big noise in the government, Minister for Regional Development and Planning, something like that." Alfie took a pace back from Steve and Steve noticed concern on the Commander's features. "Thing is, I'm not sure what she's supposed to do. We've never had a solicitor on the strength before who didn't have a specific brief. She was rolled out by the Commissioner at a meeting last week. We were told she was starting today but that was it, all very hush-hush. What did she say to you?"

"Not much. She was there before anyone else arrived, having a nosey around. Said she'd heard I cut corners to get results and I might be requiring her services in the future. That's it."

"Cheeky cow. Who says you cut corners? Nobody's said it in my hearing."

Both men shrugged their shoulders in unison and Steve left.

He'd have a long chat with Alison this evening about a move to Vice and his career in general.

***

The man with the high IQ was still mulling things over when he eventually hit upon an idea. In his mind questions began to form. What if the perfect murder wasn't a murder at all? What if the victim were killed along with other innocent victims? Then the murdered victim would be just another casualty among the rest. If a group of people were killed at the same time and his intended victim was among them, then who'd know? The rest would be just collateral damage.

He liked the idea and reached for a pen and a pad but as he did so he quickly realised he didn't have a lot of time and he didn't know how to make such a catastrophic event happen. He sat contemplating the problem. After all, someone with his IQ and intellect must be able to find a solution.

He realised he needed help and knew from films and books that it was possible to hire hitmen to carry out such things. But where to find one? He reached for his laptop. He loved surfing the web, especially what people called the dark web. He'd devoted a lot of time to working out how to access it and had even used it recently to buy a gun when he thought the simplest solution to his problem was just to shoot his target. He'd bought a .45 Smith and Wesson pistol that was now hidden in his writing desk. He knew such a purchase could be traced to him if he ever came to the attention of the police, so he had set up a mailbox using a false name. The weapon had been delivered there. Unfortunately, the gun seller insisted on a credit card for payment, but he'd been lucky. One of his cards was almost out of date so he had used it for the purchase and, after he received the weapon, he had immediately paid off the card balance from an overseas account and cancelled the card. He knew it wasn't fool proof, but it was better than nothing.

He hit a few keys, then a few more on his laptop to enter the dark web. It wasn't dark and wasn't easy to find mainly because it was full of the less savoury things most people didn't want to see or find during a normal web browser. Once he'd logged on, he keyed in 'Hitmen. London based'. He had no idea what might come up, but you had to start somewhere. To his surprise, several anonymous listings appeared. As he expected the details were sketchy and each entry was clouded in secrecy, listing some form of pseudo name and a not too obvious e-mail contact address. He decided to just pick the first one on the list that said they functioned primarily in London. The e-mail address was odd and obviously of foreign origin.

The man smiled. He liked the anonymity of this dark web. It had taken even him several attempts to gain access to this mysterious world and he doubted that the police with their inferior intelligence would ever succeed in getting in. He felt safe.

He sent the e-mail as requested, giving a telephone number, and waited with growing excitement. It wasn't long before the number he'd given started to ring. He congratulated himself on using what some people referred to as a burner phone. It couldn't be traced. He answered on the second ring and was immediately met by a gruff voice.

"Yes?"

He was taken aback and almost lost for words. Was he really speaking to a killer? He stumbled over his opening remarks. "Eh! I saw your posting on the web." He wasn't sure what to say but tried to sound like a gangster from a bad film. "I need a job doing involving killing someone. Can you do it?" He'd no idea if this was the correct approach or even if he had the correct person at the other end of the phone but, as he kept telling himself, you have to start somewhere.

"Just the one?" The voice was still gruff and unfriendly.

"Yes, but it's urgent."

"Where will he be and when do you want it done?"

The man thought he'd impress this supposed killer, so he ignored the question. "But I have a plan to hide the actual murder victim." The strained silence told the man this comment hadn't been well-received at the other end of the phone. He quickly added, "He will be in London, and I want it done tomorrow."

"Listen, I'm the one taking the risks, so I do these things my way or I don't do it at all." The voice was insistent and in control.

"OK." Despite his superior intelligence and his plan for multiple killings to hide the real victim, the man acquiesced and backed away from his plan. He was shaking from a mixture of fear and excitement. He suddenly realised this was real and not just an academic exercise. He was out of his comfort zone.

"Twenty thousand cash. Half as a deposit up front, the rest when the job's done."

"Right, twenty thousand. Agreed!"

"In cash. Be in the Tavern Pub on Peckham High Road tonight at eight p.m. Bring the ten grand and wear a scarf. I'll find you. Bring photos and an address where the target will be tomorrow night at seven p.m. Got it?"

"Yes. Eight p.m. The Tavern on Peckham High Road."

"And don't think about stiffing me out of the balance. If I sniff the cops, you won't see me, but I'll find you and that could also be very bad for your health." The connection was broken.

The hitman hung up and smiled to himself. *There's one born every minute. Who on earth would think they can just dial up a killer?* He didn't mind. Killing people was his side-line. Despite what people saw in films or on television very few people asked to have somebody murdered. He made his living quietly from driving taxis but occasionally he'd provided another service, but only for those clients who had the bottle and the money to go through with it. Most didn't, but he lived very nicely on the upfront payments he occasionally received from aborted jobs. After all, he was running a business. He laughed. But this latest one sounded weird. He didn't argue about the money, but the hired gun doubted he would ever see this client or the money.

The man sat back. He felt exhausted but elated. He'd started a process and now there'd be no going back. Ideally, he'd like his target to be dead by tomorrow evening but knew it would only be possible if everything went to the killer's plan. He was unhappy he didn't know the plan except the hitman was to use a gun. In reality, he knew he needed his victim out of the way before Friday morning. That's when the meeting that would make him rich was to take place. He knew the importance of contingency planning and to try and get this done by tomorrow night might prove difficult, but he had plenty of time to rearrange things if something went wrong. He still had Wednesday and Thursday. His brain was detached from the implications of what he'd just set up. He told himself this was an exercise in logic, management and organisation but definitely not murder. He was simply removing an obstacle to his future well-being. He shivered remembering the sound of the hitman's voice over the phone. He sounded rough. Just like a killer should.

He reminisced on his career to date. He knew he wasn't skilled in anything in particular, but he was the son of a lord and as such, certain companies and organisations had paid him handsomely over the years just for the privilege of having his name on their letterhead as a non-executive director. They apparently felt it gave them a certain kudos and lifted their status over any rivals. He was aware this was a form of prostitution. He was selling his name for money, and it had given him a nice lifestyle and he hadn't had to work, but he'd found himself short of cash, although by most people's standards he wasn't poor. He wanted rather than needed to boost his income to allow for a more satisfying and extravagant lifestyle he felt he was entitled to.

He'd recently been given such an opportunity, but it came with strings attached. He was entering a different world. A world where his name meant nothing. For the first time, he had to be seen to deliver in exchange for the massive pay day he had been offered.

He stared into space and told himself this was his chance for total financial independence. All he had to do was deliver on his commitment to his pay masters, but to do that he had to remove the one person who stood in his way. He had until ten on Friday morning.

On his sketch pad, in his almost illegible scrawl, he wrote shooting, poison, accident, explosion, mass shooting, terrorism, mass suicide and even building collapse. He'd try to discuss these options later tonight when he met the hitman. He'd show him who was the superior being.

***

Steve returned to his office and called Andy in. He handed him the brown envelope the Commander had given him. The young DC opened it, read it, reread it and looked dumbly at his DCI. "Do you know what this is Steve?"

"Yes, and it's well deserved." Steve stood up, stretched out his hand and vigorously shook Detective Sergeant Andrew Miller's hand. "Congratulations Andy, it's about time."

The new DS sat down again with a big grin on his face. "Wow! Wait till I tell Sam, she'll be over the moon."

Samantha Burns was a profiler the team had used on one of their cases. When she first arrived, she was very like Andy. Outside of work, she was shy and awkward in company plus she had the same old-fashioned dress sense as Andy. Steve knew the two got on but hadn't heard Andy mention Sam for some time.

"Andy, there's something else you should know." Steve produced the request from the NCA.

He explained to Andy the NCA offer just as Alfie had explained it to him. "It's a great opportunity. I think you'd be daft not to take it. We'll all be sorry to see you go, but it's a once in a lifetime career move." Steve handed over the piece of paper.

Andy read it and reread it. "When do they need an answer?"

"I'm not sure. It's signed by a Chief Superintendent Carlyle and there's a phone number. Have a think and give him a call. See what he says and ask for a job description. See what you're letting yourself in for." Steve laughed as Andy looked shell-shocked. "Go and have a coffee. Phone Samantha. You don't have to do anything straight away."

A happy and smiling Andy left to tell The Cap about his promotion, but not about the NCA offer.

The DCI's day was taken up in budgetary meetings and a briefing on new personnel practices being adopted across the Met. After getting over his excitement, the new DS Miller knuckled down to updating the files as he'd promised Steve. The Cap finished his notes, looked around and stated if there wasn't anything else, he'd be in the canteen interrogating one of the day's newspapers.

***

Steve arrived home early for him. He'd phoned ahead and Alison had their meal almost cooked.

A bottle of red was opened, and they both snuggled together on their sofa, enjoying their wine.

Alison, having survived a shooting, was now well on the road to recovery. They still discussed how since meeting Steve she'd been threatened with disfigurement by a less than bright piece of muscle called Micky Russ and been shot by a psychopathic security guard called Mathew Spink. "Darling, please don't allow anyone to use me for bayonet or target practice in the future. I seem to get over one incident and then I'm in the middle of the next."

They both laughed. Steve mocked. "I'll try but you know how it is. If I ever decide to knock you off for the life insurance, I only have to involve you in one of my cases."

Alison placed her wine on her side table before theatrically punching her husband on the shoulder. She stood and headed for the kitchen thinking that the roast chicken might be about done.

Over their dinner, Steve told his wife about Andy's promotion and his chance to join the National Crime Agency.

"That's wonderful for him." Alison was genuinely pleased. "I suppose Sam will be pleased. She's been nagging him about promotion."

"How do you know that?"

"We girls talk to each other." Alison gave a sly grin as she tilted her head to one side. "When I was in the hospital, Sam and Flo were regular visitors and during my convalescence, we often met for coffee and short walks. I know Sam has high hopes. Andy's the one for her but she despairs he'll ever get round to popping the question."

They finished their meal over more small talk, Alison explaining how working three days a week wasn't too bad because she didn't need to see some of her regular patients that often. "Oh! I forgot, I had lunch with Flo today. The diet's going really well. She bought some lovely new clothes, not the old tents she used to wear. She's done really well and looked good."

Flo had worked with Steve in the Special Resolutions Unit. Like Abul, she had been given a nickname, Twiggy. Steve said this was great news and he was pleased for Twiggy as she'd always be known to him. He told Alison about the new solicitor that even Alfie Brooks knew little or nothing about. It was all very strange but probably nothing for him to get excited about.

Once everything had been washed and tidied away, they settled down to watch television. Steve took the remote and turned the volume all the way down.

"Darling, there's something else."

Alison looked puzzled. "I had a conversation with Alfie today about my future. There's a Superintendent vacancy in Vice. Alfie thinks I should take it."

This simple statement started a debate between them. Alison's initial reaction was Steve should take it, but as they talked, it became clear Steve had reservations. Too much admin and politics when you broke out of Chief Inspector rank. This led Alison to declare he must do what he felt comfortable with, but if it meant more regular hours and less stress, she was all for it. She joked that, if he were working Vice, there was less chance she'd be pulled into his cases and thus would be safer unless he ever needed her for some undercover work.

It was a good-hearted debate between the two although no decision was reached. Steve switched the television off. He and Alison had been discussing his future for almost three hours.

The renovations to what had been Alison's living quarters before their marriage had gone well. Their architect had been excellent as had the builders. The living space had been remodelled to make it their home, and not just the place Alison used to live in, and the master bedroom was an especially spectacular success. It was opulent, large, comfortable and functional. As they prepared for bed Steve thought how wonderful his bride had been about making her old home their new home together and for the thousandth time since his marriage how lucky he had been to find Alison.

Chapter Three

Florance Rough had had an easy day. There was nothing urgent and she'd enjoyed her shopping trip with Alison Mills. As she drank her after dinner herbal tea, she wondered why Alison was keeping her maiden name when she was working. Flo knew she wouldn't. If she found a man and married him, she'd shout her new surname from the rooftops. She sat daydreaming that with her new shape and what she thought was a sexier wardrobe then maybe she'd find someone.

As she sat her doorbell sounded. She groaned. It had to be that Mrs Bostrom from this morning about her missing son. Flo's first impressions were that the lady was probably a domineering mother not prepared to let her son too far away from her apron strings and that the lad had most likely run off with his fiancée to escape his mother. As Flo made for the door, she shook her head and thought, *31 years old and still living with mummy.*

On opening the door Flo's fears were answered. Mrs Bostrom stood there looking pale with red eyes and wringing a moist handkerchief between her hands. Before Flo could say anything, Mrs Bostrom blurted out, "He hasn't come home yet, and you said to let you know."

Flo sighed and ushered the lady in. She sat her down, made a cup of tea and prepared to listen to the tale of the missing son.

"Mrs Bostrom I'm not sure I can help. As I said this morning, I'm not exactly with the police any longer, and this is clearly a missing persons case."

The lady seated opposite Flo smiled sadly and dabbed her eyes with her damp handkerchief. Flo passed her a box of paper tissues. The handkerchief looked saturated and was useless for mopping up Mrs Bostrom's tears. "I know but I feel if I could speak to you as a friendly face you'd understand and maybe get the police to take me seriously. All they say is he's old enough and he'll probably turn up but I know something is wrong." Mrs Bostrom started to cry again and helped herself to a handful of Flo's paper tissues. Her voice was pleading. "Can you please help? At least explain to someone, get them to start looking for him, please."

Flo knew this wasn't possible and she really couldn't get involved but with this woman clearly in distress, she decided to ask a few more questions as she knew she would when Mrs Bostrom first appeared at her door.

"OK, Mrs Bostrom, no promises but tell me everything you can, and I'll see if I can help."

"Oh! Thank you, dear, that's all I want. Someone to listen." Mrs Bostrom wiped her eyes. Sniffed and drew a deep breath. Her story was about to begin.

"Take your time, there's no rush." Flo calmed the lady down.

Mrs Bostrom sat up straight and began. Flo had her notebook out both to look official and to record anything of interest. The least she could do was speak to someone in Missing Persons tomorrow.

"Walter, that's my son's name, Walter Fredrick Bostrom." His mother smiled with pride just thinking of him. "He's thirty-one and engaged to a lovely girl. She's a bit younger than him and comes from Scotland."

Flo felt this was going to take a while.

"He was a bright boy at school. He did well in his exams and got a place at Cambridge. He did economics and advanced maths. He got a double first."

Flo was impressed. "You must have been very proud!"

"Oh, yes. His father was killed in a car crash when he was just six years old, so it's only been the two of us." The storyteller looked sad again and ready to cry. She pulled herself together.

"When he was in his final year, he was recruited by the Bank. He left Cambridge and went straight to the Bank. He's been there ever since."

Flo asked, "Which bank, Barclays, Nat West?"

"Oh! Bless you, dear, not that kind of bank, he works at the Bank of England."

Florance's head spun. Any Cambridge graduate working at the Bank of England wouldn't be a clerk, he'd be more senior. Missing Persons should have passed this guy's disappearance on to Special Branch immediately. She would have to take Mrs Bostrom more seriously and watch how she proceeded.

Gently and with a casual tone to her voice, Flo asked. "Do you know what your son did at the Bank?"

"No, he never discussed his work other than one time I asked him about his day, and he said it was top secret." Mrs Bostrom smiled remembering the incident. "He said if he told me he'd have to kill me." She laughed but her memories wouldn't allow her to relax. She dabbed her eyes again using several of Flo's paper tissues.

"Just to be clear Mrs Bostrom…"

"Please, call me Susan."

"Right, er, Susan." Flo paused. "Just to be clear. Walter went out Sunday. At what time and to go where?"

"He left after breakfast so about ten o'clock. He was going to his gym and then on to pick up his fiancée. They were booked to have lunch with some friends, but he didn't arrive at Paula's… that's his fiancée. She called me around one o'clock saying he hadn't arrived."

"And you've not heard from anyone?"

"Yes, a man from the bank phoned this morning around ten wanting to know why Walter wasn't at work."

"Do you remember this man's name?"

"Yes, give me a minute." Susan Bostrom was thinking. "Yes, it was someone called Michael Pleasance. He said he worked with Walter."

For the second time in the past thirty minutes, Florance's head was spinning. She knew Michael Pleasance was Head of Bullion Movements and was a very senior officer within the Bank. If Walter Bostrom worked closely enough with him to make the main man check on him, then Walter Bostrom was a serious player in the Bank.

Flo felt this information could put this disappearance squarely in her court as it was linked to the Treasury. She said nothing.

The pair sat in silence as Flo made some notes. "Susan, leave this with me. I'm sure there's nothing to worry about but I'll talk to people tomorrow and get the ball rolling to look for Walter. Please don't worry and I'll keep in touch."

Mrs Bostrom visibly brightened up. "Thank you, dear. I feel better having spoken to someone, but you will keep me informed, won't you?"

The two women walked to the door. "Of course, Susan." Flo opened the door, patted her visitor gently on the shoulder and again told her not to worry.

Flo may have told her neighbour not to worry but Honorary Inspector Florance Rough was deeply concerned. She knew that everyone who worked in the bullion area within the Bank had to be cleared by Positive Vetting carried out by MI5 and Special Branch. Each member of the department was privy to some of the Bank's best-guarded secrets, especially concerning bullion payments to the World Bank. If Walter Bostrom was involved as part of the team, then he had to be found, and quickly.

***

The man had dressed as he thought a rough East End person visiting the Tavern pub might look like. The weather wasn't warm, and this allowed him to wear a raincoat he'd bought that afternoon from a charity shop. His normal elegant bearing and six-foot frame were disguised not only by the coat but by the cap he was wearing. He'd considered a false beard as a disguise but settled on a pair of almost plain glass reading glasses bought from Boots. As instructed, he wore a large scarf round his neck to further disguise himself. Before entering the pub, he'd walked round the block looking for evidence of CCTV cameras. He'd spotted only one on the adjacent main road. The area around the entrance to the pub was clear. Happy that he wasn't being spotted he entered the pub. A brown box containing half the hitman's fee was safely hidden inside a pocket attached to the lining of his raincoat. His Smith and Wesson was in the right-hand outer pocket of his coat. Just in case!

The man walked into the pub displaying as much confidence as he could muster. He hadn't been in many East End pubs and wasn't sure what to expect. The area directly in front of him was busy with mostly men standing and talking. He noted that the bar itself was round and at equally spaced intervals a partition extended from the bar to split the floor into different sections. Because the bar was round it reminded the man of a bicycle wheel. The partitions were made of dark wood but had stained glass mounted on top for the last eighteen inches of their five-foot height. They didn't go all the way to the wall so as to allow customers to move between sections. The pub itself was warm and welcoming in a rough sort of way and the man approached the bar and ordered a half-pint of bitter. He didn't normally drink beer and found the taste odd. He preferred a nice mellow claret.

He checked his watch. It was exactly eight p.m. He moved between sections noticing that the walls of the building were lined in dark heavy wood. If the hired gun was here, he would make himself known. Logic dictated he was in the right place, he was on time, he was wearing a scarf, although the temperature inside the pub was hot, and he had the money, an address and photographs. The hired gun must appear. He took up a position in the less crowded section of the bar and stood by the back wall where the landlord had kindly provided a shelf for customers to rest their glasses. The man wanted to remain invisible and tried to blend in without talking to anyone. He found a copy of the Metro and pretended to read it. He waited.

By nine p.m. the man was ready to give up. His brain told him the person he was meeting must be careful and would take his time before making himself known. But to be an hour late was just too much. As much as he needed such a person, this particular hitman had proven to be unreliable, if he existed, or the whole thing was a joke. He folded his paper, put it on the shelf and left the pub.

As he turned right to walk towards the tube station a man approached him. He was big, well over six foot and in the opinion of the man, he must weigh at least two hundred and eighty pounds. He had a large dark beard, was dressed almost entirely in black and wore a ski cap.

"You the geezer?" The man recognised the gruff voice.

Now he was face to face with an assassin, the man's knees were knocking together. He couldn't remember being so scared in his life. His right hand gripped the pistol in his pocket. It acted as a comfort blanket of sorts. In a timid voice, the reply fell from his mouth powered only by gravity. "Yes." It was no more than a squeak.

"Follow me." The man in black turned and walked towards a dark alley that branched off this street.

"You got the money?"

The man was comforted by his grip on the Smith and Wesson. "Yes. Ten thousand now the rest when you've finished the job." The man felt empowered holding the money and the gun. "What do I call you? Before going into detail, I'd like to discuss—"

"Look, I told you." The gruff voice held even more aggression. "I do things my way. You can call me John. Did you bring the pictures and where I'll find this bloke?"

"Now, just hold on." The man was regaining some of his inbred superiority. After all, this rough uncouth man was no match for him. "I want to be sure you will carry out the task as I want it done."

As the two men — both six-foot, one rounded and the other slim — stood facing each other in the darkened space, an uneasy and menacing silence descended. Both stared at each other until the hired gun heaved a great sigh that shook his obese frame. "Give me the money and the details and he'll be dead by tomorrow night. If that's not what you want give me a grand now for my troubles and bugger off."

The man knew he was in over his head, but he still believed he was a superior being to this hitman. "Tell me how you will do it without getting caught!"

The hitman sighed and grabbed the photographs and the sheet of paper the man had finally taken out of his pocket. Looking at the sheet of paper with the name and address and the photographs under a faint streetlight, he asked. "This is where he'll be tomorrow evening at seven?"

"Yes. He always dines with his wife at Frederick's Restaurant on Pine Street every Tuesday evening. They get there at six-thirty sharp and leave at eight."

The hitman gave a grin that exposed his uneven and broken teeth. "It's easy, I'll shoot him." This was said matter-of-factly. "I'll break up the gun and drop most of it in the Thames. Piece of cake, you don't have to worry!"

The simplicity of this approach over his more elaborate schemes appealed to him. He had to admit that if an unconnected third party simply shot the target and escaped then his troubles would be over. There would be no connection to him.

"Nothing must come back on me."

"And remember, I'll be in touch about the rest of my money!" The hitman's gruff voice once again carried a high degree of menace.

The man pulled out the box containing the money and handed it over in silence.

The large man in black opened the box and looked inside. He didn't count the notes. He turned and walked away leaving his client shaking slightly.

This whole experience hadn't been pleasant. He told himself he was a gentle, cultured individual who in his life should never need to come across this type of man, but it had been necessary and at least he'd set the wheels in motion to his chances of becoming very rich.

Chapter Four

DCI Burt was later getting into his office this Tuesday morning. He'd had a leisurely breakfast and had continued his discussion with his wife about his future and whether or not he should take the promotion. They arrived at a compromise meaning Steve could make the decision and Alison would go along with whatever he decided.

As he entered Andy and The Cap were sitting at their desks. The DCI immediately spotted The Cap was looking a bit pale. It suggested a fair amount of alcohol had been consumed yesterday evening. Turning his attention to Andy he saw that his face was normal except his cheeks were a fiery red. This was Andy's tell-tale sign of having had one too many.

"I suppose you two were celebrating Andy's promotion last night?" Steve gave a performance of being annoyed with his team.

"Only a couple, Steve." Abul tried to wave off the criticism. "But it got a bit out of hand."

"I don't suppose you thought about waiting for an official bash with wives and girlfriends?"

"Yes, we did but it was more fun last night." The Cap grinned despite his throbbing head. Andy was a bit sheepish. "I'll still arrange a celebration, Steve. The Cap thought it might be a good idea to get in a bit of practice." He looked at The Cap who mouthed, "Snitch," but with good humour.

Once Steve was in his office, Andy knocked on the door frame of the usually open door and entered. "Can I have a minute, Steve?"

The now Detective Sergeant sat down at his boss' request. "I've given a lot of thought to the NCA, and Sam thinks it's a great chance so if you don't mind, I'll take it."

Andy had reverted to his old, shy manner. He sat with his hands in his lap stroking his fingers. Steve wasn't surprised but would be sorry to lose this slightly eccentric highly intelligent officer, but he realised Andy had a bright future.

"Well Andy, I'm really pleased for you. It's a great opportunity and Inspector in about six months after making Sergeant is incredible. We'll all be sorry to see you go but I'm sure you've made the right choice."

Both men stood up and shook hands.

"I'd like to take a week's leave before getting started. I phoned my new Superintendent and he'd like me to start ASAP but agreed to a week's leave subject to your say-so. I thought I could work this week out, have my week off and start at the NCA in a couple of weeks if that's OK, Steve?"

The DCI knew clean breaks were always best in such circumstances. "What do you have on just now?"

"Nothing really. Just one more file to update."

"Right." Steve was all action. "Finish today and take the rest of the week off as unofficial leave. We'll organise a bit of a bash for Friday and let you know. So, no ifs, no buts, finish the file and disappear. I'm sure you've got a lot to do." Steve had a sudden thought. "Where are you being based?"

Andy looked squarely into his boss' eyes and smiled. "Right here on the eighth floor."

"Ah! I see. So, we're not getting rid of you totally then." The DCI paused before calling in The Cap. He explained about Andy's elevation in status to the National Crime Agency and instructed The Cap to organise an evening out including other halves for Friday night. This was a task The Cap enjoyed.

Once the air of congratulations had died down, they went back to their desks. Steve lifted the phone and made an appointment to see the Commander.

***

As the three detectives were celebrating Andy's good fortune, Flo was sitting at her desk worrying about her meeting with Mrs Bostrom last night. She'd have to be careful not to stand on anyone's toes by not following procedure, but she'd never been in this position before.

She decided to go step by step. First, she'd try to discover how senior Walter Fredrick Bostrom was within the Bank. Then she'd review what she knew.

Flo lifted her phone and dialled zero to be put through to internal directory enquiries. She asked for Michael Pleasance at the Bank of England. After the usual electronic static and a few whistles, a man's voice came on the line. He didn't sound friendly based on his opening tone.

"Yes. Who's calling?"

Flo knew if this was Michael Pleasance, he was several pay grades above her and not a man to cross. "Is this Mr Pleasance?"

"Yes." In an even more annoyed tone, he almost shouted, "Who is this?"

Flo stuck to her guns. "Mr Pleasance, my name is Inspector Florance Rough. I'm on strength at the Treasury but seconded to the Metropolitan Police's Financial Crimes Section. I'd like to talk to you about Walter Bostrom."

Flo swore she could feel fear and hear the panic coming from the man who gulped and blurted out, "Who the hell are you?"

"I explained sir. I'm on strength—"

"Yes. Yes, I got all that but why are you asking about Walter Bostrom?"

"I have reason to think he is missing, and his disappearance is most out of character. I need to talk to you, sir."

"Why me. What makes you think I know anything about Walter Bostrom?"

"Well sir, I understand you called his mother asking where he was."

"I see." There was a long pause whilst Michael Pleasance made a decision. "Very well. I can see you this morning at eleven-thirty. Come alone." The line went dead.

Flo felt his instruction to come alone was a bit odd when he thought he was speaking to a proper police officer, but she let it pass. Now she had the appointment she didn't think there was much more to do except contact missing persons and see if they had any news.

But... she had an odd feeling. As she sat thinking about the missing man, she decided she needed help. She could alert her immediate line boss over at the Treasury or speak with the Head of Financial Crimes about her misgivings, but all she had was a feeling. She felt something was wrong. But what? She could only discuss this with one man, her ex-boss DCI Steve Burt. She decided to pay him a visit.

***

Steve was shown into Commander Alfie Brooks' office by his gatekeeper of a secretary who for once was behind her desk when the DCI arrived. Alfie as usual ordered coffee and ushered Steve to the comfortable seating area of his office.

"Well, I suppose you've made a decision about going to Vice?" Alfie was known as a man who got straight to the point.

"Yes, we have." Alfie noted the 'we'. "But first you should know DS Miller is going to take the offer from the NCA. I've told him to bugger off when he finishes today and not come back. He's signed out on a week's leave starting next week then he's straight into NCA." Steve gauged the Commander's reaction and carried on. "So that's that. He'll do really well, but the unit's a man short now."

"OK, I'm glad young Andy's taken the chance, but what about you?"

"Alfie." Steve opened his arms toward the senior officer. "You know me. I'm more at home catching bad guys instead of shuffling paper. I discussed it last night and this morning with Alison. She says it's my decision, but I know she knows I don't want to leave frontline police work. So, if it's OK with you, I'll stay put."

The Commander shook his head but managed a tight little smile. "I'd have bet the house that wife of yours would have persuaded you to go for it but there you are. On one hand, I'm sorry you're not taking the promotion but on the other, I'm glad you're staying here." The Commander stood as did Steve and both men shook hands.

"I'll better find you another admin assistant pronto then."

Steve put his hand up like a schoolboy asking a question in class. "Can you make whoever it is as good as the last one?"

Both men walked towards the door. As Steve left Alfie patted his shoulder. "I'll see what I can do."

38

When Steve got back, Andy was placing some items in a cardboard box he must have found somewhere. The Cap was sitting on his desk swinging his legs and looking at Andy.

When he saw Steve, Abul nodded towards Andy. "You know sir, it's at times like this when a young stud's off to greater and better things that he should remember the colleagues he's leaving behind and drop his little black book in the centre of his desk but in young Andy's case…" He left the remainder to hang in the air.

The DCI laughed loudly and under his breath said. "*Only you Cap, only you.*"

Florance, or Twiggy as she was known by her ex-colleagues, arrived seconds after Steve. The Cap still sitting on his desk saw her approach and immediately jumped off to face the new arrival. Abul hadn't seen Twiggy for some time. Certainly not since her weight loss and transformation.

"Well look at you." The Cap, smiling all over his face, held his arms wide. He pecked her on the cheek. "You look fantastic." He genuinely meant it. He remembered Twiggy when he'd first met her with her five or six chins, arms the same diameter as a sewage pipe and dressed in a tent. This new Twiggy was quite attractive and certainly dressed better.

Andy said hello although he'd only come across Twiggy briefly. He had finished packing his box and was set to leave, except a general discussion initiated by The Cap followed, as The Cap explained Andy's promotion and transfer, and opened up the discussion to other nonrelated topics. Andy and Twiggy wanted to get on, but The Cap seemed content to chat. After a few minutes, they wished Andy good luck and eventually Twiggy extricated herself from her two male colleagues and Andy said his goodbyes. Twiggy knocked on Steve's door frame and entered his office with a meek, "Have you got a minute, Steve?"

"Twiggy!" Her old boss was pleased to see her. "I know in this politically correct age we're not supposed to say it, but you look amazing."

Twiggy blushed. "Why thank you, sir, I feel better and, if during the next month I don't gain any weight, then Alison says I'll be ready for round two and that should take even more off."

"Fantastic. Who'd have thought it? Well, done, but you'll always be Twiggy around here." Both laughed and Flo knew she wouldn't have it any other way.

Steve became all business but in a jovial way. "Right Miss Rough, to what do I owe the pleasure?"

Twiggy sat and gathered her thoughts. "It's a bit awkward really. I've got, let's say, a situation."

She looked at the DCI and arched one of her eyebrows.

Steve took the hint. "I see, it's a bit off the books."

"Well not really, I just need some advice and a sounding board." She put on her little girl's lost face but smiled at the same time.

"OK. Let's hear it; do we need The Cap?"

"Won't do any harm." Twiggy was pleased Steve had suggested involving Abul. It would be like in the beginning when it had been the three of them against the establishment.

Steve yelled for The Cap to join them. He opened the door, put his head round and whispered, "You yelled sir?" He was grinning as Steve told him to come in and close the door.

Twiggy gathered her thoughts and began by explaining she'd just moved to a new apartment. She described her first and second meeting with Mrs Bostrom and her concern that if she was right about Walter Bostrom's seniority in the Bank then his disappearance should have been reported to Special Branch.

"I spoke to the person I think is his boss, that's Michael Pleasance. I'm seeing him this morning at eleven-thirty. I looked him up. He's very senior and Head of Bullion." Twiggy stopped to gather her thoughts. "It's nothing I can put a finger on, but people who work for The Bank of England don't just disappear. And why would a senior manager phone Walter's mother? And why haven't Special Branch been notified?" Twiggy was almost pleading for answers, but she carried on.

"I spoke with the Branch earlier, you know, Special Branch. Just an enquiry. They know nothing about a missing bank official." She stopped for effect. "So, you see I've nothing but a few odd bits, but I'd really like you to come with me to meet Michael Pleasance." This was directed at Steve. "You're a much better interviewer than I am, and you'll get to the bottom of anything that's not right, long before I would."

Steve sat back and steepled his fingers under his nose. "You're right about one thing Twiggy. You don't have much, really, think about it? What's got you so interested in this guy's disappearance?"

"I don't know Steve. All I know is that the Bullion Department within the Bank is a big thing. I suppose I've just got a feeling from talking to this Walter's mother that this is so out of character and something's wrong."

"Mm. Any thoughts, Cap?"

Abul had played his usual role of the listener in these situations. "Have you checked his credit cards? Any movements since he vanished?"

"That was one of the first things I did but nothing."

"Have you checked this Walter's bank accounts? Any unusual transfers?" The Cap was thinking.

"I've requested them, but it'll be later today."

The three sat in silence. The DCI looked at his watch. It was 10.52 a.m. He ran a few plans through his head before sitting straight in his chair. "OK Twiggy, you've got our attention, but we can't get too heavily into this. If we find something, then it's straight to Special Branch. Clear?"

Twiggy had known Steve couldn't resist a mystery. She had what she'd hoped for, the involvement of her old team.

Steve carried on. "Cap, go and see the mother. You know, a bit of background on the son and get the details of the fiancée. If she's not too far away, go and see her as well. Then do a deep background check on Mr Pleasance at the Bank of England. Let's see who he is."

The Cap was making notes and thinking that firstly he missed Andy for this stuff but secondly, it was a great feeling to be back working as the old team.

Steve stood up. "This is for today only." He looked at his colleagues. "We'll get away with this for now, but if the Commander gets a sniff that we're up to something off the books he'll crucify me and then you. I'll go with Twiggy to see Michael Pleasance now. Cap, you've got your tasks, we'll meet up later at say five p.m. off-site. Any suggestions?"

"What about the Waterman's, just like old times?" The Cap was always up for a meeting in a pub.

So, the three detectives set off for a very unofficial investigation based only on Twiggy's hunch. They'd involved themselves in unofficial investigations before but had no idea where this one would finish.

Chapter Five

Steve and Twiggy arrived ten minutes early for their appointment with Michael Pleasance. Steve thought security getting into New Scotland Yard was tight, but the Bank of England could teach them a thing or two. Not only did they have to fill in a personal questionnaire, but they also had to make their way through two body scanners where one was the norm. After successfully negotiating the obstacles to entry, they were dumped in a small waiting area that was cordoned off by a thick rope. They were now ten minutes late for their appointment.

A petite young lady dressed in what Steve thought was standard Bank dress code of white blouse, dark skirt and sensible shoes arrived to escort them to the office of Mr Michael Pleasance. Twiggy had said Pleasance was a senior manager and their escort certainly seemed in awe of the great man judging by how she spoke about him.

As she opened an office door, she asked if they would like something to drink. Water for Twiggy and no biscuits. Coffee for Steve and biscuits if there were any going.

On the other side of the office door was a grand space filled with a huge desk that took up all of the central floor. Steve noted there were oil paintings of men dressed in fashions from the last century hanging on two walls and that the windows appeared to open onto a central courtyard.

The man sitting behind the desk was in his mid-fifties at a guess. He wore rimless glasses, was balding from the middle of his head and was wearing his suit jacket. This struck Steve as odd as most people he knew removed their jackets when working at their desks.

Mr Michael Pleasance didn't look anything like his name. He didn't look overly pleasant. Steve and Twiggy approached the desk walking over a lush light grey coloured carpet. They'd agreed Twiggy would take the lead as she'd arranged the meeting.

Michael Pleasance looked up from his desk. He still didn't look friendly.

Twiggy started off, "Thank you for seeing us, Mr Pleasance. I'm Florance Rough with the Treasury seconded to Scotland Yard—"

Michael Pleasance cut her off. "Yes, I guessed who you were but who is this?" He pointed to Steve with his pen. "I told you to come alone." He succeeded by the tone of his voice in letting his visitors know he didn't appreciate surprises.

Steve tried to rescue the meeting. "I'm DCI Burt sir, a colleague of Inspector Rough." Using Florance's honorary title wouldn't do any harm in this fraught environment.

"Why are you here? I only agreed to see the woman."

Steve remained calm but Twiggy didn't. "Look, sir. We have a situation and both DCI Burt and I think we can help, but not if you again refer to me as 'the woman'." Twiggy was on a roll, and she still hadn't been invited to sit on any of the three chairs that were positioned in front of the huge desk. "I'm a member of the Civil Service attached to the Metropolitan Police and will be addressed cordially."

Steve, standing beside Twiggy was impressed. He thought, *Go, girl.* He took a small pace back to allow Twiggy the floor. Silence descended and was only broken by the petite girl entering with a tray of drinks and some biscuits. She noticed both strangers were still standing and knew something was amiss. It was not her job to become involved in her boss' meetings, so she smiled sweetly and placed the tray on the edge of the big desk. "The water and coffee you asked for. I even found a few biscuits." She smiled again and left.

For what felt like an eternity, no one moved or spoke. Eventually, Michael Pleasance tried to live up to his name. "I'm sorry, that was very rude of me." He indicated the chairs in front of his desk. "Please have a seat." Both detectives did exactly that.

"Can I see your warrant cards please before we get started?"

Once he'd examined their credentials, Michael Pleasance appeared to relax. He took his cup of coffee from the tray and gestured to Steve and Twiggy to take theirs.

"Miss Rough, you indicated earlier today that you felt something had happened to Walter Bostrom, and because I had called his mother

44

asking where he was, then I, by implication, must be worried about his disappearance. Is that a fair summary?"

"In its simplest terms yes."

"And DCI Burt you're a senior officer, but I don't know which department you represent?" The question was left hanging. This Pleasance character was no fool. He'd found Steve out straight away. Twiggy chanced a brief look at Steve. He could lie or tell the truth.

Steve began talking hoping his brain would stay ahead of his mouth. "Miss Rough explained to me her concerns and asked if I would accompany her here today. I have some experience of missing persons," he lied, "and I head up a special unit within Scotland Yard responsible for solving serious crimes." Steve thought for a second before adding, "My unit is expert at keeping our findings confidential and if you're concerned, I have signed the Official Secrets Act. I know Miss Rough's intention is to give you any assistance you feel you might require should Mr Bostrom's disappearance have an impact on the Bank."

Twiggy looked at Michael Pleasance. She was impressed by Steve's quick thinking and judging by the expression on his face Michael Pleasance was impressed too.

He sat back and picked up a pen and started to doodle on his blotting-pad. Neither Steve nor Twiggy broke the silence. The next sound would have to come from the doodle artist behind the desk.

"What I'm going to tell you must never leave this room. I'm relying on your total honesty in that regard and your unconditional discretion. There are matters here that should never be discussed, and to be honest, which I thought I would never be mixed up in." From being a confident, arrogant and rude bank official Michael Pleasance had, in the space of sixty seconds, become an obviously nervous and frightened man.

"Anything you say here, sir, will be treated in the utmost of confidence unless of course, you admit to a crime." Steve needed to get this statement in. Although this was very much an unofficial meeting it didn't do any harm to stick to interview protocol.

"I understand, but as you've signed the Official Secrets Act, and I know Miss Rough has been positively vetted by Treasury, then anything I tell you, DCI Burt, will be covered by the Act. Are we clear to continue?"

Both Twiggy and Steve nodded.

Michael Pleasance cleared his throat. He looked a shadow of the man the detectives had first witnessed when they entered his office although Steve felt the arrogance had not totally vanished.

"Do you remember the Brink's-Mat robbery in November 1983? A gang got away with twenty-six million in gold?"

"No, but I know of it. I think it's a bit before our time." Twiggy looked demure.

"Yes, it was a while ago, but we've been living with the repercussions ever since. It's not generally known but the bullion that was stolen belonged to the Bank although its origin was never admitted to. It was being shipped to the World Bank in Geneva. I don't know what you know about international finance, but the Bank makes regular payments on behalf of HM Government to settle debts and so on. A lot of those payments are made in gold. We also buy gold on the world markets when the timing is right. That's largely why my department exists. To repay government debt in bullion and to ensure adequate reserves in line with Treasury edicts.

Unlike money that can be paid or transferred by the click of a computer key, gold bullion can only be paid in its form, so if we are repaying, say interest, we have to ship the actual payment, in other words, gold." Michael Pleasance smiled to himself with satisfaction. He'd explained to these two police officers how important he was. Steve continued to detect an arrogance in this man.

"After the Brink's-Mat robbery, all kinds of additional security measures were introduced but remember it was back in 1983. The Bank is an old lady and slow to change. Over the years, the state-of-the-art security in 1983 was left behind and we've only slowly patched on improvements since then." Michael Pleasance paused for effect.

"A few months ago, we had an incident. A shipment was intercepted electronically. By that, I mean we became aware that an outside source had accessed our shipping data. As I said, since 1983 we've upgraded our systems, but certainly not to anything like the state-of-the-art security available today. Anyway, we cancelled the shipment, informed the Governors of the Bank and Special Branch."

Mr Pleasance stared into space for several seconds remembering Special Branch's involvement. "If I'd have known how Special Branch acts, I'd have thought twice about inviting them in. They treated everyone as though they were guilty. They were rude; they dug into everyone's background including our junior clerks; they had access to our most secret files and even our personal files. They opened our bank accounts, credit card accounts even looked at how we funded our mortgages and holidays. It was an awful experience." Pleasance paused to let the meaning of his words rest on the two detectives. He was clearly unhappy and unnerved by the experience.

Steve was interested but wanted to move this Bank bureaucrat on. "Did they find anything?"

"Yes, eventually. A senior clerk in our IT department was traced as the leak. Apparently, she was smitten by some gangster type, so it was all done for love." Pleasance sneered.

"Fortunately, we discovered it and no harm was done to the Bank, but several high-profile Bank employees were dismissed. I was extremely lucky to survive but was told in no uncertain manner that one more security breach and I'd be out." This man was clearly worried about his job. Twiggy felt some sympathy for him despite his earlier remark.

Steve wasn't really following. "To be clear Mr Pleasance. You're saying that after 1983, the Bank introduced more computer security, but it's only been gradually updated to allow for today's systems. You say you had a recent breach, but it was human intervention not electronic. If that's correct, where are you today?"

"Well put, Detective Chief Inspector. I'm not very good at explaining things sometimes but I've not given you the whole picture." The storyteller picked up a paperclip and started to unwind it as he spoke.

"We had a team of high-powered computer wizards in and they picked our systems to bits. Fortunately, they signed off on our efforts and protocols saying, that, given what we had to work with, we'd done a good job. But that's when the trouble started." Michael Pleasance looked directly at Steve.

"They found a deep bug implanted in our software. They said it was a sophisticated device that must have been planted in-house and by someone who knew their way around computers. The experts were able to see it but couldn't disarm it. They said when they tried it just multiplied and accessed even more files. This thing was also transmitting data to do with our bullion shipments and so far, they've found no way of stopping it, apart from scrapping our software entirely and starting again. This was obviously not a feasible option and we have to assume this bug is there to give someone information that will allow for the theft of our shipments." Michael Pleasance looked exhausted.

"I'm telling you all this to help you understand why we're here now." He paused before carrying on. "Because of the problem and the need to continue with bullion transfers, the military was called in. After all, the business of HM Government can't stop just because some crook has infiltrated our software. The military used GCHQ to come up with a system that would allow us to safely carry on shipping the gold."

He looked at both police officers to gauge their level of involvement with his story. He was pleased with what he saw. "First they told us to revert to old fashioned codes that we would make up manually until further notice. They said a twelve-digit code provided by three Bank employees would be needed, with each person contributing four characters. I chose myself obviously, Walter and my other assistant Sophia Marr as the three employees. This was our first use of this system. Are you following?"

Both Steve and Flo were following but thought the storytelling was a bit laborious.

"We were sworn to secrecy and couldn't divulge our four characters to each other. The military set up a coding machine in the Bank they called REC. This stands for Random Encrypted Characters. One by one, we entered our four secret characters into the REC. Myself first, then Walter and finally Sophia. The codes had to be put in in the correct order, me, Walter and Sophia. The REC machine scrambles the characters and stores them. When the shipment is ready and is being loaded into the armoured trucks, the convoy commander is sent the scrambled code from the REC machine and can unscramble it to give him our twelve-digit code." Mr Pleasance again looked at his visitors for their understanding. He received nods from both, but Steve needed time to fully absorb this information. He allowed the storyteller to continue uninterrupted.

"Only the military could come up with something like that. While we have this computer security problem, they are also transporting the gold until further notice in their own version of an armoured truck. Once the gold is loaded and the military commander knows the twelve-digit code the three of us, are to meet here, call the convoy commander and confirm our collective code to him and I am to give him instructions on where to deliver the bullion."

Steve was shocked and amazed at all this cloak-and-dagger. Twiggy understood better than the DCI and was aware of bullion movements both into and out of the country. She appreciated the need for top-level security and saw that if the present computer system in the Bank was compromised and if a robbery were to be avoided, then this military system appeared to be the best available. Twiggy told her two male colleagues this and Mr Pleasance agreed.

Steve was a little behind. "Let me look at this again, Mr Pleasance. You're saying your existing computer system has been hacked so badly that you can't use it to plan your gold deliveries. The Army has put in a scrambling device that takes a twelve-digit code dreamed up by you and two others and each of you only knows your own four digits. This combined code is put into a machine that scrambles and stores it. When required, this scrambled code is sent to the officer in charge of transporting the gold and he sees it in an unscrambled form. This is the twelve-digit code made up by you and your colleagues. Then before the bullion leaves, you contact the officer in charge, confirm the twelve-digit code that should match what he has and then give him instructions on where to take the gold. Is that about it?"

"Yes. It is believed this is fool proof."

Steve saw why they were sitting here today. "But it's not, is it Mr Pleasance? That's why you haven't called Special Branch about Walter Bostrom's disappearance." Steve looked triumphant while Twiggy was confused.

Michael Pleasance gave out a deep sigh. "Unfortunately, DCI Burt, you are correct. You see, provided the convoy commander gets confirmation of the code he'll deliver the bullion to any address he's given. If for any reason, let's say the three of us were kidnapped and tortured to give up our codes, then any villain could reroute the armoured cars."

Twiggy had caught up. "But if that happened, someone could cancel everything and change the codes." Twiggy wasn't referring to the fact that Mr Pleasance might be injured or dead.

"It's not that simple. You see, once a code is entered into the REC machine, it cannot be changed. The date for the next shipment is set and must happen. Processes have been put in place as part of our enhanced security protocol. So, on Friday of this week, the 21st of October at twelve noon exactly, one hundred million pounds of gold bullion will be loaded onto three military armoured trucks regardless. If the commander of the convoy gets the correct code, then that's all he needs, blind obedience. He is under instructions not to deviate from his orders."

Steve was bewildered. "You mean nothing can stop it?"

Mr Pleasance's countenance changed. "It could be stopped if the code we give the convoy commander didn't match, and that would in this case only be because Walter is still missing with his four-digit code, but frankly I'd be sacked on the spot. I've got until Friday to salvage this mess, find Walter and save my career. I'm hoping he's just wandered off."

Steve and Twiggy sat up and looked at each other. Steve's head was spinning. He still sensed something in this Mr Pleasance that he couldn't identify. He'd call it arrogance for now, but he was disturbed by this man with his finger on so much gold. He needed coffee, a place to think and a sounding board in the shape of Twiggy and The Cap. He wasn't too concerned about saving Michael Pleasance's career, but he did care about a possible threat to one hundred million pounds of gold and for the safety of Walter Bostrom.

What a mess, he thought and reminded himself to thank Twiggy for effectively dropping him in it when they got back to the office. One last thought struck the DCI. "I presume it's because you have time that you haven't followed procedure and informed Special Branch about Walter Bostrom?"

Michael Pleasance looked drained but strangely defiant. "Yes, you see if he turns up by Friday twelve noon then there's nothing to report. If he doesn't, the shipment will be stopped, and I will have to admit to concealing his disappearance and pay the price."

"But you've done nothing to set the wheels in motion to find him?"

"No DCI Burt, I haven't." This bank official was now a shell of his former self. All the initial obvious arrogance had gone as he'd told his story. Even Steve felt a stirring of sympathy for this man who was clearly out of his depth. Or was he?

Steve made a decision, good or bad. "Mr Pleasance, I really don't know what you have got yourself into, but we'll try to find Walter Bostrom before Friday. I can't tell you what to do but the involvement of Special Branch could inhibit our efforts. Do you understand?"

Michael Pleasance smiled at the DCI and mouthed a thank you.

The police officers showed themselves out. It was 13.50 in the afternoon of Tuesday the 18th of October.

***

The Cap had found Walter Bostrom's mother at 11.47 a.m. He was impressed by the new apartment building and marvelled that Twiggy had moved so far upmarket. He'd always fancied living in Greenwich. The building was clearly new and still smelt of fresh paint. The carpets in the hall and common areas felt expensive as was the plate glass entrance door that was controlled by a very sophisticated entry system. He felt a pang of jealousy.

Mrs Bostrom lived on the third floor in apartment 307. He'd announced his arrival by using the intercom at the main door and a woman The Cap took to be Mrs Bostrom was waiting by the door marked 307 as he exited the lift.

After introductions and a, "Please call me Susan," from Mrs Bostrom, Abul gently took her through the events that had led up to her son's disappearance. Over tea and a large selection of biscuits, The Cap formed a picture of Walter Bostrom as a normal young man with no obvious vices — at least according to his mother — who had a good well-paying job, had no money worries and again, according to his mother, was engaged to a beautiful and bright girl from Scotland.

51

Abul kept asking himself *Where the hell has this guy gone?* He discounted any obvious criminal involvement. The man didn't seem to have a drug habit nor any peculiar sexual orientations and lived with his mum.

After his second cup of tea, The Cap asked to see Walter's room.

"Of course, dear, it's just as he left it. He doesn't like me fussing over his things. It's through here." Mrs Bostrom led the way.

As they entered the room, The Cap asked, "You've not been here long Susan, where did you move from?"

"Oh, we had a nice bungalow over in Kent beside Maidstone but, with Walter's promotion at the Bank, he thought it would be better to be closer to his office and avoid the commute every day, so we moved here. It's very nice and so far, the neighbours are friendly, but I miss my garden." Susan Bostrom had a faraway look as she said this.

The Cap asked to be left alone while he examined Walter's room. Mrs Bostrom reluctantly agreed. Abul felt she was enjoying the excitement of having the police investigate despite the circumstances. The Cap systematically searched every drawer, shelf, book and wardrobe. He felt inside Walter's suit pockets, he searched his sock and underwear drawer even looked under the bed. He could find nothing that might give a clue as to why this man had disappeared. Even the artwork on the walls was run of the mill and neutral.

Abul returned to Susan's living room and was immediately invited to have a bowl of soup. Reluctantly he refused but he had another cup of tea, so Susan insisted he have a sandwich. Whilst he tucked in, he asked for Walter's fiancée's details. Mrs Bostrom produced a handwritten card. "She's Paula White. Lives with her parents at Great Stodding Farm just outside of Esher. She has a very good job." Mrs Bostrom was obviously proud of her son's choice of future wife. "She's the personal assistant to one of the directors of Sun Oil in the City you know."

"Really?" was all The Cap could say as he finished his tea and his sandwich.

The Cap left Mrs Bostrom with a reassurance not to worry, they were now looking for Walter and he was sure to turn up. This gave Susan Bostrom hope and she visibly appreciated the efforts being made to find her son.

***

Once outside Abul looked at his watch. Due to the number of cups of tea and a few rounds of sandwiches for lunch his watch showed him it was approaching two o'clock. He surmised that he'd learn little from talking to Miss White and he didn't fancy a trip into the City. He decided to phone her in the evening after work. Without much enthusiasm, he set off for the office and the background checks Steve had asked for.

Chapter Six

On the way back to Scotland Yard, Steve and Twiggy discussed the meeting they had just left. Neither had formed any definite thoughts, although Steve voiced his concern that he felt Michael Pleasance wasn't being totally honest.

Twiggy saw things differently. "He told us all about his job being under threat, and I follow his logic in not alerting anyone just yet. After all, if Walter Bostrom turns up there's nothing to worry about. If he doesn't then the code won't be complete, and the shipment will be stopped. Either way, the bullion will be safe." She said she felt better that at least she now understood why Special Branch hadn't been called in.

"But how do we find Walter? We're not Missing Persons and I certainly don't know anybody who is."

They stopped for a snack lunch before returning to the office. They'd agreed not to talk about the case, if there was one, until they met up in the pub at five p.m.

When they got back, Twiggy went off to Financial Crimes and Steve returned to his office. He found The Cap hard at it gathering background summaries on the main players. When Steve saw what The Cap was doing, he said, "Add a Miss Sophia Marr to the list, Cap. She's another assistant to Michael Pleasance. Better to be thorough."

"Right." The Cap looked up. "Oh, someone was looking for you. Pretty thing, might be a contestant for Miss Metropolitan Police this year." The Cap giggled. He liked a pretty face and figure. "She said she'd been told to report to you, all very official. She had her personnel file with her. Maybe she's the new Andy?" Abul said this with relish.

"Where is she?"

"I told her to go and have a coffee in the canteen and come back later. She's probably still up there." The Cap started to hit some keys on his computer indicating to his boss that for once he was busy.

***

Steve made his way to the canteen. Sure enough, sitting at a corner table was a strikingly good-looking girl. Steve looked around but could see no one else who matched Abul's description. Steve walked over and stood to one side. "I believe you were looking for me." He was looking down on a slender pale face with deep blue eyes and a beautiful unblemished complexion. Her naturally blonde hair was cut medium length and her white blouse showed her to advantage. Steve held out his hand. "DCI Steve Burt."

The girl was full of poise. The DCI saw she was a bit more sophisticated than some of the WPCs around the place. She continued to sit but extended her hand, holding it as though Steve was expected to kiss it. "Hello, sir, I'm DC Amelia Cooper but my friends call me Poppy. Please don't ask!" She giggled like a schoolgirl.

Steve sat down and noticed that this detective constable held his gaze. Her voice was pure Home Counties, and her diction was flawless. She picked up a file that was sitting on the table. "I'm posted to your unit, sir with immediate effect. Here's my file. I'd just like to say I'm thrilled to be working with you. You're almost a legend among the junior officers."

Steve was amused and scared. He didn't think he was old enough to be a legend and wondered how young these junior officers were. He put Poppy around her mid-twenties. He noted she wasn't wearing any rings and suddenly realised her flawless complexion was natural. There wasn't a hint of make-up.

"Who gave you this assignment, DC Cooper?" Legend or not the DCI had to show his new recruit that he was the boss.

"I was interviewed by Chief Superintendent Charles in Human Resources. I've just left uniform and finished my preliminary CID course, so this is my first plain clothes posting." Poppy wriggled on her chair holding her arms together and shook herself. "Oh! I'm so excited."

Steve smiled and thought, *I'd never have guessed.* Out loud he said, "What did Chief Super Charles tell you?"

"To report to you ASAP. That my role would be more administrative, and I'd find the experience of working for you very rewarding."

Steve could see she still had a bit of the upper-sixth head girl about her. He smiled at the thought of how Abul would get on with this pretty face.

Steve took her personnel file, stood and made to leave. "Welcome to the team Poppy. We're a small but dedicated unit." A vision of The Cap once more entered his thoughts as the DCI wondered what Abul would make of Andy's replacement. "I'll see you tomorrow morning, nine, sharp."

"Yes sir, thank you." She gave Steve a beaming smile that almost brought a glow to the whole canteen. The DCI waved to her, went to the self-service counter for two coffees and returned to his office.

***

At just after five p.m., all three detectives were seated in a booth in the Waterman's Pub just around the corner from New Scotland Yard. Despite its close proximity to the Yard, very few officers used it, preferring the more upmarket hostelries of the city.

Twiggy had ordered the drinks, a beer for Steve, a lager for The Cap and a non-fattening still water for her.

Steve kicked things off by updating The Cap on his and Twiggy's meeting with Michael Pleasance. Twiggy offered a comment that she felt sorry for him. After all, it wasn't his fault that his assistant had vanished, and she could now see why she may have jumped the gun. Mr Pleasance still had time to stop the shipment if Walter Bostrom didn't turn up, so she wasn't so concerned that Special Branch hadn't been alerted to Walter's disappearance.

Abul, who was hearing most of this for the first time, took a long pull of his pint of lager. "So, you think it's a waste of time and your gut instinct was wrong?"

Twiggy was a bit hurt but said, "Well I suppose so. I understand why Pleasance hasn't followed protocol, but I can't blame him."

Steve was listening to his colleagues. "That's as may be but let's look at what we've got before we declare a non-contest. Abul, did you get the backgrounds on the main players?"

"Yes boss, just as requested."

Before Steve could continue Twiggy piped up. "And after we got back, I pulled the financials on them as well."

The DCI was impressed. "Right. Let's take each one in turn. Cap, you first, then Twiggy."

The Cap produced folded pieces of paper from inside his jacket. Twiggy produced similar pieces of paper, but they were flat and inside a plastic wallet that she retrieved from her oversize shoulder bag. He took another swig of his lager, theatrically cleared his throat and began. He had a cheeky grin on his face.

"First, Michael Pleasance. Born 16th March 1967. Educated at Oxford where he got a second. His degree was in International Finance. He's married with two kids. He worked for IKI, the chemicals giant, from university and finished up as a main board member responsible for finance. Unusually he was recruited into the Bank of England from industry in 2011 when he was forty-four. I'm told it's unusual to recruit from outside into senior positions." The Cap shrugged. "He started as a manager in the International Budgetary Department and must have done well because he was promoted to General Manager in 2014 and then to Head of Bullion in 2016. He has no criminal record, not even a parking ticket. He's clean." The Cap took a sip of lager.

Twiggy took up the tale. "I got his bank details as I promised. Nothing much to report. He lives on his salary, has no mortgage, lives in Weybridge with his wife and both cars are paid for. Saves about a grand a month into a separate higher-yielding account. He plays the markets but usually with pretty safe investments, nothing flash. He seems to take two holidays a year with his wife. I checked his credit cards. Same story really. Always pays them off, never gets anywhere near his limit and has a very high credit rating. Just what he is, a servant of the Bank of England."

"So, he's clean." Steve looked doubtful.

Twiggy chided him. "What's wrong Steve, you seem to have doubts?"

"No, not really. I just didn't get the right feeling from him when we talked earlier. You had your doubts, but he satisfied you. I didn't have any doubts and he didn't satisfy me. Bloody strange."

The DCI lightened up. "Never mind, it's probably only me being me. Let's move on." But DCI Burt had one of his feelings and something at the back of his brain was telling him all was not correct. *But what?*

"Sophia Marr, Cap, did you get a background for her?"

"Yes, not much really. Sophia Marr. Born 5th September 1981. Not married. Educated at Oxford and got a second in Economics and Politics. Joined the Bank straight from university in 2003 as a graduate entrant. She's worked in various offices climbing the greasy pole all the time and in 2017 was promoted as Michael Pleasance's assistant. No criminal record, just a boring woman heading for middle-aged spinsterhood."

Twiggy took over. "Maybe not Cap, her bank statements are normal. She occasionally goes overdrawn but recently arranged a five-thousand-pound overdraft facility. She's paying off her car which is a bit flash. It's the latest Morgan Four, and costs around eighty grand. That seems her only extravagance. Her mortgage is two thousand two hundred a month on a mews conversion in Chelsea, but it's well within her take-home salary. Only thing slightly unusual is she's regularly maxed out two of her credit cards and is paying hefty interest payments each month. Nothing really out of the ordinary for a single person living in London but maybe not the middle-aged spinster she appears."

Steve was stroking his chin. From experience, both The Cap and Twiggy knew he was deep in thought, and they remained silent, knowing Steve was trying to piece something together. He needed a theory to explain some of the mystery of Walter Bostrom's disappearance but nothing that he was hearing helped him.

"Right." The DCI was back. "Walter Bostrom."

The Cap started. "Walter Fredrick Bostrom. Born 27th July 1989. Educated Cambridge got a double first in Economics and Advanced Maths. Joined the Bank straight from university in 2013 on a management trainee programme. Something of a whizz-kid. After his training, he spent six months in Clearing, a year in International Settlements and in 2017, was appointed Michael Pleasance's senior assistant. We know he's engaged to a Miss Paula White, aged twenty-nine. She lives outside Esher with her parents. I'm going to telephone interview her when we're finished here but I have something for you. But later…" he teased and grinned. "Anyway, Walter has no criminal record and is as clean as a whistle."

Again, Twiggy jumped straight in. Steve remembered seeing them perform this double act when he had first met the two detectives.

"Bank accounts clean. No overdraft and has a monthly savings plan for a grand every month. Very few standing orders and only one direct debit for his car. Credit card has never been maxed out. Overall, a good sound credit score."

Steve drained his beer and called over for another round. "Are we saying Twiggy's feeling was misplaced and there's nothing for us to investigate here?"

Twiggy looked at The Cap before answering. "I think I have to own up that my gut isn't as infallible as yours, Steve."

"All the players check out, boss. On the surface, nothing is going on except a missing bank official."

Steve looked at his two colleagues. "Yes, but a bank official with part of a code in his head that could release a hundred million in gold bullion, so not just *any* missing bank official, Cap."

"So, you think there's something to this?" The Cap was a little exasperated because he couldn't see any problem.

"I'm not sure. Let's sleep on it and revisit it in the morning. If we agree we've got nothing, then we'll pass everything onto Missing Persons and let them hunt for Walter Bostrom. Agreed?"

Both detectives smiled. "Agreed."

The Cap started up again. "When I was checking out Paula White— you know Walter's fiancée, I did a bit of digging into her family, particularly her father. All the players we know about seem clean, but if Cecil White was on our list, it might be a different story."

Both Twiggy and Steve were all ears.

"It seems our Cecil started selling second-hand cars from bombed-out lots in Glasgow in the early 1980s. He got in with some hard characters and served a five stretch for GBH. When he got out on good behaviour, a few Glasgow hard men disappeared. Cecil's car business flourished until friends of the blokes who vanished called on Cecil. I spoke with a DS in Glasgow who didn't know all the details, but Cecil left Glasgow in a hurry and hasn't been back.

"He's on record as owning a string of upmarket car showrooms across the Home Counties and there's nothing on him. He's been clean since he came south in 1989. Like I say if he were involved, he'd be worth a look. We only looked at him because of his daughter."

Steve finished his beer. "Interesting though Cap; good work." He stood up. "Right, I'm off. Let's re-hash this tomorrow." Steve took a step and stopped. He turned to look at the Cap. "Oh Cap, Andy's replacement starts tomorrow. I told her to be in by nine so look out for her."

The Cap looked at his boss with something close to amazement. "You don't mean that gorgeous thing that was in the office earlier today?"

Steve grinned. "You'll see. Till tomorrow, oh and Twiggy, I'll keep you posted, but if you want to sit in tomorrow I wouldn't object."

The DCI left.

Twiggy and The Cap followed a few minutes later. Twiggy to her new apartment and something tasteless for supper and The Cap home to his family and a telephone conversation with Paula White.

Chapter Seven

The man with the high IQ was restless. He was pacing his sitting room unable to settle to anything. It was seven p.m. He knew his victim should be in the restaurant now and in his mind's eye, he saw the hitman casually strolling up to the table occupied by the victim and his wife, removing a pistol and shooting the target squarely between the eyes.

The man knew he was fantasising, and he was nervous. He had the local radio station playing hoping to hear a breaking news story of a restaurant shooting. Each minute seemed like an hour. He just couldn't wait so decided to travel to Pine Street hoping to be just another face in the crowds, gawping at the scene of the shooting. He visualised blue-and-white tape strung everywhere, and police cars abandoned at odd angles with their lights flashing. What a sight it would be. He dressed the way he had when he'd visited the hitman in the Tavern Pub just last night. The man thought it seemed an age since he'd commissioned the hit. He told himself that's what it was called in the movies, the hit. He smiled to himself. He liked the description. As he pulled on the old raincoat, he realised his Smith and Wesson was still in the pocket.

The trip to Pine Street took about thirty-five minutes. To his surprise and disappointment, everything was normal. The blue-and-white police tape and the police cars with their lights flashing were missing. The man told himself the hitman was waiting till the target had finished his meal. He was worried something had gone wrong and he would feel the heavy hand of a policeman on his collar but then he snapped out of his self-torture. He waited in the shadows knowing he was safe but at eight-ten the victim and his wife left the restaurant and entered a waiting taxi. The hitman hadn't killed the target as promised.

The realisation upset the man. He told himself to think rationally. Perhaps the hitman hadn't had a clear shot, or it was too dangerous. He stood looking at the restaurant searching for the hitman. Maybe he was going to follow the couple home and kill the victim there.

After a while, the man knew he'd been let down. The hitman hadn't performed. The man grew more and more enraged. The man in black had taken his money. He was furious and considered all sorts of vengeance he would heap on this big fat man. His imagination knew no bounds. It wasn't the money he'd lost but the sense he'd been duped. It wasn't a nice feeling and he decided to take him to task. No one made a fool out of a man with a Mensa IQ.

The man decided to seek out his chosen hitman and thought the Tavern Pub was a good place to start. From his original meeting, he felt this man must be known in the pub otherwise why choose it? He journeyed across town and arrived in Peckham High Road at just after nine p.m. He was dressed to blend in and entered the pub with more confidence than he had the previous evening. The pub was exactly as it had been. The dividers segregated the bar into various parts and men were drinking mainly beer and the few women present seemed to be drinking either Coke, no doubt with something in it, or a clear liquid that could have been anything.

The man walked around the outer edge of the circular bar looking into each segment hoping to see the killer. He heard him before he saw him. He was standing at the bar surrounded by other men who were similarly dressed and equally large. All had huge beer bellies. The hitman was holding court so the man chose the adjoining segment and stood at the bar beside the partition where he could hear what his bought and paid for hitman was saying. He didn't want to confront him in the pub but would follow him outside when he left. From his vantage point standing by the divider, he could see and hear everything.

The killer called John was in full flow and on his fifth pint of beer and his third whisky chaser.

"You know it's the best advert I've put out there." He was loud and talking to a group of men. It also appeared he was buying the drinks. He was clearly not sober. "The world's populated by delusional people." He was laughing in between drinking large gulps of his beer. "Can you imagine!" He spat the words out and splashed beer on the bar as he banged his glass onto the counter. "Some little snivelling turd answers the ad and says he want's someone rubbed out. What an idiot." The hitman was doubled up with laughter. "Imagine thinking you can dial a hit! And he paid upfront. Easiest money I've ever made." He drained his glass and ordered drinks for everyone standing listening to him. "I'll take the missus on a holiday to Spain on the chump's money. She'll enjoy that, sun and Sangria, all paid for by a clown!" The hitman was again laughing and slapping those closest to him on the back. He drank a huge amount from his newly refreshed pint glass and again splashed beer on the countertop as he crashed his glass down. "And you know what, boys?" He grinned and tapped the side of his nose in a conspiratorial gesture. "It's all tax-free." He convulsed with laughter.

The man heard all of John's statements. He knew he was the patsy. The idiot who thought he could just dial up a killer. As he listened to the hitman's rants his anger grew again. He thought *who did this fat ugly man think he was describing as an idiot and a clown*. His pent-up anger had to be controlled. He formulated a plan to stay where he was and follow the killer outside when he left, but instead of asking for an explanation he'd demand his money back and tell the fat killer exactly what he thought of him.

***

At 9.50 p.m., the killer drained his last beer, slapped everyone near him on the back and left the pub. The man waited a minute and followed. He saw the fat hitman staggering towards the same alley they'd met last night. Tonight, instead of meeting a future client, the killer was relieving himself against a doorway when the man entered the alley.

"What went wrong tonight?"

The killer finished and as he zipped up his fly tried to focus on the man. He held out his right hand and pointed but was weaving trying to focus on the newcomer. He failed. In a slurred speech that was difficult to understand, the swaying killer tried to sound sober but failed.

"Who the hell are you?"

"I'm the guy you conned out of ten thousand pounds last night. I'm the idiot and the clown who expected you to do a job tonight. I'm the fool who wants his money back and who is going to let the authorities know your little scam."

The very drunk fat man sobered up slightly at being confronted with his client from last night. He again tried to point at the man and bring him into focus. "Look you little shit, I've got your money, and you're lucky I didn't tell the cops you wanted someone dead. Little people like you make me sick." He was slurring his words and trying manfully to stay upright without swaying. "You think your money and your comfortable life can be maintained by using people like me to get rid of any little inconveniences to your perfect lives." The killer wasn't getting better. His slurred speech now included a fair volume of spit as he spoke. "People like you don't know how to survive in the real world, so piss off and leave me alone. You're a nobody!"

The man listened to this, and his anger grew. He knew trying to reason with a drunk wasn't possible and especially this drunk. He was shaking with fury. He felt the grip of his pistol and on instinct pulled the gun from his raincoat pocket. He pointed it at the drunk fat man. "You'll give me back my money, every penny of it, or I'll kill you." The man was seeing red. He'd never been so angry both for being taken for a fool and for the way this fat slob had described him in the pub.

The killer still swaying looked at the man and the gun. "You haven't got the balls. People like you," he sneered, "get your kicks by dealing with people like me. Look at the way you're dressed. I bet you think that's how a working-class man dresses, not like your toffs and gentry. Get out of my way and take your pea shooter home. I've—"

The explosion was louder than the man had thought possible. In the darkness of the alley, there was nothing to see except the fat man dressed in black was no longer swaying. He had both hands clutching his chest and was lying on the cobbled road surface.

The man felt numb. He recalled later he felt nothing as he walked towards the fat man lying on the ground and shot him again this time aiming for the head. He had no idea if he had hit the killer in the head, but the second explosion brought him back to the present. His larger than normal brain kicked in and instantly analysed the situation. He'd shot and most likely killed this man. They were in a deserted alley so there were no witnesses. He knew there was no CCTV to worry about so the correct thing to do was just leave. No one could possibly connect him to this killing.

The man returned to his car knowing he hadn't been spotted on CCTV and drove steadily to his apartment and several large whiskies. By the time he got home the shock had set in and the alcohol helped. As he sat drinking, his thoughts returned to the need to kill his target but first, he analysed his feelings. He realised he had none. He'd just killed a human being and felt no guilt or remorse. He told himself he was probably a natural cold-blooded killer.

As he thought through the events of the evening, he realised nothing had been achieved. The need to kill his target hadn't disappeared just because his first plan hadn't worked out. He remembered the satisfaction of pulling the trigger, of the cool breeze that wafted over him as he stood over the fat man. His brain had shut down for a few minutes, but he remembered the feeling of power. The act of taking another human being's life in cold blood gave him a buzz. He was somehow detached from the act of pulling the trigger.

A new plan formed in his head that involved him doing the killing. That way it would be done right and in such a way he'd get away with it. He thought one of the advantages of being a genius was you could always find solutions to seemingly intractable problems. He'd successfully killed the impostor of a hitman. He admitted he'd enjoyed the experience and knew he could do it again.

He smiled as he sipped his whisky, then on his shelf below the television he saw the opportunity to kill his victim and soon. He was looking at an embossed card inviting him to a social dinner being given by old friends Lord and Lady Rosyth. The dinner was tomorrow, Wednesday the 19th, at their estate near Cirencester. The man had already RSVP'd but now, as he thought it through, he realised it was the perfect place to kill his target. He knew his target was going to be there and would stay over. As was usual on these occasions, a select few stayed over as guests of his Lordship, especially those who travelled from London. The guest list had been published in *The Times* newspaper. The man thought this publication was a great source of information.

He started to dream about how he would kill Sir Anthony Layburn, the so-called friend, who had refused to help him.

His thoughts drifted to university days and how different he and his friend Anthony Layburn were. He was the son of a Peer. As the eldest son, he had the title Right Honourable. His Mensa score ensured he would get a place at university but like most overly intelligent people his practical skills, including studying, weren't as good as people with lower IQs who wanted to advance in the world. He had had a place at Exeter to read geography, but quit after two years. He remembered his father ranting at him, and his weak excuse that his tutors were his intellectual inferiors. How could they possibly teach him anything he didn't already know? That had been twelve years ago, and in that time, he'd only held one real job.

He remembered his first day in gainful employment. His father got him an internship in a merchant bank in the city. The work was boring, but he did well enough in his trial period to be offered a full-time job as a client liaison manager. He smiled again. What it meant was he was a salesman, whose job it was to get wealthy families from similar backgrounds to his to part with their money, on the basis the merchant bank knew best where to invest their money. He was amazed at the power of a title and how people felt comfortable dealing with their own class.

His mind turned to his first meeting with Anthony Layburn. Anthony had gone to a Cambridge college and had earned a first in finance and politics. Layburn joined just as the man was told he had a full-time job, effectively as an upmarket salesman. Anthony had gone straight into investment banking when he joined, and it was only the man's need to understand a few buzz words commonly used when describing investments that the two men met. The man had a high-net-worth client who, unlike most of his clients, seemed to understand the world of finance and had asked a few awkward questions. The man had sought out someone in investment banking to help him. He had stumbled upon Anthony Layburn, purely by chance and instantly recognised he was a social climber, impressed by a member of the aristocracy. The title impressed him, and Anthony soon became the man's best friend, even accompanying him to a meeting with his awkward client and helping to sell the investment that netted the man a sizeable commission. Since then, they had met several times a year at social events.

The man sat and pondered how their lives had diverged. Anthony was ambitious and made steady progress within the bank. After five years, he was a director and six years ago he was elected Member of

Parliament for East Sussex, and was knighted for something or other two years ago. He conceded that Anthony worked hard and only six months ago he'd been appointed Minister for Development and Planning, but he didn't like Anthony Layburn's wife. Lady Layburn was, in his opinion, a stuck-up lawyer who'd probably slept her way to a partnership at her law firm.

As he sipped his scotch, he thought about his own career. He hadn't lasted long in the bank. He had found the work boring but when he'd tendered his resignation he was surprised to be asked to sit as a non-executive director provided the bank could show his name and title on their letterhead. He was told there was nothing really to do except attend a once-a-month board meeting that lasted less than an hour. He'd be paid ten thousand a year for a maximum of twelve hours of his time each year. The bank knew he would inherit his father's title one day and that as a member of the aristocracy he must already be well connected, and therefore useful to the bank in opening doors.

Since the first invitation from the bank, word got out that he was available, and he had been invited onto the boards of eight other companies who paid him between ten and twenty thousand a year on the assumption he was connected, and for the use of his present and future title. He calculated his income from doing nothing was around one hundred and ten thousand pounds. He refilled his whisky glass and thought life without working wasn't so bad, but **now** he had an opportunity to make some real money. Sir Anthony Layburn, Minister for Development and Planning stood in the way. He'd have to be removed.

The man would plan the perfect murder and eliminate Anthony Layburn tomorrow evening whilst attending Lord Rosyth's dinner. He just needed to work out how he would do it.

Chapter Eight

Wednesday the 19th of October started wet and cold. Steve's wife, Dr Alison Mills, was working today, and she liked him out of her hair as early as possible. The DCI was happy to oblige as it got him into the office before things got busy. He stopped at a Costa and almost ordered two black coffees. This had been his regular routine for weeks knowing his admin assistant, now Detective Sergeant Andy Miller, would be at his desk when Steve arrived.

He walked into the outer office and although he knew Andy wouldn't be there, he was disappointed to see his desk empty. He shrugged, and then remembered he'd told Andy's replacement DC Amelia Cooper, also known as Poppy, to start at nine a.m.. He knew his other permanent staff member DI Abul Ishmal wouldn't be in before nine a.m.. He took his coffee into his own office and settled down behind his desk.

He replayed in his mind the meeting the previous day with Michael Pleasance, the Head of Bullion Transfers for the Bank of England. Twiggy was not certain anything was seriously amiss after the meeting with Pleasance and had suggested dropping it. As had happened before, the DCI, having interviewed the Head of Bullion Transfers, wasn't too sure Twiggy was right. Something was niggling at the back of his brain.

He'd called a nine a.m. meeting to discuss the disappearance of Walter Bostrom and how it might play into anything untoward at the Bank of England. Twiggy was coming and with The Cap's input, they might be able to come up with something. Or they'd admit it was a waste of time and they'd drop the whole thing and push Missing Persons on behalf of Walter Bostrom's mother. Steve checked his watch. It was exactly eight thirty-five.

At eight thirty-nine, his internal phone rang. It was Commander Alfie Brooks. "Get up to my office NOW!"

The phone line went dead, and the DCI sat for a minute looking at the buzzing instrument. It was clear the Commander wasn't pleased about something. But what?"

***

The DCI knocked gently on his boss' door. Alfie's secretary-cum-gatekeeper hadn't arrived yet.

"Come in." The voice wasn't in the least friendly. The Commander was behind his desk. Raising his right arm and using his index figure, he pointed to a chair on the opposite side of his desk. "Sit and say nothing." Steve had had friendlier openings from Alfie.

"I spent a very uncomfortable fifteen minutes with the Commissioner last night. She chewed me out good and proper. She told me one of my officers was engaged in a vigilante hunt involving staff members at the Bank of England."

Steve could tell Alfie was angry, but so far, his anger was under control. He looked at a sheet of handwritten notes.

"Someone called Michael Pleasance complained that two officers interviewed him yesterday for no reason and that such officers were acting outside of their authority. The complaint finished up with The Governor of the Bank of England and in turn with the Commissioner of the Metropolitan Police. I was summoned at five minutes past five last night to give an explanation. Of course, I couldn't because I knew nothing about it, and had to sit through being told that unless I got a grip of my junior officers I could well be in traffic by the end of the week."

Steve realised he was in very hot water but had found when being bawled out by a senior officer dumb insolence worked as well as anything else.

Alfie's voice became softer. "Now, DCI Burt, please tell me it wasn't you, and from the description, that overweight woman who used to work for you, who interviewed this Pleasance character, then we can all get on with our day's work." The Commander even smiled as he sat back in his large executive chair and waited for the DCI to talk.

Steve knew that in his own jargon he was bang to rights. Dumb insolence had to come to an end at some point but Steve thought, not yet. He returned Alfie's stare and just shrugged his shoulders.

The Commander stood up and leant over his desk to be closer to the DCI. "Listen to me and listen good." The decibel level of the Commander's voice was increasing. "You work for the Metropolitan Police." Alfie looked as though his blood pressure would blow the veins on his neck. "We don't allow private-case detectives within the force. If you want to be a private dick, then leave and set up on your own." Steve thought this dressing-down was quite mild until the Commander brought his large fist down on his desk making the top shudder. "By Christ, you work for *me*, remember!"

The decibel level was off the scale. "We have a chain of command and I'm in command. From now on you don't breathe without telling me why you're doing it. I want to know each day what you're up to. I had to fight to save your career last night, MBE for services to policing or not. The Commissioner wanted you up on a disciplinary and God knows why, but I talked her out of it. You're officially on very thin ice and are not to go anywhere near Michael Pleasance again. Is that clear?"

Alfie sat down again, and his colour returned to something like normal. "Do you understand, Detective Chief Inspector, because by God if you don't, I'll have you out the door now before you do any more damage." The Commander was clearly still upset, and he looked drained.

Steve realised he was only passing on what he'd suffered last night with the Commissioner, but still, this was a serious breach and he'd have to work hard to repair the damage.

An air of tension and suspicion settled between the two men. Alfie Brooks had had his say. He sat and waited for some comment from his DCI.

Steve realised it was his turn to speak. "I'm sorry sir." The DCI was aware that the use of the senior officer's Christian name might only add oil to the fire. "Miss Rough asked me to go with her to her interview with this Michael Pleasance. She'd learnt one of her neighbour's son's, who worked at the Bank, had gone missing and Pleasance appeared not to have followed protocol by calling in Special Branch. She was suspicious and knew—"

The Commander was once again red with rage. "You *what*!" he shouted. "You got involved because some girl was suspicious!" The word 'suspicious' was said in a sarcastic tone.

Steve knew he'd have to take his medicine. "Yes sir." He spoke in the tone of voice he used to win the trust of prisoners. "You see, if something unexplained happens to any senior Bank employee, that person's immediate manager is mandated to bring in the Branch, in case there are any security implications. That didn't happen in this case so Miss Rough, knowing her interview techniques aren't too sharp, asked me to go with her."

Steve felt he was winning the Commander over. He decided to lie believing that when your back was to the wall like now, it never did any harm and most times helped. "We have a briefing session planned for this morning. If we had felt there was something to be investigated, I'd have brought it to you but yesterday I didn't see anything to investigate."

"Mm! You're sure that's it."

"Yes sir."

"How did Miss Rough get to learn of her neighbour's son's disappearance?" Alfie was thinking like a policeman again rather than a police administrator.

"Her neighbour, the boy's mother, visited Miss Rough in an anxious state. Miss Rough was just trying to help. The mother had been onto Missing Persons but thought they weren't taking her seriously. With the protocol breach, Miss Rough felt it was legitimate to speak to the boy's immediate superior and as I said, I was asked to tag along."

The Commander sat in his overly large chair. Steve hadn't noticed before how big it was. He was swinging the chair from side to side deep in thought, clearly considering the DCI's explanation. Eventually, he spoke. "Right, you'd better finish off what you've started. Hold your briefing meeting and then give me a full written report. If there is anything here, you'll be a lucky man. If there isn't, you'd better keep your nose clean for a long time." The Commander's tone of voice was reasoned. "Are we clear?"

"Yes sir, and thank you, sir."

Alfie grunted and, with a swish of his arm, indicated Steve should leave.

***

The DCI slowly returned to his office to give himself time to consider Alfie Brook's words. He also wondered why Michael Pleasance had shouted foul and informed his superiors of the visit by Twiggy and himself. His previous feeling of unease was now compounded, something wasn't right. Before going to his own office, he visited Technical Support to see its head, Inspector Terry Harvey. Terry had become a good friend of Steve's, having helped out during several high-profile cases. Steve liked the boffin who always seemed to have a solution no matter what problem Steve presented him with.

The DCI explained his problem and as always Terry agreed to investigate and to be at Steve's debrief meeting within the next thirty minutes.

As Steve arrived at his office, he could smell the coffee and hear the noise of several voices talking at once. He first saw The Cap sitting back in a chair in Steve's inner office talking to Andy's replacement, Amelia Cooper. She was sitting next to The Cap but was upright on her chair. Steve noticed that The Cap was wearing a new suit and a crisp white shirt. To Steve's surprise, even his shoes were polished, and his tie was correctly tied at his neck.

Steve smiled inwardly. Obviously, the presence of a pretty face on the team might have had a positive effect on Abul's dress code although once Mrs Ishmal met Poppy, Steve suspected The Cap would be back to his more casual and wrinkled dress code.

Twiggy was sitting at an angle to Poppy and with her new slim figure could sit comfortably within the dimensions of the chair. All three were talking but Steve couldn't work out their topic of conversation which stopped when they saw him enter.

"I take it everyone has met Poppy?"

Nods of heads all round and a big smile from The Cap. Twiggy just raised her eyes to the ceiling and shook her head.

"Let's get to it. First off, I've just had my nuts well and truly squeezed. Twiggy, the powers-that-be know about our interview yesterday with Michael Pleasance and they are not happy. I've had the riot act read about unofficial investigations and vigilante behaviour. It

72

seems Michael reported our visit, and a complaint went to the Commissioner from the Governor of the Bank."

Twiggy and The Cap looked surprised. Before Twiggy could speak, The Cap sat upright and looked at Twiggy. "Why would your man Pleasance do that? He's the one with something to hide is he not?"

"Well yes, he should have followed protocol, but I thought we parted on good terms. He even thanked us when we said we'd help intensify the search for Walter Bostrom. I'm sorry Steve, I'd no idea you'd get caught up in this or that there was anything to get caught up in." Twiggy was genuinely shocked.

Again, before Steve could say something, The Cap was in full flow. Steve wondered if Poppy was having an effect on his DI.

"From what you've told me about the interview there was nothing to investigate so why stir the pot? It doesn't make sense."

"Before yesterday, Twiggy had a hunch that something was amiss. Remember, I only went along to help out, but personally, I thought it a waste of time." Steve paused to make sure he had everyone's attention. "When we left the meeting, Twiggy was sure she had overreacted and there was nothing to look at. I, on the other hand, felt that things weren't right and had a bad feeling. Now, this morning with this news that a complaint was filed, my instinct is there may be something, but I don't know what."

Poppy, who knew nothing of the events under discussion, wisely stayed silent. Steve waited for comments from both Twiggy who knew everything first-hand, and The Cap who'd been involved and had been briefed by Twiggy.

"So that's it. We're not to do any more on this and just forget it." The Cap seemed strangely disappointed.

"Not quite." Steve allowed a small grin to appear. "The Commander wants us to debrief and say whether there's something to look at or not. He wants a report showing we've concluded our enquiries."

Steve sitting behind his desk sat back and steepled his fingers in front of his face. This was a sure sign he was thinking. No one spoke while their leader was in this state. After a few minutes, the DCI was back.

"What I don't get is Walter Bostrom goes missing the week a large bullion shipment is being arranged and his boss does nothing about it. When the police turn up, he seems genuinely relieved, appears to tell us everything he can about recent events at the Bank even the fact that without Walter Bostrom's four-digit code the shipment can't be made. We promise to put pressure on Missing Persons, he seems satisfied but then goes and initiates a formal complaint. We're now warned off even talking to him. So, what does he gain? My feeling is there's something going on; I'm blowed if I know what, but something's up."

As silence descended on the group, Inspector Terry Harvey arrived clutching a thick folder. With a cheerful grin, he nodded to everyone present, placed his file on Steve's desk and approached Poppy. She stood up and flung her arms around the Inspector's neck. "Uncle Terry, I didn't think I'd see you so soon."

The Inspector pulled away from the embrace and kissed his niece lightly on both cheeks. "I'm only here by invitation but I didn't realise you were mixed up with this lot." Terry Harvey waved his arm and with a good-humoured grin said, "You must have done something very bad."

Steve had no idea that Poppy was connected to the Inspector. It made no difference and he thought further on it might help if a special favour were required. "So, you've got a relative on the inside now, Terry, I suppose any future favours will be free." Steve laughed.

"No chance, I haven't had the beer you owe me from last time." Both men smiled and Steve invited Terry to sit down after he retrieved his file.

"I asked Inspector Harvey to check out computer viruses." Steve was now being formal. "The explanation we got at the Bank yesterday seemed a bit farfetched so I asked Terry to look at it." Steve nodded in Terry's direction indicating the floor was his.

"Right. When the DCI told me that he'd come across a virus that transmitted files and multiplied if it was threatened, I was equally dubious. I'd never come across such a thing. Luckily, we have a new lad who's just transferred in from GCHQ and is more knowledgeable about spyware and computer bugs in general. This is what he told me."

The Inspector opened his file and started to read. "Such sophisticated spyware software was developed a few years ago by the Chinese and copied by the Americans. It doesn't transmit in the usual sense in that it's not radio-controlled but can be interrogated remotely using a simple mobile phone. The thing about it is it has to be inserted on site. In other words, it cannot be installed remotely. A human being sitting in front of an active terminal has to actually introduce the bug into the system. The clever thing about this bug is that once installed it's almost impossible to get it out. If you try to eliminate it, you only succeed in firing up dormant cells and the virus multiplies. The scary thing is that it's an intelligent plant. It can think, so once it's in and you have the access codes, all you need do is ask it a question or give it instructions in plain language." Terry paused for breath. His audience was spellbound.

"For example, if this type of spyware has been inserted into the Bank's mainframe all anyone has to do, in plain language, is ask about the next gold shipment and they'd get everything on the system. That's why the next shipment has been dealt with offline so no details can be hacked." Terry closed his file.

"Bottom line, folks, is that if this is the bug that's been introduced into the Bank's software, then they have a problem, but more importantly they're dealing with some pretty sophisticated opponents."

Everyone sat silently looking at each other. It was Twiggy who broke the silence. "If you tried to remove the virus you say it will multiply, but how?"

"As I said, it's an intelligent bug. It thinks for itself so once it feels threatened it looks for other folders within the system and attacks them. Remember, it's not a disruptive virus. It won't crash your system. It's designed to gather information so shutting systems down won't do any good. It thrives on data. Also, once it has accessed other files these files can be interrogated using a mobile phone and plain language. Once it gets started, and the more people try to kill it, the stronger it gets."

"Wow! Do we know who introduced this bug?" The Cap hadn't been fully brought up to speed.

"Yes, some low-level clerk. Pleasance told us they'd had a breach a few months earlier and it was traced back to this clerk. At the time they'd no idea what they were dealing with, and it was only after Special Branch brought in their own experts that the significance of this spyware was realised. That's when they shut everything down and reverted to old-fashioned manual methods." Steve could see The Cap digesting this information.

Silence descended again. Apart from Terry Harvey, no one could guess what this meant. They were under instructions to put the whole thing to bed or show a legitimate reason for Twiggy's and the DCI's unofficial involvement yesterday.

Terry broke the silence. "Well, that's it; if there's nothing else, I'm off." He stood up to go.

Steve asked Poppy to go and get four coffees and they'd take a five-minute break. Terry approached Twiggy and introduced himself formally. Steve couldn't hear the conversation but noted as Terry shook her hand, he held on to it just a little longer than was necessary. Steve also noticed Twiggy was blushing.

Armed with fresh coffee, the DCI's team reconvened to consider how to proceed. Steve wanted to sit back and listen so asked Twiggy to go first.

"I don't know what to think. At first, I thought it suspicious the Bank hadn't called in the Branch. Then Pleasance explained the manual system for transferring bullion and Walter Bostrom's part in it." She shrugged. "I suppose the explanation that Pleasance gave about having time to see if Walter turned up, plus his reluctance to admit another breach in security and the effect it could have on his career, convinced me everything was above board. Plus, if Walter didn't turn up, the shipment would automatically be cancelled. I couldn't see a risk to the shipment."

"What about the software plant? The Inspector said it's pretty sophisticated. Any thoughts on where this might fit in. After all, if you have access to stuff like that you must be after a big payday. Could it be this twenty-ton shipment?" The Cap was on the ball.

"I suppose it changes things, but I don't see how. Remember, no Walter, no shipment, meaning the gold doesn't move."

The fog Steve had been looking through was beginning to lift as his colleagues spoke.

"Let's start with the Bank. We've got three people involved in controlling the code that will release the bullion. That's Walter, who's missing, Michael Pleasance and Sophia Marr. The Cap and Twiggy checked into their backgrounds, and nothing came up. On the face of it we've nothing, but suppose the spyware bug isn't there for any other reason but to force the Bank to revert back to a manual system for shipments. Suppose the Friday shipment is being targeted and Pleasance is involved?"

"But where would he get the spyware?" The Cap was suddenly alert. "You can't just go into a computer shop and buy it. If the origins are as Terry said, it must be government-controlled and not cheap to steal." The Cap's face suddenly lit up. "Unless we are looking at some form of international organisation. After all, if you're going to nick twenty tonnes of bullion you don't do it using a Ford Mondeo. You'd need an organisation both to steal it, handle twenty tonnes in weight, move it, fence it to some underworld gangster and have the infrastructure to set it up. Unless Michael Pleasance is somehow connected to an international gang, I don't see it. Sorry, Steve."

The DCI knew The Cap was right. His idea was a bit ill-conceived but still, there was something not right. Something he couldn't work out. Everyone finished their coffee and Twiggy said she had to go. She had a meeting to prepare for. As she gathered her things Poppy put up her hand just like the schoolgirl Steve had in his mind's eye.

"Yes Poppy, no need to put your hand up. The idea here is to speak freely."

"Thank you, sir." Her cultured voice was strong and direct. She certainly was no shrinking violet. "I read a lot of trashy girly novels. Reading them helps me sleep at night."

The Cap wickedly thought of other ways of sending Poppy to sleep but knowing that she was Terry Harvey's niece, he quickly removed all such thoughts from his head. He vowed not even to think such thoughts again.

Poppy, unaware of The Cap's thoughts, carried on. "You know, it's all romance and usually the same story told over and over with only the characters changing. The one thing they all have in common is that the hero and occasionally the villain have an affair with his secretary or co-worker. The plots never vary, much. Men and women connected usually by work, have an affair and plan some way of living happily ever after." Poppy looked at the faces of her colleagues, conscious that they didn't know where she was going with her tale.

"The point is, suppose Michael Pleasance and Sophia Marr are having a clandestine relationship and plan to steal the bullion to set themselves up for life. If we accept that then things make a bit more sense. They kidnap Walter Bostrom to get his four-digit code, then on Friday they confirm the code to the convoy commander and tell him to take the bullion to a location known only to them." Poppy was getting excited and seemed to enjoy telling her tale. "Think about the beauty and simplicity of it. Only Pleasance knows what address he's given for delivery; the convoy commander signs off that he's delivered the gold as instructed. The chances are that the alarm won't be raised until after the weekend by which time our loving couple have vanished."

Twiggy replaced her things on the floor. This was some theory from the newcomer.

"You know Steve, with a few changes Poppy could have something." The Cap gave his colleague a smile of praise. "It works up until the convoy delivers the bullion. They'd be expecting an organisation. Certainly, a secure warehouse such as at Heathrow, but suppose the delivery point was another airfield like Biggin Hill for example. If an aircraft was already chartered and standing by, all the logistics I mentioned before about transport and handling problems disappear. The convoy arrives at an airport, the airport's forklift truck loads the aeroplane, the aeroplane takes off but diverts en-route to another destination. If it's done properly and it's the weekend, no one would be any the wiser for days and no heavy mob involved at this end."

Twiggy was impressed. "You know Steve, daft as it sounds, it could make sense, except for the spyware. It was originally only set up to access the bullion shipments. I'm not sure either Michael Pleasance or Sophia Marr would have access to such sophisticated software."

Steve sat still. "Twiggy, you said you had to go. No point hanging around here; I'll keep you posted, and thanks for coming."

Twiggy was grateful to the DCI for not apportioning blame for his dressing-down by the Commander.

"You mean thanks for dropping me in it but good of you not to mention it." They both laughed. "Yeah, that too."

Once Twiggy had gone, Steve asked The Cap to show Poppy around and explain to her how things worked.

The DCI had to put his thoughts into an order that made sense and might explain his initial involvement in a missing persons case. He quickly realised Poppy's hypothesis had merit. Someone might be planning to steal twenty tonnes of gold bullion at twelve noon on Friday the 21st of October, but how to prove it and prevent it? The question of the spyware wasn't resolved. It suggested some heavyweight money and power behind Michael Pleasance if he was involved, *if* indeed he was involved, and *if* the plan existed.

The DCI had been warned he was on thin ice. Could he take the chance and inform the Commander of his concerns, knowing it might look like him trying to justify his original involvement, or did he just close everything down?

Then he thought of Michael Pleasance's complaint and asked himself again, *Why?*

For better or worse, Detective Chief Inspector Steve Burt made a decision.

Chapter Nine

As DCI Burt was making his decision on how to proceed with what he hoped his Commander would agree was now the Bank of England case, the man was just passing Reading on the M4, heading towards his destination at Lord Rosyth's mansion. He had decided on the easiest but longest route using the motorway network to get to Cirencester. He thought it would give him time to think about how he was going to kill Sir Derek Layburn. He drove at 60 mph using only the inside lane. He knew it was safer and allowed for more thinking without worrying too much about other cars.

He had spent a good part of last night listening to the local radio station, but nothing had been reported about a murder in Peckham. It was only this morning on local television news that there was a report of a body having been found in an alley off Peckham High Road. The report simply said a man had been shot and police were asking for witnesses to come forward. The man instantly knew he was in the clear. If the police had anything they wouldn't be asking for witnesses.

While listening to his radio last night he had searched the internet seeking methods of killing by accident. He knew people had died by inadvertently digesting poisonous mushrooms or drinking weed killer. The man spent over two hours researching various accidental killings. He thought rat poison sounded the safest and most deadly but gave up on this idea when he discovered he'd have to provide proof of identity to purchase some and sign a poison register. This didn't sit well with his need for anonymity.

He concluded that this form of poisoning was too hit-or-miss. People had been known to recover from such accidental poisonings plus he'd have to find a way of administering it which in itself could expose him. In the end, he decided a bullet was the most secure way of getting rid of his one-time friend.

He was making good time and decided to pull into a motorway service stop. He parked up away from other cars, lowered his passenger side window to halfway and reclined his seat. He'd often done this when he needed to think but in addition, this time, each mile took him closer to Cirencester, so his anticipation level rose. He needed to visualise the act. He sat back and allowed his mind to wander but instead of thinking about how he would shoot Derek Layburn, he found himself going back six weeks to a Board Meeting of Colonial and English Land Inc.

This was where it had all started. C and EL was one of his best and easiest board appointments. The board only met once a quarter and the meetings usually didn't last more than two hours. The get-togethers themselves were held at different venues but always ran for three days and always in the most upmarket locations. In addition to his eighteen thousand pounds retainer C and EL always took care of all his expenses and treated him well. All he had to do was sit, listen and ask the odd question. The man knew his questions, coming from someone with his IQ, always impressed the members of the board. After all, they were all his intellectual inferiors.

The meeting had been held at the Belfry near Birmingham. He'd just finished a round of golf with three members of the board and was enjoying a drink in the bar when the Managing Director of C and EL entered the bar. He ordered a small beer, acknowledged his colleagues and indicated for the man to join him on the terrace.

With their drinks safely placed on a wrought-iron table, the MD looked at the man somehow weighing him up. "Are you enjoying your time with us?"

"Well yes, your company is very progressive, and I enjoy being able to help where I can."

The MD thought this pompous fool of a Right Honourable was full of wind. He smiled and sipped his beer. "I'm glad you said that. What did you think about our discussion of the Blackwood Project?"

The man remembered the discussion but wasn't sure he could add anything. "Well, it's an exciting development and a bold one. To create a new town in a deprived area is laudable and of course, will make the company a lot of money."

"Yes, but what about the planning permission?"

"I'm sorry, I don't follow."

The MD was a large man with a wide middle. He stood around five-foot-ten and always wore a three-piece pin-striped suit even in the height of summer. He was also a man who liked getting his own way. He sat straight up on the small wrought-iron seat and drew closer to the man.

"You see, we have all the planning permissions we need from local community councils all the way up to the County and Regional Council. We even involved the Department for Regional Development and Planning at central government before we started this scheme. We were assured there would be no difficulties with planning permissions, so we went ahead and purchased 15,000 acres and started the process of realising our ambitions. This was all a few years before you joined us." The MD now sat back. "It must have been ten years ago at least."

He sat forward again. "When you joined us, everything was on track. We'd spent millions on land purchases, fees, engineers, architects, lawyers but we were getting close to what we wanted. The vision of a new town with schools, retail parks, commercial buildings even huge warehouses to attract new employers to the area plus of course 10,000 family homes. We had legal agreements with the County Council for our company to control every aspect of the project and agreements that they would pay us an annual management fee. We'd build and sell or rent everything. Hell, we would even still own the freehold and be selling leasehold properties."

The MD finished his beer with a flourish. He was clearly proud of this project. "But here's the rub, my friend."

The man had no idea what this large powerful man was talking about, but he tried to look interested and concerned.

"Two years ago, we were ready to start cutting ground. We knew because of the size of the project and the re-zoning of green belt land we'd need national dispensation but up until then, we'd been assured this would be no problem. That was until we applied to and met a new Minister. One Sir Derek Layburn, defender of the countryside, the green belt and a staunch advocate of the use of brown field sites only for all future development." The MD sat back.

"Over the past two years, we've had millions tied up in this while the Minister for Regional Development and Planning has fought us through the courts, referred our applications to committees and sub committees, stalled us at every turn. We got a score draw in court four weeks ago in our last-ditch legal appeal against the government's refusal to grant national dispensation. The judges ruled it was the government's judgement call but thought on balance our scheme should be given the go-ahead." The MD studied the man to gauge a reaction. He got none.

As he rested in his car enjoying the slight cooling breeze, he recalled the conversation and the statement that followed that would change his life.

"We know the Minister has, since the judge's comments, referred our application to his planning review committee on two occasions just to be seen to be playing the game. The final do-or-die meeting is in two weeks' time, Friday the 21st of October. If this Minister gets his way, we'll have lost a fortune, something we don't like doing."

Again, a pause, but this time it was for the MD to choose his words carefully. "In your contract, it says that in exchange for the use of your name and attending our quarterly meetings you are also obliged to assist the business by bringing to bear such influential contacts, garnered from your background, who may be of help to the business from time to time." Another pause. "You are aware of this clause?"

The man couldn't remember but surmised this director knew exactly what he had signed. "Yes of course I remember the clause," he lied.

"Good, because now it is your turn to justify your fees and help us out. I need you to use your influence, if you have any, or use your little black book of old Etonian pals, to somehow find out what it'll take to get this bloody Derek Layburn to grant us our permission!"

"Oh!" This slipped out. "You mean bribe him?"

"If that's what it takes."

The man's nimble brain was working in overdrive. "I actually know Derek Layburn, we used to work together." Not one to hide his light under a bushel the man boasted, "I'm sure Derek will listen to reason."

The MD stood, leant over the small round table and hugged the man. "Bloody brilliant. Listen, you get us our permissions and I'll personally authorise a one-million-pound bonus and increase your retainer to one hundred thousand a year."

The breeze was turning chillier as the man sat in his car. He remembered every detail of the meeting that had only occurred two weeks ago. Yet here he was now two days away from the final planning meeting.

He thought back to his meeting with Derek Layburn just after he'd been offered life-changing money to secure planning permission for the MD's Blackwood Project. They'd met for lunch. After the usual pleasantries, the man broached the subject of the Blackwood Project. Layburn had ranted on about the loss of the green belt, greedy developers, and how there were many useful brown field sites all over the UK that should be developed first.

The man admitted to Layburn that he was representing Colonial and English Land and that he would regard it as a personal favour if the Minister could see his way clear to grant permission for what was after all a wonderful scheme.

The Minister sat quietly before looking the man square in the eye. "Never think because we know each other that you can influence any decisions I make." His voice was low but fierce. "By rights, I should report this conversation. You've just tried to unduly influence a Minister of the Crown but out of respect for your father, I won't. But never, and I mean *never*, raise this or any other such topic again, for if you do then I will report you. Do you understand?"

The man sat up and adjusted the back of his seat. He inhaled the fumes around the service area. As he put the window up to the fully closed position, he recalled the moment when he realised the only way he would get his bonus, was if Derek Layburn wasn't the Minister for Regional Development and Planning. And the only way that would happen was if Derek Layburn was dead.

The man realised he hadn't thought about how to kill Layburn, but he'd cleared his head and knew he had to carry through with the plan he still had to finally formulate. He started his car and drove off. Next stop Lord Rosyth's country pile beside Cirencester and the death of a government minister.

Chapter Ten

Steve had been sitting for some time in his office thinking things through. He'd started to prepare a report for Alfie Brooks but couldn't find a sensible conclusion mainly because he was now even more convinced that something was amiss.

He phoned Twiggy who was free from her meeting and arranged to meet her in the canteen. He called out to The Cap as he rose from his desk telling him to accompany him to a meeting. As he and The Cap were leaving the DCI told Poppy her thoughts on a workable theory on what he was now calling the Bank Case were very helpful and innovative. He left her smiling with his words of 'well done' still sounding in her ears.

Seated at a corner table Steve opened the debate. "Do we think Poppy's theory stands up?"

The Cap and Twiggy considered this, but Twiggy answered first.

"Well, it's a theory and it's workable. It goes a long way to explain why Pleasance didn't call in the Branch and why he reported us. He's a man in power; she's a woman who seems to like spending money. They work together, and an opportunity presents itself. So yes, but I don't get the software nor the underworld connection they'd need to get away with it. Twenty tonnes is a lot of gold."

The Cap took over but looked at things from a different angle.

"Let's say the boss and his assistant are having it off. It's a big jump from a romp between the sheets to pulling off a billion-pound gold robbery. If we ignore the software problem and call it a lucky coincidence, why would two ordinary bank employees suddenly go rogue? Then, as Twiggy says, where would they get the expertise to handle the weight and turn gold into cash? You can't walk into an overseas estate agent and buy a luxury villa by plopping three gold bars on the desk. No, Steve, I think the theory is one thing but there are too many loose ends."

Twiggy was back.

"And what about Walter Bostrom? Do we really think the two lovers kidnapped him and are even now holding him in some dark cellar torturing him to get his four-digit code? No, I'm with The Cap, Steve, I can't see it."

This was what the DCI liked about his two colleagues. Their ability to analyse a problem and see all the faults. Also, their ability to give a free and frank appraisal. The DCI considered this and concluded that over the years in similar situations he'd listened to their thoughts but not always acted on their good counsel.

Both Twiggy and The Cap could see they had made their arguments and that Steve was weighing up the pros and cons. They also saw he wasn't entirely convinced, and both knew he was carrying some niggle about the case that was buried deep in his brain.

After a few minutes' silence, Steve withdrew several A4 sheets from his inside jacket pocket and smoothed them out in front of him. He drank what remained of his coffee but didn't suggest refills. "I hear what you both say, and I don't disagree, but I'm convinced something is up at the Bank and at least Michael Pleasance is involved. We haven't met his assistant Sophia Marr but from the background checks, she's no shrinking violet." Steve looked at his notes. "We've been told the spyware programme is so sophisticated it's almost impossible for a normal person to get their hands on it. Agreed?"

Both Abul and Twiggy nodded.

"Right, so is there something bigger going on, and maybe these two people, lovers or not, are just pawns in the game? One billion in gold is a pretty big payday and spending money acquiring the spyware software may be justified." Steve took off in a different direction for a moment. He looked at Twiggy. "Find out from Terry Harvey if he knows how much that software might sell for on the black market."

Twiggy speed dialled the Head of Technical Services. Steve and Abul exchanged glances. Their looks seemed to say, "Twiggy's got the guy's number on her speed dial." The Cap smirked but said nothing. They waited while Twiggy finished her conversation with a "Yes, that would be nice, I'll call you later."

As she hung up, she realised both her male colleagues had listened to every word she'd said. She blushed, put her phone away and pretended to be hurt. "What! Can't a girl speak to a man without you two being overly inquisitive?" She tutted and continued to act. "Oh, grow up!" But she couldn't maintain the pretence and smiled a broad happy smile.

"OK, what did Terry say?"

"He's not sure, but he followed up after our briefing this morning. He spoke to someone at GCHQ. Apparently, this stuff is all over the place if you know where to look. A Russian hacker has made a load of sophisticated and sensitive software options available to anyone who donates to his favoured wildlife cause, so in theory, if you know where to look and spend a few pounds saving a tiger, the software can be yours."

"So, going back to it." Steve began. "My thought that a bigger game was unfolding may not be the case. Maybe Pleasance got hold of the spyware for the price of a meal for a donkey." The DCI sat back thinking.

He burst into life just seconds after sitting back. "Say the software was planted as part of a plan to steal a billion pounds in gold bullion, then Poppy's theory isn't too far off. Pleasance and Sophia Marr are involved and are holding Walter Bostrom for his four-digit code. Let's say the plan was to use the spyware to close down the computer routing and shipment system in the Bank and force them to use a manual version instead. Pleasance would have more control over the manual input and if Sophia Marr is in on it, he only needs Walter's part of the code." Steve paused, awaiting comments and was met with heads nodding in agreement.

"Getting rid of twenty tonnes of bullion would be a big problem for anyone and you'd need underworld connections, but remember Pleasance is buying and selling gold every day. He'll certainly know the big players and probably a few who may not ask too many questions as to the gold's origins. If anyone can fence this stuff Michael Pleasance would be high up the list."

The Cap spoke up. "OK, so I agree, if the software isn't difficult to find, then there could be no Mr Big involved and yes, Pleasance and his lady could be acting alone and again, yes they probably know how to dispose of the bullion without getting caught. Walter Bostrom would no doubt, with a little persuasion, give up his code number so that, on Friday, Pleasance can have the gold shipped. But where? He'd need an organisation in place to handle it. You can't just deliver twenty tonnes of gold to the middle of a field." The Cap was trying to help but was seeing the weakness in the DCI's case. "Hell, even the Army might refuse to offload the stuff unless you're suggesting an armed gang's waiting for them. That reintroduces a Mr Big." The Cap was on a roll and enjoying this more academic side of police work.

All three appreciated Abul's logic until Steve spoke up. He started slowly. "Well… maybe not. Let's look at it. At twelve noon this Friday, Pleasance has to confirm his twelve-digit code to the armoured truck's commander. There will be three trucks and an escort Land Rover. Let's assume he has Walter's code, and everything looks correct. Because the computer system isn't being used, Pleasance tells the commander where to take the shipment."

"Yes, go on."

"We were told the usual place was the secure facility at Heathrow but suppose Pleasance tells the commander to go somewhere else. Not a field but like we said before, perhaps a small airfield, even a large airfield but not Heathrow. We have to assume that if the codes match, then the convoy commander will deliver and offload if the destination looks even remotely legitimate. The commander of the convoy presumably gets a signature, returns to his barracks and stands down for the weekend. All Pleasance would need is for, say, Sophia Marr to drive ahead of the convoy, meet it at the airfield, sign for the gold and have it offloaded, perhaps into a hangar or maybe even straight onto a waiting aircraft. A large forklift truck would easily take care of forty half-tonne pallets, and if the aircraft were a freighter, then there would be no problem fitting them in.

Again, the Army stands down for the weekend, Pleasance drives to meet Marr and they and the aircraft take off to parts overseas. The beauty of this is that everything would look normal until at least lunchtime on Monday when Pleasance and Marr don't report for work. You'd think someone at the Bank might check on the shipment. It could take all day Monday before the alarm's raised. They could be home free and not need a Mr Big or any other underworld gang to help them, just a chartered freight aircraft and a forklift driver employed by the airfield. Pleasance would have no difficulties in producing false shipping documents for any customs' checks."

Steve called over a waiter and ordered three coffees. He was confident that at least he had brought Poppy's theory to life. He once again waited for his colleagues' comments. No one said anything until the coffee had been served.

Twiggy was first to offer an opinion. "It's a long way from Poppy's suggestion to what you've just outlined." She sipped her coffee and grinned. "It's as though the story you've told makes this couple sound like romantic characters like Bonny and Clyde. I almost believe it could happen." She relaxed in her chair and became serious.

"Steve, I got you into this, thinking Walter Bostrom had perhaps wandered off, and now we're suggesting we stop a bullion heist worth around a billion pounds." She paused. "It's a big jump, but you've convinced me something's going on and I agree there is potential for the theft of twenty tonnes of gold bullion this Friday lunchtime. Whether it goes down as you've suggested I don't know but I think it's our duty to report our concerns."

Silence. Steve looked at The Cap.

"Oh, Christ Steve, why do you do it and why do I go along with you? Working for you is like walking a tight rope. There's always space to fall." He laughed. "I suppose I see the logic. The only problem will be convincing Commander Brooks. I think you said your instructions were to close it down or bring him the evidence. I don't think what you've described counts as evidence. It's a nice story but he might interpret it as you trying to justify your interview yesterday with Michael Pleasance. I'll back you but we'd have to get cracking gathering real evidence, otherwise I feel all our bottoms will be hanging out the window."

Twiggy faked a shocked look. "Excuse me, I haven't lost all this weight just so my bottom will hang out a window!"

The ensuing laughter told the DCI his team were with him. All he needed to do was convince Commander Alfie Brooks. Not an easy task.

***

Having finished his report, the DCI was now sitting in front of Commander Alfie Brooks. The Commander was reading the five-page document for the second time. Eventually, he finished, looked at Steve and announced, "We'd better have a coffee and decide what we're going to do with this work of fiction." Alfie was smiling and having shouted to his secretary for coffee, he ushered Steve over to the more comfortable seating area within his office.

Drinking their coffee, the Commander started. "So, what do we do now? I'm not joking when I say your report is a work of fiction and as a working theory it may have merit but you've no evidence. If you're correct, you're saying a gold bullion heist is going down at twelve noon on Friday so how do we prove it? It's not often we get a chance to solve a crime before it takes place."

"Yes, I know sir. I was thinking we should put tabs on both Pleasance and Sophia Marr. We haven't even interviewed her but if we follow them, they may lead us to the missing man, that's Walter Bostrom. If we found him and he is being held by these two then we might have leverage."

"I see your point, but don't you think this is more specialist. I'm thinking of handing it over to the Squad." Alfie knew this wouldn't go down well and raised his eyebrows as he looked to Steve for a reaction.

The morning's dressing-down was forgotten. Steve couldn't believe this. "What!" His voice was raised. "Not the Sweeny sir, you couldn't!"

"If you're right then they are the best people to deal with it."

"Yes, if we were dealing with an armed gang of thugs armed with pickaxes, but not what is more of a sophisticated crime." The DCI was almost pleading. "You do see that sir?"

The Commander sat still and finished his coffee. He had a decision to make. "If we do nothing and bring these two in for questioning on Friday morning, they couldn't carry out the robbery. If there's no one to relay the code, then the shipment would be cancelled, isn't that correct?"

"Yes, I suppose so."

"And our job is to protect the nation from crimes like this, is it not?"

"Again, sir, yes, it goes without saying." Steve could see where the cunning Commander was going with this. If you removed the suspects before the deed could be done, then the deed can never be done. Steve thought this was very clever but it wouldn't help find Walter Bostrom.

"So, here's the plan, we'll keep it in-house. Put these two under twenty-four-hour surveillance from now. I'll authorise the manpower.

Keep your people digging into anything they can find that might help identify any other players, or prove their involvement, so we can charge them. Personally, I don't believe these two would have dreamt up a billion-pound robbery without help. Your analysis is fine as far as it goes but there must be other parties involved. See what you can find. It feels unfinished and might still only be a good story." Alfie held his hand up as Steve was about to object. "We'll leave Pleasance and Marr free to wander until ten a.m. on Friday and then pull them in. Like you say, at least the gold will be safe."

Alfie could see the disappointment on his DCI's face. He knew he wanted to crack this, but he also knew he was a good officer and would see the sense in this plan.

"Yes sir, you're right of course. Can we arrange a meeting with everyone for, say, an hour's time? I'd like Pleasance and Marr under surveillance as they leave their office."

The Commander looked at his watch. "Right, three-thirty, we'll use conference room three. It's a bit bigger and has more desks. Go and get a plan put together to present to the meeting. I'll get the headcount sorted."

Both men stood. The meeting was over. As they walked towards the office door, the Commander stopped. "Oh, Steve, I'll show your report to the Commissioner. With a few well-chosen words, I think she'll see the complaint from Pleasance was a smokescreen but don't forget, you're not a private dick nor a vigilante. Work with the structure and for the moment I'm the structure. Are we clear?"

The DCI knew he was being let down gently. In a quiet voice, he replied, "Yes sir."

"Good; and it's Archie."

Both men grinned. They'd reached an understanding.

***

At three-thirty exactly, the door to conference room three opened and the Commander accompanied by the DCI, and a woman known only to one other person in the room walked in.

91

Present in the room were DI Abul Ishmal, Miss Florance Rough, DC Poppy Cooper, a DS from missing persons called Matt Conway, a DI Peter Jones from tactical liaison and various other officers; this was now a large operation.

The room fell silent as the three new arrivals made their way to the front of the room. Standing in front of a large whiteboard, the Commander made the introductions but referred to the sixteen men and women only as 'watchers'.

"We have a delicate operation to perform over the next two days or so. I know DCI Burt's team are more or less up to speed, but I want everyone's full attention. This operation called 'Operation Bank' is to be taken seriously. Any lack of concentration and we could collectively be responsible for losing this country twenty tonnes of gold bullion. To you and me that's one billion pounds we'd have to pay back if we don't all do our jobs." Alfie got the desired effect. He was a copper's cop and loved mixing it with the troops.

"Be under no illusion. This is important and if you think getting this operation together at short notice was easy, well you'd be wrong. We've got the surveillance order through in double-quick time just to show you how important this is. I'll hand you over to DCI Burt who's in overall operational command."

Steve hurried through the report he'd presented to Alfie earlier but took time to explain Walter Bostrom's part and that the operation was geared to the targets leading them to Walter Bostrom, and the need to know where the targets were at all times leading up to Friday lunchtime. He included the possibility that other people might be involved higher up the organisation if indeed such an organisation existed, but stressed this operation was only interested in keeping the two targets under observation at all times.

"It's vital that you watchers don't lose either of the subjects, not even for a minute!" He paused. "Remember, we think they may be holding Walter Bostrom and this whole operation is geared to finding him before Friday lunchtime. Clear?" It was.

The DCI gathered up a copy of a file that Poppy had prepared earlier and was now handing out to those present. Steve held up his copy. "In here is all the data you'll need to find and keep tabs on your targets.

Photographs, descriptions, addresses, car makes, and registration numbers plus certain bio details you may not need. Now." He turned to the whiteboard and wrote Michael Pleasance on the left and Sophia Marr on the right. He attached their photographs beside their names. Using his marker pen as a pointer. "I want these two picked up as they leave their office tonight. The files give the exit they normally use."

Steve's audience seemed attentive and set to examining their files. "I've worked out with DI Peter Jones," Steve pointed at the DI using the marker pen, "come on up to the front Peter, a series of shifts designed to keep you watchers fresh. You'll be double manned at all times so no excuses about comfort breaks. Peter has split you into teams of two and there'll be four teams allocated to each target." Steve nodded toward the DI. "Peter?"

Peter Jones was a rising star within the Met. He was a fast-track entrant and had impressed with his quick brain and the way he already looked and talked like a policeman. He was just under six feet tall, ruggedly handsome, slim and had a broad Welsh accent.

"Right, none of us has met but for this operation, we are one big team, OK?"

Mumbles from the ranks. "This is important." His Welsh accent was flowing like a Welsh choir. "So, we all work with each other, no solo performances. Now because I don't know any of you, I've had to randomly put you in pairs. If it doesn't suit you, then that's tough. Like I said, for the next two days we're a team."

The DI produced a sheet of paper from his folder. "In each of your folders, you have a full list of everybody's mobile phone number. This is so you can all keep in touch but especially between the teams assigned to each target. I want the relieving team to meet up one hour before handover and to make contact with the team they're relieving to make sure everything is all right. Is that clear?"

Every head nodded.

The DI's Welsh lilt was having a soothing effect on his teams. "Jenny, can you please step forward and you, Matt." Peter Jones stood to one side to allow the newcomers space in front of the whiteboard. He made sure DS Jenny Fuller was standing under the photograph of

Michael Pleasance and that DS Matt Conway was standing under Sophia Marr's.

"DS Jenny Fuller will be responsible for the A teams allocated to Michael Pleasance and DS Matt Conway will similarly be responsible for the B teams allocated to Sophia Marr. Both DSs will be available twenty-four seven. Anything happens out of the ordinary call them, day or night. Do you all understand?"

Lots of 'yes sirs'.

"Now you'll see that Commander Brooks has given us enough manpower to complete the job without any of you falling asleep on the job. Stay alert! Each team is double-handed so no excuses."

It was clear to each member of the teams that this man from the valleys would not accept any foul-ups.

DI Peter Jones took a felt-tipped pen and wrote in the space between the two photographs of the targets.

WEDNESDAY	17.00 TILL 22.00	TEAM 1 A and B
WEDNESDAY/ THURSDAY	22.00 TILL 06.00	TEAM 2 A and B
THURSDAY	06.00 TILL 12.00	TEAM 3 A and B
THURSDAY	12.00 TILL 17.00	TEAM 4 A and B
THURSDAY	17.00 TILL 22.00	TEAM 1 A and B
THURSDAY/ FRIDAY	22.00 TILL 06.00	TEAM 2 A and B
FRIDAY	06.00 TILL 10.00	TEAM 3 A and B

"That's the rota. One team keeping watch on each target round the clock. Right, those in team one you'd better get moving. It's getting close to the target's going home time. Any questions?"

A young-looking uniformed officer who had been drafted into plain clothes just for Operation Bank asked, "If they go to their homes and stay in all night what do we do?" A giggle went round the room. The DCI asked for the girl's name and with whom she was partnered. An untidy man in his fifties with bad teeth and, Steve was sure, bad breath, raised his hand. "DC Player sir, from the list she's with me in Team 2 on

Michael Pleasance. I'll keep her right." More smiles but the tension had been broken.

Steve finished off. "You've got all the resources the Met can give you at short notice. Commander Brooks has broken the overtime bank for this and drafted in enough manpower to make your jobs easy. You're double manned but look carefully at the rota. Both Team 3s should be prepared to arrest their targets at ten this Friday the 21st and bring them to the Yard. Other officers will likely carry out the arrests, but I want both teams there as backup. If the targets are in their offices, I want both teams inside the Bank, in their targets' offices and prepared to arrest them on suspicion of robbery if ordered. Does everyone understand?"

Again, lots of nodding.

"Right. Go to it and remember what DI Jones said. We're a team so act as one and use the information in the files and keep in regular contact with DS Fuller and DS Conway. Good luck."

The teams exited. The Commander patted Steve on the back. "Well done; now we wait."

"Yes, thank you, sir, for your help. I'm amazed you pulled so many officers together so quickly."

Alfie just shrugged and headed for the door. "Rank, dear boy, sometimes it helps."

The remaining officers sat randomly around the room. The Cap was excitedly talking to Jenny Fuller. Both he and the DCI had worked with Jenny on a previous case, and she had almost certainly saved the DCI's life by shooting and wounding an out-of-control gunman.

Steve approached the pair. Protocol was forgotten and Steve hugged the dark-skinned officer from Chelmsford. "You know I asked for you to be seconded onto this?"

"Yes, sir and I'm glad you did. It was a bit of a rush but I'm up to speed. Do you really believe these two people are involved in nicking a billion pounds of gold?"

Steve looked at the other officers before answering. "Yes, but we'll know for sure in around thirty-six hours."

Steve introduced everyone to each other and made Poppy blush by giving her credit for inventing the present theory. She was sitting near

Twiggy and on hearing the DCI's words she blushed and gushed out "Isn't it really exciting! All this just because I read trashy novelettes."

A few of those present didn't understand her comments but when Steve explained, the whole room erupted. All this effort and resources based on a story.

The DCI took charge and delegated jobs. "We'll use my offices as our control centre. Poppy, I want you to log everything that comes in. Set up a spreadsheet. Peter, you're in overall control of the teams but I want Abul to be involved. The pair of you should be ready to take over from any of the teams if things get out of hand. Jenny, you and Matt base yourselves in my offices and make sure Poppy's kept up to date. Every time one of your teams reports in, it has to be logged. Clear?"

Both detective sergeants agreed.

"We're in for a few extra hours over the next few days so work out a duty roster to make sure you all get some sleep. Cap, maybe you and Peter can handle that. Any questions?"

Twiggy put up her hand. "Anything for me to do?"

"Not just now Flo." Steve thought the use of her nickname in this company might not be appropriate. "We'll keep you posted as things develop but your masters at Treasury should be told—" The door opened and Inspector Terry Harvey entered. As usual, he was smiling and acknowledged everyone present including his niece.

"I just thought I'd tell you personally that the bugs were planted in the teams' cars before they left. I've checked them and they're pinging like birds. I've set a live map up in the Technical Services viewing area so if anybody needs to know where the teams are, they just have to visit or ask."

Terry was a bit surprised by the look of confusion on the assembled police officers' faces.

Steve explained. "Sorry everyone, I should have explained. I asked Terry to bug the teams' cars on the basis if we know where an active team is positioned then we'll know where the targets are. It's just a bit of belt and braces. The teams don't know these trackers are fitted."

DI Peter Jones grinned at the DCI. "Cunning sir, very devious. I'd never have thought of that." He clearly thought Steve knew his job. "But I have a question or rather a need for an explanation. We are arresting both targets at ten on Friday regardless of any information we get as a result of the surveillance. Correct?"

Steve acknowledged this. "Yes."

"But why at ten?"

"Terry, maybe you'd better explain."

"Sure. When the DCI explained the REC machine that was installed at the Bank, I was curious. It seems the machine was devised by GCHQ for the military." Terry looked searchingly at the DI. "You were briefed on this I take it?"

"Yes, I got the basics about a computer virus and the need for a secure manual system."

"Good, so you know a twelve-digit code made up of three groups of four has to be used and that three people input their own four digits independently of each other, so they don't know each other's code."

Again, DI Peter Jones agreed that he followed.

"When a shipment is set, the last thing to be entered is the twelve-digit code. Once this has been entered, the shipment is locked in. On Friday at pre-agreed times, the machine will issue shipping instructions that the automatic handling system in the Bank's vaults will obey. In this case, the twenty tonnes of gold will be removed from the vaults by automatic conveyor and delivered to a secure loading bay within the Bank ready to be loaded into armoured trucks. This process starts at ten a.m. on the day so the trucks are loaded and ready to leave the secure area of the Bank just waiting for the twelve-digit code to be telephoned to the convoy commander. If he gets the correct code, he'll deliver his load to wherever he's given on the shipping documents."

"So, all this technology but it comes down to a phone call?"

"Yes I'm afraid so."

The DI nodded his head in appreciation of Terry's explanation. Steve wanted to get things moving. It was approaching five p.m. "OK everybody, those who need to can decamp to my offices now and get set up. It could be a long night so Cap, you and Peter get that rota right. No point in everybody losing sleep."

As the group set off, and en route to Steve's office, DS Matt Conway and DS Jenny Fuller received confirmation their respective teams were in position outside the Bank. The Cap noticed Twiggy and Terry Harvey peeled off and headed for the front door of the Metropolitan Police HQ Building. The Cap always curious about other people's private lives smiled and wondered. Had the new slimmer but still not skinny Twiggy got lucky? He hoped so. Terry Harvey seemed like a nice bloke.

Chapter Eleven

At precisely 4.43 p.m., as the first two teams took up position outside the Bank of England, the phone rang in the offices of Direct Air Charter. It was a small privately run air charter company usually employed to move heavy loads throughout Europe. Business had been poor of late, and the three employees were regularly considering their future and that of the company.

The man in charge was Captain Norman Colington, a 55-year-old veteran with more than twenty-five thousand flying hours already logged. He'd started in the RAF before joining British Airways. By the end of his BA career, he was a senior training captain.

His second in command was his wife, Sally, who looked after the office and tried to keep the business afloat.

The third member of the team was Paul Stockland. Like Norman, Paul was ex-RAF but was an engineer and had only qualified as a pilot five years ago when Norman offered him a job as his chief engineer and sometime co-pilot.

Sally Colington answered the phone, realised it was a technical booking and handed the phone to Norman. The office wasn't big with only room for two desks, just a structure tagged onto the side of a large ex-military maintenance hangar at what had once been RAF Manston.

The voice on the other end of the phone was very professional. "Captain Colington, my name is Pleasance. I'm with The Bank of England and we'd like to charter your aircraft for a job this Friday, the 21st of October. Sorry it's short notice but it's a rush job, and of course, we are happy to pay your rate and perhaps a little bonus." The voice of Mr Pleasance chuckled.

"We haven't done any government work before and of course we'd be happy to quote for the shipment." Norman Colington was used to high-powered customers and understood the protocols.

"Can I ask what the cargo is and what weight is involved?"

"Certainly. It's 20 tonnes of gold bullion."

Captain Colington was suddenly sitting at his small desk with his mouth open, speechless. The voice of Mr Pleasance carried on.

"Given the short notice of our request, we are prepared to waive the usual bid and offer tendering system, Captain. If you tell me now you can handle this shipment, and have it loaded and ready to fly out by four p.m. on Friday, then the contract is yours."

Norman Colington regained his composure. "What time will the consignment arrive?"

"At approximately two p.m. and it has to be offloaded from the armoured trucks and reloaded onto your aircraft ready to take off no later than four p.m. Is that understood?"

"Yes. Where am I flying to?"

"You should submit a provisional flight plan tomorrow showing your final destination as Ankara, Turkey. You will receive your exact final landing place on Friday from one of our colleagues here at the Bank. There will be two people accompanying the shipment."

"I'll have to get back to you. I need to confirm that my aircraft can carry twenty tonnes over the distance to Ankara. I'll have to check fuel loads and get clearances for alternate landing airfields in the event of an emergency. Is that, OK?"

"Yes of course we must be safe, but such detail is why we are paying you, so no. There is no need to confirm any technical data back to me. We trust your airmanship and skills. All I need to know is can you undertake this contract on behalf of the Bank of England?"

Captain Colington thought back. When he'd set up his company, he had had to decide on a heavy-lift aircraft that would best suit his needs. In the beginning, he had envisaged a fleet but after five years he was still running his first aircraft bought second-hand from a dealer: an L100 civilian version of the military Hercules heavy-lift aircraft. It was a bit clapped out but had the inbred military ruggedness and simplicity of maintenance that Norman needed, although Paul Stockland was finding it more and more difficult keeping the old girl in the air.

Norman answered decisively. "Yes, Mr Pleasance, it would be an honour to undertake the contract."

"Splendid. Now as to your fee. We propose an allowance of thirty thousand for fuel, ten thousand for landing fees and flight plan submissions, a twenty thousand subsistence allowance for you and your crew and fifty thousand in salaries. I believe you'll find that comes to one hundred and ten thousand pounds for the one-way trip. We, therefore, propose a payment of two hundred thousand pounds for the round trip and a fifty-thousand-pound bonus. That's two hundred and fifty thousand pounds paid half upfront first thing tomorrow, the balance when we land in Ankara." Mr Pleasance waited for a reaction.

A weak voice replied. "Yes, that's acceptable."

"All I need are your bank details and half the money will be transferred tomorrow before ten a.m.. Should you wish to have the funds sent to an offshore address, we are more than happy to oblige."

Norman had been around long enough to understand the advantages of offshore bank accounts but just keeping his company going meant he'd had no time to consider such luxuries.

"Hold on, Mr Pleasance, I'll hand you over to our company secretary. She'll give you all the details." Norman passed the phone to his wife who, after giving out the bank details, passed the phone back to her husband.

The Captain had hoped to use his wife's time on the phone as a bit of breathing space, and time to think, but the man called Pleasance was back.

"One final point, Captain. You will appreciate this is a highly secure operation so I must insist no one outside of your immediate circle is aware of our transaction. Further, you will require a forklift truck with a lifting capacity of one ton and a qualified driver. The gold will be in boxes and each box will weigh one hundred weight. That means there will be four hundred boxes to load onto your aircraft. Do you have access to manual labourers?"

"That's no problem. We're used to split loads and our aircraft has a rear ramp so loading should be simple."

The voice of Mr Pleasance became less convivial and more threatening. "Remember Captain, you have two hours. Oh, and by the way, as a government shipment, it is exempt from customs regulations.

All the export documents are in order so no need to worry about anything like that."

The voice became friendly again. "Thank you, Captain, we'll meet on Friday."

The line went dead. Captain and Mrs Colington both sat back. "You know Sally, I think we've just saved the company. If that was legit, we'll have one hundred and twenty-five thousand in the bank tomorrow morning and we can get ready for Friday. If there's no money, then someone's just played a big hoax on us." He looked at his wife. "Tomorrow will tell."

Captain and Mrs Colington left for the night. Paul Stockland their Chief Engineer and sometime co-pilot had left earlier.

"If this is genuine, Paul will certainly get a shock in the morning."

The Captain joked. "Yes, he might get the salary we owe him."

Chapter Twelve

The teams picked up their targets as planned. From their files, they knew Sophia Marr used the garage located within the Bank. As a senior employee, she was entitled to a parking space. She drove to and from her mews conversion in Chelsea, so the team assigned to follow her found their task simple, provided they didn't get snarled up in London traffic.

They followed her by her direct route home only having one nasty moment when she jumped a red light meaning the officers had to let her get further ahead than they would have wished. Luckily, she was on a straight road, and they soon picked up the bright red Morgan travelling only four cars in front of them.

Sophia Marr went straight to her house in Chelsea which had a private parking bay painted on the cobbles outside her front door. She entered but left the hood of the Morgan down despite it being late October. Finding a vantage point in such a restricted collection of properties wasn't easy. One detective stood watch whilst the other sought out a parking space that would give a line of sight to the entrance to the mews. Fortunately, the mews was a dead end so anyone leaving had to exit the way they'd come in. Eventually, the second detective found a spot in a supermarket car park with a perfect view of the entrance. Both men sat back and started their task of keeping tabs on Sophia Marr.

Michael Pleasance took the tube and train to work so one officer followed on foot whilst the other drove the car to Weybridge station. Following Pleasance wasn't difficult, and the pair of detectives tasked with following Michael Pleasance were reunited outside Weybridge station car park. They saw their target walk to the car park, open his car and drive off. They followed him to his detached mid-1930s house, saw him park in the driveway and enter his house through the front door.

The watchers found a layby offering a view of their target's drive and settled in. Both teams reported that they were in position.

***

In Cirencester, the would-be murderer had arrived some hours before the surveillance operation in London had begun. He'd met his host, walked around the estate and was now enjoying a gin and tonic seated in front of a large log fire. After his drink, he would bathe, dress for dinner and finalise his plan to shoot the Minister for Regional Development and Planning.

Also, in the drawing room were the remainder of the guests. There were two other Right Honourable gentlemen enjoying a drink and talking about horses. He knew them only vaguely. Sir Derek and Lady Layburn were deep in conversation with their host, Lord Rosyth, and an odd couple called Carstairs was standing off to one side looking embarrassed. From the fact they were already in their formal gear, the man assumed they must be from the local area.

There might be a few more to arrive especially the daughters of the local social climbers. Lady Rosyth prided herself on being a matchmaker and with three young and single men present, the man knew it was odds-on that three young things from the village would be wheeled out as companions for the night.

He remembered his last visit and the girl he was paired off with. She was pleasant enough but despite his best efforts went home alone. He hoped for better tonight but knew he mustn't get distracted. He wasn't here for fun.

His plan was forming. He'd seen and now hidden a ladder just under the bedroom window of his target. He was considering breaking into Derek Layburn's bedroom using the ladder to make it look like a burglary. He'd shoot his one-time friend and his wife if he had to and simply walk back to his own bedroom which was just three doors down. He was considering his plan as he sat and sipped his drink realising it had flaws, when an old friend entered from the terrace, acknowledged everyone present, spotted the man and lifted a whisky from a tray on the sideboard as he approached him.

The man recognised the Right Hon Julian Bennet, heir to Lord Bennet the technology king.

"I didn't know you were coming to this bash, old boy. How have you been?" greeted Julian Bennet.

He didn't want to get into conversation but felt that acting normally would help throw the police off his scent, so he entered into a long conversation ranging from cars to girls. They had another drink and parted promising to enjoy Lord Rosyth's hospitality later.

As he dressed for dinner, he formed his plan. It was simple and deep down he thought it too simple but realised with his superior intellect he sometimes overcomplicated tasks he set himself. He'd examined the best way to kill Derek Layburn from many different angles and concluded his current plan was simple and as fool proof as he could make it.

He'd decided not to play burglar but to lead the police to think a burglar could be the killer. He'd wait until he knew his target and his wife were circulating in the great hall downstairs. He concluded that the curtains of their bedroom would be drawn as it was already dark outside. The man's plan was to retrieve the hidden ladder, place it against the wall below Derek Layburn's bedroom window knowing it wouldn't be spotted from inside as the curtains were drawn. He would then simply wait until everyone had left or gone to bed, silently walk the short distance to the Layburn's bedroom, shoot them and return to his own room unseen. He smiled as he thought of his attention to detail. Any normal killer would simply implement the plan, but he knew better. Before joining everyone downstairs he'd visit his target's bedroom, remove the key from inside the door in order the door couldn't be locked by the Layburn's as they bedded down for the night. This would ensure that he'd be able to enter the bedroom. Whilst in the bedroom he'd slip the window catch so the window could be opened. If the police bought the theory of a burglar killer, they'd see how it could have been done.

With the time approaching seven-thirty, he set about implementing his plan. By the time he joined the other guests for pre-dinner drinks, everything was in place. He'd left his revolver hidden in his room, he'd checked it was fully loaded and he'd even wiped the bullets to ensure there were no fingerprints.

As he circulated sipping on his champagne, he was met by Lady Rosyth who had a slightly plump girl in tow. She was her usual bubbly self and introduced him to Matilda Armstrong.

"Matilda has just returned from a wonderful adventure touring the Far East. I'm sure you'll have lots in common. Matilda's father is one of the largest landowners in the county and our Deputy Sheriff." Lady Rosyth was gushing as she always was. At around sixty years old she had adopted a matronly approach to marriage early on. He knew her husband had a reputation for liking attractive younger women so the fact his wife was happy to attend to domestic matters and play the Lady of the Manor probably suited him.

Matilda shook his hand and held it longer than was necessary. Lady Rosyth, her matchmaking duty done, floated off to find another young thing to introduce to one of her bachelor guests. Matilda wasn't unattractive with long brown hair and an elegant stance. She was about five-foot-nine with a round face and brown eyes. She was a little on the plump side for his usual taste in women, but he forgave all of that as he visually examined her most attractive feature, her cleavage. Like a lot of slightly tubby girls, she was well endowed, and the cut of her rose-pink evening gown did nothing to hide her assets. As he returned to Matilda's side with a glass of champagne for her, he realised her figure was perfectly proportioned and that she had a glow of a girl used to the outdoor life. They chatted freely on a range of topics, but he was surprised that this well-educated and endowed 24-year-old talked with so much smutty innuendo. It was clear Matilda Armstrong knew about the birds and the bees and was a girl not afraid of men. He began to think he might get lucky tonight.

***

At the ornate dining table laid out in the vast dining room of Lord Rosyth's country house, he was of course seated next to Matilda. He looked around the room and spotted Julian Bennet seated next to Mrs Carstairs. Julian didn't seem to have a female companion and the man wondered if the rumours regarding his sexuality might be true. He looked round the table and counted the guests, all of whom could be murder suspects by morning except for his victims.

Apart from his hosts and Derek Layburn and his wife, there was the couple he'd seen earlier already dressed for dinner. He now knew they were called Mr and Mrs Carstairs. He was a businessman and an apparent social climber. Then the local doctor, Dr Francis and his wife sitting towards the opposite end of the table. He noticed the two sons of peers like himself sitting as a group of four, having been presumably introduced to their female dining companions by her Ladyship. One of the girls was particularly thin with protruding teeth. Her high-pitched nervous laugh sounded like horse neighing and could be heard by everyone around the table. He concluded that this particular Right Hon wouldn't be lucky tonight and should be grateful not to have to wake up next to this horsey-looking girl.

His companion on the other hand was luckier. This other man was paired with a stunning girl with long blonde hair and a flawless complexion. She seemed engrossed in the same horse stories he'd overheard earlier when the two bachelors were talking over pre-dinner drinks. He wondered if he could somehow swap Matilda for this blonde beauty. He thought he might try later after the men had their brandy and cigars.

A couple of well-known socialites, Sir Colin and Lady Thomson completed the guest list. Their faces were always to be found in *Tatler* and they seemed to attend as many dinners as possible, so it was no surprise they were present, but as a famous criminal barrister, Sir Colin would make a good witness. He undertook to ensure he made the correct noises to Sir Colin such that he would never think he was the killer. The man counted sixteen guests at the table tonight but there would only be fourteen to make statements to the police in the morning.

The meal progressed as expected. The food was excellent as was the wine. He spoke seductively to Matilda who, after the main course, surprised him by placing her hand on the inside of his thigh. Not unsurprisingly he gave up all thoughts of swapping Matilda for the blonde. He thought things were going well for a bit of a romp later in the evening but as he allowed himself to daydream about pleasures to come, he formed another part of his plan. Matilda could become an important part of his alibi. The pair continued to flirt, and he kept topping up her wine glass without refilling his own. For his revised plan to work he needed Matilda merry if not drunk after the meal, especially if he were to enjoy a night with her but he needed her drunk afterwards, so that she'd pass out with him in bed. His revised plan was to carry out the deed as already planned but to return to Matilda who wouldn't know he'd been out of the room. When the alarm was raised, he could waken Matilda and as far as she would be concerned, he'd never left her side. The man knew using her as his alibi would potentially damage her reputation, but he thought she already had what was probably a well-earned reputation.

After proposing various toasts Lord Rosyth stood. "Gentlemen, I believe it is time for us men to enjoy our brandy and cigars. I'll now ask my wife to escort the ladies into the drawing room where further refreshments will be served."

At this announcement, a flushed and happy Matilda gripped the inside of his leg with undue force. "I'll see you later if you want."

The man wanted and said so. He whispered to her telling her which room he was in as she stood to follow the ladies. She turned and with an impish grin said, "See you later."

He hoped he would. He would have preferred to bed the blonde companion of the other Right Hon, but Matilda looked capable and would serve as his alibi.

The men gathered around one end of the large dining room table. Introductions were made where necessary, the man said hello to Derek Layburn and made sure Sir Colin Thompson heard their conversation which he kept friendly and light. The evening progressed until their host suggested they re-join the ladies. Matilda was waiting for him and immediately put her arm through his in the manner of claiming him for her own.

Eventually, the guests started to leave. Mr and Mrs Carstairs left with the thin girl who'd been paired off with one of the Right Honourables, Dr Francis left with his wife saying he had a busy surgery in the morning, and he was immediately followed by Sir Colin Thompson and Lady Thompson who whisked the stunning blonde away with them. It seemed she was there as a favour to her father who was a barrister in Sir Colin's practice. He felt sorry for her companion. He had Matilda, but at that moment he realised she too had gone.

He was philosophical about it. Easy come, easy go, but he felt disappointed and let down as Matilda would have been an enjoyable part of his alibi, plus he'd ordered a bottle of champagne to be placed in his room so that Matilda could top up her alcohol level after she'd been nice to him. He'd have to revert to his original plan.

**

The first team watching Michael Pleasance reported to DS Jenny Fuller at nine p.m. The report was routine. Pleasance hadn't moved. Almost as soon as they'd hung up, their relief team phoned asking for their location. At five minutes before ten p.m. the first team watching Michael Pleasance handed over to the second. This was the team lead by DC Player and the girl taken out of uniform just for this operation who'd made everyone laugh at the briefing with her naïve question. She suspected her older and fatter companion might sleep most of the night leaving her to keep watch. She could almost have been clairvoyant, but all remained quiet.

The first team watching Sophia Marr reported to DS Matt Conway at three minutes past eight saying all was quiet, but they were getting funny looks from the supermarket security. They'd been reminded they were only allowed to park in the supermarket car park for three hours. The DS and his reporting DC had a laugh about paying the parking fine.

At ten minutes past eight, Sophia Marr's car exited the mews and turned left heading towards the Embankment. The car with her two watchers scrambled to follow. They realised that although using a supermarket car park for observation gave them a good vantage point, exiting in a hurry surrounded by late-night shoppers wasn't so easy.

They caught a glimpse of the Morgan as it headed over Tower Bridge but lost it on the far side. The detective in the passenger seat called into DS Matt Conway. "Sorry skip, we've lost her." He explained about the difficulty getting out of the car park and tried to maintain it wasn't their fault. The DS was livid, told them to carry out a box search of the area immediately south of the bridge.

As he hung up, both The Cap and DI Peter Jones knew something was wrong. Matt Conway explained. "We'd better find her quick. The DCI will go spare. It's one thing to say we lost her and found her. It's another to say we lost her all night." The Cap was thinking how Steve would react. He was at home but on call. Poppy had already recorded the facts into her log.

The Cap as the senior man made a decision. "Poppy, you hold the fort. Peter, you and I will get out there and try and spot the car. It's a bit flash so shouldn't be too difficult. Jenny, you and Matt do the same thing but cover the west side, we'll cover the east. Poppy, get onto the two clowns who lost her. Tell them we're on our way and to give us all ten-minute updates." The four detectives were up and leaving when The Cap stopped. "Oh! Unless the DCI calls in don't phone him unless it's a major issue. Got it?"

"Yes sir, I understand."

***

With three cars covering a wide area south of Tower Bridge, it was hoped the Morgan could be spotted but after two hours The Cap called it off. He instructed team one to return to the supermarket car park and told team two to meet them there. He also instructed one member of team two to keep the mews house under surveillance and that meant on foot. He wanted to know exactly when Sophia Marr returned.

It was now ten-thirty in the evening. The first teams had been relieved, and their replacements were now in position. The Cap instructed both DSs to stand down, but to keep their mobiles switched on. He and Peter Jones headed back to the office. When they arrived, The Cap saw that Steve was in his office talking to Poppy.

"What the hell happened? I see from Poppy's log you've lost Sophia Marr." The DCI wasn't happy, and the two DIs knew it. "How the hell could it happen and who are the two idiots responsible? I'll have them back directing traffic if Marr's even now torturing Walter Bostrom."

The Cap explained about the supermarket car park exit, he tried to defend the two officers saying it was difficult to find an observation site. The DCI wasn't impressed.

"They should have had enough common sense or been ordered to have one of them with eyes on the house. Not both tucked up in the car." This latter comment was a direct criticism of both the DIs present and DS Matt Conway as the team leader.

The Cap tried again. "Sorry Steve but these things happen. I've told the relief lads to keep watch on foot and let me know as soon as she returns."

Steve seemed to mellow. "Yeah, I suppose so. Poppy, you get off home, see you tomorrow as early as you like."

Poppy gathered up her things, said goodnight and left.

"You two had better get off as well. It's almost eleven and I've a feeling tomorrow's going to be a long, busy day. I just hope I don't have to tell Alfie Brooks we've lost Sophia Marr."

As his two colleagues left the DCI had no way of knowing how prophetic his words were. Tomorrow would indeed be a long and busy day but not because of Operation Bank. He sat alone drinking his coffee.

Chapter Thirteen

The man helped himself to another small whiskey. He was the last of the guests to retire for the evening. Lady Rosyth had retired but Lord Rosyth seemed happy to keep him company. His Lordship wasn't too sober but not so drunk that he would forget all the nice things the man was saying about the Minister for Regional Development and Planning, praising his stand on green issues and making the suggestion he might one day be Prime Minister.

Lord Rosyth wasn't such a big fan of Sir Derek Layburn, thinking him a snob and a social climber with no real class, but agreed that his stand on green issues was welcome within the government. Lord Rosyth would repeat this conversation to the police, proving he had no ill will towards the Minister.

Their conversation came to a halt when Lord Rosyth spoke about the man's father and started to reminisce about their time in the Army together. He did not get on with his father. Every time they met, he was quizzed about his lifestyle, his need to settle down and his mother's constant and ongoing topic, the need for a suitable prospect as a wife.

As he climbed the stairs his heart rate increased as adrenaline pumped through his body. He was within hours of gaining a fortune and becoming financially independent. His only regret was that Matilda had vanished. Just remembering her outsize curves and her hand on his thigh brought him to a state of excitement over and above his adrenaline rush. He shrugged as he approached his bedroom door. He turned the handle and realised something was different. He'd left the main light on but now the room was illuminated only by the bedside lamp. As his eyes adjusted to the gloom, he spotted the figure of Matilda in his bed. She was clearly naked and covered only by a thin silk sheet. As she lay there, he observed the rise and fall of her chest and acknowledged that she was shaped in all the right places.

He had a mission to perform tonight in addition to Matilda. His brain went into overdrive calculating how the next few hours would play out. Here was his delightful alibi waiting to give him pleasure. He realised he had two for one, a companion for the night and an alibi.

"I thought you'd run off."

"Well, here I am darling, just waiting for you to take me," Matilda spoke in her sexiest low voice that further excited the man.

He approached the bed and bent down to kiss his plaything for the night. Matilda returned his kiss and grabbed the back of his neck daring him to come up for air.

He started to strip off his clothes but remembered he had preparations to make. Dressed only in socks and underpants he separated himself from Matilda, walked to a chest of drawers and lifted the key to his victims' room. He carefully wiped it using a face cloth from the bathroom to remove his finger prints, laid it on the side table together with a clean handkerchief to wrap it in when he replaced it after he'd killed his victims.

"What are you doing darling, Mattie's waiting?" asked a sleepy Matilda but using a very deep sexy voice. She put her arms out pleading for the man to come to her.

The man observed she'd opened the champagne and the glass was on her bedside cabinet. He thought this was good, but he didn't want her falling asleep just yet. He checked the drawer for his pistol. He didn't want Matilda to see it, so he examined it with his back to her. Happy everything was in order he closed the drawer, removed the rest of his clothing, including his socks and was immediately carried away to a world of ecstasy only a girl of Matilda's proportions could offer.

As he lay exhausted, he looked at his watch. It was 01.47 a.m. Matilda was still active allowing her hands and thighs to perform minor miracles. His brain told him he had time to allow Matilda to perform all over again, so he lay back and once more entered a world few people outside of Matilda's acquaintance even knew existed.

His brain said stop. He pushed Matilda aside, kissed her passionately several times and reached for the champagne. This part of his plan was easy. The lady apparently had an enormous appetite for all things.

Persuading her to drink most of the bottle of champagne wasn't difficult and almost as planned she passed out as the man's watch said 02.57 a.m.

He rose still naked, gathered up the key wrapped in his handkerchief and retrieved his pistol from its hiding place in his top drawer. Matilda was snoring gently.

Opening his bedroom door, he saw no one; the house was quiet. He'd read about DNA evidence and microscopic forensic science breakthroughs. His brain told him if he didn't wear any clothes, he couldn't leave behind any trace evidence. He smiled to himself. He was too smart for PC Plod.

At the door of the room occupied by Derek Layburn he stood and listened. Hearing nothing, he quietly opened the door, closed it and replaced the bedroom door key. He held his revolver in his right hand, his handkerchief in the other. He noticed his hand was shaking and his breathing was irregular. He was about to end two peoples' lives, but he felt no remorse, only nervous excitement.

Both victims were asleep side by side on a king-sized bed. They'd left a light on in their en-suite bathroom and left the door slightly ajar. The man thanked them for being so considerate. He looked around and saw a cushion on one of the side chairs. He had read that in the absence of a silencer shooting through a cushion helped dampen the noise. Although not part of his original plan this small deviation seemed to be sensible. After all, a quieter shot would give him more time to return to Matilda before someone investigated the noise.

He approached Derek Layburn with the cushion in front of the barrel of his gun. In a strange way, he hoped Layburn would wake up and understand why he had to die and how he could have carried on living if he'd only helped out his old friend.

The man counted to three. At 03.03 a.m., he pulled the trigger. The brain matter that had once been the brain of Sir Derek Layburn Minister for Regional Development and Planning exploded across the bed linen and the pillows. Some even sprayed the wall behind the bed. The man was momentarily in shock. The explosion was louder than he imagined or remembered. Clearly, the cushion as a silencer didn't work too well. Lady Layburn woke with a start and before she could scream, the man fired a shot into her chest. He walked around the bed and calmly shot

Amanda Layburn in the head just like her husband. He used the cushion again despite thinking it didn't work too well as a suppressor of sound but decided he needed two shots to make sure the lady was dead. He couldn't afford to leave a witness.

Even more adrenaline coursed through his brain, urging him into action. His breathing was erratic; he was sweating from fear but with his IQ he knew he'd overcome the fears of mere mortals at times like this. He even allowed himself a few seconds to slide up the bedroom window using his handkerchief to further perpetuate the story of an intruder. He calmly used his handkerchief to open and close the bedroom door and walked smartly back the dozen or so yards to his own bedroom and the comatose Matilda.

After wiping down the gun again and placing it back in the drawer he decided to take a quick shower in case anything had stuck to him, but in his nude state, he knew this was impossible. He reasoned better safe than sorry, so he quickly stood under the shower letting the water flow over him.

He slid into bed, pulled Matilda toward him, put his arm around her shoulders and lay still awaiting the discovery of a murder. He was surprised nothing happened. He thought that the sound of the loud explosions must waken someone in the household but there was no alarm and no frantic activity to discover the source of the sounds. With Matilda sleeping and no activity, he really didn't need her as an alibi, except to confirm they'd spent the night together and he hadn't left the room. He knew he had to do something about the gun but first, he'd pleasurably enhance his alibi. He gently woke Matilda and, being a lady with large appetites, she took little persuading even in her intoxicated state to be nice once again to the man. He made a point of asking what time it was and confirming with Matilda that it was just 03.30 a.m.

The pair slept until around eight a.m. As he woke, he heard nothing to suggest two murders had taken place in the house only a few hours previously. He rose, showered and shaved, dressed in his finest country gentleman tweeds and woke Matilda. The girl was seriously hungover and didn't want to see daylight. As far as the man was concerned, Matilda had done her bit and would provide his alibi but as a bonus had given him pleasure beyond his wildest expectations. Although he wouldn't abandon her as he needed her alibi, he decided she wasn't his responsibility. He shrugged, said he was going down to breakfast and left a naked and still very drunk girl to sleep it off.

Most of the house guests were already present in the breakfast room. The man didn't know if anyone present was aware Matilda was in his room, but he chose not to mention it. As they were finishing, Lord Rosyth asked if anybody had seen Sir Derek and his wife. A uniform negative led him to ask his butler to enquire if Sir Derek and Lady Layburn were joining them for breakfast as it was now after nine'. The man pretended to be reading *The Times*. He'd finished his breakfast and adjourned to the lounge next door for more coffee. He waited.

As he was in the adjoining room, he only heard the exchange between Lord Rosyth and his butler. The poor old butler had been physically sick at what he'd witnessed when he knocked and entered the bedroom of Sir Derek and his wife. The man grinned behind his newspaper. Being physically sick meant the crime scene would be contaminated making it even more difficult to prove who had killed the couple. The man relaxed and wondered if Matilda was ready for another round of bedroom antics. He thought better not.

As soon as the butler had reported to his master, events moved quickly. The police were called; Lord Rosyth ordered that no one should enter the bedroom of the dead couple and, as an afterthought, cancelled the morning's rough shoot telling his guests they'd better not leave the estate.

The man went to his room and gently nudged Matilda awake. As she came to, she reached out for the man, placed her arms around his neck and made noises that got the man once more excited at the thought of what she could do to him with her body. Reluctantly, he pulled back.

"You'll never believe it, my dear, there's been a double murder here. It seems two of the guests have been shot. It must have happened around three-thirty just as we were enjoying each other for the last time last night. Remember, I asked you the time?"

Matilda was surfacing from her alcohol-induced coma and vaguely remembered their final romp but not the time. "My memory goes but if you say we were romping then you must be correct; alcohol does that to me." She pulled the sheet to one side showing her naked body and held out her arms imploring him to join her for more bedroom frolics. The man took in the vision of nudity and admired the girl's sexual appetite. He looked her over with more of an analytical eye and concluded she was a bit heavy for his tastes and in clear daylight wasn't such a conquest as he had thought the previous evening. He wrote her off as a useful, promiscuous and enjoyable one-night stand but nothing more.

"You'd better get up and dress. The police are on their way."

The man removed his revolver from his drawer, where he had hidden it still wrapped in his handkerchief, after shooting Derek and Amanda Layburn. With his back to Matilda, he slipped it into his jacket pocket. Once again, he told Matilda to get up and said he was going for a walk.

As he walked around the grounds looking for a place to hide the gun, he saw the first of several police cars arrive speeding up the drive. He smiled inwardly thinking *poor buggers, they won't have a clue*. He spied an old tree that had obviously been struck by lightning some time ago, and saw it had a hole not dissimilar to a rabbit hole. He casually approached the tree, thought this was a good hiding place and after carefully looking around for witnesses, placed the gun in the hole and removed his handkerchief.

He was pleased with himself. He had his own back on a hitman who'd double-crossed him, he'd carried out this task to get his bumper payday. He'd procured an alibi that he was sure couldn't be broken and with his enormous brain, he felt he had calculated everything to the last detail. He told himself he'd committed the perfect murder, and no one would ever suspect him.

He looked at his watch. It was 10.28 a.m. Almost exactly seven hours since he'd committed a double murder. He acknowledged to himself he felt no remorse or guilt. In this world, you look after yourself. Everybody needed money and would do what he'd done to make themselves wealthy. He'd nothing to feel guilty about.

He casually strolled up to the house to have his fun with the plodding policeman some other plodding policeman would have put in charge to try to solve these murders. He laughed out loud as he thought, *Well, good luck*.

Chapter Fourteen

The sergeants had gathered in Steve's office early on Thursday morning the 20th of October.

The second surveillance teams had been successfully relieved by their third team colleagues. It was seven a.m. and Poppy was updating the logs, although in truth, apart from losing Sophia Marr for several hours there was little to report. Marr had remained in her mews house after returning and Pleasance had been home all evening.

The team watching Pleasance had been briefed about his movements by the first team and were aware he would probably drive to Weybridge Station Car Park, leave his car and travel by train to central London. The watchers decided to reverse the procedure used yesterday. They followed him to the car park. One officer boarded the train and followed him to his office whilst the second watcher drove into central London, parked the car in the Bank's private car park and met his colleague in reception. Michael Pleasance was at his desk at 08.47 a.m.

Sophia Marr was observed leaving her mews house and getting into her car. The team now watching her had learnt from the mistakes of their colleagues. One of the two watchers had been in a position to watch the property all night whilst his colleague remained in the car. They had alternated every hour throughout the night. On seeing Marr exit her house, the watcher called up the car that was still parked in the supermarket car park. As soon as Marr's little Morgan exited the mews, the watchers were only two cars behind. The drive to the Bank was uneventful and after allowing time for her to park, the team followed her into the Bank's car park.

At 09.03 a.m., all four watchers were seated in the Bank's large reception area. Commander Brooks had arranged security passes for those officers who needed to be inside the Bank to keep watch on the two suspects. This allowed for periodic walks past their individual offices to ensure they hadn't somehow escaped the building. The four officers who would be on duty till twelve noon decided to split up allowing for two at anyone time to be present in the reception area keeping watch on who came but more importantly who left. They swapped over every hour.

The watchers reported back to both Jenny and Matt Conway who in turn updated Poppy. Everything was quiet. There seemed a lot of bodies within Steve's office suite. Apart from himself and Poppy, both Jenny Fuller and Matt Conway had positioned themselves behind desks. The Cap was at his own desk whilst DI Peter Jones just seemed to be hanging around. Steve told everyone except Poppy to go to the canteen and get out of his hair. As things developed, they should update Poppy, and he reminded both detective sergeants that the relieving teams should be in position well before noon. "If anything is to develop it could be over the cover of a lunch date or even an afternoon off. Make sure both teams on the twelve-to-five shift understand and make sure they are alert. You might even want to back them up just in case."

Both sergeants nodded their agreement.

As the team shuffled out The Cap held back. "Steve, what if we're wrong? What if these two are innocent and not holding Walter Bostrom? What if this is a complete waste of money and manpower?" The Cap looked dejected.

"I suppose no one can say we didn't try but if you're right and this is all for nothing, for Christ's sake, don't ever tell anyone it was based on one of Poppy's stories." The DCI laughed. "We'll be a laughing stock for months."

The Cap obviously wanted to talk. He pulled up a chair. "Look, Steve, you and the Commander have stuck your necks out. I wasn't with you and Twiggy when you interviewed this guy, Michael Pleasance, so I can only go on what you've told me but we're acting on your gut instinct that this guy's a wrong one, we've no evidence."

The DCI appreciated his colleague's concern. "Yes, you're right, but you know sometimes you get your copper gut. It tells you to be suspicious and that's what I feel about Mr Michael Pleasance. Not *for* his reporting our interview, but *because* he reported it. I had a feeling when we left him and it's even stronger now, but you're right. We've no evidence but twenty tonnes of gold bullion is due to be shipped tomorrow at twelve noon and it might be at risk."

The Cap stood. He could see his boss was concerned so in an attempt to lighten the mood, he confirmed the party to celebrate Andy Miller's promotion and transfer was all arranged for eight the following evening. "Do you think we should invite Poppy?"

"No reason why not. She's part of the team and your missus will be with you, so Poppy should be safe." The DCI grinned.

"That's not fair sir. I only ever look; I appreciate a beautiful lady but I've…"

Twiggy arrived out of breath. It was 10.32 a.m. "Thank goodness you're both here," she panted. "I've had a call from Susan Bostrom, Walter Bostrom's mother. She says Walter called her half an hour ago. He said he was OK she wasn't to worry, and he'd see her soon."

The Cap was the first to respond as only he could. "Bloody hell, where does that leave us?"

"For once, Cap, you're right. Bloody hell!"

***

Activity at Direct Air Charter at Manston Airfield in Kent had never been greater. They were preparing to receive twenty tonnes of gold bullion the next day and fly it to somewhere in Turkey.

Fuel had to be ordered and Captain Colington was busy calculating the fuel load needed to get them there without stopping to refuel. The old L100 aircraft had a long range but with such a heavy payload it would mean skimping on the amount of reserve fuel they carried if the trip was to be made non-stop.

Captain Colington sat back, having calculated that unless they experienced headwinds, the non-stop journey was possible. He allowed himself to think about the money sitting in the company bank account. He smiled. One hundred and twenty-five thousand pounds with the same again to come and the promise of further Bank of England contracts. Life was at last looking good for the struggling airline.

The Captain shook himself, pulled flight plan submission paperwork towards him and set to work with maps and navigational instruments to prepare a flight plan for submission to European Air Traffic Control.

His engineer and co-pilot for the trip, Paul Stockland. was happily working on the inner starboard engine. It had developed a slight oil leak and needed to be repaired. Paul didn't mind as he worked on the engine. He'd just been given a cheque for his back pay and a five-hundred-pound bonus for late payment. He knew there was a big lift to Turkey on Friday, but Norman Colington hadn't given him any details.

***

"Let's get the other three back." The DCI needed clarity and thought the best way was to hear the thoughts of those officers who had already been briefed about the operation. He considered telling Commander Alfie Brooks of this development but decided to wait.

Once everyone was seated in the outer office, Steve called for their attention. "We've just heard from Flo that apparently Walter Bostrom is alive and free to call his mother. As you know we've been working on Operation Bank based on a theory that Walter Bostrom's being held and possibly tortured for his four-digit secret code." The DCI looked at the blank faces in front of him. "If he's free to call his mother then where is he, and have we got it totally wrong?"

Twiggy spoke. "I didn't get much sense from Susan Bostrom other than he'd called. I asked if she knew where he was but all she said was he's alive and will be in touch."

DS Matt Conway spoke up. "Is it possible all three of them are in on it and plan to nick the gold?"

The Cap had been thinking. "It's possible but these guys aren't seasoned criminals." He let his voice convey his irritation. "They'd have no idea how to pull off a job like this. No, I don't see it, but I think it's possible they're all involved, and someone with criminal contacts might be pulling the strings." The Cap looked at everybody in turn. "And another thing, how could three bank clerks organise to snatch the gold from the armoured trucks? That takes muscle."

Steve allowed the debate to continue. He was pleased to note everyone except Poppy contributed and openly discussed various theories. He held his own counsel and was still convinced Pleasance and

Marr were involved in some way in a plan to steal the twenty tonnes of bullion. After ten minutes or so, Steve called the open forum to a halt.

"Let's look at this. We now know Walter Bostrom is free, but we don't know where. Flo, can you do a search of his credit cards, to see if any have been used over the past few days?"

"Right, will do."

"Cap get over to Mrs Bostrom's again. Do a call back on her phone. See if we can get the number he called from and pump her for details of what he said, any background noise, you know the thing." Steve had a sudden thought. "Cap, did we ever check his mobile?"

"Yes. I think so."

"Don't think. Get it checked out to see if it's active. Ask Technical Support."

Before Steve could continue Twiggy chipped in. "I'll do that if The Cap's going to see Mrs Bostrom."

The Cap had shared his thoughts about Twiggy and the Head of Tech Support with his DCI. They both liked Terry Harvey and Steve had dismissed it as The Cap's imagination but now, as he smiled to himself, he wasn't so sure. "Fine, that'll let The Cap get started, but remember, we're looking for activity over the past few days. Any and all masts his phone may have pinged." The DCI had another thought. "I suppose we have his mobile number?"

Twiggy smiled. "First thing I got from his mother."

Twiggy nodded. The Cap grinned.

Steve was still in control. "We carry on with Operation Bank." He addressed the two sergeants. "Make sure your teams stay on them. As I said, lunchtime could be crucial, so they'd better not lose them. Understood?"

Jenny and Matt Conway said they understood.

"Peter." Steve singled out DI Peter Jones who'd been attached to the operation from Tactical Liaison. "With The Cap following up with Walter's mother I need you to hold the fort as senior officer present. OK?"

"Yes, boss. No problem…" Steve's internal phone was ringing. With an angry movement, he crashed into his office and lifted the receiver. He was about to shout a *Yes* when he stopped. It was

Commander Brooks instructing him to drop everything and get himself up to the Commander's office three minutes ago.

With no more information from the Commander and before going to his twelfth-floor office, Steve told his team to carry on and reminded Jenny and Matt that they should back up the handover between the teams before twelve noon.

He watched as The Cap set off to see Mrs Bostrom, Twiggy to meet Terry Harvey in Tech Support and then look into Walter Bostrom's credit card activity, Poppy was updating the files as the teams reported in and Detective Inspector Peter Jones was holding each strand together.

Steve felt he could do no more but decided to come clean with Alfie Brooks and tell him about Walter Bostrom's appearance. He examined his watch. It was 11.04 a.m.

***

As he entered Alfie's office, he noted the presence of a man he recognised from television. He was dressed in a blue pinstriped suit, his hair was slicked back, and he carried himself like someone with all the problems of the world on his shoulders. Also present was the Deputy Commissioner of the Metropolitan Police who didn't look happy. All three were seated around Alfie Brook's conference table.

The DCI acknowledged Alfie with a "You sent for me sir?"

"Yes, I did, Inspector. I don't know if you've met the Deputy Commissioner Phillipa Cartwright."

Steve nodded. "Ma'am, a pleasure." The woman didn't smile and barely acknowledged the DCI's pleasantry. As a detective, Steve deduced this was not a happy woman and he wondered apprehensively why he had been commanded to attend.

Alfie carried on. "And this is the Home Secretary, Julian Covely."

Steve nodded, but the Home Secretary, always the politician, stood and offered his hand which Steve shook.

The Commander appeared to be running this meeting whatever it was about.

"Steve, there's been an incident in Cirencester at the estate of Lord Rosyth. It seems there's been a double homicide. The reason the Home

Secretary is here is one of the victims is a member of the government, Sir Derek Layburn." Alfie paused to gauge Steve's reaction to the name. He got none.

"The second victim is his wife, Lady Layburn, but you know her better as Amanda Layburn, our newly appointed internal solicitor." Alfie watched as Steve's face registered recognition.

Steve knew from experience to remain silent in such company. He was here to be ordered what to do. Anything he said would be a waste of breath.

Phillipa Cartwright spoke up. "DCI Burt, you are aware one of your unit's tasks is to assist outside forces as required. Well, this is a case you are to take on. With the Home Secretary's blessing, you are to run the investigation into the murders of Sir Derek and Lady Layburn. Is that understood?"

"Yes, Ma'am."

The Home Secretary was next to speak, but in a far gentler tone than the Deputy Commissioner's. "Mr Burt, when a government minister is murdered, the government must consider every angle including state security. Fortunately, Sir Derek's department didn't handle any state secrets, so we are happy that this be dealt with by the Met.

I'm told you are a very accomplished officer and one who has proved to be discreet in the past. I'm asking for your discretion here. I don't want unsubstantiated gossip in the newspapers. Keep the press away from this as best you can but find this murderer."

All Steve could say was, "Yes sir, I'll do my best." He knew the real briefing still had to come.

"DCI Burt, remember Amanda Layburn was almost one of us so spare nothing to get to the bottom of this. I expect a quick result and an early trial. Clear?" The Deputy Commissioner wasn't known for her deductive skills having spent most of her career in administration, but Steve just acknowledged the instruction. He could do no more.

The visitors rose followed by Steve and Alfie Brooks. Julian Covely wished Steve good luck while the Deputy Commissioner just scowled as she left. Steve and Alfie resumed their seats.

"Bloody hell, Alfie, I've got enough on with this gold thing. How do you expect me to run a double murder at the same time?"

Alfie sat back. "Look, Steve, you're the best bloody homicide detective we've got. Your Special Resolutions Unit was set up for just this very thing, so don't bitch about being overworked. We all are at certain times." Alfie crossed his arms. "Now look, your man DI Ishmal, you've given him some glowing reports so I'm assuming he's capable of taking over the bullion job. It's only until lunchtime tomorrow anyway."

Steve interrupted the Commander to tell him of Walter Bostrom's reappearance.

"I see how that might complicate things but are you sticking to your theory that someone's going to try and steal that gold tomorrow?"

"Yes sir."

"Well, there you go. Get your people reorganised, leave DI Ishmal in charge. You can keep an eye on things from a distance. We do have phones and other modern technologies you know." The Commander said with a smile.

"Get down to Cirencester as quick as you like but before five this afternoon. The local man's a DI Halliday, he's expecting you. He's already taken statements from the guests. It sounds like a bloody Agatha Christie get together so most likely you'll find the butler did it."

"Very funny sir." Steve was more formal. "If you don't mind, I'd like to take DS Jenny Fuller as my number two. We've worked together before, and I know I can trust her."

"Yes, with your life if I recall. Well, she's on secondment from Essex for the Bank case so I suppose I can extend her stay until you've solved this thing but Steve," the Commander was looking the DCI squarely in the eyes. "Watch your back. You've already seen how political it is, and this guy Lord Rosyth is a big noise on the opposition benches in the Lords, so tread carefully. Use all the Met's resources and stay down as long as you think you need to."

Both men stood. Steve was in a daze thinking of everything he had to put in place before going off to Cirencester. The two men shook hands and with a 'good luck and report in regularly' ringing in his ears, the DCI set off to solve a double murder but first he had to regroup his troops.

***

The first thing he did on arriving at his office was to bring Poppy up to date. He told her to open a new set of files marked Cirencester and to contact DI Halliday and have him send any statements he'd already taken. He asked her to arrange hotel accommodation for himself and DS Jenny Fuller and to keep in contact as events on the bullion case developed. He called Jenny Fuller, explained the situation and told her she'd be relieved by Peter Jones and to make her way independently to Cirencester. He'd meet her at Lord Rosyth's mansion at five o'clock.

Next, he contacted DI Peter Jones and again explained the situation and was relieved by the DI's response. He would talk with Jenny Fuller and take over from her in half an hour. Lastly, he called The Cap. He brought him up to speed and agreed once he'd interviewed Mrs Bostrom, he'd base himself in Steve's office. "But keep me posted. Let me know what goes down and when."

The Cap agreed, wished his boss good luck and assured him the investigation into the potential bullion robbery would carry on as though the DCI were still in his office.

DCI Steve Burt having organised his troops as best he could, set off to his home to pack a bag and inform his wife he might be away a few days. His wife Dr Alison Mills was seeing patients, so he left a note and set off for Cirencester and into one of the most perplexing cases he would ever work on.

Chapter Fifteen

The drive to Cirencester was fairly straightforward. The weather was kind, and the traffic was light. The DCI had time to stop at a roadside services station for a coffee and a ham sandwich. With his stomach fuller and not making rumbling noises he set off on the final part of his three-hour journey to Lord Rosyth's country pad.

He approached the impressive, gated drive, pressed the intercom, informed the detached voice who he was and would they please open the gates. The voice obviously knew who the DCI was as they immediately swung open. Steve drove up the long driveway marvelling that such obvious wealth still existed, even more so when he saw the house. From what little he knew about architecture he assumed the style was early Victorian. It was square, built of light-coloured stone and in Steve's estimation must contain twenty bedrooms. To the front was a large circle planted with flowers, bushes and small trees. This was obviously to allow visiting vehicles to turn without having to reverse. The drive was covered with loose pebbles of various colours and there were four wide steps up to the large double door that was painted in a high gloss grey colour.

The whole appearance and ambience were of wealth and privilege. Sitting in his car with the engine running and the heater still giving out warm air, Steve determined not to be overwhelmed by this grandeur and obvious wealth. He was here to investigate a double murder.

There were several cars parked at various angles around the planted circle. Some were clearly police patrol cars and others were unmarked police vehicles obvious by the array of antennas fixed to the boot lids. Several uniformed officers were searching the grounds which seemed to go on for miles around each side of the house, but Steve knew the light would fade in another hour or so, and the search teams would have to be stood down. Steve looked at his watch. It was 16.07 p.m.

At first glance, the DCI was impressed by the efficiency of DI Halliday, an officer he had to still meet but who was clearly capable.

Reluctantly the DCI exited his warm car, pulled his fleece-lined coat tighter around him and set off for the front door of the house. After sitting for so long in a nice warm car experiencing the late afternoon temperatures on a mid-October day was a shock to the system. He hurried up the front stairs and tugged on the bell-pull handle that disappeared into the wall by the left-hand door.

The door was opened by a rather sickly-looking but well-dressed butler who, after enquiring in a friendly manner the purpose of this stranger's business, immediately ushered Steve into an average-sized room that the DCI thought might be Lord Rosyth's man cave due to the smell of cigar smoke and the masculine design of the furniture. The butler had explained in his cultured voice that his Lordship had kindly given his den up to the police to use as an incident room. Seated at various temporary tables were several uniformed officers and a few people dressed in civilian clothes. As he entered, a tall thin man broke off from a group of three people standing in the middle of the room and approached Steve.

The tall thin man extended his hand as he closed in on the DCI. "Good afternoon, sir, I'm guessing you must be DCI Burt from the Yard. I'm DI Arthur Halliday." The two men shook warmly. "I'm from the local nick and my Super's told me to give you all the assistance you need."

The DI looked behind him before continuing in a low conspiratorial voice. "To be honest, no one around here is happy with this mess. Lord Rosyth is the Sheriff for the county and a big noise. When he calls the Chief Constable comes running. I think everybody's happy the Met is taking over."

Steve made no comment. DI Arthur Halliday was over six feet tall with a full head of unruly brown hair. His suit looked well-used as though he might occasionally have slept in it, his once-white shirt was now grey and the stains on his tie could be a bacteriologist's worst nightmare. Steve put him in his early forties and his slight accent sounded local. From the activity he'd witnessed as he arrived, DI Halliday seemed to Steve to be a well-organised individual.

"Where are the house guests now?"

"I've told them they can come and go locally, and I've arranged with his Lordship that they can stay in the house until you tell them otherwise. The household knows the Yard are in charge and the house guests have been told to be in the sitting room at six." Steve thought this last comment was to reinforce the fact that Lord Rosyth was a big noise in these parts and needed to see police activity.

"Oh sir, I had a call from your DC Cooper asking for the witness statements. I've had them e-mailed to her." It took Steve a few seconds to realise that DC Cooper was in fact Poppy.

"Good." Steve looked around. "How do I get a cup of coffee around here?"

DI Arthur Halliday smiled. "If you'd like to follow me, sir, I'll introduce you to the housekeeper, a Mrs Stocks. She makes the best coffee I've ever had."

"Right. Bring the files and we'll go over what we have while we sample your Mrs Stocks' coffee."

The pair of detectives went down a set of stone stairs that started in a cupboard under the grand central stairway that dominated the beautifully decorated entrance hall and led them, after a few tight turns, into a vast kitchen. There were two uniformed officers seated at a large well-scrubbed kitchen table drinking tea and helping themselves to what looked like homemade cakes. When they saw the two detectives enter from the backstairs, they gulped down their mouthfuls of cake, quickly finished their tea and stood ready to leave. Steve smiled inwardly. Skiving off was an art form among certain police officers but at least these two had the sense to know when they'd been caught.

"Just having a five-minute break, Inspector," the older and probably more experienced of the two stated. "Our shift was up at two p.m., but we volunteered to stay on and help." This was obviously said to gain some sympathy from their senior officer.

"Yes Stevens, I know. Now get back out there, the pair of you, and pass the word. This kitchen's off-limits until further notice. I don't want you going home from here pounds heavier than when you arrived." The DI nodded towards the tray full of homemade cakes. The two uniforms smiled, said "Thank you, sir," and left.

Steve was impressed by DI Halliday's relationship with his troops.

Mrs Stocks was a stereotypical grand house cook. She was as round as she was tall, had a ruddy complexion and a spotless starched apron. When she spoke, it was obvious she was from the southwest. "Now, sirs, I suppose you'll be wantin' a cup of coffee and a few of me new cakes." She didn't wait for an answer. "Just thee sit yourselves down and I'll put the coffee to brewin."

DI Halliday, who'd obviously been treated to Mrs Stocks' coffee and cake before, spoke up. "Mrs Stocks, this is Detective Chief Inspector Burt from New Scotland Yard. He'll be in charge, and we need to discuss a few things in private." The DI pointed towards a fairly large room that had a glass-panelled door and was being used as an office. "Do you mind if we have our coffee and cakes in your office?"

"Not at all deary, you make yourselves comfortable. I'll have you tasting me coffee in minutes."

The pair settled into two upright chairs that had been placed around an old table that was obviously now being used as a desk.

Steve took charge. "Right, Arthur, tell me what we know. I'll interview everyone once I have a better understanding of events and who's who."

"We haven't much, sir. The Minister for Regional Development and Planning was staying in the house with his wife, Lady Layburn, as guests of Lord and Lady Rosyth overnight on Wednesday the 19th. That's last night." Arthur Halliday looked at Steve to make sure he understood the timeline. "His Lordship was hosting a dinner party for a few people. Some live locally within the village and others like Sir Derek travelled here and stayed the night. It was the butler who found the bodies when he was told to give the couple a shout at around nine this morning. Lord Rosyth called us, and we got here around ten-fifteen. I sealed off the bedroom, told everyone in the house to gather in the sitting room, called in the circus and was told to wait for you to arrive to take over. I've also started a search of the ground. I couldn't see a weapon in the room so it's possible it was dumped by the killer somewhere in the grounds. It's a long shot but you never know."

"Has the pathologist looked at the bodies?"

"Yes. She confirmed Sir Derek was shot once in the head and Lady Layburn was shot twice. Once in the chest and again in the head.

Probably from a pistol and probably .45 calibre but she'll confirm that at the post-mortem. Looks like the killer used a cushion to suppress the noise of the shots. The bodies have been left as we found them, but the mortuary wagon is on standby to move them once you've had a look."

"Good. Anything else?"

Before Arthur Halliday could open his first file Mrs Stocks entered with a large wooden tray. On it was a square plate of cakes, a large pot of hot coffee and two mugs. "You help yourselves dearies and if you needs anything, just shout." She looked at each detective in turn and a large red-cheeked satisfied smile appeared on her face. "I'll leave you in peace. Nobody will disturb you in here." She closed the door and the two policemen helped themselves to the contents of the tray.

Once they had settled down and only as they were halfway through their second cake and on their second cup of coffee, did Arthur Halliday open a file.

"Right, a house full of guests staying over, there's the list." The DI presented an A4 sheet of paper to Steve who scanned it and read out the names.

"We have Lord and Lady Rosyth." Steve looked at Arthur who nodded. As he read out each name the DCI paused and sought confirmation from the DI.

"Sir Derek and Lady Layburn, the victims." The DI confirmed.

"The Honourable Clarence Strum; The Honourable Cedric Blake; The Honourable Richard Pardew and The Honourable Julian Bennett."

Again, the DI nodded but added "It seems Lady Rosyth sees herself as a bit of a matchmaker. Each of these Honourable gentlemen had a female companion, except Julian Bennett, provided to accompany them at dinner, but they all left once the evening was finished."

"So, apart from the servants, these are the only people who were in the house overnight? That's his Lordship and his Lady, four Right Honourable gentlemen and our two victims. That's eight overnight including the two that have been murdered."

"That's about it, sir."

"What about the live-in staff?"

The DI opened a second file. "There are three live-in staff: Mrs Stocks, the cook, Mr Percival Lomond, the butler and a Miss Henrietta

Drummond, the housekeeper. The rest of the staff such as gardeners are contracted in."

"So last night we had eight people and three members of staff inside the house when the murders took place. Is that correct?"

"Yes, unless you buy into the theory that an intruder may have been present."

The DCI considered this but carried on. "And you've taken statements from them all including the staff?"

"Yes sir, and as I said, I've e-mailed the statements to your DC at the Yard."

"What about the other guests who didn't stay over?"

"I had a couple of DCs interview them and get their statements. They didn't seem to know much."

The DI produced another sheet of A4. "That's a list of the other guests with their addresses and contact details." He handed the paper to Steve.

"So, Mr and Mrs Carstairs live locally and left at around eleven with a Miss Annabella Carson, one of Lady Rosyth's young ladies?"

"Yes sir."

"Dr Francis and his wife, the local GP. They also left just after eleven and finally, Sir Colin and Lady Thomson, local socialite and London lawyer. They left at more or less the same time with another young lady, a Miss Ivory Blanchard."

Steve was considering this when there was a tap on the door, and he saw DS Jenny Fuller. He checked his watch and noted it was 4.50 p.m. Jenny had made good time.

Steve introduced Jenny to Arthur Halliday and told her he'd bring her up to speed when he'd finished being briefed by the local DI. He suddenly realised someone was missing from the list of guests.

"You said there were three female companions, so who was the third?"

The DI looked at his notebook and took the paper back from Steve. He looked crestfallen.

"Sorry, sir, it looks like we forgot about the third one. We forgot to put her on the list." Arthur Halliday had sudden colour to his face from embarrassment.

"Her name is Miss Matilda Armstrong." He used his pen to add the name to the list of guests.

"How did she get home?"

"Sorry sir, she seems to have been forgotten about. I'll check but she probably drove herself."

Steve was tolerant but only up to a point. "Arthur, in a murder enquiry, *nothing* gets forgotten. I'm not saying this woman is important to the case but until we can eliminate her, she's still a suspect. Is that clear?"

"Yes sir," the DI replied but without making eye contact with his senior officer.

"Have we got the statements from these outside people?"

"Yes sir, I've read them. They don't say much but I can get them e-mailed to the Yard if you want.

"Yes, better do that, Arthur."

Steve had to admit the coffee was good as he helped himself to another cup. He suggested Jenny should seek out Mrs Stocks and get a cup for herself. He saw the cakes had somehow vanished. "Maybe ask for a few more buns while you're at it." Jenny smiled and left to look for the cook.

"OK. We have eight people in the house overnight including the victims, three live-in servants and six guests who were here only for the dinner. Plus, three lady guests who were here to entertain three of the four Right Honourable gentlemen. Was there anything else out of the ordinary?"

"There was."

DI Arthur Halliday went on to explain that a ladder had been found propped up outside the bedroom window of the murdered victims' room and the sash cord window was open. The DI further explained that the local CSIs had examined the area around the foot of the ladder and found no evidence that it had been used. The feet of the ladder were in soft earth and any weight placed on the ladder would have meant the feet sinking into the earth, but there were only slight indentations in the ground.

"Another strange thing, sir. The key for the victims' bedroom door was in the lock but there were no prints on it. It had been wiped clean."

"Mm, interesting. Did forensics come up with anything else?"

Arthur Halliday opened another file. "They're still processing the scene but so far there's nothing. Whoever killed these people appears to have been very thorough. There are no prints except the victims and a range of secondary smudges that we think come from the maid. There's nothing on the cushion our killer used to deaden the sound and nothing on the window. They've checked the ladder but there's nothing to suggest anybody used it last night. No mud on the rungs and only odd, smudged prints. Our scene-of-crime boys aren't even sure if it had been used recently."

"So, you think the ladder was a plant to put us off?"

"I'd say so sir, based on our findings, but we can't be sure. It could have been a very lightweight murderer." The DI looked at his colleague from the Yard for a reaction. He got none. The DCI was considering this seriously. Women had been known to kill, but even a slender woman weighed something, and any weight would have meant the feet of the ladder would have sunk into the soft earth. Steve determined to check this out.

"What about the females who were at the dinner? Have they been spoken to?"

"Not yet, sir, we're getting addresses for them from Lady Rosyth, but to be honest, I'd be surprised if they knew anything. From what I gather, Lady Rosyth likes to bring in the local social-climbing talent to hang on the arms of her single male guests. You know sir, horsey types who may not be too bright but are looking for a titled husband."

"Yes Arthur, I know the type, so they're probably not a high priority."

Steve's mobile rang as Jenny returned with Mrs Stocks in tow. She was carrying another tray containing a plate of freshly baked cakes, another large pot of coffee and three mugs. She fussed around the detectives, clearing away their original cups and leaving the tray on the edge of the table. She smiled at everyone and gently closed the door.

"Sir, it's Poppy. I've booked you and DS Fuller into the Brook Arms for tonight. I've processed the statements as you asked and the surveillance teams on The Bank operation are due to report in. The changeover at five p.m. has already happened so I think everything is under control. Miss Rough wants to speak to you and DI Ishmal says

134

he'll call you before you turn in for the night, but everything looks good at this end and tomorrow has been set up."

"Thanks, Poppy; now, this case down here. Have you set up the files?" Steve didn't wait for an answer knowing so far Poppy had proved efficient. "You have the details from the statements of the four men who stayed in Lord Rosyth's manor last night. I need you to do a full background check on them plus his Lordship. I also want a detailed background on the victims and please look into the staff as well. I don't suppose they're involved but let's take a look. Have you got that?"

"Yes sir, will first thing tomorrow do?"

"Yes. You've got enough on with the Bank just now; tomorrow will be fine. Tell The Cap to call me around nine tonight. Also, Poppy, get hold of Twiggy... sorry Flo. Ask her to look into the financial backgrounds of Lord Rosyth's house guests. Get her to call me later this evening when she can with anything she gets."

With her now usual bubbly self, Poppy signed off with a "Righto" and she was gone.

The DCI worried about the Bank operation. He knew Commander Alfie Brooks had stuck his neck out in providing so much manpower and cost. Steve wished he were there now keeping an eye on things but knew The Cap was capable. Still, he fretted in case things went wrong and knew the arrests were planned for tomorrow. He realised the murder of a government minister probably took priority, but felt uncomfortable being so far away from the action.

Chapter Sixteen

At Direct Air Charter in Kent, everything was ready for the morning. The aircraft had been thoroughly checked over by Paul Stockland, each engine had had an oil change and Paul was satisfied there were no longer any oil leaks.

The provisional flight plan to Ankara had been filed and approved, the fuel tanks were full although Captain Norman Colington would have liked more reserve capacity. A heavy-duty forklift truck with a driver had been hired for the afternoon from another larger air freight operation based at Manston and the galley was fully provisioned.

Mrs Colington had been busy ensuring the passports, visas and general documentation were all current and had even paid a stack of outstanding bills from the money they had received that morning.

Everything was ready at Direct Air Charter. The three closed the doors at five p.m. exactly and went home for a relaxing evening in anticipation of a long day tomorrow.

***

DCI Steve Burt, accompanied by DI Arthur Halliday and DS Jenny Fuller, entered the bedroom where the double murder had taken place. Two men in white paper all-in-one suits were busy dusting for prints and examining every corner of the room in minute detail.

The bodies were still in situ. The three detectives noticed the splatter of brain matter on the headboard and the wall behind the bed but just standing looking told them nothing.

"This is how they were found?" The question was directed at Arthur Halliday.

"Yes sir." The DI produced his notebook and read from it. "The butler Mr Lomond was told to enquire if the couple required breakfast. All the house guests had assembled for breakfast before nine a.m., but

Sir Derek and Lady Layburn hadn't appeared, and his Lordship wanted to get on with his day." Arthur stopped to make sure both detectives from the Yard followed. "This is how the butler found them and that stain by the door was the poor man's breakfast."

"Apart from the forensic people, no one has been in here after the butler raised the alarm?"

"No, Lord Rosyth came up to confirm what his butler told him, but he says he didn't enter more than two feet into the room. He closed the door and forbade anyone from entering. He called us and we arrived within the hour."

The DCI wandered around the room careful that his blue plastic shoe coverings didn't stand in anything that looked like evidence. He examined the window and saw the ladder propped up outside. With his gloved hands, he raised the sash window and examined the top of the ladder.

"Forensics have examined the ladder and the window?"

"Yes sir, there's nothing on either the window or the ladder. The window catches and the handles have been wiped clean. there are only a few smudged prints but according to SOCO they are probably old, but they can't get anything for comparison anyway."

"Why would anybody put a ladder against the window and open the window?"

"Maybe to throw us off the scent?" Arthur Halliday surmised.

"But by wiping the window handles he's telling us he might have come in that way and certainly didn't leave that way. The handles are on the inside. If he left by the window, he'd not be able to wipe the handles from the outside and would surely have left something behind even if he wore gloves, but you say forensics found nothing."

"Yes, that's about it but I suppose if he was supple and wore disposable plastic gloves, he could have done it."

Jenny smiled, knowing she was about to win a point. "But you said forensics said the handles had been wiped. If you wear gloves the surface pattern is different."

DI Arthur Halliday thought for a moment before conceding the point.

"So, are we saying the ladder and open window is a plant?"

Jenny spoke up. "Yes sir."

Followed by Arthur. "Looks like it, sir."

"Right. We discount the ladder but what about the door key? Arthur, you said it had been wiped?"

"Yes, I did, we would have expected some prints. It's a door key for goodness' sake but it's clean. Why do you think that is, sir?"

Steve thought as he walked around the room. "I'm not sure but I think it's significant."

Silence descended as the three busied themselves looking for anything that others might have missed. The bathroom had been emptied of the victim's personal toiletries so there was nothing to see in there.

"Right Arthur." Steve burst into life. "Get the bodies removed. I want the post-mortems done as early tomorrow as can be arranged. Give your hard copy files to Jenny and we'll take it from here, but I'd like you to hang around in case we need your local knowledge. Tell your pathologist a Home Office pathologist will be with them first thing tomorrow and he'll carry out the post-mortem. Your guy won't be surprised given the high profile of the victims. DS Fuller will attend the post-mortem, so you need to liaise with everybody. Clear?"

The DCI was clearly in charge. The DI nodded he understood.

Steve looked at Jenny. "You OK with that?"

"Yes sir, no problem."

"And get what you can from forensics. They must have found something that would help."

"We'll talk to the live-in guests at six as you arranged, but first I think we need to meet his Lordship."

"Right you are, sir." DI Halladay looked a bit disappointed at being dismissed from the case. He liked what he'd seen of both these Met officers and thought he'd like to work with them. He reluctantly handed over the files he'd discussed earlier with Steve and reminded Jenny that copies had been e-mailed to the yard already.

Steve recognised the DI's disappointment and encouraged him by asking him to make sure the uniformed officers he had seen searching the grounds earlier were back first light tomorrow.

DI Arthur Halliday brightened up at this confirmation that he still had a part to play in the investigation. "I'll show you the way, sir. Lord

138

Rosyth likes to have his butler introduce anyone who calls on him."
Arthur shrugged and smiled with a look that said, *The landed gentry for
you.*

***

The handover between the surveillance teams was carried out at 16.44
exactly. Everyone knew the importance of keeping these two Bank
employees under full-time surveillance. The teams taking over the watch
were the same teams that had started the surveillance at this time
yesterday. The team watching Sophia Marr had received a good talking
to from DS Matt Conway and had learnt from their mistakes.

Michael Pleasance was picked up first and he followed the same
route home as the previous evening. As before the team split up with one
constable tailing him onto the tube and train whilst the other drove the
car to Weybridge Station Car Park. Michael Pleasance was logged by his
followers as having parked in the driveway of his 1930s house at exactly
18.27 p.m. The watchers took up the same vantage point as before and
settled in for a boring, few hours until their relief arrived at 22.00 p.m.

The team watching Sophia still had the DS's words of censure
ringing in their ears when they spotted the Morgan exit the Bank's car
park and take the same route to Chelsea as yesterday. Following the little
sports car was easier today. The traffic seemed somehow lighter, and
Miss Marr wasn't driving so fast. They logged her into her house at
18.49. Having learnt from their previous mistakes, they set up a rota such
that one of them kept watch on the mews house from an opposite
doorway whilst the other constable remained with the car. Also, as they
had eyes on the house and the car driver could be alerted by phone to any
movements, the car was now parked in a spot where exiting the car park
would be easy. Although the driver could not see the house, his colleague
could. Like the other team, the two watchers settled into their routine and
looked forward to being relieved at 22.00 p.m.

***

The Cap was in Steve's office briefing Poppy about his conversation with the missing man's mother. He wanted an accurate statement on the file. Poppy listened carefully with a look of concentration on her pretty face. The Cap spoke while Poppy took notes.

"Mrs Susan Bostrom had a call on her landline from her son Walter at ten this morning. I did a 1471 and confirmed that the call was made from a number outside London. I asked Technical Support to trace the number. Because of the new electronic exchanges, all they can tell us is the number is somewhere in the Esher/Surrey area." The Cap stopped. "Have you got that Poppy?"

"Yes, Sergeant."

"Poppy, we're not too formal around here, call me Cap. Every other bugger does."

Poppy giggled. "Righto... Cap."

"Get that written up into the Bank file. Have you heard from Twiggy? She was chasing up a couple of things."

"She called earlier and said she needed to speak to the boss."

The Cap smiled and puffed out his chest slightly. "Well, until the DCI gets back, I'm the boss on the bullion case."

Poppy stood up to go and update the file. As she left, she looked at The Cap. "Yes, boss."

The Cap sat back and thought about what the DCI would do now. He decided to call Twiggy.

She answered on the second ring of her internal phone. The Cap began by congratulating her on her new flat. "Very upmarket; they must be paying you more at the Treasury than a common DI like me!"

"Ha, ha, I'm a single woman earning the same as you, but you have a wife and kids to support. I only have to consider me, so my cash is all mine." She made the statement with a force that The Cap realised this was the end of this topic of conversation. He moved on.

"Twiggy, you know Steve's in Cirencester. I've to brief him tonight on our gold case. How did you get on with Terry in Technical Support, you know, the mobile number?"

"It hasn't been switched on much, so it was difficult for Terry and his lads to get a ping from any masts. But..." Twiggy left The Cap guessing what was to come after the 'but'. "He made two calls around lunchtime today. Tech Support got a ping from a mast in Esher, and they traced the calls. One was to a number in London belonging to Sun Oil. The second was to a number in Kent, belonging to a company called Direct Air Charter. The second call only lasted just over a minute, so they didn't say much."

"Right. What about Walter's bank account, you know, credit cards; all that financial stuff you're good at?"

"I got it all back. There's nothing unusual. His current account goes from black to red like a yo-yo, but he's always covered it. He used his credit card on Tuesday of this week, the 18th. Looks like he booked a very expensive trip. I haven't got details yet, but the payment was to British Airways and was over ten grand. I'll try and get details, but it won't be easy."

As an afterthought, Twiggy added, "I'm waiting for financial checks for Steve on this murder case he's on, but the bullion case has priority."

The Cap was beginning to understand how his DCI felt trying to analyse all these different facts and make sense of them. "Thanks, Twiggy; if you get anything else pass it on. The teams are due to pick up both Marr and Pleasance at ten tomorrow morning. I wish Steve were here because I'm not sure what I'm supposed to do. I might need your help with the financial side, but I'll call you."

"Fine Cap, you'll be OK. Just do what you've seen Steve do a hundred times."

"Yeah! Thanks for that Twiggy. See you tomorrow for sure."

They both hung up. The Cap was desperate to talk to his boss about the operation tomorrow but had said he'd call at nine p.m.. He'd wait and worry while trying to figure out what this latest intelligence meant.

***

The butler, Mr Percival Lomond, walked Steve and Jenny to Lord Rosyth's study. It was now almost fully dark outside and all the lights inside the common areas of the house appeared to be on, including the large crystal chandelier that was suspended above the great entrance hall. As he ushered the pair along, he couldn't help going on about how dreadful it was, that a thing like murder should occur in his Lordship's house. "It's just terrible sir, and of course I found the bodies." Mr Lomond tutted to himself. "Just terrible, I shall have nightmares for months."

Steve remained silent knowing that, like most people faced with violent crime, all this butler wanted to do was talk of his experiences to someone in authority.

They walked on until Mr Lomond stopped outside a large solid-looking door. He tapped reverently, opened the door and took one and a half paces inside the room. He covered his mouth, coughed gently and announced. "The police are here to see you, my Lord." He stood to one side to allow the two detectives to enter yet another grand room.

Lord Rosyth was sitting in a comfortable and well-used armchair. He was reading a newspaper as the butler announced the arrival of the two detectives from London. He stood immediately and approached the pair with an outstretched hand. Steve noticed his grip was firm and he spent more than a few seconds admiring his DS.

"Terrible thing this, Inspector. I've told my guests and staff to be available for you at six in the drawing room and I've arranged for our four young gentlemen to stay over an extra night. I hope that's in order."

Lord Rosyth was obviously a man used to organising other people. He wasn't particularly tall and sported a full grey beard. He was dressed in a tweed suit favoured by the hunting and shooting set although Steve noted his Lordship's had been mended many times.

"Thank you, sir, we'll try not to disturb the routine of the household too much."

Lord Rosyth smiled a warm and genuine smile. "Very kind of you, Chief Inspector. We haven't had a murder in this house in over a hundred years and overnight we get two." He laughed. "Just like London buses. You wait forever and two come along at once." He continued to chuckle at his own joke. Steve didn't.

His Lordship invited them to sit. It was very masculine and smelt of cigar smoke. The furnishings were dated but comfortable. Steve and Jenny sat on a long Chesterfield sofa whilst his Lordship seated himself on another worn armchair opposite his guests. Jenny took out her notebook ready to record anything his Lordship said.

"Why were Sir Derek and Lady Layburn here last night, sir?"

"No particular reason, Chief Inspector. My wife likes to host small dinner parties once a month. We have a regular circle of friends, acquaintances and political types we tend to invite. Layburn fell into the political expedient camp."

"Can I ask in what way was he an expedient?"

"Well, he's the Minister… sorry, *was* the Minister for Regional Development and Planning and on the wrong side of my politics. He's the sort who needs to be constantly told he's getting on in the world. We invited him to boost his ego and gain a few points should we need to cash them in in the future. Personally, I couldn't stand the man, but before you ask, I didn't shoot him."

Steve smiled openly and gave a slight chuckle. "I don't think I suggested you did sir, but can you tell us where you were between say one and four this morning?"

Lord Rosyth looked perplexed. "Do you think that's when they were killed?"

"Yes sir, our pathologist has provisionally put that timeframe on the shootings."

"Well, I was in my room with my wife from around midnight. Our local guests had all left by then and our staying guests had all gone to bed. The staff had tidied up and I dismissed them for the evening just before midnight. The house was quiet. Our butler, old Lomond, would have set the alarms before he went to bed. I read, as is my usual practice, for thirty minutes or so, said goodnight to my wife who was almost asleep, put the light out and I believe I was sound asleep within five minutes of my head hitting the pillow."

Steve was impressed by his Lordship's recall. "Thank you, sir, that's very helpful."

The DCI launched into another line of questioning. "The four young gentlemen who stayed the night. Why did they stay and why were they invited?"

"No particular reason, other than my wife likes to have younger people around." His Lordship looked quizzical. "Surely you don't think any of *them* could have done this?"

"I'm just asking questions at the moment, sir." Jenny who hadn't worked this closely with Steve, nor seen him in action, was impressed by his interviewing technique.

"The four of them are the sons of friends of mine. I've known them since they were born. One of them even works in our estate office in London. They are just young men who appreciate a good dinner and know my wife will try and fix them up with a bit of local skirt." Lord Rosyth gazed into the distance for a second. "Her count so far is three. She's claiming three marriages as a result of introductions she's made here. The boys all live in London so it's easier if they bed down here for the night. Under normal circumstances, they'd stay till after lunch and be off around mid-afternoon."

"What about the girls who were here?"

"My wife's doing, Chief Inspector. She sits on all sorts of committees and meets local mothers, keen to promote their daughters into a marriage with a title. There's never any shortage of takers for our dinner parties."

Steve considered this and moved on. "Do you know if any of your guests had a reason to kill the Minister and his wife?"

"Good Lord no!" His Lordship spluttered at the thought. "He and his wife weren't universally liked. Too clever by half the pair of them, and a bit snobbish, especially after he was knighted and got the government job, but most of my guests hardly knew him or his wife. I can't think that anyone here last night would want the fellow dead."

"Thank you, sir. So, just to recap before I meet your overnight house guests, you're saying everyone was in their rooms by midnight last night; you turned in around midnight and read for half an hour while Lady Rosyth was already in bed trying to sleep. The guests from the local area plus the three girls left before, say, eleven-fifteen. Your butler set the burglar alarm before he went to bed just before midnight and none of your dinner guests was particularly known to the victims. Does that about cover your statement, my Lord?"

"Yes, Chief Inspector, I think that's a very fair summary of events."

The DCI was preparing to leave when a question jumped into his head. "How did a Miss Matilda Armstrong get home last night? We know her two companions left with Mr and Mrs Carstairs and Sir Colin

Thomson but we've no information as to how or when Miss Armstrong left."

"All I can tell you is that everybody was gone by midnight. Either this girl got a lift possibly from Dr Francis or she had her own car. I'm sorry I can't help, but if it's the girl I'm thinking of she was very friendly with the Right Honourable Clarence Strum at the dinner table last night. He may be able to help you."

Steve finally stood, followed by Jenny. He checked his watch. It was 06.05 p.m.. "Thank you, sir, perhaps we'll be able to interview Lady Rosyth tomorrow when she's feeling better?"

"Yes, thank you; she's taken this very badly."

Steve and Jenny made their way to the drawing room. They spotted DI Arthur Halliday hanging about in the hall. Steve knew he wanted to be part of the investigation so invited him to join them interviewing the four titled gentlemen.

Steve asked Jenny what she thought. "It's a can of worms, sir. Whoever did this was smart. We've no forensics yet, we've no weapon, we've no prints and a ladder stuck outside the victims' bedroom." She smiled at the DCI. "I suppose you'll tell me we're only getting started."

"Yes, we are Jenny. It's a mystery but everyone makes mistakes. We've just got to find the mistake our killer made."

Steve stopped just outside the drawing room door. "It's not a criticism Arthur but it's not good procedure to allow suspects to mingle with each other before they give their statements. I know you took their statements but now we have to unpick what they told us. We'll just carry out a general debrief and talk to them individually tomorrow morning. OK?"

Jenny and Arthur agreed. "Right Jenny, you lead and get what you can. I'm off to see a man about a ladder."

With that Steve left the two detectives standing outside the door. "I'll only be half an hour and I'll meet you in the drawing room."

The two detectives walked into the drawing room to meet the four sons of titled fathers at exactly 18.07 p.m.

Chapter Seventeen

Steve left the house and walked around the outside to where the ladder was propped against the wall under the victim's bedroom window. The area was festooned with police blue-and-white crime scene tape. Floodlights had been erected and washed the whole area around the ladder in bright light. A man in a white paper suit was studiously examining the lower rungs of the ladder. The DCI ducked under the tape and approached the forensic technician.

The technician stood back from the ladder. Steve noticed he had been using a cotton bud on the end of a large stick and seemed to be rubbing the cotton bud along each lower rung on the ladder.

"Evening sir, I wondered how long it would take you to find me."

"I'm sorry. I wanted a chat about this ladder. Do you think it's a plant?"

"Not for me to say sir but I was in the bedroom when your attractive sergeant put our DI in his place." The technician took a pace towards Steve and removed his blue plastic gloves. "Name's Munroe, Dougal Munroe." Dougal stretched out his hand which Steve shook.

"Hello, Dougal. I'm DCI Steve Burt from Scotland Yard."

"Yes, I know." Dougal paused. "Whoever did this hasn't made it easy for you. So far my lads haven't got much and there's nothing on this ladder to help you."

Steve considered the forensic technician's statement. "What did you mean my sergeant put your DI in his place?"

"Just that she's been trained. The window catches and handles had been wiped. Gloves leave a smear especially if they're rubber or plastic. The surface of the material transfers onto the surface. It's not a fingerprint but the chemical deposit from gloves shows up under ultraviolet as a deposit once we chemically spray the surface. If the surfaces are wiped, we see no deposits but usually draw marks from the cloth used to wipe off any prints especially if a rough cloth has been used. She's a smart girl that one."

"It's not new." The technician was obviously from Scotland and retained a thick Scottish accent. "We've developed the ultraviolet light combined with the chemical spray technique over the past few years. It's helpful to know if a perpetrator wore gloves or wiped surfaces after him."

"So, tell me, Dougal, what do you think?"

"As I said, Chief Inspector, it's not my job to speculate. At least not officially, but I think this ladder was planted and hasn't been used to carry out the murders. There's no indentation in the ground where the feet of the ladder would have sunk if anybody had put their weight on the ladder climbing up, and the rungs I've checked so far have no new material on them. What I've found is days or weeks old."

Steve could feel the heat coming from the high-intensity lamps. He was considering what Dougal had said. This seemed to be the consensus. The ladder was only there to throw them off the scent.

"What about the window. Is there anything on it?"

Dougal stepped outside the crime scene tape. "Come on sir, let's go and have a look. I'll try to educate you in the ways of forensic science then you'll be as good as your sergeant." Both men laughed and Steve followed the technician up to the victims' bedroom.

After discarding his outside overshoes and gloves, Dougal replaced them with new ones. Steve simply put on overshoes once inside the house.

"Right, DCI Burt." Both men were standing in front of the window. It was still raised about four inches. Dougal lowered the window to its closed position giving a clear view of the catch.

The technician sprayed a liquid onto the catch, fired up a blue light machine and asked Steve to put the room lights out. After adjusting to the dark, Steve saw what looked like fine scratch marks on the catch. He nodded to Dougal. Next Dougal repeated the process on the two handles that were used to lift and close the sash window. Again, Steve saw fine scratch marks on both handles.

Dougal crossed the room and put the light on. "Tell me what you saw."

The DCI thought. "Well, only what looked like fine scratch marks."

147

"So, from our previous conversation, which tells us our killer didn't wear gloves but wiped down the surfaces or more likely held a cloth in his hand and used the cloth to avoid leaving prints."

Dougal had a peculiar look on his face which was round and ruddy. At around five-foot-seven, the Scotsman wasn't tall and in his ill-fitting paper suit looked to be more than a little overweight. "I might have something for you."

Steve decided he liked this forensic technician. "Go on."

"Well. What are the catch and the handles made from?"

Steve shrugged. "I don't know, probably brass by the colour."

"Exactly, brass, and in big houses like this with servants, anything that is made from brass gets polished. Look at the shine on these handles."

The DCI wasn't sure where this was going but he felt Dougal had something to tell him.

"You remember the scratches we saw under the ultraviolet?"

"Yes."

Dougal was enjoying himself feeding the DCI small scraps. "Did you notice how fine they were?"

"I suppose so, but what's your point?"

"If the killer had used a rough piece of cloth, the scratches, as you call them, would be wider and not so fine." The technician paused and looked the DCI squarely in the eye. "But… if he used something finer like a handkerchief, probably an expensive finely woven one, we'd expect to get these finer marks."

Steve was about to speak but Dougal held up his hand to stop him. "If our killer touched either the handles or the catch with say his handkerchief to avoid leaving any prints then it's odds-on we'd have transference from the polish used to buff up these brass fittings onto the handkerchief. Looking at these marks I'd lay odds he used a fine handkerchief."

The DCI looked at the Scotsman with renewed admiration. "You're saying if we find a handkerchief and it has traces of metal polish on it, we may have found our man?"

"I'm saying it's not conclusive but why would someone use a perfectly good handkerchief to polish window fittings? Get us the handkerchiefs and we can run them through our spectrum analyser. If there's any evidence of metal polish, we'll find it."

"Dougal, that's brilliant. Any other little gems you'd care to give me?"

"No. No, that's enough, but we can't have a DS knowing more than a DCI can we?"

Steve left to re-join his colleagues in the drawing room. The time was 19.03 p.m.

***

Before he reached the drawing room door, his mobile vibrated in his pocket. It was Twiggy.

"How's it going, Steve?"

"Slowly but we're making progress. What's up? I got a message you needed to talk to me."

Twiggy giggled at the other end of the line. "I had a call from The Cap reminding me he was now the Senior Investigating Officer on the gold case. He was quite sweet really. He went through the motions but didn't ask any follow-up questions. He just seemed to write everything down. He's calling you later to update you on everything so no doubt between you, you can sort it out, but that's not why I'm calling."

"Didn't think it was. Did Poppy talk to you?"

"Yes. She has a way with her. She manages to make a simple message from you sound like a royal command." Twiggy giggled again. "I tell you what though, she knows how to get through the work. She's no Andy yet but one day soon… sorry, I'm rambling. She asked me to do financial checks on the people who stayed at the Hall last night including Lord and Lady Rosyth."

"I did ask her and suggested she call you as being the best person to get the data quickly."

"Oh! You old smoothie you." Twiggy became serious and gathered her thoughts. "First, his Lordship: as you might expect, plenty of money, all inherited. I don't think he's done a productive day's work in his life. He draws his Lord's attendance allowance three days a week but lives off his investments. He's not poor and has a net worth in the tens of

149

millions. The wife just seems to do good works and spend his money. They have no credit card debt, their accountant seems to control their day-to-day bills, and they're a platinum-rated couple at Coutts Bank."

"I suppose it's only what we'd expect. What about the four Right Honourables?"

"Completely different story. First Julian Bennett... he's the only one who has a proper job. He works for Lord Rosyth in his London estate office. He's paid eighty thousand a year which he spends. He's up to his limit on most of his credit cards and more than a few transactions are for a gay club off Soho. He's overdrawn at the bank, runs a car on finance and is in arrears with his rent. That's all I got in the time."

"Well done, Twiggy, that's fairly comprehensive."

"Thanks. Now Cedric Blake... no real source of income. Gets a monthly allowance from his family of five thousand but according to his bank records, he constantly gets a top-up from his family when he goes seriously overdrawn. He lives in Pimlico at a top-end address, but the family owns it. I don't see any rent being paid by him. Certainly not from his Nat West account. His car was bought by the family, his credit cards are all maxed out and he likes to spend big on horse racing and strip clubs."

"How old is this guy?"

"Don't know, Steve. You're there, maybe you should ask him."

Steve heard Twiggy shuffling papers at the end of the line. "Now, Clarence Strum... seems to generate a healthy income from sitting on company boards. He banks around ten grand a month although some months it's half of that. He runs an overdraft of five thousand, is paying off his car on credit and, like the others, is almost maxed out on his credit cards. He rents his apartment in London and from his credit card entries likes upmarket clubs and dines out in some of the most upmarket restaurants. He's not poor but could probably do with a cash injection."

"Right, thanks, Twiggy. What about Richard Pardew?"

"More of the same. He's not employed at present although up until three months ago Riviera Homes were paying him. Seems it's a timeshare scheme and he operated as a salesman in the UK for them. From his bank statements, he only received payments from them for four months, so I suppose that's the length of time he was employed."

Twiggy stopped for breath and a sip of water she was drinking. "His overdraft is up to its limit; his credit cards seem reasonable although he has a habit of maxing them out every so often. His family appears to support him when he gets in over his limits. The credit cards are mainly used to buy theatre tickets and entertaining what I'd take to be rich young things in swanky restaurants. His flat is rented but he's not behind with his rent and his car is leased." Twiggy paused.

Steve remained silent.

As the silence became embarrassing, Twiggy commented. "You know Steve, none of these four appears to like working."

Steve was lost in his own thoughts, but Twiggy's comments brought him back. "Yes, thanks Twiggy, that's good work." He paused. "Are you lined up for tomorrow?"

"I'll be in and available. I've told my boss at Treasury I'm seconded to your team for the bullion case. He'd go ballistic if he knew I was ferreting around in a murder case for you."

"I understand but keep your nose clean. The Cap will probably need your help tomorrow with the interviews so please keep him and me posted."

"Will do. Good luck in Cirencester. Looking at the backgrounds of your suspects you'll need it."

As Twiggy hung up, a thought hit the DCI. Twiggy had referred to the four titled gentlemen in the drawing room as *suspects*. It dawned on him they probably were and one of them could be the killer. This realisation sharpened his senses. He strode into the drawing room with new purpose, viewing these four in a different light.

As the DCI entered, he saw Jenny seated in the bay window talking to a young man. Arthur Halliday was by the far wall also speaking to a young man while two others sprawled on the chesterfield sofas that were positioned opposite each other and at ninety degrees to the fire that was burning nicely.

Steve called his colleagues over and stood just inside the door. "Anything?"

Jenny answered. "Not really. They're only repeating what they said in their statements. You know, went to bed, slept, woke and showered, down to breakfast then all hell broke loose. They claim not to know anything."

DI Halliday agreed. "They know nothing."

The DCI lowered his voice. "For the time being, we will regard one of these fine gentlemen as our killer. Don't ask, I've no evidence but that's why we're here. If we discount the staff and Lord and Lady Rosyth, these are the only other people who were in the house. The butler set the burglar alarm and the ladder outside the window is a complete red herring. No one could have got in unnoticed. It has to be one of them but which one? I don't want speculation but evidence."

Steve gave a broad smile and whispered. "Stay with me on this. Arthur do we still have uniforms on-site?"

"Yes, until we release this lot, I've arranged for a permanent presence."

"Good. Go and get four in here now please." Arthur was about to ask why when Steve raised his hand. "All in good time."

The DCI called the four Right Honourable gentlemen together. "I'm sorry for this inconvenience but with your cooperation, we should be able to allow you to return to your own homes sometime tomorrow."

The four visibly cheered up at this news.

"Now, I want you to accompany one of these officers" — Arthur had returned with four constables — "back to your rooms and give them all the handkerchiefs you have with you. You'll be asked to put them individually in a clear plastic bag. You'll be given a receipt and your handkerchiefs will be laundered and returned to you once our laboratory is finished with them. Please also put any soiled handkerchiefs into a bag. Once you've done that the officers" — Steve pointed to the four uniformed policemen — "will search your rooms to establish that you have handed over all your handkerchiefs. Is that clear?"

Julian Bennett was the first to react. "This is a bit of an imposition. We have our civil liberties and I'll wager you don't have a search warrant." Julian Bennet looked pleased with himself. He was the oldest and appeared to be acting as spokesperson for the group.

"You are?"

"The Right Honourable Julian Bennett." A smug grin creased the Honourable gentleman's face. Steve decided to be confrontational. He'd taken an instant dislike to this upper-crust arrogant son of a Lord.

"Mr Bennet," — he emphasised the 'Mr', — "you are of course correct. We find innocent people with nothing to hide usually cooperate with the police. However, if you're not happy, we can all stay here for another three hours while I get a warrant, and believe me if I have to do that, then we'll be looking for more than handkerchiefs. Do you understand?"

The DCI allowed his voice to rise an octave as he stared straight into this pompous gentleman's eyes.

"Oh! Well, I suppose you are only doing your job." Bennet slowly walked towards the door.

Clarence Strum stood immediately. "Well, I've nothing to hide so come along, one of you people in a blue suit, and you can rummage through my handkerchief drawer all night if you wish."

Steve noted this Right Honourable was acting the part of a gay man too well, although Twiggy hadn't found anything to suggest he was.

After the constables and the suspects had left, Steve told his colleagues about his meeting with Dougal Munroe and the possibility metal polish residue could have transferred onto a handkerchief. His colleagues were impressed. "Remember Jenny, every criminal makes a mistake. If we find metal polish on any of their handkerchiefs, then it's odds-on the handkerchief was used to prevent our killer from leaving behind his fingerprints."

"This Dougal's a smart guy." Jenny was impressed.

"Yes, he is. Now Arthur, when your officers have collected the exhibits can you get them rushed to Dougal at his lab. He's offered to process them as soon as he gets them within reason. With any luck, we'll have a firm suspect in the frame by mid-morning tomorrow."

All three detectives sat back and sighed. It had been a long day. Steve spoke up. "It's now ten minutes to eight. When we get the exhibits, let's all adjourn to the local pub and have a drink. I have a feeling this night's not over by a long way."

Chapter Eighteen

With the handkerchief exhibits on their way to Dougal Munroe's laboratory, the three detectives settled down to a quick dinner washed down by a bottle of the house white. Nothing too extravagant in case their expense claim was thrown out.

They discussed the case but didn't reach any conclusions. Each detective accepted that Dougal Munroe could hold the answer to at least setting them on a course of action. Otherwise, they had nothing and would have to start again from the beginning. With their plates cleared and their glasses empty, the three split up, Arthur Halliday to his bachelor pad just outside of Cirencester and Steve and Jenny to their own rooms.

Steve had just removed his jacket when his mobile rang. It was The Cap.

"Hi, Steve. How goes it?"

"It's a bit of a slog. Our killer's been clever, but we'll get him. Look, sorry Cap but let's not discuss this case. My head is having problems being in two places at once." An unintended sigh was heard over the phone coming from the DCI. "What's happening at your end?"

"I feel a bit overwhelmed, to be honest, but Twiggy tells me just to do what you do, so I am." He gave a chuckle that was louder than he'd intended. Steve thought this was due to nerves but said nothing. He let The Cap carry on.

"Twiggy had Tech Services track down Walter Bostrom's mobile. He made two calls from it today. One to a number that belongs to Sun Oil in London, I'm guessing that was to his fiancée. The second was to a Kent number. It's registered to a commercial air charter company based at Manston Airport."

Steve interrupted. "I'm beginning to think Walter Bostrom's not a victim in this."

"Well, you could be right. Terry Harvey, you know Twiggy's fancy man," — The Cap laughed at his own joke, — "got a ping from a tower near Esher when Walter made these calls."

Steve was pensive. "Anything else?"

"Yes. I did a call back from Mrs Bostrom's phone. The number Walter called her from is in the Esher exchange area. I had it traced..." The Cap paused for effect. "It's registered to a Cecil White. He's the father of Paula White who in turn is the fiancée of Walter Bostrom." The Cap sat back pleased with himself although it was Twiggy who had given him the information.

"Hang on. Are we saying Walter Bostrom's been holed up at the home of his fiancée's father since Sunday?"

"We don't know, but it's possible."

"Does that mean we're putting him in the frame as a player in this robbery?"

"I don't know, Steve. I'm hoping you can think this through. I've got a theory but I'm not sure it stands up."

"Don't be shy Abul, let's hear it."

The Cap took a deep breath. "Well, suppose the fiancée's father, Cecil White, is behind this. After all, he has form and probably still has connections and certainly the money to mount a heist like this. Let's say he knows where his future son-in-law works and persuades him to come up with this plan. What if Michael Pleasance and Sophia Marr are either innocent or just bit players. If Walter has the twelve-digit code, he could release the shipment. Remember we were told it's all automatic until the code is given, so the gold is loaded, ready to go, just awaiting confirmation of the code. Walter could easily issue the code."

Steve cut in. "But how does Walter get the other two four-digit codes?"

"Maybe Pleasance and Marr have been bribed. Maybe they are getting a cut. Remember we think Pleasance has the contacts to fence the bullion so it's likely he's in on it."

"Yes, I see that. So, your theory is Cecil White is the money behind this job, Walter Bostrom is somehow working for his future father-in-law and has put the plan together. He's involved his boss Pleasance and his colleague Marr to get their part of the twelve-digit release code."

"That about it."

"Hmm… Who put the bug in the Bank's software that meant this manual system was put in place?"

"Not sure, but I'm thinking Cecil White probably has the connections. It's possible that he orchestrated it with Walter's help. And remember Walter called from the Esher area where Cecil White lives."

"What about the call to this air charter firm in Kent?"

"Well, I'm thinking if they give the correct code to the convoy commander it would be easy to tell him to take the gold to Manston Airfield in Kent. The guy in charge of the convoy doesn't know where to take the bullion. If he's told Manston, he'll go to Manston." Steve could hear tiredness in The Cap's voice.

"So, you're saying the gold goes to Manston to this air charter company, gets loaded onto one of their aircraft and flies out of the UK?"

"More or less, yes."

"It's a good theory, Cap and almost works. But twenty tonnes are a lot of weight for an aeroplane to lift. Do we know anything about this air freight company?"

"No."

"First thing tomorrow, have Poppy do a search." The DCI paused. "The other thing is where do Pleasance and Marr fit in and why would Cecil White suddenly take up bullion robbery?"

"I don't know Steve. As I said, it's only a theory."

"Right. But look at what we have. Walter Bostrom might not have been abducted. He seems to be living with his future father-in-law, who's a known criminal from way back. He's spoken with an air transport company and it's not the sort of airline that would take you on your summer holidays. Michael Pleasance should have reported Walter's apparent disappearance but didn't. There's a valuable gold shipment planned for tomorrow and Walter Bostrom, Pleasance and Marr hold the keys to whether it leaves the Bank or not, and its destination once it leaves the Bank. The only reason we think they're so heavily involved was the virus that was planted in the Bank's bullion shipment software. It cost money to obtain it and Cecil White's a rich man." Steve sat back thinking.

"So, you think the theory stands up?" The Cap suddenly felt proud.

"Mm. Yes, it does Cap, well done. The connection between Esher and Manston can't just be a coincidence. Are the teams still watching Pleasance and Marr?"

"Yes. The ten p.m. teams have already relieved the five p.m. lot. So far nothing has been reported out of the ordinary tonight."

"Cap, it's been a long day. Get Poppy to check on this air charter company and ask Twiggy to do a financial background check. Leave them messages if they don't pick up tonight. Tell them it's urgent. You need the information first thing. After all, you are the SIO."

Steve remembered Twiggy's comments about The Cap being in charge and smiled to himself. They signed off.

Steve was exhausted having had a full day. He called his wife and spent fifteen minutes talking about domestic and work matters. Dr Alison Mills was now back to full fitness after being shot during one of Steve's previous cases. Her private practice was back to full-time working and she was once again happy in her work. She didn't like the hours her husband gave the Metropolitan Police but realised that, like her, he enjoyed his work.

Steve hung up, showered and climbed into the most comfortable bed he could ever remember sleeping in. Within two minutes he was in a deep sleep expecting not to waken until at least six the following morning.

How disappointed he'd be. It was 20.21 on Thursday the 20th of October.

**

The team watching Sophia Marr had been in position since 22.00. The constable in the car was dozing on and off and struggling to stay awake. His colleague positioned in the doorway with a view of Sophia Marr's front door was struggling to stay warm. He and his colleague had swapped positions each hour on the hour. He looked at his watch. It was 03.06 a.m. on Friday the 21st of October. He thought only another fifty-four minutes before he could return to the warmth of the car. He noted his feet had already started to feel as though they were blocks of ice and his hands despite being encased in warm fur-lined gloves were beginning to scream for more heat. The constable stamped his feet to maintain circulation and consoled himself with the thought of his overtime payment.

A taxi turned into the mews at exactly 03.56 a.m. The watcher in the car was still floating between consciousness and sleep. His colleague was about to call him on his mobile to confirm his stint at being away from the car was over. Instead, he quickly alerted his partner. "Get the car ready, something's up. A black cab has just arrived, and it's stopped outside our target's house." There was a pause before the watcher continued. "I can't see any lights on inside the house but the cab driver's knocking on the door." Another pause lasted several minutes. The watcher was back and excited. "Right, we're on, bring the car. She's just climbed into the taxi with a large suitcase." The watcher noted the taxi registration number and slid deeper into the doorway to avoid being seen. As the taxi approached the end of the mews, it turned right. The unmarked police car collected the officer at the mouth of the mews and followed the black cab.

After a debate as to what they should do, they triggered a series of events by calling their designated team leader Detective Sergeant Matt Conway. DS Conway in turn called Detective Inspector Abul Ishmal who decided to wait and elected to get constant updates as to where the target might be going. Once the taxi entered the M4 heading west out of London and with the evidence of the suitcase, everyone agreed she was headed for Heathrow.

The followers wanted to know what to do if this woman entered one of the terminals at Heathrow. DS Conway couldn't answer so asked DI Ishmal who also couldn't answer. Reluctantly he called DCI Burt at 04.22 a.m. on the morning of the Friday 21st of October.

Once Steve had regained his thoughts and shaken himself awake, The Cap gave him the facts. "And she's definitely heading for Heathrow?"

"Looks like it, Steve. The boys said she has a large suitcase with her."

The DCI was fully awake despite having had only six hours' sleep. "Keep the watchers on her. Tell them to follow her into the terminal and find out what flight she's on. It should be simple enough if she's checking in that suitcase, but you'd better explain it to them. They should watch her, quiz the attendant manning the check-in desk. I want to know where she's going and the time of her flight. Have you got that?"

"Yes, Steve."

"They should only shadow her until we figure this out. They've got warrant cards so tell them to use them, if necessary, but she is not to board any flight. Clear?"

"Got it, Steve. I'll call you with updates."

The officers continued to follow the taxi and when it turned off the M4 onto the Heathrow slip they knew she was heading for the airport. They called DS Conway who said he was on his way to Heathrow to provide backup. The DS called the DI who in turn called the DCI again. The chain of command was working.

"She's definitely headed for Heathrow Steve… hold on. Matt Conway's on the other line."

The DCI heard a mumbled conversation before The Cap was back. "She's at Terminal Five. Could be booked on BA. The lads have her in sight and Matt Conway's headed over there now."

"Good. Keep me posted. I wonder what she's up to." Steve was more or less speaking to himself. "If she's not involved, she could simply be going on holiday. We've no hard evidence against her, but she was supposed to be in her office today. If we get it wrong, we'll be back on traffic after the weekend."

The Cap replied, "That's a cheery thought. Remember I'm SIO on this so you'd better steer me in the right direction."

They both nervously laughed. "Just keep me updated. Let's work it out as we go."

At 05.23 a.m. The Cap phoned back.

"Good news. Matt Conway is now with the watchers. Sophia Marr is checked onto the 06.45 a.m. BA flight to Istanbul. She's not gone airside yet. What do you want to do?"

"Bugger me, Cap. We're wrong if we lift her, and she has nothing to do with this, and we're wrong if she is involved and we let her take that flight."

Steve was torn on which way to jump. The Cap, although notionally in command, stayed quiet. This was not a decision he wanted to make. After a full three minutes of agonising over his decision, Steve spoke.

"Arrest her on suspicion of conspiracy in planning a robbery. Make sure she doesn't use her mobile to alert anybody. I'll sign the forms and take responsibility. I'll finish here as soon as I can this morning and get back."

The Cap admired his boss' decisive actions and was happy for him to put his name to the arrest. As was his way, in times of crisis The Cap usually found some humour. "You're not getting back early just to be at Andy's farewell party tonight I hope… sir."

"Christ, Cap! I forgot all about that. Let's hope we don't have to cancel."

Steve was running through everything he'd been told. "Cap, get the lads from Heathrow over to Esher. I want them to stake out Cecil White's place. They're due off shift shortly so get their relief over to Esher as soon as. Get Poppy to text them the details when she gets in. If anything moves, they should call it in."

"They won't have to wait, Steve, Poppy's here already. She's been in since five a.m.."

Steve made no comment but made a mental note. Poppy was beginning to fill Andy Miller's shoes.

Detective Sergeant Matt Conway arrested Miss Sophia Marr at exactly 05.33 a.m. at Heathrow Airport, Terminal Five.

The two constables who had followed Sophia Marr set off for the home of Cecil White in Esher. Although both had put in a full shift, the adrenaline rush of the chase was still coursing through their veins. They also knew they would be relieved within the hour.

The team watching Michael Pleasance knew nothing of developments at Heathrow. Their night had been boring and uneventful. The overnight watchers reported nothing unusual and were relieved by their colleagues. The new team settled in and at 07.23 a.m., Michael Pleasance left his house and was followed on his usual route to work. The watchers reported that he had arrived at the Bank at exactly 08.51 a.m.

They followed the same procedure as before, entering the Bank and walking around to ensure their target was at his desk in his office. This was reported to DI Peter Jones who had been briefed on events at

Heathrow. He brought his two constables up to date with events. They had been instructed to arrest Michael Pleasance at exactly 10.00 a.m. Peter Jones would be with them to carry out the arrest.

Chapter Nineteen

DCI Steve Burt was sitting in his bedroom drinking bad instant coffee. He wondered why people drank the stuff when there were other better-tasting alternatives. He knew he wouldn't get back to sleep, so he'd showered and sorted himself out.

He was fully dressed and awake and had an A4 pad on his knee as he sat on the edge of his bed. He doodled as he thought. He realised he was trying to run two cases at the same time. The Cap was notionally in charge of the gold case but needed help. This was something he'd been told by Commander Alfie Brooks not to do.

He was aware his priority was the double murder, but he realised until he got some forensics, he was stuck. He convinced himself he could handle both cases without jeopardising either investigation. Steve was conscious The Cap was panicking a little and not comfortable with the extra responsibility of being SIO on the gold case. He stopped scribbling and started to list the facts he had on the case. He told himself the murders were his priority, but he would work the bullion case with The Cap.

He looked at his watch. It was 06.36 a.m. Too early to get stuck into the murder case anyway. The DCI started by listing the names involved. He'd just written 'Michael Pleasance' when his phone rang. It was Poppy.

"Morning, sir." She sounded bright and breezy although Steve knew she hadn't had any more sleep than he'd had. "I've got the data on the air charter company you wanted, and Flo's passed on some financial stuff."

"Well done, Poppy. Let's have it."

"Right." Steve heard her clearing her throat as though she were about to deliver a speech. "Direct Air Charter was founded by Captain Norman Colington and his wife five years ago. It's a small one-plane operation. Flo says it's run on a shoestring. There's only one employee, that's the maintenance engineer, someone called Paul Stockland."

Poppy continued to read from her notes and was delivering the information as though she were reading the news on radio. "There's nothing showing for any of them, not even a parking ticket. Flo says their bank account has rarely been in the black but two days ago a large deposit of one hundred and twenty-five grand was deposited into it. She says the funds came from an offshore account she hasn't had time to trace yet." Poppy stopped talking and silence descended on the phone line.

Steve was in deep thought and Poppy had been around her new boss long enough now to know the signs and not to interrupt.

"Is that it, Poppy? A five-year-old company with one aeroplane that's been struggling financially and now suddenly has a hundred and twenty-five thousand pounds in its bank account? A bit suspicious don't you think?"

"Yes sir, but there's more." Now Poppy's voice wasn't reading the news. She was more excited. "I checked with Euro Control. That's the European wide air traffic control centre. It seems Direct Air Charter has filed a provisional flight plan for a journey to Ankara in Turkey leaving Manston around four this afternoon."

"You never fail to amaze me, Poppy. How did you get on to that?"

She giggled her schoolgirl giggle. "I used to have a boyfriend who was a pilot. He would bore me for hours about flying but I picked up a few bits of information. I also checked up on the aeroplane Direct Air Charter operates. It's an old civilian model of a military heavy-lift aircraft. Before you ask, it can comfortably transport twenty tonnes of anything, if you're thinking what I'm thinking."

Again, Steve was quiet and again Poppy didn't interrupt. "You're a very clever girl, DC Amelia Cooper and I think we're thinking the same thing." Silence again fell on the phone line momentarily.

"You're thinking if the gold does get shipped from the Bank, the plan is to transport it to Manston to this air charter company and have them fly it to Turkey?"

"Yes sir, but there's more to it. Turkey is not in the EU and the flight plan to Ankara is only provisional to make sure they have an air traffic control slot to Turkey. They could change the final destination and land at any of the terrorist bases in the east of Turkey."

Steve was on his feet with his phone firmly pressed to his ear. "Hang on a minute! Are you suggesting there might be a terrorist implication here rather than a straightforward gold heist?"

Steve could tell Poppy was considering her reply. "All I'm saying, sir, is if they get the gold onto that aeroplane, the military version is capable of landing on rough runways. If they get into Turkish air space, they could land anywhere."

"Bloody hell Poppy. If it isn't theories from reading trashy novels, it's James Bond-style theories. You are a wonder but I'm not sure I'm buying your terrorist story. There's nothing to support it but..." The line went quiet. The DCI was once more in deep thought.

"Poppy, don't discuss this with anybody except The Cap. I'll get back to you."

Rather rudely, Steve instantly hung up. His brain was in overdrive. He needed to talk to someone to better understand Poppy's latest theory.

***

Dougal Munroe had been in his laboratory in Cheltenham police headquarters since before seven a.m. He saw the evidence bags containing various handkerchiefs sitting on his desk. Each bag was sealed and a signature in black ink had been written over the flap that sealed the bags thus showing no one had tampered with the bags since being delivered to Dougal's office. The name of the owners of the handkerchiefs had also been added to the front of each bag. He was alone but had asked one of his technicians to come in early to assist him with the analysis of the handkerchiefs.

A tall, slim lady in her early twenties called Jane arrived just after Dougal, and once both were dressed in their white lab coats, they started the analysis of the cloth. As Dougal had indicated to Steve, they had a new auto-analyser that once set up could quickly provide results. The only flaw was it needed human input to extract any contaminant substances from the surface of the handkerchiefs, and this is where Jane came in. She was skilled in dousing the materials with the appropriate chemicals that would extract chemical residues and inserting them into a large centrifuge that spun so fast it forced any liquid out of the cloth giving the scientists a clear liquid that could be analysed for a variety of substances.

The whole process took less than forty minutes. Dougal inserted the various ampoules of liquid he had received from Jane into a turntable that slowly went round allowing the machine to analyse each sample in turn.

By 08.10 a.m. the forensic scientist had his results.

***

At eight a.m. exactly, Steve called an old friend, or at least someone he'd worked with before. Not only had this man tried to recruit Steve but he was someone who was indirectly responsible for getting Alison shot and placing Steve himself at the wrong end of a pistol, which at the time was being held by a deranged killer. Despite all this, Steve and the Head of MI6 had struck up an acquaintance that verged on friendship.

"Patrick Bond speaking. Who the hell's calling when I'm at my breakfast?"

This was a typical response from the country's chief spy. Steve knew Sir Patrick Bond had his number in his phone and it would have registered on his screen as soon as he answered.

"If you're having a full fry up then it's the cholesterol police, calling to save you from yourself."

The pair usually tried to start off in a light-hearted mood despite the severity of the issues they normally discussed. After a few pleasantries, Steve got to the point.

"Patrick, one of my DCs, who admittedly has a vivid imagination, has just suggested something I need your thoughts on." Steve went on to explain how Walter Bostrom had started the whole thing off by apparently going missing, how the computer software controlling bullion shipments had been compromised and how this led to a more manual system having to be implemented. He explained the introduction of the new system had put more control in the hands of Bostrom, Pleasance and Marr and how Bostrom had reappeared unharmed and seemed to be living in Esher with his prospective father-in-law who just happened to have a criminal record.

"My team found that Bostrom, or someone using his phone, had called an air charter firm that runs some kind of military heavy-lift aeroplane and that a provisional flight plan has been submitted for a flight to Turkey this afternoon. My young DC has a theory that the aeroplane has military rough-landing capabilities, and it might finish up landing in eastern Turkey. Even I know that's terrorist country. I'm not sure I buy it, but I thought I'd run it by you. If there's anything to it, it's obviously well above my pay grade." Steve paused. "Any thoughts?"

Sir Patrick Bond was quiet for a long time. "My goodness Steve, once again you have given me a serious problem. I'll ask the Turkish desk if they've heard any chatter, but the theory could be viable. At the last briefing I attended, the Turkish Government were concerned the rebels in the east were becoming better armed and more organised. Also, a pact seemed to be developing with other groups in Syria and Iran. I suppose something like this could be on the cards but this man, White, the car dealer, why would he finance something like this? You haven't said he was a terrorist sympathiser or had any terrorist leanings. I think all you have is this girl's thoughts."

"Yes, I know, but it sounds plausible, that's why I wanted to run it by you just in case they succeed in getting a billion pounds into the hands of terrorist groups."

"OK Steve, I agree it's possible, so leave it with me, but you said the noon shipment of the gold can't happen because you're arresting this Pleasance person before he can give the confirmation code."

"Yes, the gold shouldn't leave, so it's pretty secure, but what if there is a conspiracy. You'd want to do something about it, wouldn't you? In case they try again."

The Head of MI6 was silent. Steve could hear him breathing deeply before he was back on the line with a curt "I'll call you back." With that, the head of Her Majesty's Secret Service hung up.

***

On reflection, Steve felt he may have made a fool of himself. Apart from Poppy's imagination, there was no evidence suggesting a terrorist connection.

Steve went down to breakfast to find Jenny had eaten and gone. Clearly, the post-mortem was being carried out earlier than the DCI had thought. As he enjoyed a good breakfast, the sort he'd warned Sir Patrick Bond about, his mobile vibrated. He didn't recognise the number but answered anyway.

"Good morning Chief Inspector, it's Dougal Munroe here." The forensic scientist's Scottish accent seemed to be stronger down the phone. "I was just wondering if you'd like the results of the analysis of the gentlemen's handkerchiefs?"

Steve stopped eating and pulled out his notebook. He took a long sip of excellent coffee before telling Dougal to carry on.

"Well, we've tested every hanky your lads could find on the four gentlemen. Every hanky was clean, and I don't mean laundry clean." Steve might have expected a joke here from the Scotsman, but he didn't get one. Dougal Munroe was being very serious leading the DCI to hope he had something. He did. "Only one of the hankies tested positive for metal cleaning polish." Dougal paused and now gave out a small chuckle. "Turns out it was common or garden Brasso." Again, a pause. "Now I'll be back this morning and sample the window catch and handles. With luck, we'll get a chemical match to what's on the hanky. If his Lordship uses Brasso we've got him. At least we'll have a definite link between the hanky, the window and the owner of the hanky."

Steve smiled to himself. Like all technical people, Dougal saw the excitement that was in the science. A slightly exasperated Steve said, "Dougal that's great, and please follow it up, but whose handkerchief had the polish on it?"

"Oh! Sorry Inspector, didn't I tell you?"

Dougal went on to say who owned the handkerchief. Steve explained he wouldn't be too long at Lord Rosyth's place this morning, gave Dougal the e-mail address for Poppy, with a request to send his report to Poppy as soon as he could, and thanked the forensic officer for his help and initiative.

The DCI slowly finished his breakfast. He had his first solid piece of evidence even though it was purely circumstantial.

After checking out of his room he arrived at Lord Rosyth's country manor just before nine o'clock. He entered through the rear door to find

Arthur Halliday deep in conversation with a uniformed sergeant. The sergeant left and Arthur approached the DCI.

"Morning sir, that was Sergeant Albertson. He's one of the best in our force. I've had him brought in to pep up the outside search teams. He'll get twice the ground covered in half the time." Arthur looked pleased with himself. "He takes no excuses and rumour has it he doesn't even allow toilet breaks."

Both men nodded. "He sounds just what we need." Steve was conscious he needed more evidence. "Let's go to our office in the kitchen and see if Mrs Stocks has any coffee on."

Over a large mug of steaming hot coffee, Steve brought the Inspector up to date, following his conversation with Dougal Munroe. "I'm going to let the four gentlemen go. They all live in London, so it'll be easy enough for us to keep tabs on them. We'll keep quiet just now about the Brasso on the handkerchief and wait for Dougal's final report. Meantime you and your Sergeant Albertson keep searching for the murder weapon. The killer has probably ditched it, but if it was one of our Right Honourable gents, there's a chance he's kept it and we need to find it."

Detective Inspector Arthur Halliday looked confused. "Are you saying one of the four gents who stayed over on Wednesday night is the killer according to the metal polish lead?"

Steve considered this. "Yes, unless you think the staff are involved, or that either Lord or Lady Rosyth go around bumping off their guests." Steve paused.

"Look, the house was sealed up for the night. The alarm was set and there's no evidence of a break-in even though someone wanted us to believe the ladder under the victims' bedroom window was important. The ladies who were here all went home together with the local guests leaving only these four toffs inside the house. One of them must have killed the Minister and his wife. We've got a finger pointing at one of them thanks to Dougal, but we need to know why. The post-mortem might tell us something and I think Dougal's coming back to finish off all the forensics. Make sure he arranges for a sweep of the four bedrooms used by our Honourable Gentlemen and not just the window metalwork. Nobody can kill like this and not leave traces."

"Yes, I see that, sir. I'll make sure the bedrooms are sealed. So, what do we do now?"

"We'll go see all four gents and release them with a warning not to go more than twenty miles from their home addresses without telling me. I'll get someone on to do a deep forensic check into the background of our handkerchief man, we'll get the post-mortem and forensic results later today and apart from that we're back to good old police work."

As Steve and the local DI walked towards the breakfast room door Steve stopped. "Arthur? Where are we with the four girls who were at the dinner?"

"Nowhere just now. Until I interview Lady Rosyth, I won't have their details."

"Fine, but as soon as you do, get them over to DC Cooper at the Yard."

After sending the young gentlemen on their way with his warning about not travelling more than twenty miles from their homes still ringing in their ears, and DI Halliday set to interview Lady Rosyth, plus continue the search of the grounds and talk to Dougal, Steve took his leave of Lord Rosyth, thanking him for his assistance. He informed his Lordship that DI Arthur Halliday would speak with Lady Rosyth later in the morning just to take her statement. Lord Rosyth was somewhat surprised the DCI was heading back to London so soon. "We've uncovered a link we are following up, sir. I've all the details I need on your guests and the investigation will proceed faster if we have all the resources of Scotland Yard behind us."

"But surely, Inspector, you can't think anyone in the house did this thing?"

"As I said, sir, we have a link that needs following up, plus our forensic teams are still collating evidence. I'm sure our senior officers will keep you and your Chief Constable apprised of developments."

Steve could see his Lordship wasn't happy, but he also saw that Lord Rosyth now suspected the truth. That only one of his house guests could have shot Sir Derek and Lady Layburn as they slept.

***

As the DCI drove back to London, The Cap accompanied by Twiggy had their first meeting with Sophia Marr. They kept it very low-key in the hope of developing a bond with the suspect, but Miss Marr was using her "no comment" privilege and after an hour, The Cap and Twiggy left her in interview room two. "We'll wait for Steve to get back."

The Cap returned to the office to find Poppy hard at work keying data into her computer. The Cap looked at the clock on the wall. It read 09.19 a.m.

***

In the offices of the Department for Regional Development and Planning located just off Whitehall, the two civil servants responsible for arranging committee meetings were busy laying out files containing the briefs on the items for discussion at the upcoming meeting. Neither man was aware that the minister in charge of the department would not be attending, nor that the meeting would be unusually short.

Once news of Sir Derek Layburn's murder had been relayed to the Prime Minister, and the Cabinet had been satisfied there were no national security issues at stake, the Prime Minister had happily passed responsibility over to the Home Office, who in turn had happily passed responsibility over to the Metropolitan Police.

The Head of the Civil service had been tasked to look at Sir Derek's immediate schedule and in conjunction with the most senior civil servant in Sir Derek's department, to set about ensuring continuity of government.

The Prime Minister had done his bit to ensure the work of government carried on by appointing Sir Derek's number two as the new, if temporary, Minister for Regional Development and Planning.

The room for today's meeting was now set out. Five places had briefing note files laid in front of them. One was set at the head of the table to be used by the chairman of the meeting and the other four were spread two either side. Jugs of water and glasses were placed on the table, and all was ready for the ten a.m. meeting to start.

Chapter Twenty

At nine-thirty a.m., Detective Inspector Peter Jones accompanied by the two constables who had kept watch on Michael Pleasance entered the office of the Assistant Deputy Governor of the Bank of England.

DCI Burt had instructed the Welsh DI to inform senior management of the Bank of the events of the past week and advise him that Michael Pleasance was to be arrested at ten. He explained the background and as instructed apologised for keeping the operation secret but stressed they were operating first and foremost to prevent a robbery.

The Assistant Deputy Governor whose name was Rupert Naismith was shocked by the news. He talked about how loyal Michael Pleasance was, how dedicated he was to the Bank and how he couldn't believe one of the Bank's most trusted employees could be mixed up in anything like this.

In his lilting accent, Peter Jones explained. "We have Miss Marr in custody and with Mr Pleasance alongside her, your gold shipment will be safe. The gold won't even have to be moved until you sort out the next date."

"Oh, but you're wrong, Inspector; I thought you knew. As of eight this morning that shipment has been underway. The whole process is automatic due to the weights involved. The Bank is known as The Old Lady but over the years we have invested in technology and less than two years ago we installed a completely robotic gold handling and shipment system. Michael Pleasance helped set it up." Rupert Naismith wiped his now sweating brow and continued.

"You see we need four hours for a twenty-tonne load. The robot's computer would have been instructed last night to prepare a twenty-tonne shipment. No matter what, the gold will be delivered to the north loading bay precisely thirty minutes before the due time. Once there, the security doors will open, and the pallets will be automatically laid out on the loading dock to be loaded into the armoured cars. At that point, the only thing between the gold and the outside world is a door in the exterior wall of the bank. Although it's reinforced it has been identified as a weak spot. Anyone knowing a shipment was being dispatched would only have to break down this outer door and the gold would be just sitting there waiting for them." Rupert had told his tale quickly and continued to wipe his brow.

DI Jones listened with interest. "But if you know this is a weak spot, what have you done to tighten security?"

Rupert waved the comment away. "We employ armed guards around the armoured trucks while the gold's being loaded but in truth, they have orders not to open fire, so you see, if Michael Pleasance wanted to steal the gold, that's where he'd do it." Rupert now looked ill. "Not dream up some elaborate science fiction scheme."

Peter Jones had his orders. "Yes sir, I'll mention your observations to my DCI. Meantime, we will go and meet Mr Pleasance."

At 09.55 a.m., Mr Michael Pleasance was arrested on suspicion of conspiring to steal twenty tonnes of gold bullion from his employer.

He was taken to the interview suite at New Scotland Yard and placed in interview room three next to Sophia Marr.

***

The new and temporary Minister for Regional Development and Planning entered the conference room that had previously and meticulously been prepared by the two low-level clerks attached to the department. Four senior career Whitehall would-be Mandarins were already seated. Each was dressed in the same way. It seemed the dress code for senior civil servants was compulsory: dark suits, white shirts and a formal but not flashy tie.

The new and temporary chief was an old-school politician from the north of England. Miss Gloria Shaw had been a Member of Parliament for over twenty years. She was unmarried, was known to hate men and had a reputation for being able to match most men pint for pint in any drinking contest. Her love of beer had taken its toll on her body which sagged in all the wrong places and no amount of clever tailoring could disguise her shape.

She uttered a curt "Good morning," and waddled to the head of the table where she slowly and with great difficulty lowered herself into her chair. The four assembled suits looked at each other with questioning stares.

As a Northerner, Miss Shaw was known for her blunt forthright speech and today would prove no exception. In her broad Mancunian accent, she opened the meeting.

"If you don't already know, Sir Derek and his missus were shot in the early hours of yesterday. The PM's asked me to take over for now so you lot had better get used to it."

She looked at each member in turn. "Bloody hell, a woman in charge, whatever next!" Miss Shaw theatrically performed with her arms making sweeping gestures in the air. "Don't worry lads, it's only temporary but let's be clear, the work of the department carries on."

One of the suits started to talk, saying he felt he spoke for all those present how sorry they were to hear the sad news, and how they would give 100% support to Miss Shaw.

Miss Shaw had no time for such sickly sentiments nor such insincere assurances.

"Just do what I tell you and everything will be fine."

The new Minister for Planning and Regional Development opened her file. "Right, let's get to work. I'm up to speed on all these, but we'd better go over them one at a time."

Gloria Shaw took her pen and ticked the first item on the agenda. "Item one. Extension to experimental cycle lanes in Norwich." She looked around the table.

One of the four suits, a little man whose compulsory white shirt was clearly two collar sizes too big for him raised his hand to speak.

"It has been approved by Norwich City Council and Treasury have confirmed a grant of five hundred thousand pounds to support the extension. The last meeting voted approval subject to today's sign off."

Gloria looked at the little man. "Waste of space and money. All cyclists are a menace on the road, and they don't pay road tax. If I had my way, I'd ban the lot of them from the public highway." Gloria was clearly not a fan of lycra-clad people on two wheels. "Not approved and Treasury can keep its money for something else more worthwhile."

The little man's jaw fell. This was obviously one of his pet projects. He was brave enough or silly enough to challenge the new Minister.

"Excuse me, Minister, but we usually debate such matters before voting whether to approve or reject…" He saw the look Miss Shaw was giving him. He fell silent.

"As I said, waste of money and not approved." The new temporary Minister smiled inwardly and thought to herself, *Bloody red tape. This lot need to get a life.*

"Item two. Building of a techno park in Peterborough…"

And so, it went on. Item three. A car showroom and workshop on green belt land in Kent. Item four. A leisure and bar sports club in Liverpool. Item five… etc., etc.

After forty minutes of Miss Shaw singlehandedly deciding the fate of some half a dozen projects, the committee came to item seven, the Blackwood Project.

"Item seven. Redevelopment of green belt close to Bury known as The Blackwood Project." The new Minister reached for a thick file marked Blackwood. The four suits did likewise.

Without being asked to comment, the more intelligent-looking of the four spoke up. "Minister, this project, as you may know, has been under discussion for some time. Your predecessor was against the intrusion into the green belt and felt, in my opinion quite rightly, that the local authorities who granted local permissions were only looking at one side of the argument. Very limited social or ecological impact studies have been carried out and we feel the economic argument only favours the developer. The previous Minister was minded to refuse permission."

Gloria Shaw didn't take too kindly to being lectured. She hadn't asked for a commentary and didn't particularly like what she'd heard.

"It looks like Colonial and English Land have already invested heavily in this project. Do you know how much they've spent so far?" Her remark was addressed to the previous speaker.

"Eh, no Minister but I could find out."

"No need. You see, while you and your colleagues sit around tables pontificating about planning theory and risk assessments, some people are out there in the real world trying to make a difference. You're happy to reject something that's had millions and millions poured into without even bothering to understand how much of its own money this developer has spent." Miss Shaw allowed her disgust at what she saw as intellectual arrogance that was common throughout Whitehall.

"This Blackwood Project will bring jobs and prosperity to the area. Something the local politicians understand. So, what if a bit of green belt gets used up, the men on the ground know the extra housing and jobs are needed." She paused. "I've got an idea. Get the head of this Colonial and English Land in on Monday morning. We'll make a joint press announcement about a new town under this government's watch. You know, jobs, prosperity, affordable housing all backed by the government." She pointed to the younger of her four officials. "You set it up."

Miss Shaw continued to review the file. "I see from the file you've even been to court spending taxpayer's money trying to justify the unjustifiable. You've held this project up for years just because you could. There is no justification except political dogma to reject this project."

She looked at her committee of four daring them to challenge her. None of the four did but they all knew the idea of a press conference announcing government participation in this project wasn't true although it sounded good. Each man independently decided not to raise this discrepancy in the Minister's thinking.

"Right. Item seven is approved."

At the stroke of a pen, Miss Gloria Shaw had unwittingly made a triple murderer a very wealthy man.

***

The watch team sitting outside Cecil White's house in Esher were bored. Since their arrival, there had been no evidence of any movement. The flasks of coffee they had brought were empty and they needed the toilet.

Just as they'd decided to drive off and chance leaving their post for five minutes the large metal electronic gates opened, and a late model Land Rover appeared. It turned in the direction of London, but the darkened windows meant neither watcher could identify the occupants.

A call was made to DS Matt Conway who was sitting with The Cap in the DCI's office.

"Hold tight and wait," was the response from the DS.

"What do you want them to do?"

The Cap was afraid something like this might happen. He had his two suspects below in the interview rooms awaiting the DCI's return. This other new dimension was something he couldn't deal with easily. He was conscious that DS Matt Conway needed an answer.

"Tell them to follow and if possible, identify who is in the car."

This was relayed to the watchers, who set off in pursuit.

The Cap had used the time to think. "Matt, get the other team that was watching Pleasance over to Esher. Tell them to keep watch and they'll be relieved when we can but to report any movements. It's safer to have two units in case someone else goes for a drive."

Matt Conway left the office to set the watchers up as per The Cap's instructions.

Poppy arrived in Steve's office. "The boss has been on. He wants an update so can you call him. He reckons he'll be here by eleven-thirty, subject to traffic."

The Cap called Steve and brought him up to date. Both arrests had been made. Sophia Marr wasn't talking. Michael Pleasance was in shock at being arrested but wasn't talking. The Cap explained in more detail how the gold was handled and that the collection of the shipment had been going on since eight that morning. "Should we have Kent Constabulary present at this air charter business just in case?"

"Not a bad idea Cap, but you'd better see Commander Brooks first. That's his call, so bring him up to speed. We've spent a lot of money either preventing a robbery or wasted a lot of money on a non-event. I'm making good time I'll be there in about thirty minutes." The DCI hung up.

The Cap was unhappy about seeing the Commander but bit the bullet, made an urgent appointment and ten minutes later was seated in front of Commander Alfred Brooks.

Alfie was a copper's copper and knew how to put junior officers at their ease. He offered the DI coffee which was accepted. Both men sat weighing each other up before Alfie began.

"Don't just sit there, man, you asked to see me, so you must have something on your mind."

The Cap once more hid behind his boss. He blurted out talking very fast. "Well sir, DCI Burt suggested I should meet you and bring you up to speed on the Bank job."

"Did he indeed? That's the likely gold heist from the Bank of England you are running?"

Sheepishly The Cap looked at the Commander. "Yes sir."

"And no doubt with DCI Burt's assistance?"

The Cap seemed to brighten up. The Commander obviously knew Steve had been running the case but not officially. "Yes sir."

"OK, let's hear it. We've got enough invested in this operation, so it had better be good."

"Well, sir, you know Walter Bostrom was reported missing by his mother, first to her local nick and then to Miss Rough."

The Commander was impatient. "Yes, yes I know Miss Rough, carry on."

It took The Cap a while to relax in front of this senior policeman. "The DCI was a bit suspicious of Pleasance especially when he learnt that a twenty-tonne gold shipment was due to be transported today."

"So, you're saying there isn't a lot of firm evidence, except we're stopping a twenty-tonne gold shipment leaving the Bank at twelve noon today in case there's a plan to heist it?" The Commander didn't look pleased.

"Not exactly sir, although our first priority has been to protect the gold." The Cap explained about the aircraft sitting at Manston with a flight plan to Turkey, the payment into Direct Air Charter's bank account, and Poppy's idea that the aircraft once in Turkish airspace could land almost anywhere.

"The thing is sir; we've got both Pleasance and Marr downstairs but they're not talking. We've no real evidence as to Walter Bostrom's whereabouts, other than his two phone calls originating near Esher. His prospective father-in-law lives in Esher, and we've got a watch on the house. This guy Cecil White has form from way back and the wealth to fund an operation like this." The Cap paused and looked a bit sheepishly at the Commander. "But he's been clean for years and we can't figure out why he'd suddenly get involved in bullion robbery."

Commander Brooks interrupted The Cap's flow. "Money son, the oldest motive in the world. For some men, enough is never too much. The more they have the more they want."

"Yes, I see that sir, but here's the thing. We have a theory that there might be a terrorist connection, but White has no links to any organisation, not even the SNP." The Cap allowed himself a slight smile and was pleased to see Alfie Brooks show his teeth. "If this aircraft got to Turkey and did land in the east of the country, then terrorism worldwide could be one billion pounds richer. The DCI has spoken to someone he knows in intelligence and they're checking out the theory, but I'd like Kent Police to sit on this air charter bunch today from say noon until we can safely stand them down. We don't think the bullion can be moved, but if we have shut down their ultimate escape then we're doubly safe." The Cap felt exhausted having to talk so much and provide so much detail.

Alfie Brooks sat behind his desk in silence for fully three minutes. "So, you want me to alert Kent and have them place a squad at Manston?"

"Yes sir. I'd leave it up to them, but I'd prefer if they were sited inside the company's offices with the pilot in full view."

Alfie considered this. "Yes Cap, very sound." He stood up. "OK, I'll speak to Kent. I suppose the DCI's on his way back?"

The Cap also stood, noting the use of his in-house nickname. "Yes sir, he should be here now."

"Right. Off you go and keep me posted. It's coming up for twelve o'clock when hopefully most of this will be over."

As The Cap got back to the office, he saw Steve in his office talking with Poppy. He knocked on the door frame and entered.

"The watchers are reporting that the Land Rover seems to be driven by a woman who's doing the weekly shop. It's only been to a supermarket and a few local stores. It's now back at the Esher house." As Steve explained this to The Cap, his mobile sounded. It was Patrick Bond.

Steve put his phone on speaker in order The Cap and Poppy could hear both sides of the conversation.

"Sir Patrick. Just so you know you're on speaker so if there are any state secrets you want to share now's the time." Steve as usual started these conversations with a light-hearted remark. The usual light-hearted reply was missing on this occasion.

"Fine." A long pause, unlike Sir Patrick. He was clearly choosing his words carefully. "Where did you pick up on this intelligence?"

"I told you. My DC had a theory but she's listening in, so ask her yourself."

"Well miss, how did you get the information?" Sir Patrick sounded intense as though he were carrying out an interrogation.

Poppy was stunned. What had started as a wild story based on a few facts now sounded real. This was, after all the head of Britain's secret service she was being questioned by. "I didn't really get any information. I just sat and thought if the flight plan to Turkey is provisional and it's to Ankara then it's only a few miles to the rebel Kurds in the east of the country. The aircraft can land almost anywhere so I just thought what if!"

"And you've no connection to any Turks living in this country? No boyfriend, no friend of a friend?"

"No sir, nothing like that. It was only my imagination running a possible scenario."

"Steve, we've got evidence that a house in Esher, a place called Great Stodding Farm, has been at the centre of some seriously heavy-duty terrorist chatter. Our Turkish desk didn't have it but our communications analysts at GCHQ have been monitoring it for days. They say it started on Monday of this week, the 17th. So far it's only chatter but the word gold has appeared too many times for this to be a coincidence."

The DCI looked at his two colleagues as he answered Sir Patrick. "Patrick, that address, that's Cecil White's residence. We've got it under observation, but the latest report said it was all quiet."

The Cap banged his hand on his desk. "Hold on sir." Turning to Poppy. "Has the second surveillance team reported in? The one we sent when the first one left to follow the Land Rover."

"No sir, it's all been very quiet."

The Cap was standing up. "Poppy, get onto the surveillance unit that followed the Land Rover. Ask them if they can see the second unit and try calling them."

Poppy rushed from the room.

"What are you thinking, Cap?"

"I don't know, Steve, but with this information from Sir Patrick I'm a bit worried."

Poppy came back. She was clearly excited. "I can't raise the second unit and the first unit says there's no sign of them or their car."

With Sir Patrick still on the phone having heard everything the DCI and the DI looked at each other and like a double act said "Oh! Shit!"

Chapter Twenty-One

The realisation that two police constables appeared to be missing caused a certain amount of initial panic and uproar among the officers assembled in Steve's office. Everyone seemed to be talking at once. The DCI called for quiet and brought a sense of order to the gathering.

The line to Sir Patrick Bond was still open. "Patrick, what do you want to do about this suspected terrorist situation?"

Sir Patrick responded immediately. "MI6 only has limited powers within the UK. It's a job for MI5 and your anti-terrorist unit. I'm not sure whether your missing officers complicate things or not, but I think you have a multitask job on your hands. Leave any terrorist threat to me. I'll talk to Five and your Commissioner and we'll sort something out. The security of the gold and the search for the missing officers are up to you." The Head of MI6 paused. "Sorry Steve, I think that's as far as my remit goes."

"No problem, Sir Patrick. Just keep me posted." Steve was almost pleading. "I don't want to walk into something I'm not prepared for." The line went dead.

Steve's mind was buzzing but he was prioritising as he went. "Poppy, it's more than likely our officers are inside Cecil White's house in Esher. Get a search warrant now, officers in danger." Poppy immediately left.

"Cap, are the two watchers still outside the Esher house?"

"Yes."

"Get on to them. They're to stop anybody who tries to leave. In fact, tell them to park over the entrance. We'll get troops there even before the warrant's issued. Also, they should treat anybody they come across as armed and dangerous."

"Right Steve. What about armed response?"

"Yes, good idea. Get them rolling and get Poppy to put an all-ports for Walter Bostrom and Cecil White."

The DCI stood. "I'm going to brief the Commander. As soon as I'm back we're off to Esher."

Commander Alfie Brooks wasn't pleased with the DCI's report. Sir Patrick Bond's counterpart at MI5 had already been onto the Metropolitan Police Commissioner and explained about a possible terrorist connection involving a suspected gold bullion robbery the Met's Special Resolutions team were dealing with. The Commissioner knew nothing of this, had alerted the Anti-Terrorism unit and immediately contacted Commander Alfie Brooks as Department Commander of the Special Resolutions Unit for an explanation.

Alfie had just lifted the phone to summon Steve as he walked in.

"What the bloody hell are you up to now? I've had the Commissioner on my neck about a terrorist conspiracy that none of us knows anything about, the Anti-Terrorism unit has been put on standby..." The Commander's phone rang.

He grabbed it and shouted "Yes?" He listened and made no comment to what he was hearing from the other end of the line. Steve knew it wasn't good news as Alfie's face was getting redder and his eyes were boring into the DCI's skull.

In what Steve took as a bad sign, the Commander slowly replaced the receiver, sat back and looked squarely at his DCI. "Now you've called out an armed response unit." The decibel level of his voice suddenly increased as he hit his desk with a closed fist. "For Christ's sake Detective Chief Inspector, what the hell's going on? Your man DI Ishmal briefed me not long ago that there could, repeat *could*, be a terrorist implication to the gold case but it was far away from MI5, the Commissioner, Anti-Terrorism units or Armed Response. Just tell me now."

Alfie's voice was now at shouting level and his blood pressure was obviously up. "What is going on and why have you disobeyed a direct order to stay away from this and concentrate on the murder of a Government Minister and his wife?"

Steve was in very hot water, but he'd been here before. He quickly but calmly explained the events of the past several minutes. He didn't relish adding to the Commander's list of complaints against him by admitting two officers were missing but knew he had no choice.

"You see sir, we now believe the house in Esher is the headquarters of some terrorist gang who intended to fly the gold out of the country this afternoon. The supposed missing man, Walter Bostrom, could in fact be a leading player as could his prospective father-in-law, one Cecil White. "We believe they must have seen our watchers; they diverted one set away by sending a maid on a shopping trip knowing we'd follow, and somehow lured the remaining watching pair into the house so they could escape. We've put out an all-ports and are getting a search warrant for the Esher house. I'm just off there now in case our lads are in there." Steve made to go.

"Hang on Steve." The Commander appeared to have calmed down, possibly soothed by the DCI's explanation. "I see all that and I did suggest you keep an eye on this gold thing but told you specifically your priority was the double murder."

Steve could see Alfie was again building up to explode. "What the hell am I to tell the Commissioner or the Assistant Deputy. Shall I just swan into their offices and say don't worry?" The decibel level was once more rising. "Detective Chief Inspector Steve Burt, MBE, AKA Supercop, has everything under control from the murder of a Government Minister to a foiled bullion robbery, to thwarting a terrorist cell set to get its hands on a billion quid. Oh! and by the way, he does 'missing persons' on the side and for an encore, he's lost two valuable police officers and he's managed this all on his own without help. But the good news is the gold, which may not have been at risk in the first place, is safe. Is that what I tell them? For Christ's sake Steve, give me a break."

Alfie had slowly worked himself into a temper and was shouting. His blood pressure was once more rising. "Well! Is that what I'm to tell them? That you're a bloody one-man police force?" Alfie picked up a pen and threw it across his office. With a huge sigh, he slumped his oversize body further into his executive chair and stared red-faced at his junior colleague.

Silence descended but only for a few seconds while the Commander got his breath back. He started up again. "You're a bloody loose cannon. I tell you to concentrate on the murders and you ignore me. We've kept the press away so far, but they've started to ask questions. Now I've got the press office asking for a statement for the Commissioner's TV broadcast. The murder of a Government Minister is big news once it gets out and what have I got for the Commissioner to tell the press?" Alfie glared at the DCI. "Bugger all, that's what."

Steve knew when to be silent without appearing to be insubordinate. He'd had dressing-downs before but not like this. His mind was looking for a way out, but his temper was also rising. Alfie's last remark triggered something in the DCI that he couldn't control.

"Sir. You're being bloody unfair. I told you I was up to my neck in the bullion job, but you insisted I look into the murders." Steve was now also shouting. "I've done everything you've asked. I haven't had a decent night's sleep in days; my teams are working eighteen-hour shifts and to be honest, Alfie," — Steve deliberately used the Commander's Christian name — "I've just about had it. You can stick your press release and the Commissioner's TV broadcast."

He knew instantly he may have gone too far with this last statement, but he ploughed on. "Just so you know, in less than 24 hours I've got a suspect in the frame, forensics are still working on something, and Jenny Fuller is on her way back with the PM report."

The DCI paused more for effect than to calm himself down. The Commander had a furious look on his face and was about to say something when Steve resumed. "You can tell the Commissioner and the press that Supercop expects to make an arrest within seventy-two hours, and he'll have done it with no help from senior management in the Met."

Steve headed towards the door. "I'll expect to have Internal Affairs on my doorstep later today armed with the disciplinary you'll no doubt file as soon as I leave. But don't worry, *sir,*" — Steve put as sarcastic an emphasis on the 'sir' as he could — "I won't fight it. So, if you'll excuse me, I have two missing officers to find and if I'm allowed, I also have a murderer to apprehend."

The Commander was mad. That was obvious. In response to Steve's request to be excused, he waved an arm in the direction of the door. "Bugger off and don't come back without our missing officers."

***

184

Steve and The Cap sped towards Esher with all lights on and sirens screaming. The two watchers confirmed they'd parked across the entrance; armed response was already on the scene awaiting the DCI, and Poppy confirmed the search warrant had been granted. She had faxed it to the local police substation and a local officer was on his way with it. Everything looked set.

The Cap and Steve discussed the case as The Cap drove at top speed.

"Where are we, Steve? I'm a bit confused, especially over the past hour. I'm the one supposedly in charge but you're the one that got blasted by the Commander."

"Don't worry Abul, I've got broad shoulders." As Steve said this he began to wonder if his shoulders were broad enough. He'd done what he thought was for the best and finished up getting a roasting from a man he liked and admired. He allowed an element of self-pity to creep into his thoughts. Maybe it was time to take the promotion, to sit behind a desk and shuffle paper and not expose himself to criticism as he always did with each new case he took on. He smiled inwardly, thinking, *If I have a career after this.*

He shook himself out of his daydream. "Sorry Cap what did you say?"

"I was wondering where you think we are with this case?"

Steve shook himself again and tried to organise his thoughts.

"Well, first, I think Walter Bostrom being reported missing was a red herring, designed to confuse everybody. I think he's probably mixed up in the planned bullion heist with his future father-in-law. We've got two bank officials who are likely having an affair and see this robbery as a way of escaping. It seems probable that the bulk of the gold was to be flown out of Manston Airport and delivered to terrorist groups in Turkey and, once we'd shut down the robbery side by arresting two of the players, the rest would have done a runner."

"You don't think Pleasance and Marr are terrorists?"

"No. I suspect they were promised a nice payday that would've allowed them to settle down in a non-extradition country in the sun and live happily ever after."

The Cap was swinging around cars and vans and driving at breakneck speed. "It makes sense, but what about Walter Bostrom? There's nothing in his background to suggest terrorist sympathies."

"Mm." Steve was stroking his chin. The Cap knew this was a sure sign he was thinking. "Yes, you're right. He's a puzzle but he's definitely involved. Maybe he's getting a payoff as well. Maybe he'll marry his girlfriend and, like Pleasance and Marr, jet off and live happily ever after."

The pair sat in silence apart from Steve calling out on a few occasions. "Watch that car!" or, "There's a cyclist up ahead for Christ's sake! Watch it." In the end, Steve would not describe his journey to Esher as uneventful but they made the trip in record time.

***

As they arrived at Great Stodding Farm just on the outskirts of Esher they were surprised to see two armed-response cars parked by the side of the road. Steve was also surprised by the address because although it was Great Stodding Farm it was in fact number 116 Esher Road. He presumed the address was to make the place sound grander than it was.

They immediately recognised both DI Peter Jones and DS Matt Conway standing talking to one of the armed response team. A minibus was also parked outside the high stone wall of the property and Steve saw half a dozen uniformed officers obviously drawn from the local force.

A uniformed inspector approached the two detectives as they got out of their car.

"Inspector Brian Cole, armed response, sir. I take it you're DCI Burt?"

"Yes, Brian. Have you had a look around?"

Brian Cole opened the laptop he was carrying and placed it on the bonnet of the pool car Steve and The Cap had just arrived in. He fired it up and the two detectives saw an aerial view of the house and gardens. Brian Cole pointed skywards. A drone was hovering over the property and Inspector Cole nodded in the direction of a uniformed constable who was obviously controlling the machine.

"From what we can see, it's all quiet sir. It's your shout but from a tactical perspective, I'm not seeing anything to suggest my lads will be needed to gain entry. My assessment is you can just ring the bell, flash the search warrant and enter. We'll be within the grounds to back you up if things turn nasty. We've seen some person hanging out washing around ten minutes ago so it looks like domestic bliss in there."

"Thanks, Brian. We'll go with your assessment. Have your lads stand by."

Brian Cole marched off, calling out orders to the teams under his command. Steve walked towards Peter Jones and Matt Conway. Before he could say anything, Peter produced the search warrant. "Hand-delivered less than five minutes ago sir."

Steve took the warrant, scanned it and passed it to The Cap. "What the hell happened here, Peter?"

"To be honest it's pure speculation but we think the first team was lured away and somehow whoever is in the house got our boys inside and are holding them. The tracker in their car says it's inside the gate. The drone suggests it's all quiet, so they probably grabbed our lads and then legged it."

"Hm! Yes, that seems to be possible." Steve rubbed his hands. "Everybody, get your stab vests on." The officers from the Yard complied. When everything was ready and Brian Cole — who was tasked with carrying out a risk assessment for the operation — gave the nod, Steve rang the bell attached to a pillar that supported large fairly solid metal gates. After a few minutes, he rang again and noted the drone was still in position overhead presumably to give early warning of anything unexpected.

No voice came through the intercom, but the gates slowly opened. When there was a sufficient gap, Inspector Cole and four of his team of armed policemen rushed through and took up strategic positions around the house, weapons at the ready. Steve, followed by The Cap, Peter Jones, Matt Conway and the two constables who had been watching the property, rushed forward after the armed officers.

The house was a grand affair despite being significantly smaller than Lord Rosyth's place. Steve took it to be fake Tudor probably no more than ten years old. The outside was dressed in stone and the black-painted beams were obviously false. There were three steps up to a porticoed canopy supported by two round pillars. This covered the double front doors and clearly was there to protect visitors when it was raining.

The left-hand door opened, and a little Asian woman appeared. The team didn't stand on ceremony. Without any preamble, Steve showed the warrant to the lady, said they were there to search the premises and stood aside as first the detectives from the Yard rushed in, followed by two of the uniformed officers from the minibus parked outside.

The maid looked frightened and after a few seconds, it was obvious she didn't speak much English. Steve called over another uniformed officer from the minibus. "Take her to my car and stay with her." The constable gently led the maid away.

Steve entered to find something he remembered from an old Keystone Cops movie. People were dashing everywhere. Up and down stairs, from room to room all looking for some obvious evidence their colleagues had been in the house. The DCI decided to base himself in the smallish square hall with several doors leading off it.

"Steve, down here." It was The Cap and the DCI guessed that 'down here' probably meant the cellar. The DCI found a door by the side of the staircase and descended. Sitting tied hand and foot to upright chairs were the two missing watchers. Their mouths were taped but they looked in good shape. The Cap had begun to release them as Steve arrived. Once they were free and had stretched themselves back into shape, Steve asked what had happened.

"I'd not say no to a cup of tea and a toilet first sir." The older of the two spoke. Steve smiled, relieved that they had found the two officers, and kicking himself for not suggesting this before questioning them.

"Yes. I'm sorry; there must be a kitchen." From somewhere in the house, a loud voice called out, "Mr Burt, sir, can you come now?" The voice had an air of desperation about it that worried Steve. He reacted straight away but before dashing off asked The Cap to organise things for the two kidnapped victims and said he'd see them in the kitchen.

Steve ran up the stairs to the hall. Matt Conway was rushing around looking for the DCI.

"This way sir." The DS went ahead of Steve and bounded up the stairs two at a time. Steve followed and Matt ushered the DCI into what was obviously a bedroom. Lying on the bed was a man who had obviously taken a real beating. His face was covered in bruises, his nose looked to be broken and both eyes were almost fully shut due to swelling. He wasn't wearing a shirt, and everyone present could see burn marks all over his body.

This person, whoever it was, had been severely tortured. Peter Jones was by the bed. "I've called for an ambulance sir. He's still alive, but God knows what his internal organs are like. He's taken some heavy blows."

The DCI looked at the victim. "Do we know who he is?"

"Bloody hell! It looks like Walter Bostrom." Matt began to search a jacket lying near the chair and found a wallet. "Yes, this confirms it, this is Walter Bostrom."

Steve was speechless. If this was Walter Bostrom then his theory about Walter being involved was now completely shot. Matt Conway handed him the wallet containing the driving licence as though for confirmation. As Steve saw the licence and tried to rearrange his thoughts, his mobile vibrated. He saw it was Commander Brooks. Despite still being in a state of shock and his brain racing with theories he decided to answer and at least give the Commander the news that the two officers were safe.

"Yes sir."

"Steve before I say anything, I want you to know I'm completely calm. I need you back here an hour ago." The tension between the two men could be felt down the phones.

Steve wasn't sure he liked this sinister-sounding Alfie Brooks. "We've got our two lads sir and we've found Walter Bostrom. I'm—"

"You're not listening, DCI Burt. I want you here ASAP." Alfie was still talking in a controlled way that was unnerving Steve.

"You remember the gold bullion that you told me couldn't be shipped and was safe? Well, it left the Bank of England as planned and on time at four minutes past twelve this afternoon. The Deputy Governor called asking for DI Peter Jones because Jones had spoken to him before he arrested Pleasance this morning. He wanted to tell DI Jones the shipment of twenty tonnes of bullion had left the Bank and just wondered if we knew." The quiet, threatening tone coming from the other end of the phone alarmed the DCI as did the news that the gold was missing. "Oh! And in case you're interested, the Commissioner has a date with the media at five this afternoon to explain what we're doing about the murder of a government minister and his wife. That's the small insignificant case that you're SIO on, remember? The case I ordered you to concentrate on." Commander Brooks was still talking quietly and in a tight, controlled manner, but the DCI knew there was pent-up anger just below the surface. He wished Alfie would just explode and get everything out in the open between them.

Steve decided to ignore the murders for now and concentrate on the missing bullion. "There has to be an explanation for the gold being shipped, sir. I'll leave right away but can I ask you to do something?"

"So now I'm a messenger?" The Commander exploded. "What the hell do you take me for, I'm your senior officer, not someone you can ignore. Oh, this had better be good."

Steve ignored the implied threat. "Can you contact Kent? Make sure they have men at the air charter company. If the gold has somehow been released and it's been redirected, then that's where it's going, sir. I'll be there in less than an hour." Steve terminated the call without any formality.

He looked at Matt and Peter. "The gold's been moved. I've no idea how or why. It should have been impossible. DI Jones, I want you to tidy up here." He looked at the broken body of Walter Bostrom. "Get a local bobby to go with that poor sod to the hospital and arrange a guard. I don't suppose we'll be able to interview him for a day or so."

Steve was obviously upset at the condition of Walter Bostrom and embarrassed that he could have been so wrong about this man. He shook himself back to the present. "There's a forensic unit on its way and a search team. Look for anything that might tell us where Cecil White has gone. I'll take DI Ishmal back to the Yard with me. Get statements from the two officers downstairs, and you'd better get them checked over by a doctor." The DCI paused, thinking. "Once everything's checked here make sure you write it up and get the full reports over to Poppy so she can update the file. The maid is outside in my car. Matt, you go and get her, bring her in and when you're done here bring her into the Yard and get an interpreter. Any questions?"

Both detectives looked at each other and shook their heads. Matt Conway left to collect the maid as instructed.

Steve found the kitchen and brought The Cap up to speed. "I've asked Peter Jones to hold on here. He'll take the statements from these two." Steve nodded towards the two constables who were enjoying their tea and biscuits that The Cap had obviously found. "We're wanted back at the Met. The Commander isn't my biggest fan just now, so God knows what we're going back to. You concentrate on the bullion job and when Matt Conway gets back, he'll help you."

"You're sure that's Walter Bostrom upstairs?"

"I am unless his driving licence is a fake."

Both men were feeling low as they set off at breakneck speed to Scotland Yard. Not even The Cap could find any humour to exploit. All he could say as he drove was, "We've truly ballsed this up."

Chapter Twenty-Two

When the DCI and The Cap arrived back at Scotland Yard, they found DS Jenny Fuller talking to Poppy who was busy entering information onto her laptop. It was obvious that Jenny was telling Poppy about some event important enough to be included in the murder file.

Poppy saw her boss enter and immediately stopped typing. She looked excited and was gushing. Obviously, she had something to say but Steve remembered her last gushing statement and where it led.

"Sir, the Commander has called a case conference for three o'clock." She looked at her watch.

"You've just got time for a coffee, but I've got something."

Steve ignored his DC's obvious enthusiasm and tried to concentrate on the case. "Just a minute, Poppy."

Before The Cap could sit down, Steve was back as the man in charge. "Cap get onto the Kent boys. Find out if our missing bullion has turned up at Manston, will you?"

A dejected DI Abul Ishmal did as he had been told.

Jenny knew Steve and The Cap well enough to see they were at a low point so volunteered to get the coffees. Before she left Steve spoke. "Jenny, did you get everything we need from the post- mortems?"

"Yes sir, plus effects and some forensics."

"Good. Look, I know the murders have priority, but I don't seem to be able to get away from this blasted bullion thing. Can you keep the wheels turning on the Cirencester murders until I can get clear of this Bank case?"

"Shouldn't be a problem, but I know that Scottish forensic bloke is keen to talk to you."

"Right, I'll call him later."

Steve sat behind his desk and tried to think but Poppy was now in front of him with a notebook in her hand. Reluctantly, the DCI gave in. "OK Poppy, let's have it."

Without being asked, Poppy pulled a chair to sit opposite Steve. The Cap stood despondently by the door. "Well sir, remember a few nights ago the team watching Sophia Marr lost her and despite everybody going out searching she wasn't found until she got back to her place? I think it was around midnight."

Steve wasn't in the mood for another one of Poppy's entertaining theories. He sighed. "Yes."

"Well…" She had a twinkle in her eye. "I got my Uncle Terry, you know in Technical Support, to pull up all CCTV images he could from the end of Tower Bridge going south. It took a while, but we spotted her car parked outside a restaurant in Bromley, Kent."

The DCI was interested but didn't see how the fact that one of their suspects had eaten in Bromley helped their case. He said so and Poppy smiled an even bigger conspiratorial smile.

"Parked beside her Morgan was a Range Rover. We traced the number plate to none other than Cecil White." Poppy closed her notebook with a flourish. "How's that for a coincidence?"

The DCI was slow to arrive at a conclusion. Slowly his eyes widened. "You mean… Sophia Marr and Cecil White are an item and in this together?"

"Yes, sir. That's what Uncle Terry — sorry, Inspector Harvey and I both think. On the CCTV footage, we saw them leave the restaurant together, go to their cars together, have a goodnight smooch and drive off."

The DCI needed time to gather his thoughts as he sat behind his desk, but suddenly everything happened at once. The realisation that he had misread this case from the beginning dawned on him and caused him to reflect on what they now knew. Then his mobile started to buzz, and Jenny arrived with the coffee.

The DCI answered his phone. It was DI Peter Jones. "Sir, it's me." The DCI wasn't in the mood for small talk. "Yes, Peter."

"Oh! Sorry sir but I thought you should know we continued to search after you left and guess what?"

"Peter. You're trying my patience, just tell me! It's not a good time right now."

"Sorry sir, it's just that in the attic bedrooms we found two other people. They're not hurt but were tied and gagged. It was Michael Pleasance's wife and daughter and they've been held here since Monday."

Steve drank some coffee, too amazed to allow himself to think. "You're sure they are who they say they are?"

"Yes sir. Nobody could make that up or use that name."

"Yes." The DCI went into deep-thought mode for what appeared to be a long sixty seconds. "Get Matt to bring them here to the Yard. We've got Michael Pleasance downstairs. If this is what it looks like he'll probably talk to us now, knowing his family are safe."

Steve was about to put the phone down when he had another thought. "You'd better double-check every room in that damned house. People seem to be popping up all over the place."

Steve felt as though his whole world was imploding around him. The Cap, who was feeling the same way, entered and sat in front of Steve's desk holding his coffee. "There's no sign of any gold shipment being delivered to Manston. Kent has a team in place but so far nothing."

Steve pondered this information and suddenly had an idea. He called out. "Poppy, come in here."

Poppy, not being as sensitive as the others were to Steve's moods, arrived with a not too happy look on her face. "You only had to say please, you know sir." In other circumstances, the DCI might have read her the riot act considering the mood he was in but on this occasion, Poppy's naivety broke the spell of doom and everyone roared with laughter. Poppy stood embarrassed and slightly shocked. She'd no idea why a rebuke to her boss had caused such hilarity.

Once everyone had dried their eyes and settled down, Steve looked fondly at Poppy. "Never mind Poppy, you're a tonic. Look, get onto Terry. Ask him to use the national CCTV database and search all possible routes from the Bank of England to Kent. He's looking for a convoy of four armoured trucks. Then, at the same time, get him to look for the nearest camera to the Bank and start from twelve noon. He's looking for the same four trucks and I want him to follow them as best he can, no matter which direction they go in. Have you got that?" Poppy had and sped off to find her relative.

"Right Cap. Let's see what we've got and try and make some sense out of this mess. I'll no doubt have to explain our cock-ups to the powers that be."

"Rather you than me, Steve."

The DCI was stroking his chin in thought. "You know, Cap we've been behind this thing from the start. If it is Cecil White who's behind it, he's been clever. He's thrown us bits and pieces knowing we'd overreact and head off in different directions."

"What do you mean?"

"Well, in the beginning, Walter Bostrom was a missing person, and that alerted Twiggy. Then he calls his mother from an Esher number. This leads us to think he's not missing but involved in the heist and probably staying with Cecil White. Twiggy finds a charge to his credit card to British Airways that in our minds confirms he's not a victim but in reality, it's another clever diversion. Then there's the call to the air charter company using his mobile. They know we'll trace it to Esher and assume because it's Bostrom's mobile he had made the call. Everything has us looking at Esher, but Cecil White has another plan.

"When we raid his Esher house he's gone, and we find Walter Bostrom beaten and tortured, meaning he's a victim again. You see by having him call his mother this led us away from thinking of him being a victim." Steve was getting involved now in this narrative. "I think he was tortured for his four-digit code. Then we've got Michael Pleasance. We thought he was having an affair with Sophia Marr but that was our conclusion. In reality, Cecil White had snatched his family presumably to put pressure on him to hand over his code. Cecil White's been luring us to Esher all along and has handed us all the parts of his plan, Walter Bostrom, the Pleasance family. We get our watchers back but by then he's flown."

Steve paused. "I think Poppy finding the connection between Sophia Marr and Cecil White was pure luck but great police work. I don't think our finding out was part of White's plan. Now that Poppy's shown that Sophia Marr and Cecil White are in this together, we know she would have had no problem handing over her four-digit code. Are you following?"

A suspicious Cap nodded. "Yes, so far."

"Right. So now the gang, or whoever they are, have the code that releases the gold. They know we're looking into Walter Bostrom's disappearance which they weren't expecting. I bet Pleasance was told not to contact us and not to follow protocol at the Bank. Once they know we're involved, they hatch another plan to throw us off the scent. They charter the aircraft from Direct Air Charter to make it look like they're flying the gold out of the country to Turkey. We don't know, but I bet they knew we'd spot a possible terrorist connection, another red herring." Steve sipped the last of his now cold coffee.

"It cost them a lot of money to make it look real which means we're more likely to believe that's their plan." Steve paused and sat back. "Don't you see? It's been one red herring after another, and we fell for it." The DCI looked at The Cap.

"They'd no intention of using Manston to get the gold out. I'll also bet that the twenty tonnes of gold haven't moved very far."

"OK. I see all that, so where is the gold and where are the soldiers who drove it from the Bank?"

"Good point Cap, I don't know, but I bet if you go down and sweat Sophia Marr and let her know we have evidence that she's in this with Cecil White, you might get more than a 'no comment'. Also, when Poppy's finished with the CCTV, get her to check with the MOD. Let's see if we can talk to any of the troops who moved the gold."

It was The Cap's turn to become a deep thinker. This was an unusual experience for him and one he really didn't enjoy. He knew he wasn't as fast at analysing events as his boss, but he also knew he always got there in the end.

"Right, so Matt Conway's on his way back with Michael Pleasance's family plus the maid. I suppose I need Pleasance to confirm he handed over his code. Then I'm to put pressure on the Marr woman in the hope she lets slip where the gold has been taken and get Poppy to speak to the MOD? I'll leave Matt to get an interpreter for the maid, but I don't suppose we'll get much from her."

Steve smiled to himself. He knew The Cap wasn't the brightest, but he was a good steady cop.

"Brilliant, Cap, I couldn't have put it better myself."

196

Another thought struck the DCI. "Cap… I suppose you've checked with the Bank that the gold shipment isn't where it's supposed to be?"

The Cap looked shocked. "Bloody hell Steve, I hadn't thought about that. If the bullion's been delivered to the warehouse at Heathrow after all this, we won't even be directing traffic next week. I'd better check." A very nervous Cap left.

The DCI checked his watch. It was approaching three p.m. and time to face the Commander. Steve felt more relaxed. The pandemonium of the past half an hour hadn't played well with him. He had felt he was drowning in information but getting nowhere. Poppy's timely reprimand had in many ways changed everything. She'd lightened the mood and allowed the DCI to see clearly through the maze that Cecil White had created, and set The Cap off on a proper investigative path.

He considered the money that had been spent booking the aircraft from Manston. It had been very clever. Everyone knew or thought they knew that this was the route the gold would take out of the UK and, provided it was covered, then the gold would be safe. Everyone would feel more secure. The DCI once more marvelled at how clever Cecil White appeared to have been.

***

At three p.m., precisely as the DCI was preparing to enter the office of Commander Alfie Brooks, his phone buzzed. It was The Cap.

"Christ you scared me, fortunately, there's no sign of the gold at Heathrow."

Steve smiled. "Better safe than sorry Cap. Get on with Sophia Marr, try to break her. See what she knows." The DCI hung up as he pushed on the office door.

He expected to see a gaggle of senior officers and was surprised to find the Commander and a very attractive lady Steve knew as Helen who worked for the Media Relations Department seated at Alfie's conference table. This was clearly no case review meeting.

The Commander saw the confusion on his colleague's face. "I decided against a full-blown case review. Thought I'd save your blushes.

Helen's here to help quietly get us all out of your mess." Alfie clearly wasn't ready to forgive and forget, but Steve thought he was mellowing.

Steve had known Helen for several years and had had to rely on her good advice several times in the past. Apart from being easy on the eye, Steve knew she was married to a newspaper man, she had a daughter and lived somewhere north of London.

"Afternoon Steve. The Commander's been telling me of your exploits and how guilty he's feeling that he didn't give you more support on the cases you're handling."

Alfie coughed and spluttered. "Good God woman, I told you that in confidence. I don't want this great lump thinking I'm getting soft."

"Well, sir, you said it, and in the context of your remarks, I think DCI Burt deserves to know. After all, isn't that why I'm here? To pour oil on stormy waters." Helen looked sweetly at both men who just stared at each other. Each was determined not to be the first to register any form of apology. Eventually, Steve as the junior officer gave in.

"Well, Helen. I suppose I might have ignored a few things the Commander told me, but he did throw me into the deep end knowing I had the bullion case ongoing."

Even Steve knew this sounded a bit childish but before Alfie could respond she held her hand up. "Gentlemen you're not children. Can you please agree to a truce and let's move on? The Commissioner has a TV date at five and I have to write something for her to say."

Commander Brooks cheered up. "Yes Helen, you're absolutely right. Steve and I will sink a few beers later and have a laugh about this." He suddenly broke off and became scarily serious again. "But only if both cases reach a satisfactory conclusion."

The fact he smiled after this statement didn't improve Steve's sense of foreboding if either case fell apart.

With the initial skirmishing over, Alfie Brooks asked the DCI to update him on the bullion case. Steve repeated his discussion with The Cap pointing out again that in his opinion Cecil White had cleverly guided the investigation down several dead ends.

He explained that The Cap was now interviewing Sophia Marr and would use the knowledge Poppy had supplied to press her harder, and that a full search of CCTV from the Bank from twelve noon was being carried out. He added that the MOD was being contacted to assist them to find the soldiers who were involved in loading and transporting the gold.

"Apart from that sir, there's not a lot we can do for now. DI Ishmal is on it. We'll see what he gets from the Marr woman. We can interview the soldiers once we get their details and the allports is still in operation."

Helen had been making unofficial notes. "Gentlemen, for obvious reasons neither the Bank, the government nor MI5 want this getting out, so you have a bit of breathing space. Steve, have you completely discounted any terrorist involvement?"

"You can never totally discount it in something like this, Helen, but up till now, there's been nothing to suggest Cecil White would be involved in terrorist activity. I'll have my admin assistant forward the file to Anti-Terrorism just in case something develops."

"Yes, do that Steve. So, for now, let DI Ishmal get on with this."

Alfie glared at his DCI. "Watch my lips. Help him if and when you can but not at the expense of the Layburn double murder. Are we clear?"

"Yes sir."

"Good. Now Helen here needs to be briefed on the Layburn murders so she can put something together for the Commissioner to spout."

Steve considered how best to reply. "Sir, I need an hour or so to put things together. I've got a definite suspect, but I need more proof. There's a very good forensics man working on things in Cirencester, and he left a message to say he needs to talk to me. Plus, I need information on my suspect's background and have asked Miss Rough to get into his financials. I think I can give Helen a full picture in an hour. Just now, I wouldn't be so confident that I could give her the whole story."

Helen nodded her agreement followed by the Commander. "Right Steve, back here at four." Alfie waved his arm towards the door and the DCI left.

Chapter Twenty-Three

When Steve got back to his office, he called Jenny Fuller in to join him. There was no sign of Poppy, and Steve knew The Cap and Matt Conway were interviewing Sophia Marr. The DCI was conscious that Jenny might not be fully up to speed on the case. He set about highlighting what they knew for her benefit.

"We know the victims were shot, one bullet for him, two for her. We haven't recovered the gun. DI Arthur Holliday still has search teams out looking for it in the grounds so let's hope they find it."

Jenny interrupted. "I brought the spent bullets back and they are with ballistics. I've asked them to check for a match from previous cases. I'm not hopeful, but as you say, you never know."

"Good work Jenny." The DCI knew Jenny Fuller was efficient and could be trusted to pick up on any loose ends. "Moving on. Dougal Munroe, the forensic boffin, found metal polish on one of the handkerchiefs from the gentlemen who stayed in the house overnight. Remember, the house was alarmed and shut up tighter than a drum. The handkerchief in question belonged to the Right Honourable Clarence Strum, so at the moment he's our main suspect, but only because there was polish on his hanky. It's a bit flimsy, so I asked Dougal to go back."

Steve picked up his phone and dialled the number for the Scotsman. As it rang, he switched on the speaker on the phone. Dougal Munroe answered on the fifth or sixth ring without any preamble.

"About bloody time you called. I thought you said this was urgent. I've had my lads on overtime, and I've put more miles on my car than I can claim for just running back and forward trying to help you out."

The DCI hadn't expected such an outburst from the scientist but thought it best not to respond. "I've been up to my neck with another case, but I'm all yours now, Dougal. What have you got?"

The forensic man calmed down, realising the DCI probably had other calls on his time." The atmosphere coming from the other end of the phone changed. "Right, we checked the rooms of our four honourable gents. Gave them a good going over, but I did the hanky man's myself. All other three bedrooms were clean, but in our hanky man's room I found something you'll like."

Steve remembered from the previous day that Dougal liked to be centre stage and dragged out his stories.

"In the U-bend in the shower, I found a feather." Steve heard a note of triumph in the Scotsman's voice. "Not just any feather. Oh no! It's a match for the feathers used to stuff the cushion the killer used to silence his shots. It must have stuck to him and been washed off when he had a shower. It's only a fragment but it's a positive match."

"Brilliant Dougal, so you can put this guy in the victims' bedroom with the cushion in his hands?"

"Definitely, unless a dead feather can fly between rooms."

"Very funny Dougal. Next time I'm over your way, you and I will split a bottle of good scotch."

"I never say no to a dram or two especially if someone else is paying."

The DCI was excited and was about to say goodbye when Dougal spoke up. "Don't you want the rest?"

Steve froze. He couldn't believe his luck. "You've got more?"

"Oh! Yes, your idea to seal off the four bedrooms was inspired. The maid hadn't been in to tidy up or change the beds, so the rooms were largely untouched. I found bodily fluids on our Honourable gentleman's sheets and not just a drop. He had a female companion, and they didn't practice safe sex nor static sex. They were both all over the place including areas of the bed I couldn't even get to. I've got good DNA so find me a sexual acrobat and I'll match her DNA."

Steve knew instantly that this complicated matters. "Dougal, can you say whether this happened Wednesday or Thursday night? Could he have had a woman last night?"

"I only found evidence of one him and one her. I time-lined the degradation of the samples and I'm ninety per cent sure they both gave their all in the early hours of Thursday morning, the 20th."

"You know what this means?"

"Apart from the obvious, I'm afraid so, but I've got more."

Steve was feeling a little deflated and hoped Dougal could produce a miracle.

"It's not much, but I found gun oil in the top drawer of the chest of drawers. Without the gun, I can't match it, but it shows there had been a weapon in that drawer, and if Arthur Halliday can find the gun, I'll be able to place it in that drawer."

"Good work Dougal and I'm sorry I was slow getting back to you. This is all good stuff. I think you've put the Right Honourable Clarence Strum squarely in the frame. I'll be in touch." Both men hung up.

"Let's get out of here. I need a coffee. The canteen should be quiet."

Before Steve could get out of his chair, his mobile rang. It was Twiggy. She said she had something for Steve, who in turn said he was headed for a coffee with Jenny. Twiggy said she'd join them.

***

As the three detectives made their way to the canteen in New Scotland Yard, the Temporary Minister for Regional Development and Planning was exiting a taxi outside a plush block of flats in fashionable Mayfair. A uniformed doorman stood forward and opened a shining door that reflected the afternoon winter sun. Gloria Shaw hadn't been here before so asked for apartment number 600. The doorman escorted his visitor to a desk occupied by a well-groomed middle-aged man dressed in winged collar and tailcoat. Gloria Shaw couldn't see his lower body but bet herself he would be wearing pin-striped trousers. She was informed that unit 600 was the penthouse and was asked if she had an appointment. After confirming her name, the man in the winged collar telephoned the occupant of the penthouse, confirmed she was indeed expected, rose gracefully from behind his desk and escorted the Temporary Minister to the lift that silently whisked her to the sixth floor.

She had met her host a few times at various functions over the years but wouldn't claim to know or like him. As she exited the lift she stepped into the heart of the penthouse, and was greeted by a largish man, casually dressed in jeans and a t-shirt holding what looked like a gin and tonic.

Roddy Glass was the CEO and majority shareholder of Colonial and English Land Inc. and the recipient of planning permission given today by the Department for Regional Development and Planning that would make him even wealthier than he already was.

***

Seated at a table away from other officers, Steve, Twiggy and Jenny were enjoying their coffee.

"Right…" Steve consulted his watch. He had forty-seven minutes before he had to be back in the Commander's office. He shared this timeline with his colleagues. "We're under a bit of pressure to show we're on top of this double murder, so no deviating into the other case." The DCI entered his lecturing mode as though he were talking to a class at Hendon Police College. "It seems the press is on to it, and we need a statement for the Commissioner to give to the TV at five p.m., OK?"

Both women seated with Steve remained silent and looked serious.

"Twiggy, I've already briefed Jenny about the initial forensics and the metal polish on a handkerchief so you'll have to catch up. The hanky belongs to The Right Honourable Clarence Strum, so he's our main suspect. Forensics found a feather from the cushion he used to shoot our victims in the U-bend of his shower. They've also got fresh gun oil smudges in one of the drawers in his room but so far we haven't found the weapon." Steve paused for effect before carrying on. "These things in themselves give us grounds to bring him in, except… it seems he had a female companion with him at the time of the shootings. Plus, we don't have any motive." The DCI sipped his coffee. "Why would a person like Strum shoot a Government Minister and his wife?"

Steve left the question hanging. Twiggy spoke first. "I've no idea, Steve, but you have enough circumstantial evidence to at least bring him in for questioning. As for his lady friend, he could have slipped out while she was asleep, shot the couple, returned to his room, showered and got back into bed." Twiggy looked keenly at her colleagues who were both nodding. "Do we know who this woman was, and have you interviewed her yet?"

"No to the last question." Jenny Fuller was consulting her notes. "But according to DI Halliday, it's likely she's called Matilda Armstrong. She has an address in Dulwich. Of the four women, three were definitely escorted home by other guests. No one can account for this Matilda. Apparently, she's a bit of a goer; Lady Rosyth said she was only invited because her father is desperate to get her off his hands."

"So, we're discounting the other ladies and concentrating on Matilda. Right?" Steve looked at Jenny who was officially his number two on the case.

Twiggy gave Steve one of her looks that said just a minute. "Is there any suggestion Matilda and the Right Honourable are in this together? Maybe she helped him and is giving him an alibi."

"Oh! Christ, Twiggy. Why do you do this to me? I've got a straightforward bad guy in the frame, and you introduce Bonnie and Clyde into it." Steve was obviously not chastising Twiggy. In fact, he realised he should have thought of it himself. "But it's a fair point." The DCI finished his coffee. "Any thoughts?"

Jenny Fuller understood the implication of an alibi, but she told herself the circumstantial evidence was too strong to be ignored. "Steve, all this is good stuff but we've no motive."

Twiggy dug into her oversize shoulder bag that she always seemed to carry. She produced her laptop and keyed away for a few minutes. The DCI looked at his watch. Twenty-four minutes left.

Eventually Twiggy looked up. Steve and Jenny had used the few minutes silence to gather their thoughts. Twiggy held centre stage.

"There's nothing known on our man Strum except he has an IQ off the scale. He's a bit of a playboy and doesn't get on with his family. He makes his living sitting on company boards but only as a title on the letterhead. From what I'm seeing, he doesn't contribute much." Twiggy hit a few more keys. "Wow! He's pulling in around a hundred grand a year in fees from sitting on seven company boards. His bank and credit cards are normal for such a guy who lives in society in London but... ah, here it is. There's no mention of a steady girlfriend. In fact, he seems to play the field. I'd say the Bonny and Clyde idea is off the mark. I can't see a one-night stand helping out in a double murder."

"No, neither can I. Good work Twiggy. I won't ask where you got all that stuff."

"It's simple, Andy Miller set it up. It's a programme that scans all news and social media traffic, collates everything and if you need information on an individual, you just key in their name and the programme scans all the data and gives you all it has."

"I'm not sure if that's legal but we can ask Andy tonight if we ever get away from here." Steve sat back and once more consulted his watch. He had eighteen minutes left.

DS Jenny Fuller had been listening and analysing everything she knew. "Steve, it sounds like we have our man but not enough to take to the DPP. The Director will need more hard evidence and a motive." Jenny gathered her thoughts. "If this guy is, as Twiggy says, just a playboy, and a man about town then something caused him to become a killer. Unless we're missing something, his only contacts are with the companies he works for. The corporate world is the only place a person like this could be corrupted. His high-class chinless wonder friends are unlikely to be the reason he killed two people."

Steve liked Jenny's analysis. "So, you're saying the motive lies somewhere within the seven businesses that pay him?"

"Makes sense to me. We only have to find it."

"Good work both of you." After a few seconds' pause, the DCI was in charge again. "Jenny, get hold of the watchers from the bullion job at The Bank of England. Peter Jones has their details and technically they're still seconded to us. Get him to set up surveillance on Clarence Strum. I want round-the-clock coverage." The DCI waited for Jenny to acknowledge his order. "Then get an address for Matilda Armstrong over in Dulwich.

"The teams out at Lord Rosyth's place are still searching the grounds for the weapon but I'm sure they'll be called off after today."

Jenny nodded.

"Twiggy, if Jenny's right and our motive is in one of these seven companies can you dig deep into all of them. Let's see if anything pops up that might be an obvious motive for murder." Steve had nine minutes left. "Anything else?"

Jenny shook her head, but Twiggy raised her hand. "I know you didn't want to talk about anything other than the murder case just now, but I've got a lot of stuff on the bullion heist. I need to go over it with you and The Cap as soon as."

"OK Twiggy, but not now. It's one thing at a time. We think the gold's safe somewhere in the country, so it has a lower priority for us, compared to the Commissioner's fifteen minutes of fame at five p.m. Once The Cap's finished with Sophia Marr and the Commissioner has her statement, we'll take a look at the gold job. OK?" Steve waited for Twiggy to agree. "But get onto those seven companies. I've a feeling we're getting close."

"Yes, Steve. No problem, but you'll like what I have on the heist."

The DCI entered the office of Commander Alfie Brooks at exactly four p.m. The Commander and Helen from Media Relations were still sitting around the table Steve had sat at less than an hour ago. Both looked up with an expectant glint in their eyes.

***

As Steve entered the office of Commander Alfie Brooks, Mathew Conway was arriving back from Esher with Michael Pleasance's wife and daughter. Once he had been informed that his family was safe, he had agreed to give his statement and it became obvious he had been coerced into giving the details of his password. He had had a very traumatic experience but being reunited with his wife and daughter eased his anxiety. A family liaison officer had been called in and had escorted all three to the family home.

The Cap and Mathew Conway had tried different techniques to break Sophia Marr but even the fact that they knew she and Cecil White were connected failed to get anything other than a 'no comment' from her to all their questions. They'd been at it for over an hour without success.

Taking a break and seeking inspiration they wandered up to The Cap's desk in Steve's outside office to try to relax before dealing with another round of 'no comment' answers. The Cap wished Steve Burt were here to help him. He knew the DCI had a way of ferreting information out of people and this was a skill he didn't have. As he sat staring blankly at the wall, coffee in hand, and with Matt Conway slouched in a chair, Poppy arrived, accompanied by Inspector Terry Harvey. Poppy was her usual bubbly and excited self.

Without any preamble, she launched straight into her news. "We've looked at all the CCTV footage we could get from just outside the Bank to Ramsgate in Kent." Poppy was like a schoolgirl when she had something to pass on that no one else knew. She almost shrieked with delight. "We saw the four trucks leaving and followed them on the cameras." Before Poppy could carry on, the Inspector from Technical Support butted in.

"It wasn't easy, Cap. A lot of the cameras around London are old and budget cuts mean they are not being maintained as they should be, but Poppy's right. We got the trucks heading east out of the city. They headed for the Blackwall Tunnel to presumably go into Kent. We saw them as far as the slip roads for the Dartford crossing but lost them there. The cameras were all down at lunchtime today and still aren't working. We got images from the M2 heading into Kent but there was no sign, so I'd bet they didn't carry on into Kent. We got images as far as the M25 and M26 intersection but again there was no sign of the trucks. We'd no coverage over the Dartford Crossing nor into Tilbury but we caught up with the cameras again at the A12 and M25 junction. Again nothing." Before Terry Harvey could continue, Poppy was back.

"We think the trucks must have turned off at the Dartford Crossing and headed into Tilbury." She was smiling a broad, happy, innocent smile. "Otherwise, we'd have seen them at the other side of the bridge." With a triumphant flourish of her arms, she announced. "The gold must be in Tilbury, probably in the docks."

The Cap looked at Terry Harvey for confirmation. He'd experienced Poppy's dramatic conclusions before. The Head of Technical Support, simply shrugged his shoulders and put his hands in his pockets. Terry knew what The Cap was asking without forming the question.

"I'd say she's right. All the CCTV we could get suggests they didn't cross into Essex; they didn't carry on into Kent and they didn't head towards the southern side of the M25. We've got them around Tilbury but no further."

The Cap was now sitting bolt upright. Matt Conway stood up and joined The Cap.

"Poppy, get a map of Tilbury and find out about storage around the docks. I want to know if any short-term rental agreements have been finalised recently and get the name of the security chief for the docks. I want to talk to him."

"No need for a map Cap. I've got Google Earth on the big screens in the department. You can see everything you want on the screen."

"Thanks, Terry I'm right with you. Let's go Matt." As the three men were leaving The Cap stopped and turned to Poppy. "Any news from the Army about the drivers of the convoy?"

"No sir. I've chased them but apparently, once the vehicles are returned to Aldershot, the troops sign out for the weekend. None of the eight personnel lives in married quarters so they could be off doing anything. The Captain I spoke with said he'd check if the vehicles had been returned and he'd try and get the name and address of the convoy commander but so far I haven't heard."

The Cap was disappointed, especially given his latest information concerning Tilbury. "Get back onto the MOD. Explain that it's urgent. Tell lies if you have to but get me a name and an address."

Poppy sprang into action and before the three policemen had left the room, she was dialling the Ministry of Defence.

***

The DCI, having been invited to sit by the Commander, explained everything, including a lack of motive and a possible alibi in the shape of Matilda Armstrong, but admitted she hadn't yet been interviewed.

"So, you've a strong suspect but not enough for the DPP or the CPS? And you think putting him under surveillance might get you somewhere?"

"Yes, sir, I'm sure Clarence Strum's our man. We've got forensics but it depends if Matilda can give him an alibi."

Helen from Media chirped up. She had a shorthand notebook in her hand and had started taking notes the second Steve started to speak. "Can we say you expect to make an arrest within the next forty-eight or seventy-two hours?"

Steve considered this. He glanced at Alfie who was slightly shaking his head warning Steve not to commit.

"Helen, if Clarence is our man, I don't want him spooked. He's got money and could run if he thinks we're on to him. He's a clever bugger who has tried to put us off his scent by using diversions. I'm sure we'll get him, but we can't operate to a timetable to suit the press."

Alfie smiled at the DCI and nodded his head.

Helen wasn't too pleased by Steve's response but accepted it. After all, a DCI couldn't censure the Commissioner of the Metropolitan Police and Helen had heard enough to suspect an arrest was imminent. She continued to take her shorthand notes. When she'd finished she looked at her watch. "It's four ten, I've just got enough time to write this up and get the Commissioner briefed." She stood up, gathered her files and left the two policemen looking at each other.

There was a tension in the air. The Commander broke it by shouting to his secretary-cum-gatekeeper for two cups of coffee. Both men relaxed during the silence that descended.

"Look, Steve, your outburst earlier could have got you suspended." Alfie paused. "You know that don't you? We have a chain of command and it's that chain that allows an organisation like ours to function."

The coffee arrived. Both men concentrated on their drinks, trying to avoid eye contact.

"Yes sir, I realise I was out of line, but I still believe I was dropped in it." The DCI tried to lighten things by smiling a faint self-deprecating smile.

"Well, you might be right. Christ, with these budget cuts, we're short-staffed as it is. I had to beg and borrow those watchers you got for the surveillance teams on the bullion job and don't think I missed the fact you're using them to keep tabs on your murder suspect." It was the Commander's turn to smile in an attempt to mend fences. "Just don't run up any overtime."

"No sir." Steve was about to stand up knowing this meeting was over but before he could leave, Alfie spoke up.

"You're a bloody good detective, Steve, and because of that, we all ask too much of our good men. You need more permanent staff in your unit. I'll have a look and see if I can get you a few more bodies but remember what I said. No more vigilante work and get these murders put to bed as soon as."

Steve walked towards the door. As he looked back to say a thank you to Alfie, he noted the Commander suddenly looked very old slouched in his chair with his hands resting on the table. He was staring into the distance. The DCI left quietly.

***

DI Peter Jones, on hearing from Jenny Fuller that Steve wanted a 24-hour watch on the Right Honourable Clarence Strum, gathered his troops and collectively they worked out a rota to achieve Steve's objective. The DI reminded his watchers that they must not lose sight of their target and to maintain contact when they were on shift.

On this occasion, he handed out cameras with high-end telephoto lenses attached so they could take pictures to back up any future court action.

Their target lived in Wimbledon. He rented a large apartment in a newly developed block of flats. DI Jones emphasised that it had an underground car park so both the garage entrance and the main pedestrian entrance would need to be covered and a car parked in a suitable location to cover the garage exit. Details of the suspect's car were given out based on information from DVLA.

Everything was set. The Right Honourable Clarence Strum couldn't blow his nose without the watchers recording it.

Chapter Twenty-Four

Steve walked into his office to find Poppy talking on the phone. As soon as she saw Steve, she brought her conversation to an end. The DCI had seen an excited Poppy before, but she somehow looked positively bursting with excitement. Steve wondered what had happened but knew he would soon find out. He also knew an overexcited Poppy needed calming down, if he were to learn anything the first time she told her tale.

"You'd better come in, Poppy." The DCI walked into his inner office. Before he could sit down, Poppy was there clutching a pile of papers. Steve concluded she had something big and felt his own excitement level rise.

Poppy sat down and launched into her tale. "Right sir, The Cap's with Miss Marr again trying to get her to talk." Steve thought Poppy might have been watching too many detective programmes on television. She continued. "He asked me to get in touch with the Army to see if the drivers and the armoured trucks had returned. It took a bit of persuasion, but I eventually got a name and phone number for the commander of the convoy." Poppy ferreted through her pile of papers before drawing out the one she wanted. "His name is Sergeant Cummings. I just spoke with him. As far as he's concerned, everything was normal." Poppy's excitement level was increasing as she spoke faster. "They collected the gold, got the correct twelve-digit code and get this…" she could hardly contain herself. "They were told to take it to warehouse B16 in Tilbury docks!" With a flourish, Poppy stood up and her papers spilt onto the floor. "That's where the gold is. The sergeant said he was met by two men who showed him Bank of England IDs, they offloaded the gold onto pallets, got a signature and left to go back to Aldershot."

Poppy sat down again, breathing hard. She collected her papers and sat back a little disappointed with the DCI's calm response to her news that they'd cracked the case. At least that's how Poppy saw it.

"Anything else?"

Poppy, now a little deflated, sifted through her papers. "Yes, I spoke with the head of security in the docks. He confirmed that storage unit B16 had recently been leased and he has CCTV of the armoured trucks arriving and leaving. Don't you see sir, we know where the bullion is!" Poppy was working up to an excited state again. "Surely we only have to raid the place and we'll get the gold and the crooks."

Again, the DCI sat and started to stroke his chin. "It's all too easy Poppy. This gang have led us up too many blind alleys. They must know we'll talk to the Army and be told about their renting of B16." Steve was still thinking out loud. "The gold won't be there—but where? How do you handle twenty tonnes of bullion so as not to attract too much attention?"

Both police officers sat in silence for two minutes. The calm was broken by the arrival of Twiggy. She swooped into Steve's office and without any formality pulled up a chair and sat beside Poppy.

"You two look as though you're lost." Twiggy had her oversized shoulder bag on her knee and was extracting a small blue file.

"We're not exactly lost, but we do have a problem," Steve explained Poppy's findings and his theory that the gold would not be found in unit B16 at Tilbury docks.

"Mm, you're usually right about these things but I've got stuff here for you."

Both Steve and a now crestfallen Poppy sat up with their attention on Twiggy. "I've been doing a deep background check on Cecil White. First off, he's dead."

Both the DCI and Poppy stared in disbelief at Twiggy. Steve was shocked and was the first to speak. "*Dead?* How the hell can that be?" He could see from the twinkle in Twiggy's eye's that she had paused for effect.

"He died in 1967 aged two years in the Glasgow Royal Infirmary. The death certificate gives the cause of death as respiratory complications following open-heart surgery. Your man Cecil White isn't Cecil White but an impostor."

"So, he got a copy of little Cecil's birth certificate and set up a new identity. But why?" Steve couldn't see through this information and hoped Twiggy had more.

212

She carried on. "I've traced as far back as I could, and the new Cecil White first appears opening a bank account in 1999 in Glasgow. He next appears in 2001 in the Sherriff's Court in Glasgow charged with grievous bodily harm. He is given five years but only serves two." Twiggy raised her eyebrows at this piece of information but carried on. "The next time I find him is when he moves to Esher in 2004 and starts his car business. He's been clean since he came down from Glasgow." Twiggy was reading from her notes. "When I say clean, of course I mean he hasn't been arrested for any offence." Twiggy looked at her audience of two for confirmation that they both understood her meaning. "I checked on the purchase of the Esher house. How could an ex-con just out of prison afford a house in Esher even at 2004 prices?"

Twiggy searched for another page in her file before carrying on. Her audience was spellbound. The DCI remembered the Twiggy of old loved to be the centre of attention.

"He started his company with a sleeping partner. It was the partner who supplied the cash to get the business going." Twiggy paused and pulled another piece of paper from her file. "Now you've got to remember that back then money laundering and offshore bank accounts weren't so frowned upon as they are today, and were a lot more secretive, so it took some digging."

She again paused letting her information sink in. "I traced the start-up cash to a Cayman Islands account in the Blue Water Bank. It belonged to none other than Mr Joshua Ibinginy, the then leader of the African People's Republic of Cambow. He was overthrown, but his son also called Joshua, has taken over. Over the years there have been regular unexplained payments into Cecil White's company bank accounts and a lot of transfers from him into an account in Lloyds Bank in London. The name on the account is APRC. In my world that's The African People's Republic of Cambow. You see APRC is obviously a money-laundering operation and not a very subtle one at that."

Steve who'd been listening and thinking, held up a hand to stop Twiggy's narrative. "Are you really saying that Cecil White who isn't Cecil White is somehow mixed up with this African country, and not to put words into your mouth it sounds like you're suggesting the gold heist might be the work of the Africans?"

Twiggy beamed a huge smile and nodded. "That's what it looks like to me. There's a strong connection between the two but there's more. Whoever Cecil White was originally, his file in Barlinnie Prison in Glasgow declares him as originally being from Africa. His prison photo clearly shows he's African."

"Bloody hell you two, between you I think you've solved this thing." Steve went into his deep-thought mode. "Poppy, check with Tilbury. See if they have any ships leaving for any African ports or have any already left? I'll get Kent Police to check out unit B16."

As Poppy made the call, Twiggy looked at Steve. "I heard you had a rough time over this double murder. Are you and Alfie back on speaking terms?"

"Only just. I know he was right to tear a strip off. I screwed up, but hopefully, we'll get the son of a bitch who shot them soon, and all will be forgiven." He paused and smiled at the slimmer but still bulky Miss Rough. "I hope."

***

At five p.m. exactly, the Commissioner of the Metropolitan Police stood in front of a bank of microphones. She was dressed in her best uniform and had her statement on small, easily held cards. She stood back as Helen took control of the main microphone within the cluster.

"Ladies and gentlemen, the Commissioner will make a pre-prepared statement concerning the unfortunate murders of Sir Derek Layburn and his wife. We will take a maximum of six questions and only from those people I point to. I hope that's clear."

The ranks of journalists mumbled their disagreement with Helen's arrangements and vowed to ignore her request. They all knew the drill on these occasions. The Commissioner would give a dry statement and each person present would shout as loudly as they could hoping to out-shout their colleagues and have their question heard and then answered.

The Commissioner stepped forward as the throng of journalists quietened down.

"At approximately three a.m. yesterday, Thursday the 20th of October, Sir Dereck Layburn and his wife were brutally murdered while staying as house guests of Lord and Lady Rosyth. When the murders were discovered at approximately nine a.m., the Metropolitan Police were called. An experienced team of detectives was dispatched immediately to Lord Rosyth's country home in Cirencester where enquiries are ongoing. Good progress has been made in the investigation and the Senior Investigating Officer has reported he hopes to make an arrest within the next forty-eight to seventy-two hours." The Commissioner folded her piece of paper she'd read from and stood back from the microphone.

The assembled press corps, as expected, erupted with questions, each journalist shouting louder than the next. Helen stood forward and tried to control the pack eventually pointing to a few people she knew and affording them a question. As usual, none of the questions was too demanding and the Commissioner batted them away with ease.

The briefing was over by ten minutes after five on the afternoon of Friday the 21st of October.

***

As Twiggy was delivering her news, DI Arthur Halliday was packing up the search of the grounds of Lord Rosyth's country estate. Arthur had noticed it was his Lordship's custom to walk his two black Labrador dogs each afternoon around the grounds usually at five p.m.. This practice had annoyed the search teams as the dogs and Lord Rosyth were prone to walk across areas that still had to be searched. The DI didn't think this mattered as the teams had found nothing during their two days of searching. Arthur had been looking forward to working with senior officers from the Met on a high-profile murder case but had been disappointed to have been left with the more menial tasks.

He was removing his rubber boots when a cry caught his attention. Although it was almost dark, he could make out the shapes of his Lordship and his dogs standing beside two uniformed officers one of whom was shouting and waving his arms in the air to attract the DI's attention.

A reluctant DI Halliday pushed his feet back into his boots and trudged towards the group that was clearly seeking his attention. As he approached them one of the uniforms stepped towards Arthur holding a plastic evidence bag. The DI could see in the bag was a pistol.

"His Lordship's dogs started to yelp and bark by the old tree stump over there sir. He went to investigate what they were excited about. He thought it might be a rabbit and it probably was, but he put his hand into the stump and found this." The constable held up the bag as if it were a trophy.

Arthur took the bag with a grateful smile. He thanked the constable, thanked his Lordship, told the older officer to get a statement from Lord Rosyth and walked back to his car, this time with a spring in his step.

DCI Burt received the news of the find at 5.06 p.m. He ordered the weapon to be rushed to the Yard and delivered to ballistics. He called the senior ballistics officer who promised to run all tests on the weapon including fingerprinting this Saturday morning.

***

Steve visited interview room two where The Cap and Matt Conway were interrogating Sophia Marr. As he entered, The Cap acknowledged his arrival for the tape recording and Matt gave up his chair for the DCI. Although he tried not to show it, The Cap was relieved to have Steve with him. Miss Marr was not being cooperative and her constant replies of 'no comment' were annoying both The Cap and Matt Conway. The Cap could see that even the duty solicitor sitting beside their suspect was looking bored by the proceedings.

The first thing Steve noted was that Sophia Marr was of mixed blood. He guessed her mother was from Africa and her father probably from the UK. The second thing he noted was her beauty. She didn't look at him when he entered nor acknowledged his arrival.

The Cap didn't speak but shrugged his shoulders in a gesture that said, 'nothing doing' and rolled his eyes toward Marr in a move that meant 'it's your turn'.

The DCI knew Marr had been held since early morning so wanted to establish for the tape that she had no complaints and to try to get her to say something other than 'no comment'.

"Is everything OK, Miss Marr; do you need anything? I realise you've been with us for some time now."

Sophia Marr glared at the DCI, but for the first time in hours said something other than her standard response to The Cap's and Matt's questions. "I wouldn't mind a glass of water and maybe a sandwich."

Steve nodded to Matt who left to fulfil their suspect's request.

The DCI looked at his watch. It was approaching five-thirty p.m. He wanted to get home before going out again to Andy Miller's leaving party so decided to play a hunch.

"Miss Marr, we know about your connection to Cambow and Joshua Ibinginy. We also know about Tilbury and warehouse B16. You see you've been caught, and it's only a matter of time before we round up Cecil White and your fellow countrymen. Why not just fill in the blanks for us? We already know most of it including the fact that Cecil White isn't Cecil White."

Sophia Marr stared at Steve and then at the solicitor. It was clear this new information that Twiggy had uncovered was something she hadn't thought the police would unearth. The Cap remained outwardly calm but was inwardly glad Steve had this information and he too spotted, for the first time, uncertainty in the demeanour of their suspect.

"No comment."

"Miss Marr, I appreciate you're trying to buy your friends enough time to get the gold out of the country but the game's up. We have officers all over Tilbury docks." Steve paused and thought a few more guesses might help, maybe even the odd untruth. "We've stopped all ships leaving Tilbury and teams of maritime specialists are boarding every ship and searching them." The DCI opened his arms wide. "So, you see Sophia, it's only a matter of time. Help yourself here. Tell us what you know and I'm sure the judge will be prepared to be more lenient when it comes to sentencing."

For the first time, Sophia Marr admitted something. "Fine, you know about Tilbury. You know about the ship but everything else you know is only because my brother led you to it."

Steve picked up on this information. "You're saying Cecil White or the man calling himself White is your brother?"

"Yes. He's my older half-brother and is really smart. Our father died not long after he was born. Our mother got married again to an Englishman called Marr and I was born. That's why Joshua is a true African, not like me."

The DCI sat back and clutched at another piece of information. He'd have to be careful with his next question. "Miss Marr," Steve spoke very deliberately, "is Cecil White really Joshua Ibinginy, the leader of Cambow?"

Sophia Marr looked straight at Steve. After a minute's silence, she nodded her head. "Yes, I thought you knew. Joshua set up as Cecil White in this country years ago while still ruling Cambow. Cambow's a poor country and the leader is seldom seen, so Joshua lives here most of the time and goes back to his country twice or three times a year. Nobody misses him and what money the country gets from foreign aid he can divert through the car business."

The Cap was amazed. After hours of getting nowhere, the suspect was suddenly admitting everything. "Why are you telling us all this now? You could have told us hours ago."

Matt Conway arrived with a small bottle of water and a cheese sandwich. Sophia Marr acknowledged Matt but didn't thank him. She sat back and started in on her sandwich, pleased with her performance so far.

Steve touched The Cap's arm. "No, Cap, she's been buying time. Telling us all this now is another smokescreen. The gold's been moved so they can play their little game with us. The Kent boys won't find anything in B16, and I bet it's not on any ship in Tilbury docks." He looked squarely at the suspect. "Where is the gold, Sophia?

"No comment."

The DCI arranged for their suspect to be kept in a cell overnight and intended to begin questioning her again in the morning.

Chapter Twenty-Five

With an all-ports warning out to look out for the gold, Steve stood down his team in order they could attend Andy Miller's farewell. The Cap had organised a private room and after interrogating Sophia Marr most of the day, he was ready to party.

When everyone had gone, leaving only The Cap and Steve, the DCI asked, "What do you think, Cap? Are we being led up another blind alley?"

"I don't think so Steve, it's all a bit cloak-and-dagger. But look at what we've got thanks to Twiggy and Poppy." The Cap opened his notebook and read. "Looks like Cecil White — who's actually Joshua Ibinginy, the leader of an African country I've never heard of — is the mastermind behind the gold heist. His sister works at the Bank and probably helped him plan the job from the start. This Joshua seems to be getting aid money to help his country but set himself up years ago as Cecil White, a respectable car dealer, so he could divert most or all of the money to himself. I'm not sure I understand all of it and he has deliberately left us clues that are false just to put us off the scent."

The Cap paused. "We know the gold was in Tilbury... Hang on Steve." The Cap dashed into the outer office and arrived with a yellow post-it note stuck to his fingers. "It's from Poppy. There's a ship due to leave this evening for Lagos and another tomorrow morning for Istanbul." The Cap waited for Steve's response.

"I wonder if we're being double-bluffed, Cap. This Cecil character has been one step ahead of us the whole time letting us think all kinds of things including possible terrorism and a flight to Istanbul from Manston. It's all been rubbish." Steve, as he always did when analysing a problem, stared at the far wall and effectively talked to himself. "What if it's all been designed to show us how clever and devious, he is? How he's clever and doesn't do anything obvious... but what if..."

Steve was on his feet. Pacing around and seemingly unaware that The Cap was still in the room. "What if he's bluffing? He's shown us he's no fool, so we'd think it's too obvious to put the gold onto a ship leaving Tilbury. But is that his bluff… I wonder?" The DCI walked back to his desk and jolted himself back to the present. "What do you think Cap? The gold could be on one or even both of these ships. It's so obvious it's a brilliant double bluff." Steve was almost shouting. "It's bloody brilliant."

The Cap didn't know how to respond but he'd found over the years that when the DCI became convinced of something, he was usually right.

"Sounds possible, but how did they get twenty tonnes of gold out of warehouse B16 and onto one or both of these ships?"

"I don't know yet, Cap, but remember they paid that air charter company as a blind. If anyone splashes enough cash around, even honest ships' captains can be bought."

"Fair enough but what do we do?"

"No, my friend. What do *you* do? Remember Alfie's got me on his watch list for being a naughty boy. It's your case but you might want to call in the river police units, get a warrant to stop and search both ships, get Kent and Essex forces to swamp both ships with search teams and get a stop warrant to stop the ship sailing for Lagos tonight from leaving. If you're quick you might just catch Alfie Brooks before he goes." The DCI looked directly at The Cap and in a low voice said, "I bet the leader of Cambow and his henchmen are tucked up in cabins on one of those ships."

The Cap suddenly felt very tired and didn't like the position his boss was putting him in. He thought, if the gold isn't on these ships, his career might be over but if it is then it could be promotion and glory. *Still,* he thought, *I wish Steve were in charge and fronting this.*

The Cap made a decision. "Right sir, I'm on it but I just hope you're right." As he walked away, he turned to Steve. "Tell Andy I'll see him next time and I'm sorry I'll miss his bash."

With that, The Cap set off to solve the bullion heist based on the logic of his DCI.

***

Steve arrived home to find his wife Dr Alison Mills just coming out of the bathroom in their Knightsbridge house. She was wearing a fluffy white bathrobe and was drying off her hair, having luxuriated in a hot bath for the past thirty minutes. She saw her husband and realised he looked exhausted. She gave him a long lingering kiss and went into the kitchen to make some coffee and prepare a sandwich. "I don't suppose you've eaten much over the past twenty-four hours. Look at you darling, you need a shave and I swear you've lost weight."

Steve followed his wife into the kitchen and held her close to him. He reminded himself as he had in the past, how lucky he was to have met this doctor who was now his wife.

With a second cup of coffee in his hand and having wolfed down his sandwich, Steve sat on a stool that served the breakfast bar area of their open-plan room.

"Darling," Alison was towel drying her long fair hair. "I've got something to tell you."

Steve wasn't listening and was planning a long hot shower before their taxi arrived to take them to Andy's party. He barely heard what Alison said, finished his coffee and set off to their bedroom. Alison stopped drying her hair, smiled and waited. There was a shout from the bedroom. He had heard Alison's news.

***

When DCI and Mrs Burt arrived, the party was in full swing. Steve was pleased to see that Twiggy, who had become a good friend of his wife, was there along with Terry Harvey, the Head of Technical Support. Steve thought The Cap might have been correct. The new slimmer Twiggy had pulled a man. Alison approached Twiggy while Steve split off and saw the guest of honour, newly promoted Detective Sergeant Andrew Miller, now with the National Crime Agency. His star was in the ascendency. Next to Andy stood Samantha Burns. Sam had been brought in as a profiler on a previous case and the shy but brilliant couple appeared to hit it off from the start. Steve was pleased to see them as a couple, especially when Andy in his shy and awkward way, announced to Steve that he and Sam were to be married, but Andy asked the DCI not to say anything until he announced it officially later in the evening.

Steve moved on and saw Matt Conway was there on his own. They exchanged greetings and although he wasn't strictly a member of Steve's small team, he seemed like a nice guy and Steve had appreciated his help on the bullion case. He was standing with Poppy who was dressed in a low-cut pink dress that made the most of her assets. She was drinking a funny coloured drink and was already giggling and giving a good impression of a sixth form pupil at an all-girls school. Peter Jones had been invited but said he couldn't come. He was busy managing the watchers assigned to Clarence Strum. As Steve scanned the room, he noted Alison was deep in conversation with DS Jenny Fuller. Steve recognised her husband who was now the Deputy Director at the DPP. He was obviously destined for greater things.

With The Cap down in Tilbury searching ships, it was a smaller gathering than had been hoped for but at least the Unit was giving Andy a send-off.

Just as everyone was beginning to head to the table that had been beautifully set up for their meal, Commander Alfie Brooks and Mrs Brooks arrived. Dressed in what looked like a new suit, Alfie introduced his wife around, congratulated Andy on his promotion and apologised for being late.

He guided Steve away from the other guests. "Any news from Tilbury?"

"No sir, The Cap will call if he gets anything."

"I hope to hell you're right, Steve. My ulcer's playing up and it's all due to nerves. I pushed for the warrants, so my neck is on the line along with Abul's. I smell your DNA all over this as well. The Cap's a smart guy but he'd never come up with bluff and double bluff."

Steve noticed Alfie was wearing what looked like a new cream-coloured shirt and that the collar was just too small. It was cutting into his neck. "I've alerted the Foreign Office in case you're right and this Joshua Ibinginy is really the head of an African country. We could have all sorts of problems if Abul arrests him tonight. The first thing he'll do is scream diplomatic immunity and you know where that'll take us."

The DCI didn't know but he guessed it could start a political storm that police officers weren't equipped to handle. The Commander sighed and looked at his watch. "It's nine o'clock. They've been at it two hours."

With that, Alfie joined his wife, and the second part of the evening began.

The food was good and the wine even better. Everyone seemed to be enjoying themselves. Alfie's wife, a rather large lady dressed in a floral creation that smacked of the 1960s was laughing and talking with Poppy and Matt Conway who had managed to seat himself beside the detective constable. Steve deliberately avoided drinking too much. He noticed Matt Conway was similarly passing on the many top-ups being offered by the waiting staff.

He felt confident about the operation going on tonight, although he worried about The Cap, and wondered how he was getting on in Tilbury. He also allowed himself to consider how the bullion heist had come about. He hadn't had time to figure out exactly how it had happened and decided to make understanding it a priority for tomorrow when he interviewed Sophia Marr again.

He scanned the table and saw his wife sitting next to Alfie Brooks. He thought she looked radiant and again told himself he was a lucky man. The Commander proposed a toast, wishing Andy every success. Steve said a few words recounting Andy's early career in Special Resolutions and generally everyone was in fine form.

The food service came to an end and coffee was offered and accepted by most of the guests. People started to rise from the table and Andy approached Steve with a request.

Once everyone had returned and were either seated or standing around the table, Steve rattled a glass to get everyone's attention. "Ladies and gentlemen, I have two pieces of information to pass on tonight." He paused for effect and to let the room fall silent. "First, please raise your glasses to not only celebrate Andy's promotion… again." There was laughter in the room as they had toasted Andy's promotion several times already. "But to congratulate him and Samantha who have told me tonight they plan to be married."

The room erupted with goodwill statements, calls for another toast and a speech from Andy. The new Detective Sergeant rose and helped

Sam to her feet. The pair looked well-matched although Steve noticed Sam still seemed to do her clothes shopping at charity shops. Andy spoke for a few minutes. He was no public speaker but managed to say the right things, finishing with, "'Everyone's invited to the wedding when Sam tells me where and when it's to be." This final remark got a round of applause.

Steve was still on his feet and looked to where Alison was sitting. They looked at each other and Alison gave a slight nod. Steve rattled the glass again and once more the room fell silent. "I said I had two announcements." He paused to gather his thoughts. He looked down at the table before continuing. "Alison and I want you all to know that we are expecting a baby in about seven months."

The DCI had a tear in his eye and was surprised how emotional this simple statement had made him. Alison came round the table to join him as the room erupted with applause and calls for more wine to celebrate both pieces of news. Steve felt his right hand would fall off if another person came forward to shake it. It was clear that all present were very happy for both couples.

Everyone was now standing around and mixing, discussing the news. The Commander arrived at Steve's side and shook his hand. "Congratulations Steve, a baby completes the family, at least that's what we found." It was clear to Steve that Alfie, although genuine in his congratulations, had another reason for standing next to the DCI. "Have you heard from The Cap? It's after eleven. We should have heard by now."

"Yes, you're right. I'll call him although he won't thank me for it."

The Commander shrugged his shoulders as though to say, "so what?"

The Cap answered on the first ring. "Evening boss, how's the party?"

"The party's fine but the Commander and I are wondering how it's going at Tilbury?"

"I'll tell you in person in exactly five seconds." The Cap hung up as he walked into the room. "Good evening, sirs." He addressed the Commander and Steve. He had a great grin on his face that both senior officers, thought was a good sign. Steve knew The Cap of old so stepped in to avoid a long-winded report.

"Just give us the facts, Cap; did you find the gold?"

The Cap was disappointed at not getting his time in the spotlight but went along with Steve's not too subtle instruction.

"The gold's locked and guarded in two containers on the ship and Joshua Ibinginy, together with two of his countrymen, plus the Captain and First Officer of the MV Moyra, have been charged and are locked up in Dartford nick." The Cap smiled at his audience. "A bit of poetic justice, don't you think? Kent police are keeping them overnight and transferring them to central holding in the morning. I suppose someone will tell the Bank we've got their gold in the morning."

The Commander put his hand on The Cap's shoulder. "No Inspector, my job is to tell the Governor now, well done!" The Commander walked off to make the call.

Still grinning and receiving plaudits and handshakes all round from the assembled guests, The Cap made his way towards the table. "How do I get a drink in this place?"

Alison joined Steve as the Commander returned. "Well husband, we've made a baby, you've almost married off Andy and The Cap has found your gold. Let's go home." She kissed her husband on the cheek.

The Commander smiled. "You're right of course Doctor, but he's still got a double murder to solve. I suppose you'll be in tomorrow?"

"Yes sir, I've told the team, and with your permission sir, I'm going to try to understand this gold heist."

***

While good news was being dispensed at Andy's farewell party and before The Cap arrived to give his news that they'd found the gold, Clarence Strum was having a night in. He'd called an old friend who worked as a civil servant and learnt that the Colonial and English Land project had been given final planning permission at the morning meeting. Not only that, but the new Minister had recommended that the company be awarded a Regional Development grant of some ten million pounds to help with set-up costs. Clarence looked around his plush Wimbledon flat. He thought maybe he'd move up to something grander with his million. After all, a man of his standing and superior intelligence should have a home that matched his intellect.

Clarence was delighted. He had fulfilled his part of the bargain and more. He'd got away with murder. He had known the police would be no match for his superior intellect. He'd killed three times and the police had no clue that it was him. He was feeling good and started to dream of spending his bonus. He tried to visualise what one million pounds looked like. Eventually, he gave up and knew it didn't matter what it looked like. All that mattered was that it was his.

Clarence had been sitting most of the night dreaming and drinking very good brandy. He'd found in the past that a quiet night in somehow cleared his head and allowed him to think more rationally. It turned out tonight was no exception.

His thoughts turned to his future. His father was always on at him to marry well and settle down. The man knew this was good advice but had felt that his father had pushed the point too early on in his life. As he approached another birthday, Clarence thought about marriage and who he might take as a wife.

He had recently been introduced to a very plain and ordinary girl called Suzanne Baird. He smiled to himself as he thought of the stick-thin woman with the schoolgirl hairstyle. He admitted she had been decent company and hadn't tried to dominate the conversation nor tried to stop him drinking. He'd been with friends so hadn't paid much attention to his date. He told himself this might be a good sign and something to look for in a wife.

He had collected her from the family pile in Harlow and been introduced to her father. Even Clarence was impressed by the size and opulence of the family home set behind high stone walls and accessed through a heavy electronic gate.

After the evening, he'd looked her father up on the *Times* Rich List. Mr Baird was said to be worth over 150 million pounds and ran his electronics empire from his home. Clarence had dug deeper and discovered Baird was a widower with one daughter who might realistically inherit her father's fortune when he passed away.

When he'd gathered this information, Miss Baird had suddenly become more attractive, especially as at their only meeting, it had been very obvious Mr Baird would like his daughter to marry a title.

Clarence grappled with the thought. It was true that Suzanne Baird, at five foot nine inches tall and with the upper body of a sixteen-year-old schoolboy, was no beauty and could never excite him sexually. Certainly not like Matilda Armstrong had at Lord Rosyth's. She seemed to wear heavy tights and flat shoes that made her feet look more like flippers than feet. Her dress sense wasn't sexy or exciting, but practical and dull. However, Clarence dreamt of marrying one hundred and fifty million pounds, not Miss Universe. He surmised he could keep a few more exciting women on the side to satisfy his desires. He laughed out loud when he thought he might include Matilda. He also thought that if Mr Baird ever sensed he was only after the money, then Derek Layburn was an example of what might befall him.

As he sat enjoying his brandy, he hatched a plan to court Suzanne Baird. He'd invest some of his one million into impressing not so much her as her father. He'd charter a cruiser and whisk her away for a few weeks' holiday. He'd take her on a shopping trip to New York and fly BA first class. He'd take a box at Epsom racecourse for the whole of the next meeting. Clarence's imagination knew no bounds.

He told himself if he had to splash out a fair slice of his windfall to impress Mr Baird and show him that he had the money to maintain his daughter's living standards, then a few thousand in exchange for one hundred and fifty million wasn't a bad investment. He took his writing pad and made a note to invite Suzanne to dinner one day next week. The brandy had had an effect.

He also made a note to call Roddy Glass of Colonial and English Land. He wanted his money, especially as he was going to get married.

Clarence Strum let his pad slip from his lap as his brandy intake finally got the better of him and he entered an alcohol-induced sleep still sitting in his armchair.

The watchers had been positioned outside his Wimbledon flat ready to follow if Clarence moved. They were bored and had seen no activity. DI Peter Jones had passed by a few times to check if anything was happening. The two watchers had only come on shift an hour ago and were already cold and fed up, but they'd keep watching.

Chapter Twenty-Six

Saturday the 22nd of October started like any other day for DCI Burt except the topic of conversation at breakfast was the upcoming arrival of a little Burt. Alison said she didn't know the sex of the baby and didn't know if she wanted to before it was born.

A light-hearted debate took up most of Steve's coffee and toast before he left at 07.14 a.m. to walk to his office. The weather was fair and promised to be sunny so a brisk walk would do him good. Or at least that's what his wife had told him.

Steve was pleased and surprised to see The Cap and Poppy were already in. Poppy was learning and she pointed to a large cardboard cup of coffee on his desk.

"Right, let's get to it. Come on in and we'll get started."

Just as the three entered Steve's inner office, Twiggy appeared bearing another four cups of coffee. She saw her colleagues already had theirs. "Oh well, I know these won't go to waste the way you lot guzzle this stuff." She joined the meeting.

"Cap, you first. Have you had a chance to write up last night's operation?"

"No, but I'll do it later today."

Steve looked seriously at his friend. He was sometimes annoyed by The Cap's slack attitude to time-sensitive events, but he let it pass. "Don't forget. Now, tell us about last night."

Although The Cap would have preferred to tell his tale in front of last night's larger audience, he pushed on knowing this audience was the one that mattered.

"I saw the Commander, who asked a lot of questions before he agreed to sign the warrant applications. He was very good and phoned both Kent and Essex forces. He used his position and got them both to agree to send search teams into Tilbury docks. He made sure they knew it was a Met operation and I'd be SIO." The Cap's chest swelled just a little.

"When I got there, the uniforms were waiting. Essex had sent a sergeant and five men. Kent sent an inspector and seven men. The head of dock security was also there. He's an ex-copper so didn't object too much. We boarded the first ship, that's the MV *Moyra*. She's registered in Panama. The Captain wasn't happy. He refused to recognise the warrants and threatened to throw us overboard. The Inspector from Kent was a huge guy. He got the Captain and his First Officer to see sense." The Cap drew breath and raised his eyebrows. "Don't ask."

He carried on. "The Captain denied he had any passengers and that his paperwork was in order." The Cap drank his coffee. "You can imagine. It was one of those times when everything I asked him the answer was no. Eventually, the river police arrived, and their sergeant seemed to communicate better with the Captain. Anyway, he became less obstructive but was as nervous as hell. The lads were split into two-man search teams and were briefed to seek out any passengers on board." The Cap laughed. "It was like a Keystone Cops movie. All these officers running around the ship. Anyway, I showed them a picture of Cecil White and they started searching first in the bowels of the ship and then worked their way up. I posted guards on the gangway in case our suspects tried to escape." He drank more coffee.

"I tell you what. It was bloody freezing last night on the bridge of that old tub. Then I got a shout from the Kent Inspector. There were two containers strapped down on the forward deck. He thought this was odd and had asked the Captain to open them up. When I got there the Captain was refusing and showed us his ship's manifest. It said the containers were full of machine parts." The Cap needed more coffee so reached for the fresh supply brought by Twiggy.

"He wouldn't budge on opening them, so we cut the padlocks and guess what...? Each one had boxes on pallets in them and when we opened the first box, it was the gold. We counted two hundred boxes in each container."

"How many boxes did you open?" This was from Twiggy.

"Not many, it was obvious this was the haul. The Bank guys can sort it out. We just found it for them." The Cap smiled at his audience.

"OK, Cap, go on." Steve wanted the whole story.

"The teams searching the ship found three men in what they took to be the Captain's cabin. The senior guy on the search team recognised Cecil White and called me down. I recognised him from his picture, and he was with another two gentlemen who I took to be from Africa. It was all pretty straightforward after that. I asked them to identify themselves, but they refused to say anything. I arrested them, read them their rights and had the local lads take them to Dartford nick. Just for good measure, I also arrested the Captain and his mate. They denied any knowledge, but those containers didn't just turn up. They had to know and be in on it." The Cap sat back.

"That's about it. I arranged for a security detail to guard the gold until the Bank could arrange to retrieve it. We've got eight men on a twenty-four-hour shift pattern guarding the containers that now have new padlocks on them. The head of security at the docks has a key for each and the others are with the Inspector from Kent. Both men will be in the docks this morning if we need to speak to them."

The Cap was enjoying his time in the limelight and the plaudits he was getting from his colleagues. "I went to the nick and saw the prisoners processed. I've arranged for all five to be transferred to central holding awaiting a court appearance and being interviewed. Then with everything tied up, I dashed back to Andy's party to give you the good news."

"Well done, Cap, but make sure your actual report is more complete."

"Yeah Steve, of course."

Twiggy spoke up. "I had a call from my boss at Treasury. He's arranging the pickup of the gold by armoured car this morning." She looked at her watch. "Actually, it's probably already been collected. I told him it was evidence but he's more concerned with security. He did agree to keep it segregated until we have forensics go over it."

Steve finished his second cup of coffee. "Poppy, have Sophia Marr put into an interview room downstairs. I want to understand how this happened. Cap, you're the SIO, so you'd better sit in. Then Poppy, get on to uniform. I want Cap's prisoners from last night brought from central holding to our cells here so we can interrogate them. Got that?"

"Yes sir." Steve noticed Poppy wasn't too bubbly this morning and she looked a bit pale. He knew the reason but didn't comment.

"Good work everybody. Now let's put this thing to bed." The DCI stood up, but Twiggy held up her hand. "Steve, have you got a minute to discuss the double murder?"

Steve almost groaned as he remembered Alfie's words. "I suppose I had better. Change of plan, Cap: you interview Marr and take Poppy in with you. It'll be good experience. I'll come down when I'm finished with Twiggy."

The two friends sat looking at each other, one behind his desk the other holding her oversized shoulder bag on her lap.

With a sigh, Twiggy dug into her bag. "You asked me to do a thorough search on this Clarence Strum."

"Yes, but I didn't mean for you to do it this quickly if that's what you're going to tell me." The DCI considered Twiggy's enthusiasm to The Cap's more laid-back style.

Twiggy smiled. "You know me, Steve, once it's in my head it has to be done... Anyway, I've got what you need." Twiggy flipped through a notebook. "I'll give all this to Poppy to put in the file." The DCI nodded and waited for Twiggy to start.

"The Right Honourable Clarence Strum sits on the boards of seven largish UK companies. I don't think he actually works but seems to lend his name to the businesses, so they look better connected. You know the thing. One of our non-executive directors is a Right Honourable and one day will be a Peer of the Realm. All rubbish but these companies seem to need to do it." Twiggy saw Steve was listening but had a get on with it look. "Sorry, I digress. Anyway, all seven companies appear clean. I couldn't find anything hooky about any of them. They file their accounts on time, pay the taxes and generally are good to their employees."

Steve sat forward. "Come on Twiggy, I know you've got more. Can you speed it up?"

"Sorry, and yes I have more. Of all the companies Strum is a director of, only one has a connection to our victims. Colonial and English Land has been involved with Layburn's department for years over a planning application for a new town called Blackwood. Layburn was dead against it, despite it being supported by all the local councils, but because of its

232

impact, it needed government approval. There was a meeting on Friday, that's yesterday, that was likely to finally squash the project especially with Layburn in the chair. Colonial and English have used up all their options. If Layburn rejected it on Friday that was that; no more appeals, nothing. Millions would have been wasted."

Steve was interested and had forgotten he'd asked Twiggy to hurry up. He was sitting back with his hands steepled in front of his face.

"Colonial and English had invested millions so far and even had a judge recommend the project be given approval but apparently Layburn was refusing. I dug a bit deeper into Strum and found that he and Layburn had worked together for a short time, so they clearly knew each other and were both at Lord Rosyth's get-together." Twiggy raised her eyebrows and stared at Steve awaiting his analysis.

"So, you're suggesting because Strum is on the board of this development company that he was somehow persuaded to bump off the Minister who was blocking this development to get the planning approval they needed?"

"That's about it. It makes sense especially if Strum needed money and they promised him something tasty."

The DCI sat back looking sceptical. "It's a bit of a jump though Twiggy, to assume just because Strum sits on this company's board, and they need planning permission from someone Strum knows…" The DCI went into one of his deep trances as he found something in what he was saying. Twiggy knew the signs and waited. Steve was back in less than a minute.

"Unless… Twiggy! I think you've just given us motive. With all the circumstantial evidence we have against Strum, this theory of yours might just clinch it." Steve suddenly looked worried. "But we have this woman who is alibiing him. I've still to interview her but unless she admits she can't confirm he was with her all night we've got a problem."

"Well. That's why I'm in finance now. I'll leave all the brain work to you full-time detectives."

Both friends laughed and this broke the tension that neither had felt creep up on them. Steve knew he was close to cracking the case and Twiggy had just helped. He told himself Strum was under surveillance so wasn't going anywhere and could wait. Steve had to clear his brain of the bullion job. He needed to interview Sophia Marr. Something still didn't feel right but he couldn't quite see what was bothering him.

As Twiggy was leaving to meet Alison, for an appointment that would help her carry on with her slimming regime, she stopped in the doorway. "Oh, Steve, I almost forgot. It seems Walter Bostrom is still in an induced coma. I saw his mother this morning. The poor woman is in a terrible state but get this… Paula White, Walter's fiancée and daughter of our gold heist mastermind, is staying with Mrs Bostrom at her place. Seems she's been almost constantly at the hospital with Mrs Bostrom."

"Christ! I'd forgotten about her. It sounds like she's not involved but we'd better interview her." Steve adopted a pleading pose. "I don't suppose when you're home you might just meet this Paula White and get the inside information? Just to say we've ruled her out." Still pleading Steve added, "You know you're very good at this kind of thing."

Before Twiggy could answer, Steve was making notes. "Thanks, Twiggy."

They both smiled. Twiggy knew she'd been conned but didn't mind. She knew her old boss was busy and under-resourced.

Steve went down to the interview room holding Sophia Marr. He wasn't happy. This bullion job was preying on his mind. He sensed something still wasn't right and he had been a bit sloppy on the double murder case. He told himself he'd get to the bottom of things now and then concentrate 100% on the murders.

***

While Steve and Twiggy were discussing Twiggy's theory on the murders, the technicians in the ballistics labs were examining the gun found by Lord Rosyth and his dogs. The senior lab technician — a man called Rodney Blunt — had promised the DCI he'd work Saturday morning and process the weapon, including having the fingerprint technicians dust it for prints.

Rodney had worked most of his life in this laboratory. He'd joined the forensic service after spending six years in the Army and had immediately found himself specialising in weapons. He was due to retire and thought this might be his last case.

234

He had already examined the spent bullets the lovely Detective Sergeant from Essex had delivered to him and now only needed to see if those bullets came from this gun. He loaded a round into the weapon and with his ear protectors in place and all other health and safety measures complied with, he fired a round into a long, reinforced tube. At the end of the tube, a wad of foam-like material caught the round. Rodney could now compare any marks on this round with the rounds he already had. Each gun left its own unique markings on the bullets it fired. Even the mark left by the firing pin told its own story.

It was a slow process that required years of experience, but the advent of computer-driven electron microscopes speeded up the process and made the technician's life easier. The senior technician immediately saw that the striations on all rounds were the same. He compared the firing pin marks and again got a match. Without hesitation, he confirmed that it was this revolver that fired the rounds that killed Sir Derek and Lady Layburn.

Rodney was a quiet and thoughtful man, but he had one quality that suited him to his profession. He was thorough. Most technicians would have written up their report, but Rodney went a step further. As requested by Jenny, he called up images of all spent rounds recovered from shooting incidents in the past six months where the weapon used had not been identified. He began comparison examinations with the rounds from this weapon and after only a few minutes, found a round that matched. It had been recovered from a murder victim found in a London alley only a few days ago. The victim was a London taxi driver called John Bradford.

Rodney continued his search but found no other matches. He sat down and wrote up his report linking the weapon not only to the double murder but also to the London alley killing. He appended the report from the fingerprint tech that stated the only print was a partial. Lord Rosyth's prints were found on the gun as expected as he had found the weapon.

Rodney Blunt finished his report and as already directed, e-mailed it to Poppy.

***

Steve knocked on the door of interview room three and entered. He saw Sophia Marr sitting beside her youthful solicitor; The Cap and Poppy were seated opposite while a uniformed WPC stood to one side of the door.

Steve signalled for The Cap to stop the interview and step outside. Poppy remained.

"Any joy?"

"Not really. We keep going over the same ground but at least she's talking. It's a change from 'no comment'."

"How much have you told her?"

"Everything. We've recovered the gold. Her brother and his henchmen are in custody and that she'll be charged as an accessory."

"Hm." Steve paced a circle. "And she's still not talking?"

"No. Nothing that helps."

"Something's not right, Cap. Most people in her position, knowing we've got her bang to rights would cough. They'd want to try and get a lighter sentence. So why isn't she?" Steve continued to pace and talk. "This whole thing's been a game of bluff and double bluff. If she's not admitting to anything then we've missed something."

The Cap remained silent. He knew the DCI was a master at working things through and asking the right questions during an interrogation.

"Let's go back in. I'll have a crack at her. Poppy can go back to the office. She's still looking a bit green around the edges. I don't think the drinks last night did her much good."

The pair re-entered, Poppy left, and the dual tapes were updated.

Steve, as he always did, started by being friendly. "Did you get a decent breakfast this morning, Sophia?"

"Yes. It was all right."

"Tea or coffee? I prefer coffee but I know a lot of people like a nice cup of tea. I only ask because police tea isn't usually the best."

"It was fine." Sophia stared at the DCI. "Look, I know you can't keep me here indefinitely so either charge me or let me go." She looked defiant and turned to grin at her solicitor.

Steve decided to change tack and tell a few half-truths. "Oh, we'll be charging you. The only thing is we're not sure what with. You see if

Walter Bostrom dies it'll be murder. If he lives it'll be attempted murder. Then again if—"

"Hold on." Sophia Marr had lost some of her composure. "Murder! No, no, I'd nothing to do with that."

The Cap who was taking notes smiled to himself. The DCI certainly had a skill.

"You've already admitted some involvement, but unless we know exactly what your part was, we've no alternative but to think the worst and charge you accordingly." Steve paused to let his words sink in. "Then there's the kidnapping. The courts take a very dim view of holding anyone against their will, especially children. The money laundering will get you another bunch of years. All in all, if you can't or won't explain your involvement, we'll have no choice but to throw the book at you."

Steve could see this woman was devious. He could almost hear her brain working out what to tell him. He didn't want her to have time to think so he carried on with a few more half-truths designed to upset her and get her talking.

"You know we've arrested your brother and his pals. They are next door now singing like birds, probably asking for diplomatic immunity and laying the whole thing on you. We've got you down as the brains behind the heist. It makes sense. After all, you worked at the Bank." Again, Steve paused. "Any way you look at it, Sophia, you are in it up to your neck, unless you explain to us how this all came about and who did what."

The DCI saw for the first time he'd hit a nerve. Sophia Marr was on the point of talking.

"Let's hear it, Sophia, from the beginning."

"Will you talk to the court? Tell them I helped you and I'd nothing to do with any murder?"

"We can't do deals Sophia, but the court will know you cooperated."

She looked at her solicitor who nodded.

"OK, I'll tell you."

Steve saw something in her eyes that suggested she was cunning and still working her answers out. He'd listen to her but wasn't sure they would get the whole truth. He sat back to listen.

"I told you Joshua is my older half-brother. Our father was a politician and when colonial rule was ending all over Africa, he basically grabbed a chunk of land and called it Cambow. He set up a government from nothing, and at that time because the land he grabbed was poor and the people living within its borders were badly educated, he wasn't challenged. I think he latched onto richer nations' foreign-aid money and that's what he lived on.

"He came to the UK with Joshua after his first wife died and settled in Glasgow. He met my mother who was a nurse, and I was born but he didn't like the weather, so he returned to Africa, effectively abandoning me and my mother when I was less than two years old. My mother left Glasgow and settled in London. She was originally from Canterbury in Kent." Sophia was telling a sensible tale efficiently but took a handkerchief from her pocket and dabbed her eyes.

"I didn't see Joshua again, but he told me he changed his name to Cecil White and that his father helped set him up in business. I don't know the details except Joshua said his father cheated him, so he went back to Cambow and with the help of a few soldiers got rid of his father and installed himself as ruler. I think Joshua senior... my father, is dead." Again, a dab of her eyes.

"Joshua has always been a crook. He's been stealing money from the country for years. He contacted me out of the blue a few months ago. Said he heard I worked in the bullion section of the Bank and said I could do him and myself a big favour. We met a few times and the more he talked, the easier and more exciting it sounded for us to become mega-rich overnight. I'm not naturally a crooked person. I've not even had a parking ticket, but Joshua made the whole thing sound so simple—"

Steve reluctantly interrupted. "Tell me what Joshua said."

"He had a friend who could get a piece of software that I could insert into our dispatch control system. This would create chaos to our deliveries of gold and that would allow him to form a plan to steal some gold."

Again, Steve interrupted. "So, in the beginning, you planted the spyware, but didn't have a plan to steal the gold?"

"Yes, Joshua said the Bank wouldn't stop shipping gold. They'd just find another way of arranging it. When the twelve-digit system was introduced, and I told Joshua, he said he could put pressure on both Michael and Walter to get their codes. Michael explained how the Army was involved and how the code was to be verified. It became obvious that if we had the code, I could use my access to call the convoy commander and direct the shipment to Tilbury. It was easy."

"What was to happen at Tilbury?"

Sophia Marr suddenly became defensive. "I don't know, you'll have to ask Joshua."

The DCI was quiet for a while. No one spoke. "Why did you pay so much money to the air charter company just to throw us off the scent?"

Immediately Steve saw this question had startled Sophia. She wasn't as good an actress as she thought. "I don't know anything about that."

Steve pressed on. "How was the gold to be fenced?"

"I have a few contacts, people the Bank deal with legitimately, but who might be prepared to take more gold than they appear to be buying."

"Is the deal to sell the gold set up?"

Again, a look of fear crossed Sophia's face. "No."

"You're lying Sophia." Steve felt on fairly solid ground. He'd been reading her body language. "If you don't tell us the truth we can't speak to the judge."

Sophia Marr stared down at the table. "No comment."

Steve looked at The Cap and shook his head. He twisted in his chair and spoke to the WPC. "Take her back to her cell. We'll arrange to formally process and charge her then get her over to central holding. She'll be remanded on Monday morning."

Steve and The Cap stood. The DCI nodded an acknowledgement to the duty solicitor while The Cap removed the tapes and handed one to the solicitor. Interview room three emptied very quickly.

Steve was very quiet as he and The Cap climbed the stairs back to the offices of Special Resolutions. With the DCI in thought mode, The Cap kept his opinions to himself. As they turned to climb from the first to the second floor, Steve's phone vibrated. It was the Commander.

It wasn't good news. Firstly, Joshua Ibinginy was screaming for diplomatic immunity but more importantly, the gold was still missing. All hell had broken out and the Commissioner, together with the Prime Minister, wanted heads on blocks.

Steve told The Cap who just stared in shock. Luckily, the DCI had worked it out. Their careers and reputations were safe.

Chapter Twenty-Seven

When Steve and The Cap walked into the office, the Commander was waiting. He was dressed in his civilian clothes but not the new suit he had worn to Andy's farewell. It was obvious he had a lot to say.

"I've got the Commissioner, who in turn has the Prime Minister on her back, plus I've just had a minion from the Home Office saying your prisoner is screaming diplomatic immunity. The Governor of the Bank wants a meeting on Monday and an explanation. I hope you've got…" Steve held up his hand before the senior officer could say any more.

"Please sir, just a minute." Steve turned to Poppy. "Get onto Kent constabulary right now and speak to the most senior officer you can. Tell them you're acting on instructions from Commander Brooks of Scotland Yard."

At this Alfie almost choked, but Steve continued. "Tell them we need armed response at Manston Airport immediately. They need to occupy the offices of Direct Air Charter and under no circumstances are they to allow any aircraft to take off, or anybody to enter either the offices or hangar. Tell them to deploy the nearest units, probably Margate. Have you got that, Poppy?"

Poppy looked more like her old self. Her hangover was gone, and she found this new urgency exciting. "Right, sir."

The DCI ushered the Commander into his office and signalled for The Cap to join them.

"I'm sorry sir but this is urgent. Everything fell into place a few minutes ago."

"It had better be bloody good, DCI Burt; I don't appreciate being taken for a mug." Alfie was red in the face with anger.

"Understood sir, but can I explain?" Steve knew he'd once again overstepped the mark with Alfie but this time he felt it was justified.

"Sophia Marr admitted only so much. When I pressed her on how the gold was going to be sold and why they paid so much to the air charter company she became very defensive. She's admitted so much and knows she'll do time, but she's still in it with her brother." Steve saw the Commander was listening as was The Cap.

"The so-called gold The Cap found in Tilbury was another decoy. I bet it was lead ingots sprayed with gold paint. It worried me from the start, why they would have paid the charter company so much money just to lead us up a blind alley. The buggers have been very clever. Once we'd searched Manston and the gold didn't turn up there, why would we go back and look again, especially if we think the gold is on the high seas? By the time we'd stopped the ship at sea and discovered the bullion wasn't bullion, Cecil White or Joshua would be home free. It's another bluff.

They paid the air company all that money to keep them on standby. They loaded the lead onto that ship but trucked the real gold to Manston." The DCI heard Poppy finish her call to Kent police, so he shouted to her. "Poppy, get onto Euro Control and ask if another flight plan has been lodged from Manston."

The Commander was obviously thinking so Steve continued. "I don't think this Cecil or Joshua expected us to be at Tilbury so quickly. He was supposed to be on his way to Kent and the ship in open waters before we worked it out. I don't know what he was doing on the ship but no doubt we'll find out. I think he'd planned to fly out with the gold just as we thought before, only he planned it for two days later."

The Commander was about to say something when Poppy interrupted. "There's a flight plan to Ankara in Turkey on file. It was submitted yesterday for a late departure, but it didn't take off and has been cancelled."

"Thanks, Poppy."

The Commander tried again. "So, all this bluff and double bluff has only been about getting the gold out before we could find it?"

"If you're right, then they have been very devious and clever. I don't think in all my years in the Force I've heard of anything like it. Plus, we've got the ruler of another country operating here openly selling cars." Alfie sat down and laughed. "It's un-bloody-believable. Where do crooks of today get their ideas?" He paused but no one answered. "I'm getting too old for this. If I hadn't promised…"

Poppy arrived and looked at the Commander. "Sorry sir, it's urgent. There's a Chief Superintendent from Kent Force on line one asking for you personally."

The Commander sprang to his feet and lifted the phone. He was standing to one side of Steve's desk. The assembled audience in Steve's office only heard one side of the conversation.

"And you're sure?"

"How many?"

"Good."

"Paul, thank you. I know a lot of senior officers wouldn't have acted as quickly as you did. I'll make sure your Chief Constable is made aware."

"Yes. We'll arrange that, but can you have armed officers there round the clock until they get organised?"

"Right. I'll get everybody's details to you and pass on yours."

"Yes, and thanks again." The Commander hung up.

Alfie surveyed the expectant faces. "Kent are at Manston. They've arrested another two men who were with the gold and yes, it's the proper gold this time. They'll put an armed guard on it until the Bank arranges to collect it."

The Commander looked directly at Poppy. "DC Cooper, can you please send by secure routing, details of all officers who have been involved in this case, to Kent Constabulary administration for the attention of Chief Superintendent Jack? Also include contact details for the Bank of England people."

Poppy looked pleased to be helping. "Right away, sir."

Alfie rubbed his hands. "Right DCI Burt, I'll forget your latest insubordination, but only because it looks like you've had a result. I'd better go and inform the Commissioner who in turn will no doubt inform the Prime Minister. I'll leave her to worry about the Home Office. As far as you're concerned, you plough on and charge whoever needs charging. If this Joshua Ibinginy is responsible for putting that boy in a coma, then throw the bloody book at him. Diplomatic immunity or no diplomatic immunity. Got that?"

243

Alfie didn't wait for a response but carried on. "When I've done what needs to be done, I'll come back here so make sure no one leaves." The Commander left.

Steve and The Cap collapsed into two chairs. They could hear Poppy on the phone carrying out the Commander's orders.

After a few minutes of heavy breathing and a lot of sighing, Steve went to work.

"Right Cap, you'd better go and interview Cecil White or Joshua Ibinginy. We've got his sister's confession implicating him, so I think you only want a statement. Same for the other two you found him with. I suppose we'll have to let the Captain and First Officer of the ship go. We can't charge them with transporting lead without a licence, can we?"

"No, I suppose not." The Cap looked crestfallen. "Steve I just want to say…"

"No need Abul, we work as a team. Now go and see what our crook with two names has to say and remember to come back here when you're done."

The DCI walked to the canteen and sat by himself drinking a coffee. He realised how much the gold robbery enquiry had taken out of him. He decided to take his wife off for an overnight stay in Rye, West Sussex and get away from it all for one night. He had met Alison in Rye, so it held fond memories for both of them. As he remembered the Bull Hotel, he determined to book it as soon as Alfie Brooks gave the all-clear.

Steve returned to his office to find Poppy sitting back staring into space. He gave her the coffee he'd brought and as he put it down, she turned round startled, almost spilling her drink.

"I'm glad you're back sir. I've got something you should see."

In Steve's inner office, Poppy explained about the bullets coming from the gun found by Lord Rosyth and the link to the murder of John Bradford, the London taxi driver.

"I've got the file on Bradford. It seems the murder squad are stumped. But I've got something else." She opened a notebook similar to Twiggy's that Steve had never seen Poppy use before.

"I read in the forensic report from Cirencester that the technician had found traces of gun oil in a drawer in Clarence Strum's room. He'd attached the chemical analysis so I asked our techs here if they could say if this gun used the same oil."

Steve was impressed by Poppy's initiative. "And?"

"Well, they can't say for sure the oil in the drawer came from the gun, but they have confirmed it's the same brand of oil." Poppy looked a little crestfallen. "I'm sorry sir, I'd hoped it might say the gun was in the drawer."

"No Poppy, this is fine police work. You've given us another piece of circumstantial evidence. Every bit we get takes us closer to a conviction." Steve drank his coffee. "Are you up to date with everything else?"

"Yes. I've just finished updating the file with The Cap's report."

Steve thought for a few seconds. "Poppy... in The Cap's report, I want you to change a bit. I want you to put in that when he saw the gold in the containers on the ship in Tilbury, he wanted the Bank to check the purity. Say he was suspicious of the colour. Can you do that?"

"Yes of course but is it not against the rules?"

"Only technically." Steve winked. "And only if we're found out. The report hasn't gone off to the CPS or the DPP yet so it can still technically be amended. It'll look better for The Cap if he's seen not to be fully taken in by the fake gold."

Poppy wasn't totally convinced but if her boss told her to do it then she would. She left to update the report.

The Commander appeared, having been away for about an hour. Steve looked at his watch. If his plan for a night away was to work, then he needed to get home soon. It was 11.06 a.m.

"I've spoken with the Commissioner, explained everything and she's broadly happy. She made me wait until she'd briefed the Prime Minister and The Governor. I think she laid it on thickly enough to make sure you and The Cap aren't being held responsible. I told her about the bluff and double bluff and how difficult the case was. I may have overdone it though. I think she wants to give The Cap a commendation that I know isn't really deserved." Alfie looked at Steve with an apologetic expression. "I know you figured it out, but he was SIO. I exaggerated a bit and said DI Ishmal was suspicious of the gold on the boat and had asked for a purity test before the Bank realised it was lead."

A loud sound came from the outer office. Poppy had been listening and couldn't contain herself. Now she knew the DCI and the Commander both knew how to work the system.

The Commander carried on. "I think we're done, Steve. I'll pass it on to robbery. Have your girl send over the files. Where's the DI?"

"He's finishing off with our politician…" Just as Steve said this The Cap appeared carrying three cups of coffee. "He… ah … was taking a statement."

The coffee was distributed and as Poppy had already had enough coffee, Alfie drank her cup.

"He's a slippery one that Cecil White. I've charged him in both names with robbery, conspiracy and GBH to be getting on with. His sister's statement should be enough to get a conviction, but he says he has diplomatic immunity and has been set up by his sister. He's on his way to central holding and should be remanded Monday morning. His two sidekicks say they've done nothing except obey orders. I've charged them with aiding and abetting for now."

"Good work DI Ishmal." The Commander was happy.

The Cap smiled with pride. It wasn't often these days he was congratulated about anything.

The three discussed the case again as they finished their coffee.

Alfie sat back in his chair. "Oh well, I suppose all's well that ends well. Everything is to be sent to Robbery for them to finish up Monday morning. Make sure they get the files. I suppose the Commissioner will delegate someone from International to deal with the Home Office and the deportation issue." Alfie laughed. "Rather them than me. From what you've said it's a real can of worms."

"No doubt Rupert Naismith, the Deputy Governor of The Bank, will arrange to collect his gold?" The Commander looked at the DCI.

"I suppose so." Alfie had a sudden moment of panic. "It's still under armed guard in Manston isn't it because I don't suppose it will be collected till Monday."

"Yes sir, everything's under control. I'm just glad this case is over. It's been brutal." Steve looked tired.

"Yes, it has but it's over now. I'll deal with the legal stuff but you both might have to meet with the DPP and the CPS before the trials."

Everyone looked satisfied.

"I'm off to the football this afternoon. I might even allow myself a few pints after the match. Well, done, you two, but Steve, the Commissioner is still on record saying an arrest will be made within seventy-two hours and that clock started ticking yesterday."

"Bloody woman! She was told not to put that in!"

"Well, she did and was always going to. Get everyone out of here and turn up fresh on Monday." With a wave, Alfie Brooks was gone.

Poppy needed The Cap's report to complete the file before sending it over to Robbery. They decided to stay and get it done.

***

The DCI left them to it, thanked them again with a 'well done' and set off for home.

His offer of a night in Rye was well-received by his wife, and after a quick lunch, the pair set off. The weather wasn't bad, but the forecast was for rain. Alison saw her husband was somehow elated but tired. As Steve headed the car in the direction of the coast, she asked, "Is everything all right?"

Steve took a few seconds longer than normal to answer. He looked over at his wife. "Yes darling, everything's just perfect."

They drove on in silence, but Alison could tell Steve's mind was elsewhere. "Are you thinking about a case?"

"You know I'm always thinking about a case, but no. We've just finished the gold bullion robbery case. You remember it was Twiggy's neighbour who brought it to us. Her son's still in an induced coma and according to Twiggy his mother is in a real state."

"I saw Flo. She's doing really well with her diet regime. I've referred her to a sports trainer. She doesn't need to do much but the last ten pounds or so are the most difficult to shift."

Alison was looking slyly at her husband. "Darling, I don't suppose you know anything about a man in Flo's life?"

Steve looked straight ahead at the road. "Why do you ask?"

"Oh, only curious. She mentioned the name Terry, I only wondered if you knew him."

Steve laughed and shook his head. "You women, you're so nosey."

Alison tapped him lightly on the shoulder. "Yes, we are, but I'm only looking out for her."

The DCI sighed. "OK. He's the Head of our Technical Support Unit. He's a really nice guy and you met him at Andy's party."

"That's who he is!" Alison slipped further down in her seat making herself more comfortable. "I wasn't sure because I didn't get a lot of time to speak to them both at the same time." She closed her eyes and was sleeping within minutes.

Steve slowed down and tried to avoid the inevitable potholes on the back roads leading to Rye.

He gently woke his wife up at exactly 4.12 p.m. "We're here darling, rise and shine."

***

As the DCI and his wife were driving to Rye, the watchers were sitting outside the apartment block in which Clarence Strum lived. They had nothing to report but had religiously checked in with DI Peter Jones every hour.

The only activity was when the target had exited the front door of the apartment block and started walking away from the watchers. One of them scrambled out of the car to follow on foot whilst the other drove the car at a snail's pace following. It turned out that Clarence was only going as far as the local off-licence to buy a bottle of something, then to the newsagents for a paper and then he walked home again.

This small meaningless bit of excitement was nonetheless logged at 2.55 p.m. and reported to the DI on the hour. The pair settled down once more to continue with their boring brief.

***

After checking in and relaxing for a few hours, Steve and Alison took a long slow walk by the river before enjoying a very good dinner in the hotel's restaurant. Despite her condition, Alison allowed herself a glass and a half of a rather pleasant house red leaving Steve to finish the bottle.

248

They had coffee in the bar and were sound asleep in their comfortable bed before ten-fifteen p.m.

***

The watchers had just changed shift when they spotted a taxi arrive outside Clarence Strum's Wimbledon apartment. They observed the man himself exit the building and climb into the taxi.

The police car followed as the taxi headed for the West End. They saw their target get out of the taxi and go into an upmarket members-only club just off Brompton Road.

They called DI Peter Jones for instructions. The DI despatched another team and told the team on-site to make sure they always had sight of the front door ordering one of them to de-bus and take up a position on foot.

It was 10.27 p.m. when the second set of watchers arrived. There was little they could do. It was a private members-only club and they weren't members. They could show their warrant cards and force an entry, but the target would be spooked. They discussed how to proceed amongst themselves and concluded it was best to sit and wait, although the officer standing in a doorway opposite the club didn't entirely agree with this decision.

The Right Honourable was observed leaving the club at 01.36 a.m. on Sunday morning the 23rd of October. He reversed his journey and arrived at his flat at exactly 02.07 a.m.

The second team stood down, the first team logged the target's movements and reported in to DI Jones's answering service at the Yard on the hour.

They had both grabbed a coffee and a sandwich whilst observing the club so felt better. They relaxed and thought of the overtime and what a complete waste of time this surveillance job was.

***

After a good night's sleep, Mr and Mrs Burt went down to breakfast. Last night they'd discussed their first dinner together in this very restaurant and grabbed their original table for breakfast. Although it wasn't dinner just sitting there made them both feel happy and contented. As usual, the breakfast was delicious, and they discussed what they should do. Looking out the window, they saw it was raining, and the trees appeared to be leaning at a funny angle, being bent over by the strong wind.

"Doesn't look like a day to walk anywhere." Steve was worried his wife might suggest just that.

"No. Let's go down to the nursing home where I used to volunteer. See if any of the old staff are still there. We haven't been back for ages."

After checking out and packing the car they set off to visit old haunts. The View Nursing Home was still there but few of their previous acquaintances were. Steve had met Alison at the home when he was working on a particularly difficult case and an old soldier who was a resident at the home had helped Steve with his current case. Alison had been volunteering as a doctor at the home and having been introduced to her he met her again by chance that evening in the Bull's restaurant.

They decided to drive back to London but to stop at a nice pub on the way for lunch. Steve felt relaxed. He knew the gold bullion case was behind him and he could concentrate on what was now a triple murder. He had already formed a plan for Monday morning and hoped the case might be over within twenty-four hours.

They arrived home at just before nine p.m., watched television for half an hour and after a snack for supper, they had another early night. The DCI was grateful for all the extra sleep he'd had and suspected his wife had arranged their schedule to achieve this.

Chapter Twenty-Eight

Monday the 24th of October — just five days since the killing of Sir Derek and Lady Layburn — started wet and windy. Steve decided to drive to his office and avoid getting drenched although he told himself he'd miss the exercise.

He walked into his office at 08.11 a.m. Both Poppy and The Cap were behind their desks. The Cap handed Steve a coffee as he passed on his way into his inner office. Steve noticed Poppy's hair. "Get caught in the rain?"

"How can you tell, sir? My bus was late, and I stood in a great puddle at the bus stop." She shook her head to dislodge some of her curls. "I'll soon dry out. What do you want to do this morning, sir? I've sent everything off and our murder files are up to date."

The Cap looked up from his notebook. "And if anyone's interested, my feet are wet through, and I need a holiday."

Steve remembered The Cap's ability to lighten the mood when any form of depression crept in.

"OK. First things first. You two go off to the canteen via the restrooms, sort out your wet hair and feet. I'll see you in the canteen in ten minutes. It's warmer than in here and we can get things started." Steve started to walk towards his office when over his shoulder he asked Poppy if she'd heard from Jenny Fuller.

"No sir, not so far."

The Cap and Poppy gratefully left to dry off.

With all three police officers seated in the warmth of the canteen and enjoying yet another coffee, Steve started what he hoped would be a meaningful discussion of the now triple murder case.

Just as he was about to start DI Peter Jones arrived holding a cup of coffee in his hand.

"I went to the office and when you weren't there, I guessed you'd be here." He pulled up a chair and sat down.

As he did so, The Cap spoke up. "I suppose you've come to tell us the watchers have cracked the case?"

"Well no. I just left the surveillance reports on Poppy's desk so she can update the file. I'm afraid it's all been fairly quiet. The lads are beginning to grumble."

Steve took charge. "I understand that, but I want him watched until we pull him in. Are you still using the two who got themselves kidnapped at Esher?"

"Yes, we're a bit short on manpower for this watching brief."

"Well tell them from me that they are lucky I didn't put them up for a disciplinary. They'd better not slip up again."

"I think they know that, sir, but don't worry. I've pulled a strip off them already. They won't screw up again."

Satisfied he'd made his point, Steve moved on.

"We now think Clarence Strum has committed three murders. The Minister and his wife plus a taxi driver. We'll discount the taxi driver until we understand what happened to make him kill the Layburn's." Steve sipped his coffee and started counting off on his fingers as he spoke.

"One, Twiggy has come up with a possible motive. Our suspect is involved with a company called Colonial and English Land." Steve smiled at his audience. "It's a bit of a mouthful so we'll call it CEL. Twiggy found out they've been arguing with our deceased Minister for years over a planning application to build a new town up north. They had been to the courts, but it looked like Derek Layburn was against it and it was feared that, at the meeting planned for last Friday the 21st of October, he'd kill the project. CEL would have run out of options to challenge the government's decision and stood to be out of pocket to the tune of millions." Steve looked around and paused in case anyone had a question. They didn't so he ploughed on.

"Twiggy discovered that Layburn and our suspect knew each other, and our working hypothesis is that Strum was somehow instructed by CEL to get the planning approved at all costs. I know it's a stretch but as a theory, it fits the facts." The DCI took another sip of coffee and was about to continue when Poppy spoke up.

"Surely a person like Clarence Strum wouldn't suddenly become a cold-blooded killer over a planning application?"

"I know it's difficult to take in and I could be wrong but at the moment that's our motive, unless anyone has a better one."

Everybody around the table looked blank.

"So, if we go with that as our motive just now, we come to the circumstantial evidence." Steve again reverted to his fingers to count off.

"Two, the handkerchief with the polish on it. We think it was Clarence who put the ladder outside the Layburn's window, possibly late afternoon, to make it look like an intruder had shot them. We think he must have entered their room sometime in the early evening while they were downstairs and removed the key from the lock and checked the window catch. Remember there were no prints on the key. Likely, he couldn't take the chance that the bedroom door would be locked from the inside.

We believe he entered the Layburn's room in the early hours, shot them, opened the window using his handkerchief and replaced the key on the inside of the door. He didn't know about the trace transfer of the metal polish. Dougal Munroe over in Cirencester tested the trace on the handkerchief and it's a match for the polish used on the window." Steve again paused and sipped his coffee.

"So, there's no doubt the hanky belonging to the Right Honourable was in contact with the window catch and the handles, meaning we can place him in the Layburn's bedroom?" The Cap was on the ball.

"Yes Cap, although any defence would argue he could have been in the room on a previous visit."

"But not used his handkerchief to open the window."

"It's a stretch but defence lawyers do make those connections no matter how unlikely."

No one else seemed to have a question. The DCI continued.

Holding up his fingers again. "Three, the feather. We know the killer used a cushion to deaden the sound of the shots. The cushion was filled with duck feathers. There were feathers all over the crime scene from the holes the bullets made in the cushion. We found a feather in the U-bend of the shower in Clarence Strum's bedroom. Dougal says it was a small fragment but that it definitely came from the cushion used in the killings."

"Excuse me, sir." Poppy was obviously enjoying this briefing and was keen to contribute. "How could the feather get into the shower?"

"Good point Poppy. Obviously, Clarence had it on him and didn't realise it."

Poppy came back at Steve. "But sir unless he was naked and took a shower immediately after the killings then the feather couldn't have got into the shower. It would have stuck to his clothes."

Steve pondered this for a few seconds. As he was thinking The Cap chirped up.

"I suppose he could have been naked thinking he was less likely to leave any trace evidence behind."

Steve listened and reached a conclusion. Slowly he looked around the table. "So, we're now thinking that our suspect carried out the shootings in the nude, returned to his room and showered, in the belief that he'd left nothing behind, that forensics could pick up on. But the feather fragment somehow stuck to his body and was washed off in the shower."

The Cap and Poppy both nodded. Peter Jones, who had been listening, looked at Steve. "It sounds logical sir."

The DCI sat up. "Yes, it does Peter. Well, done, Poppy. We go with this theory for now to explain the feather. OK?"

Again, everyone agreed.

Steve then held up his third finger. "Three, Dougal found gun oil in a drawer in the Right Honourable gent's chest of drawers in his bedroom. It was fresh. The oil used on the gun Lord Rosyth found was a match. At least it's the same brand but again it doesn't conclusively mean the oil in the drawer came from the gun. The gun has been tested and it's definitely the murder weapon."

"I presume the gun's clean. No prints?" The Cap realised everything they had was circumstantial. He knew they needed hard evidence.

"I got a note when I came in." Poppy was looking embarrassed. "But with my wet hair and feet, I haven't updated the file. Forensics got a partial from the gun on Saturday. You'd gone sir so I asked them to check it against Clarence Strum's prints. It's a thumbprint. Unfortunately, they only got a 60% match and that's not enough for the court."

"No, but it's another piece of circumstantial." Steve considered how to proceed. "Now, we've got a motive, four good pieces of circumstantial evidence which is probably enough to pull him in. But... we have a problem in the shape of a Miss Matilda Armstrong. Our suspect says she was with him all night and neither of them left the bedroom. Dougal says he found enough fresh DNA to categorically state she was in the bed in the room at the time Strum says. Unless we can break this alibi, we'll have problems with the CPS."

"Have we interviewed her yet?"

"No Cap, we'll take a trip to Greenwich shortly and interview the lady, so here's hoping. Meantime, Peter," Steve turned to the Welsh Detective Inspector, "keep your watchers on their toes. This guy has money and if he suspects we're on to him he might leg it."

"Understood sir."

"Right. Let's get to it, now we're all dry and warm again."

***

While the DCI was holding his meeting in the canteen in Scotland Yard, the watchers observed a taxi pull up outside Clarence Strum's apartment and saw the target get in. This was logged at 09.05 a.m. on Monday the 24th of October. As before, they followed and despite heavy Monday morning traffic, they easily kept the cab in sight.

It stopped outside a grand glass-fronted building in Central London. As the watchers pulled up behind but some way from the taxi, they saw their target get out and hurry through the revolving doors into the building. One watcher got out of the car and followed Clarence into the building while the other set off to find a parking spot.

The name emblazoned on the building in large letters said COLONIAL AND ENGLISH LAND INC.

The watcher held back as he saw his target approach a circular reception desk, sign something and walk through an airport-style security screen gaining access to the other side of a glass barrier. The policeman noted a few settees obviously for the use of waiting visitors had been set out on his side of the glass. Without trying to look too conspicuous he sat down and called his colleague. They decided one would keep watch from inside the building while the other stayed with the car. If the target hadn't reappeared after an hour, they would swap over in order not to attract the attention of anyone inside the building. This was logged at 09.42 a.m. and called in with the ten a.m. report.

Clarence had phoned ahead and arranged to meet Roddy Glass, the CEO of Colonial and English Land and the person who'd promised him the one-million-pound bonus. Clarence felt good as he entered the lift that would take him to the top floor. He daydreamed about walking out of the building with a briefcase full of money. He'd even brought his own briefcase that he carried to meetings for show, although it was always empty except for the odd A4 pad and a few pens. He told himself today his briefcase would be more than a prop.

He suddenly realised Rodney might prefer to pay him his one million by banker's draft or transfer. He knew he had his bank cards with him so even this wouldn't delay him getting his hands on his money.

A super confident non-executive Director of Colonial and English Land stepped out of the lift that opened onto the executive floor of the Company. A small reception area housing a secretary sitting behind a large desk greeted him and he was directed to the CEO's office.

Rodney Glass' office took up the entire west corner of the floor. It was surrounded on two sides by floor-to-ceiling glass while the other two sides were made up of the outside walls of the building. Within each wall were large windows giving a spectacular view over the rooftops of London. Roddy was sitting at his desk and immediately rose when he saw Clarence enter his office.

"Clarence my boy, how good to see you. Come, let's sit in comfort. Has anyone offered you anything to drink?" Rodney ushered his guest towards two large comfortable sofas that faced each other with a smart glass-topped coffee table between them. They were positioned at ninety degrees to one of the windows giving a spectacular view over London.

"No, but a cup of tea would be nice."

The CEO called the order for tea through to his secretary and both men settled opposite each other on the sofas.

"I presume you've heard the good news. We got our planning. Everyone here is totally delighted. We can't wait to get started. The official document was couriered here this morning first thing."

Clarence smiled and expanded his chest. "Yes, I heard, I'm only glad I was able to help."

"Well Clarence, let's not get carried away. Whoever bumped off Sir Derek Layburn did us a favour. If he'd still been around, I don't think we'd be celebrating."

"Yes, well Rodney, these things happen at the most opportune moments. I'm just glad I was able to be of assistance."

The tea arrived for Clarence and a glass of water for the CEO.

"I'm sure you did your best, but it was the new Minister who was on our side and pushed the approval through."

Clarence was beginning to feel uneasy. It was as though Rodney Glass wasn't giving him the credit for getting the planning passed. "But Rodney, the new Minister was only there because Derek Layburn wasn't. That was my plan all along. You asked me to make sure we got the go-ahead at the Friday meeting. Well, I did, and you got the permission."

"I'm sorry Clarence, but we got our approval without you."

Clarence began to feel unwell. "Rodney!" He had now raised his voice. "You told me to use my contacts to make sure you won through, and I'd get one million pounds when you got the approvals. I'm here now to collect. After all, I've lived up to my part of the bargain."

It was clear that Rodney Glass wasn't following. "Clarence, in business we always hedge our bets. The new Minister for Regional Development and Planning has helped us out before. We're not stupid enough not to have an arrangement with the number two in the department. I offered her the same deal as I did you. A million pounds if we got our permissions."

"What! You mean you've given my money to Gloria Shaw just because she chaired the meeting?" Clarence was not happy and was showing his anger.

Rodney Glass recognised Clarence wasn't happy but was determined to keep the meeting cordial. "It's not as simple as that Clarence. I didn't just give her your money as you put it. It wasn't yours in the first place. You both had the same offer. Get us the approval and we'll give you a million. It's just that she came through. As I said, it's good business to cover all your bases. Gloria's been paid handsomely in the past to help out. This was just another transaction for her."

Clarence was close to tears. He could see all his plans disappearing in front of him. In a final attempt to convince the CEO that it was his plan that won in the end, he threw caution to the wind. "Listen you overbearing pompous idiot, don't you understand? I took care of Derek Layburn so Gloria Shaw *would* chair the meeting. I didn't know you'd bribed her, but I knew from one of my chums that she was more liberal than Layburn. You idiot." He pointed directly at Rodney. "I killed him so either she would chair the meeting, or the meeting would be postponed and buy you time to work on the new Minister. It was my plan that got you what you wanted. Gloria Shaw had nothing to do with it!"

Clarence was standing and shouting. Tears were welling up in his eyes and spit formed at the corners of his mouth. "I did what you wanted. You've got your permission and I want my money!" Exhausted and in a highly emotional state, he fell back into the sofa.

The CEO sat in disbelief. Silence descended while Clarence regained his composure and Rodney absorbed what he'd just heard.

"Clarence, I'm afraid I can't have you on our Board any more. I didn't ask you to kill anyone, least of all the Minister." Then Rodney remembered, "But you also killed his wife."

Silence again descended as Clarence sipped his tea.

"Clarence, are you telling me the truth, did you really murder the Minister and his wife?"

He nodded and spoke very softly. "Yes, I made a plan after Layburn told me to get lost and not to try to bribe him again. I knew you were desperate, and I wanted the million. My plan was to kill him so he couldn't chair the Friday meeting. I did it for you and the firm, Rodney. You said you'd already invested millions so far and couldn't afford the loss."

Both men sat looking at each other. Each was sad but for different reasons. The CEO spoke first.

"Clarence, I'll say nothing about this conversation, but you had better leave. This firm cannot be involved with any of this." Rodney stood and placed a hand on a broken Right Honourable gentleman's shoulder, easing him upright. As both men stood, Clarence whispered, "But you're not above bribing a Government Minister with my million."

Rodney chose to ignore this remark and walked Clarence to the lift. As the lift doors closed the CEO asked his secretary to call security and ensure Clarence left the building.

***

It took Rodney Glass fifteen minutes to digest his meeting with Clarence. After a lot of soul-searching, he made a decision. He called his head of security, an ex-thug and gang member called Ron Dunlop. He'd served time for all kinds of physical attacks. He'd once worked as an enforcer for a large London gang but had been straight since Rodney employed him initially as his personal bodyguard. When Roddy had first set up his construction business, things were rough between competing contractors and Ron served his purpose. When Colonial and English Land became bigger and moved away from construction into land deals Ron had stayed as head of security.

"Come in Ron, have a seat."

The large Ron Dunlop stood over six feet tall and had the body of someone who knew about gyms. He sat where Clarence had sat only a few minutes before.

Rodney began. "I think I've dropped us in it, Ron. I've just had that prat Clarence Strum in here looking for his payoff. I'd offered him a million to get us our approvals for Blackwood. He came to collect but told me he murdered Sir Derek Layburn and his wife as a way of getting us our licences. He's a pretty weak character and if the police arrest him, I'm sure he'll talk and involve us."

"What do you want me to do?"

"We can handle anything he throws at us." The CEO paused. "No, it's what I told *him* that worries me. I admitted we'd bunged Gloria Shaw, the new Minister, a million to push through the project and I told him we'd bribed her before to get what we wanted."

Rodney looked out the window. "If the police pick him up, he'll tell them everything. Not just try and say we were somehow involved in the

259

murders but that he knows about the bribes. Whatever happens, if the police arrest him, we're in trouble."

The head of security sat and said nothing.

"Do you still have contacts who might make this problem go away?"

"You mean if he's not around he can't be arrested and he can't talk?"

"Well put, but nothing must come back to us."

"Understood. As it happens, I know someone who's looking for work. Ten grand should do it. Leave it with me."

Ron Dunlop stood and left to arrange a hit on the Right Honourable Clarence Strum.

***

The watchers reported Clarence Strum exiting the glass-fronted building at 10.11 a.m. The watcher seated in the lobby called his colleague and relayed Clarence's movements and location. The target walked east from the building and stopped in a coffee shop. He drank coffee for a quarter of an hour, left the shop and hailed a taxi. The watchers scrambled to come together to follow the cab which dropped their target outside his apartment block at 11.27 a.m.

The watchers took up their previous position and included their recent log entries in their next hourly report.

Chapter Twenty-Nine

Steve and The Cap arrived at Matilda Armstrong's flat in Greenwich to find she was still asleep. A few loud bangs on the door not only woke her up but had a few neighbours out looking to see what all the commotion was about. It took Matilda several minutes to open the door that was secured by a chain. With the door open only a few inches because of the security chain Steve introduced himself, showed his warrant card and asked to be let in.

It was clear that Matilda was a night person. From what little Steve could see of her face it was obvious she was either badly hung over, drugged or had only recently gone to bed.

"I'm not dressed; you can't come in. I'm a lady on my own. I can't have strange men in my place. What would the neighbours say?"

Steve thought back to Dougal's comments on the number of bodily fluid stains in Clarence's bedroom in Cirencester and the location of some of them. If this was the female half of that coupling, then Miss Matilda Armstrong was no shrinking violet worried about her reputation with her neighbours.

"We're police officers, miss. We just want to ask you a few questions in connection with the deaths of Sir Derek and Lady Layburn."

Matilda seemed not to comprehend. "What deaths?"

"If you'll let us in, miss, we can explain. It'll only take a few minutes." The DCI lied.

Matilda's brain must have absorbed something of what Steve had said. She closed the door, and the detectives heard the security chain being removed so the door could be fully opened.

As they entered, they could both smell marijuana. Matilda walked in front of them wearing what even from the rear the detectives could see was a flimsy very short, see-through dressing gown. It was equally clear she didn't wear a lot of clothes to sleep in. Over her shoulder, she called out, "Close the door."

Matilda led the two officers into her kitchen. She put the kettle on, sat on a high stool beside a breakfast bar and did her best to cover herself up. The Cap, who appreciated women, looked at Steve and shook his head.

"Miss Armstrong, perhaps you should put some clothes on."

Matilda seemed not to hear but jumped from the stool, spilling most of her body out of her scanty dressing gown. She didn't seem phased by this striptease show and sauntered back to her bedroom. "Make a cup of tea when the kettle boils. I'll be back in a minute."

"Christ Steve, we should have brought a WPC. This one has trouble written all over her."

Steve laughed. "Don't worry, I'm here to chaperone you if you get carried away."

The Cap looked shocked. "What, with that! She's probably had more men than I've made arrests."

"Oh, that few." The DCI smiled as did The Cap.

The kettle boiled and as instructed; The Cap made three cups of tea.

Matilda returned wearing a low-cut smock dress that only just held her assets in and just reached the top of her thighs. Without speaking to either Steve or The Cap she took her tea and wandered into her living room waving to the police officers to follow her.

The living room was a mess. It was large enough with little furniture, but clothes were scattered everywhere, and empty whisky and brandy bottles seemed to cover every surface. Magazines of various styles were scattered and added to the general air of a room nobody cared about.

Matilda lifted a few pieces of clothing from the sofa and indicated the two detectives should sit. The Cap noticed among the clothes she gathered up were several pairs of frilly knickers. He wondered how they'd ended up in her living room.

Once everyone was seated, Steve began. "Miss Armstrong, we believe—"

"Please call me Matilda," she said, with a flourish of her arm. "Everyone does."

"Fine, Matilda. We understand you were a dinner guest at Lord and Lady Rosyth's house in Cirencester last Wednesday evening. That's the 19th of this month?"

Matilda seemed to be trying to recall. "Oh! Yes, Johnny had a bash. I was invited to make up the numbers. Johnny and I have been good friends in the past." She looked at the officers with a 'you know what I mean look.'

Steve had heard that Lord Rosyth liked to keep a few ladies on the side, but he couldn't visualise this brash, slightly overweight woman being with his Lordship.

The Cap, on the other hand, had heard the same thing and he could definitely imagine his Lordship with this girl whom The Cap thought had sex screaming to get out of every part of her ill-concealed body. Nothing was said between the two detectives.

The DCI carried on. "When you were there, you were in the company of the Right Honourable Clarence Strum. Is that correct?"

"Oh yes." Her voice was now low and conspiratorial. "We had a great time."

"Can you please explain that?"

The Cap had his notebook, but her cleavage was distracting him so much he dropped it. The DCI gave him a look that said, *get a grip*.

"Well, there's not much to say. We had dinner, I, as usual, drank too much. I finished up in Clarry's bed. We had sex, drank champagne, had more sex and I fell asleep. I felt like crap in the morning. That's it. A normal night out at someone's dinner party."

"Was Clarence Strum with you all night?"

"How would I know? I passed out after our second go." Matilda stopped suddenly. She was obviously remembering something. She giggled. "Oh no, I remember, we did it three times. He woke me at some ungodly hour and wanted to start again."

"Do you know what time this was?"

She thought. As she did, her breathing quickened and her chest seemed to expand. Her low-cut smock was only keeping her from an embarrassing experience.

"Yes, now you mention it he told me the time. To be honest, I can't really remember, but I think he said it was after three in the morning."

This wasn't helping the case. "Do you remember anything else?"

Again, as she thought, her dress took the strain. "Not really, although I remember his hair was wet. I thought he must have been for a walk, and it was raining."

The DCI's ears pricked up. "Matilda, are you saying you were so drunk you thought Clarence might have left the bed, gone for a walk and returned to wake you up for more sex?"

"I suppose that's what I thought because his hair was wet."

"Matilda, please consider this very carefully. Could Clarence have left the bed without you knowing?"

"Oh easily, I was completely out. I don't really remember very much but his hair was wet."

The Cap looked at Steve who in turn had a look of triumph on his face.

"Thank you, Miss Armstrong, you've been very helpful. Now, a nice WPC and a colleague will call for you at three this afternoon. They'll take you to Scotland Yard where my colleague Detective Inspector Ishmal over there," — Steve pointed to The Cap — "will take your statement. I want you to repeat it just as you have said. Can you do that?"

"I suppose so. Will they bring me back? I need to be somewhere tonight at seven."

Steve could imagine where she might be going but told her she'd be home in plenty of time.

Once outside and walking to their pool car, the detectives compared notes.

"Her alibi won't hold up in court. She can't categorically say he was with her all night. Think about Poppy's and your theory earlier. He was naked when he shot them. He returned to his room, showered and left the feather in the U-bend then woke her up so she could confirm the time."

The Cap interrupted. "And his hair was still wet from the shower." The Cap almost did a jig. "We've got him, Steve, his alibi's blown."

"Yes, it is Abul. Let's get her statement into the record this afternoon and see how we present this to the CPS. With any luck, we'll arrest him this evening."

***

264

The Right Honourable Clarence, having returned to his Wimbledon flat, was dealing with a combination of emotions. He was livid that Rodney Glass had backed away from their deal. He told himself it was his plan that had worked. He thought it grossly unfair that some politician should get his money for doing nothing.

He sat in his favourite chair with a glass of brandy in his hand. As he sipped the golden liquid, he allowed his oversize brain to have free rein. He considered what had happened and how he would get even. He told himself that no one got the better of Clarence Strum. With his IQ, few people could better him and Rodney Glass certainly wasn't one of them.

As he poured his second brandy, his brain finally told him what to do. He analysed where he was. He laughed as he spoke out loud. "You think you're a clever sod, Mr Glass. Well, I'm the one who'll come out on top when I get my hands on one hundred and fifty million. Your million will look like petty cash money."

His plan was forming. It was simple. He would invite himself back to Lord Rosyth's for lunch and maybe take Suzanne Baird. Now he didn't have the funds to go overboard impressing her and her father he'd use his aristocratic contacts. When he was at Cirencester, he'd retrieve his gun from the dead tree stump and simply shoot Roddy Glass. He told himself nothing could be simpler. He'd killed three people already. One more wouldn't matter. It was true he'd not be any wealthier by shooting Glass, but he'd have the satisfaction of proving that no one double-crossed Clarence Strum.

He phoned the not so lovely but potentially very rich Suzanne Baird. When she answered he laid on the charm perhaps, in his later opinion, a bit too thickly. Still, it seemed to work. He had to make sure Mr Baird was aware of his interest in his daughter. "You'd better ask your father, dearest. I don't want him to get the wrong impression of me. After all, we hardly know each other but Lord Rosyth is like a second father to me and is very keen to meet the new lady in my life."

"Daddy won't mind. You're such a gentleman, Clarence. I'll just go and tell him."

She was gone only a minute. When the phone was picked up again it wasn't Suzanne but her father who was talking.

"Clarence, Suzanne has told me you're taking her to meet Lord Rosyth for lunch. I just want you to know, my boy, that I hold you in high regard and I'm sure you'll be the perfect lunch companion for Suzanne. When are you going?"

This was a tricky question as Clarence hadn't yet spoken with his Lordship. "Oh, soon Mr Baird, probably later this week or the weekend."

"Splendid, I'll pass you back to Suzanne." Mr Baird was gone to be replaced by the voice of the new love interest in Clarence's life.

They spoke for a few more minutes. Clarence found playing the lover easy. After all, he'd played it many times before but not for such a rich prize.

Once he had hung up, his mind turned to the next part of his plan. He dialled Lord Rosyth's mobile. He knew his Lordship travelled around his various properties during the week and his mobile was the easiest way of contacting him. Clarence was aware his Lordship's constant travelling within London was to keep Lady Rosyth off the scent of the various women he kept.

"Good afternoon, sir, it's Clarence Strum."

"Ah! Clarence, how are you, my boy?"

"I'm very happy sir. I've met a wonderful girl and would love to introduce her to you and Lady Rosyth. I was hoping I might be able to come down to a luncheon at Cirencester one day this week?"

Silence. His Lordship said nothing for what seemed a long time. "You mean you've got another bimbo in tow and want to impress her by bringing her to the Cirencester house?"

Clarence hadn't expected this response. "No sir, she's not a bimbo. Her father runs a multimillion-pound electronics empire. Suzanne's a sweet girl and I just thought you'd like to meet her."

"Clarence, I've known you since you were born. I've known your father most of my life. He's in no doubt you're a wastrel and a spendthrift but he's keen to see you married off." Lord Rosyth suffered from a lung condition and paused for breath. "I'll have to check with Lady Rosyth. I know we're having people for Sunday lunch, so I suppose another two won't upset anyone. Make it one p.m."

"Thank you, sir." As an afterthought, Clarence added. "Any news from the police on the murders?"

"No, nothing. I found the gun you know, or rather the dogs did. It was stuck in a dead tree stump in the grounds. I gave it to the police, but I've heard nothing since. Look, Clarence, nice to talk to you but I must go. See you Sunday." The line went dead.

It was as well Lord Rosyth ended the call because Clarence had slumped back further in his chair. His brow was wet with perspiration and his stomach felt as though it were in knots.

This was the closest he'd been to panic in years. Again, he knew he'd have to rely on his IQ to process this new information. He was shocked the gun had been found. He allowed himself a few minutes of deep breathing before summoning his brain to work things out.

He drank some more brandy. He told himself there were two issues he had to deal with. The first was the police. He searched his memory banks and went over everything he'd done the night of the shootings. He relived each minute and quickly concluded the police couldn't tie him to the gun. They were after all his intellectual inferiors. He continued to think of the murders and could find no chinks in his armour. He was still safe and congratulated himself. He'd committed the perfect murder.

The second thing of concern was his lack of a weapon to kill Rodney Glass. Clarence thought hard. He considered buying a new gun but remembered his previous experience. On reflection, he decided not to shoot Glass. He closed his eyes and let the brandy and his brain work together.

The next thing he knew it was four-thirty p.m. and he'd been asleep for two hours. He shook himself awake and realised he had the answer. He'd poison Roddy Glass.

He remembered his plan to take Suzanne to Cirencester. There was no real need now as the gun was no longer in the dead tree stump. Still, it fitted his longer-term plan to win the one hundred and fifty million. He lamented the loss of the gun. With a smile on his face, he realised that if Mr Baird became a problem, he could no longer just shoot him. He'd have to resort to something else. Maybe the same poison he would use on Roddy Glass.

He convinced himself everything was now back on track although he was a million pounds out of pocket. He realised he had time to work out how to poison Roddy Glass and what type of poison would give the most excruciating death. Revenge would be sweet. Murder was easy for a highly intelligent superhuman like himself. He was attending a friend's birthday party that evening and had arranged to be collected by taxi at five-thirty p.m.

***

Steve and The Cap returned to the Yard and had lunch together in the canteen. After a very ordinary plate of ham, egg and chips, they went to the office.

The DCI arranged to see the Commander to discuss the arrest of the Right Honourable Clarence Strum. The Cap prepared for the arrival of Matilda Armstrong while Poppy, who didn't eat lunch, was updating the file following the interview with Matilda.

"If she confirms her story, we'll plan to arrest him at six p.m." Steve was speaking to The Cap. Poppy was listening and seemed excited. "You mean you're actually going to arrest a triple murderer?" She was still a schoolgirl at heart. Steve smiled as he left.

Alfie Brooks was in a jovial mood as Steve entered his office.

"I've come to give you an update on the Layburn case, sir."

"Good, good." Alfie was happy but seemed distracted." "I hope you're here to tell me you've solved it but before you do, I thought you'd like to know Sophia Marr has been remanded in custody. Her next appearance is in four weeks, so you'll have to attend then."

Steve acknowledged this. He knew it was the bugbear of every officer's life, having to attend court.

Steve smiled "Yes sir, but we've still to run it by the CPS after we have our suspect in custody and you know how difficult those pen pushers can be."

"Now, now Steve. They do a job." With a glint in his eye and a broad smile on his face, Alfie continued. "But I know what you mean. Right! Let's hear it."

The DCI outlined the enquiry and explained the circumstantial evidence they had gathered. He went on to offer their theory that Clarence had been nude when he killed the Layburn's as a way of explaining how the feather came to be in the U-bend.

"The problem has always been the alibi but after this morning I don't think it'll stand up. The woman's being brought in this afternoon to give a formal statement. I know we've enough to arrest and charge him but I'm a bit worried about the CPS. All joking aside, I'm not sure we've enough solid evidence to guarantee a conviction."

The Commander sat with his elbows on his desk. "I don't suppose he'll cough?"

"No sir, I think it's unlikely."

"What about the taxi driver? I've spoken to the murder squad dealing with it and they've got nothing other than he was a bit of a lad and fronted as a hitman from time to time. They say he'd just duped someone out of a bundle of cash before he was murdered but they've no clue who paid the money. I don't suppose you've found a connection?"

"No, but we know his gun killed the guy so it's something to sweat out of him."

"OK, go for it. If you're convinced that he's your man then let's put him in the frame. Personally, I think you've got enough so let's not worry just now. Get him in and charged. We'll go from there."

Steve went back downstairs knowing the Commander had his back.

***

An hour later, the DCI was in his office finishing off his notes to give Poppy on the case when the phone rang. It was Alfie Brooks. He didn't seem to be in the same mood as he had been when Steve met him an hour ago.

"Sorry Steve, the powers that be have called for a debrief on the gold bullion robbery for four this afternoon. I tried to postpone it, but it's gone political. The Commissioner is insisting and Philipa Cartwright, our esteemed Deputy Commissioner, will be in the chair. You and DI Ishmal are to present yourselves to conference room four at four p.m."

The DCI was annoyed. "Christ Alfie, what do they want? I'm set to arrest a triple murderer at six and some pen pusher wants a four p.m. chat, about a case that's closed."

"That's about it. Look, you've got this Clarence bloke under surveillance. He's not going anywhere. Leave him out there until tomorrow morning. Pick him up then. Another day won't make any difference."

Reluctantly Steve agreed. "Yeah." A big sigh. "I suppose so."

"Right. Don't be late and smarten yourself up and make sure The Cap does the same."

At 3.51 p.m. The Cap arrived back from taking Matilda's statement. "All done Steve, although she's a bit hazy on the detail. She says it's possible Clarence didn't leave the bed but then says she's not sure. Either way, his alibi's blown."

"Give it to Poppy. We have an appointment upstairs in exactly eight minutes. Get your notebooks on the bullion job." Steve had his on his desk. "And comb your hair. I'll brief you as we go."

***

Conference room four was one of the largest in the building. As Steve and The Cap walked in, they saw the Deputy Commissioner at the head of the long conference table. To her left was a civilian neither man recognised but they later learnt was Rupert Naismith, Assistant Deputy Governor at the Bank of England. Sitting at Philipa Cartwright's right was Commander Alfie Brooks.

Beside the Commander sat a uniformed Chief Superintendent whom Steve recognised as CS Charles, Head of Human Resources at the Met. Next to Rupert Naismith sat another civilian who, from his dress, was obviously a civil servant. It transpired he was called Soames and dealt with immigration issues at the Home Office. The DCI felt uncomfortable with this meeting but had no choice but to see it through. He and The Cap were invited to sit opposite each other but further down the table.

"Now gentlemen. This enquiry has been set up to establish exactly what took place when recovering the one billion pounds of gold bullion recently stolen from the Bank of England. We have been charged with identifying weaknesses in the Bank's security and recommending improvements." The Deputy Commissioner was a fearsome woman used to being obeyed and it was clear how she intended to run this meeting.

"There is also the matter of police procedure and how senior command dealt with the case. We will examine how this whole thing was conceived and executed." Looking directly at the DCI and The Cap, she said, "You gentlemen were responsible for the conduct of the case and the apprehension of the miscreants so are best placed to answer our questions."

Without waiting for comments, Philipa Cartwright opened her folder and started.

"DI Ishmal, you are on record as the SIO. Perhaps you'd tell us what happened from the beginning."

Steve could see it was going to be a long haul. The Cap started but was obviously light on facts. Steve was acutely aware that he had taken charge of the initial and parts of the enquiry although he'd passed the credit on to The Cap.

The members of the enquiry prodded The Cap on many issues on which he only had superficial knowledge. Steve found himself having to step in and answer the more detailed questions on his behalf. The enquiry insisted on detailed answers concerning the fake bullion at Tilbury and when it was suspected as being painted lead. The Cap floundered over this and forgot Steve had told him he'd amended his statement on this point with the Commander's blessing. The DCI had to remind the DI that it was him who was suspicious of the quality of the gold and that he had asked it to be checked by the Bank. On this point, it was obvious The Cap had no knowledge, but Steve tried to recover the situation by saying his DI had worked an eighteen-hour shift and was exhausted. He offered this as a reason for The Cap's confusion on this point.

He felt no one believed him.

They asked about Cecil White and how much The Cap took into consideration when arresting him knowing his international status as a diplomat. Steve answered for The Cap. "He's a crook, so we arrested him. His status isn't any of our concern. Next question please." Steve saw Alfie glare at him and subtly wave a finger. The message was he'd overstepped the mark again.

By six p.m., the meeting was winding down. Steve was annoyed at being called into what looked like a witch-hunt against him and The Cap. He was asked if he had any final statement to make. He saw the Commander shake his head and his look dared the DCI to say anything negative.

Steve was about to speak when his phone pinged. Despite annoyed looks from the top of the table, he answered it. It was DI Peter Jones. The watchers had a problem, and the DCI was needed.

"I'm sorry Ma'am, but I'm needed on a small murder case that the Commissioner told the press would be solved by today. If you'll excuse us, we have to go."

Without saying anything, Steve and The Cap left. The Deputy Commissioner wasn't pleased while the Commander laughed inwardly and thought, *Good boy Steve.*

Chapter Thirty

As the watchers continued their surveillance of Clarence Strum's, they had noticed a black motorcycle drive slowly past. The rider was dressed completely in black leathers and wore a black crash helmet complete with a tinted visor. The bike stopped about a hundred metres past the apartment block, turned and slowly came back again.

The watchers became suspicious when the rider stopped, parked his bike just short of the entrance to the building and dismounted, all the time looking at the building. The uniformed concierge who the watchers had noted patrolled the entrance hallway appeared from the building, obviously taking a smoke break. He stood at the top of the steps looking down the entrance path and the small gardens to either side.

The bike rider removed his helmet and sat sideways on his bike looking at the building. In itself it was innocent but the older detective of the two watchers was one of the team who had lost Sophia Marr last week for a few hours. He was close to retirement and didn't want a young DI reading him the riot act again. He confided to his younger colleague that this looked a bit suspicious. "If I didn't know any better, I'd say that guy's sussing out the place. Maybe planning a job. I'll think I'll play safe." His younger less-experienced colleague didn't object to anything the senior man did.

The bike rider levered himself off his bike and started walking past the building and appeared to be heading for the path that ran up the side of the building and which led to a side service entrance used mainly by cleaning staff. The watchers saw him slow his pace and casually turn as if to walk up the path.

"Can I help you?" The concierge had seen the rider appear to turn into the path.

The watchers couldn't hear despite having lowered their windows. The leather-clad figure appeared to feign confusion and waved his leather-gloved hand at the keeper of the main entrance. He slowly retraced his steps back to his bike.

The senior watcher had his mobile phone resting on the wing mirror of their car and took several photographs of the rider without his helmet. "It might be nothing," he confided to the younger watcher, "but I'll pass it on just in case." He used his phone to send the images of the rider to DI Peter Jones.

The incident was logged at 4.57 p.m. and included in their hourly report to the DI.

***

The watchers settled down and noted the motorbike and the rider had driven off at 5.10 p.m. A taxi arrived outside the main door at 5.32 p.m. and Clarence Strum, dressed in his dinner jacket, was recorded as driving off in the taxi. The watchers prepared to follow but as they were about to get in position, the black motorbike cut in front of them and appeared to be following the taxi. The watchers held back not wishing to let the bike rider know they were there.

The older watcher was more convinced something was up and called in the registration number of the bike. The PNR check came back in minutes. The answer alarmed the older man who called DI Peter Jones immediately.

The DI had been busy with Technical Support analysing the photographs of the bike rider using the latest facial recognition software. Inspector Terry Harvey was presenting his findings as the senior watcher called in.

"The bike is registered to Tommy Gunn. He's a real villain and he appears to be following our target."

"Right. The photos confirm it is Tommy, so we know it's him on the bike." Peter Jones thought for a second. "You're on the spot. What do you suggest?"

After being torn off a strip by the DI, the older watcher felt better being asked for his opinion.

"Let's see where our target's going and see what Tommy does but I'll bet he's armed."

"Yes. I've got his file. He's a bloody dangerous nutter so don't get too close. I'll call the DCI and see what he thinks but call me every five minutes until we figure something out."

***

Peter had called Steve at six p.m. just as his grilling was coming to an end.

The DI explained the latest development. "I don't like the sound of this, Peter. Listen, see if you can round up one of our own motorbike boys but one who is firearms trained. Get him over to the watchers. At least we'll have some way of following Tommy Gunn and match his firepower."

"Sir, a traffic motorcycle cop who is firearms trained will be like hens' teeth. Also, we'd need a plain bike. It's gone six on a Monday night. There's no chance."

Steve could hear Peter's breathing down the phone. "Listen, sir. I'm firearms certified and I've got my own bike. If you give me time to draw a weapon and get into my leathers, I could be on my way in ten minutes."

"You are a man of many parts." The DCI was grateful the DI was working for him even though it was only temporary. "Right, off you go, Peter. I'll write an authorisation but for God's sake, be careful. This Tommy Gunn seems to be a bit of a nut."

"Don't worry sir, I've read his file."

***

The watchers followed the bike and the taxi to Russell Square. The taxi pulled off into a side road leading off the square and immediately stopped on the left-hand side of the road. The target got out and entered a building that looked like a nightclub, despite it only being 6.43 p.m. Two large men were guarding the door — whom the watchers took to be bouncers — dressed in dinner jackets.

The motorbike rider, seeing the taxi turn off the square, stopped and pulled up on the left side of the road that circled the square. As it was a one-way system the watchers pulled up on the right-hand side of the road

275

further back from the bike but still far enough forward to see the taxi drive off and have a view of the door. The bike rider disembarked his machine and removed his helmet. He scanned the area before setting off to investigate where Clarence Strum had gone. The junior watcher left the car and followed on the opposite side of the road. He observed the leather-clad figure walk past the bouncers before turning and returning. He stopped to talk to the door guards for five minutes and returned to his bike. As before, he leant against it and waited.

DI Peter Jones arrived just as Tommy Gunn returned to his bike. The DI arrived in stealth mode, freewheeling into the square and stopping behind the watchers' car. The junior watcher arrived at the car at the same time as the DI and both got in, the DI in the back. The other watcher was in front in the driver's position.

Once the DI had been briefed, he asked the senior watcher to walk past the door Clarence had been seen entering to get the name and address of the club. "But don't take any chances and don't get rumbled. The number and street name will do."

The watcher was gone no more than five minutes. Tommy Gunn still stood by his bike, smoking. It was now 7.21 p.m. and was dark and cold.

DI Peter Jones called Steve to update him. The watchers were due off shift at ten and he said he would brief the replacement team if nothing had changed. Just as he spoke, Tommy Gunn started up his bike and prepared to set off.

"Peter, follow him. We need to know what's going on. I'll brief the replacements if our man hasn't moved. Now go but be careful."

Peter Jones was an experienced driver of powerful bikes and had no difficulties in mounting his machine, putting on his helmet and firing up his beast. As Tommy Gunn pulled away from the pavement Peter followed at a discreet distance. The gun under his leather gave him confidence that if things got nasty, he'd be all right.

***

Steve took the hourly checking-in calls from the watchers. It was clear Clarence was in for the night, so at 9.22 p.m. the DCI headed out for Russell Square to meet and brief the next set of watchers. Alison wasn't happy to see her husband leave at that time, especially as she'd overheard that Tommy Gunn was usually armed. She worried about Steve and told him to be careful.

At 09.55 p.m., the watchers changed over. There was no sign of a black motorbike and Steve hadn't heard from Peter. He was a bit concerned but not yet worried. After briefing the new team, he left. As he drove his phone pinged. It was Peter Jones.

"I followed him to a block of flats in Putney. He's garaged his bike, so I think he's in for the night. I waited an hour just in case but everything's quiet. Whatever he's up to, it won't be tonight."

Steve thanked Peter and asked him to be equally prepared tomorrow and suggested they meet outside Clarence's flat at eleven to arrest him. Steve, for some reason, asked Peter to retain his gun and not return it to the armoury as was the standard operating procedure. When asked about this afterwards, he said he just had a feeling, and they were going after a man who had already shot three people.

***

The watchers were cold and tired. They saw a succession of taxis arrive outside what they now knew was the Vault Private Members Club. They saw a procession of dinner-jacketed men climb or fall into the back of these taxis. It was difficult to spot their target and were fearful of missing him. One of the watchers was about to get out of the car and walk to the club in the hope of spotting and signalling that he'd identified their target. But at that moment there was a lull in the taxi Grand Prix and a sole taxi arrived. Clarence Strum appeared and poured himself into the back seat.

Confident they were following the correct taxi, the watchers logged this at 03.02 a.m. Clarence Strum was on his way not only home but to a bad hangover later in the morning.

Chapter Thirty-One

Tuesday the 25th of October started bright and dry. It was a day DCI Steve Burt hoped to add to his tally of solved murder cases. Over breakfast, he outlined his plan for the day to his wife. Mrs Burt had always taken an interest in her husband's work and had even been shot because of it.

It all sounded very simple. First, sort out the files with Poppy for the CPS. Second, visit the CPS, explain the files and inform them of the imminent arrest and finally, arrest their suspect for three murders. That done, he'd be home for dinner.

Alison laughed at the absurd simplicity of her husband's statement. She'd been married to him long enough to know that he might not be home for dinner and there was even a chance he wouldn't be home before morning.

"You're a terrible liar DCI Burt but I love you just the same." She kissed him fondly. "Now off you go and catch your murderer but be careful. I don't want to visit you in hospital."

Steve kissed his wife again and set off for Scotland Yard. He arrived bearing coffees, but as usual someone else had already bought three cups so his offering would be the second cup of the day. Poppy and The Cap were discussing something that sounded to Steve as though it had nothing to do with the case.

"Poppy, when's my appointment with the CPS?"

"There was a message last night. One of their lawyers is coming here. You just have to give them a time."

This wasn't unusual but it was rare for a CPS lawyer to venture into the den of the police.

"Fine. Cap, what've you got on?"

"Nothing much. I've written up my notes and Poppy's put them on the file. I'm really standing by for the arrest of our man."

"Any news from Peter and his watchers?"

"Nothing so far, I'll call him if you like."

As he picked up the phone Peter Jones walked into the office, looking very tired and obviously in need of sleep.

"You look awful!" Poppy knew how to win friends. "You don't look as though you've had any sleep."

"Thank you, DC Cooper, remind me to compliment you one day." The lilt in the DI's Welsh voice sounded out of place as he smiled at a red-faced Poppy.

"She's right, Peter. We were supposed to meet at eleven outside Clarence Strum's place."

"Yes, I know sir, but I couldn't sleep." He gave Poppy a smile.

Steve was grateful he had everyone in and ready to go. "Poppy, call the CPS. Tell them nine would be good. We'll have to be out of here by ten at the latest, so I've got an hour for them."

Poppy lifted her phone.

"Cap, call up uniform. We'll need a few officers on standby. We'll let them know when we are ready to leave."

The DCI was counting off the tasks before the arrest. "Peter, anything from the watchers?"

"Not as of eight a.m. I just took their report."

"OK everyone, relax for a while. Get ready and make sure everything on the case is watertight. I don't want the CPS picking holes."

Poppy arrived in Steve's office, to confirm his nine a.m. meeting with the CPS. "Oh sir, there was a message from Human Resources. DS Conway has been returned to general duties and DS Fuller has returned to duty in Chelmsford. They said unless you needed DI Jones, he is to return to his normal duties tomorrow. If there is anything else you need, you're to call a Chief Superintendent Charles."

"Thanks, Poppy, I suppose it's not unexpected."

A rather demure lady lawyer from the CPS arrived on time at nine a.m.. She refused the offer of something to drink and scowled when Steve asked for another coffee. She was carrying a huge bundle of thick files that Steve couldn't imagine all referred to his case.

She introduced herself as Ms Hancock and told the DCI she was the leading solicitor for the Crown. Steve quickly realised trying to befriend Ms Hancock would be a waste of time so got straight down to business.

"I've reviewed the file DCI Burt and I have a few reservations." Ms Hancock was now wearing her reading glasses. "Some of your analysis appears to me to be flawed and certainly cannot be supported by facts."

"Such as?"

"Well, let's take them one at a time. Your assertion that your suspect was naked. There is no evidence of this. It is pure speculation contrived to fit a theory."

Steve could see this was not going to be a happy meeting. He explained about the feather in the shower and that the killer being nude and showering after the murders was the only explanation. He stopped short of denying they'd theorised this to explain the feather in the U-bend.

"I see; well, it's feasible." Ms Hancock appeared to concede. "Moving on, I take your point about the metal polish on the handkerchief and it's good your forensics officer matched the polish but it's not conclusive. Such contamination could have been picked up anywhere. I think it's flimsy at best."

"I'm sorry, Ms Hancock, but I disagree. It clearly shows our suspect used his handkerchief to avoid leaving fingerprints. The make of the polish is no longer a common brand and it's unlikely he would have been in contact with this product anywhere else."

"Yes of course I see that, but a good defence barrister will argue as I have. It's not conclusive."

Steve shook his head but said nothing.

Ms Hancock moved on. "Mr Burt, I'm not saying you haven't made a case but there's one big flaw. Unless you can put the gun in your suspect's hand, I'm worried our case is weak and he could walk. We need to connect him to the weapon or obtain a confession. You have a 60% partial fingerprint match from the gun but it's not enough to be admissible as evidence."

"But you're saying we have enough to proceed?"

"Oh! Yes, but be careful. I think that…"

Peter Jones opened the office door unannounced. "Sir, we've got a problem. We have to go now!"

The DCI stood, apologised to Ms Hancock and rushed out. "What the hell's going on?"

The Cap was nowhere to be seen and Poppy was looking lost.

"The watchers just called in. Our motorbike man's back outside Clarence's building. I think we need to move the arrest timetable up and see what this Tommy Gunn's up to."

Everything kicked into action. The Cap was off mobilising a uniform team; the watchers continued to watch, and Steve and Peter Jones ran for the garage and their pool car. As they ran, Steve used his phone to call up an armed response unit. He hoped the communications officer understood him as he was running, breathing heavily and talking at the same time. He vowed to take out a gym membership after this was all over.

**

The watchers had recorded the arrival of the black motorbike with its black-clad rider at 09.49 a.m. They had immediately called it in. The rider had repeated his performance of yesterday although the watchers this Tuesday morning were different officers. He had dismounted, removed his helmet and casually strolled past the entrance and stopped by the service path to the right-hand side of the building. He continually looked around and had eventually casually walked up the path.

The watchers reported this as Steve and Peter were speeding out of the garage at New Scotland Yard at breakneck speed headed for Wimbledon. The watchers were instructed to do nothing except watch and were reminded the bike rider was to be treated as armed and dangerous.

These particular watchers were old-school uniformed constables and stuck to the rules. At ten a.m. exactly, one of them called in their hourly report.

**

As the pair of detectives sped out of the garage, the DI's phone buzzed. Steve answered and received, in very formal clipped tones the watchers report. The phone was on speaker. "Reporting all is quiet as at ten hundred hours Tuesday 25th October. As per our previous report, the motorcycle remains parked outside the building." The watcher hung up.

Despite the speed of travel and the seriousness of the unfolding situation, both Steve and Peter laughed. "You can always rely on the British bobby not to panic." When Peter said this, it set both detectives laughed again. It took them several minutes to calm down and wipe the tears from their eyes. With the blues and twos on, they were cutting through the morning traffic. The laughter had lifted their spirits and they were now fully focused on arresting Clarence Strum.

They arrived at the apartment block just as The Cap arrived in a minibus with four uniformed constables and a uniformed sergeant. The watchers explained again what they'd observed, and Steve accompanied by Peter, who was checking his gun, entered the main door of the building. The Cap and the uniformed officers were close behind. There was no sign of the armed response unit.

The lift arrived and Steve had a decision to make. They suspected Tommy Gunn was with Clarence and that he was armed. In such circumstances, the standard operating procedure called for the presence of armed response. If Steve went up and something went wrong, he'd be in all kinds of trouble. He decided.

"Everyone into the lift."

The lift opened at floor ten and the team walked towards Clarence's door. The door had been smashed and the lock broken. Steve held up his hand asking for quiet. He pushed the broken door gently open. There was silence. The DCI pointed to himself, then Peter and then The Cap as the order they were to enter. A sudden cry came from inside. They could now hear voices mixed in with sobs and furniture being disturbed.

The DCI went in and opened the door into what turned out to be the living room. As he advanced, he called out, "Armed police; we're coming in."

As Steve opened the door, he saw a man dressed in black leather standing behind another man dressed in pyjamas. The man in leather had his arms around the other one in such a way as the man in pyjamas couldn't use his arms. The pair were struggling and the French windows that opened onto a Juliet balcony were open. It was clear to Steve that Tommy Gunn was intent on forcing Clarence Strum to the open window.

The man in pyjamas was Clarence. He was crying and sobbing. On seeing Steve, he called out "Please, don't let him do it. Please stop him!"

Peter was right behind Steve and had his gun in his right hand. He pointed it at the leather figure they all took to be Tommy Gunn and shouted, "Let him go, Tommy."

The sight of The Cap and the uniformed officers also entering appeared to give Tommy pause for thought. Clarence was still crying, and a large stain appeared at the front of his pyjama bottoms. He'd wet himself."

"Come on, Tommy, we're here to arrest this man. So far all you've done is kick in a door. It's a police caution at best." The DCI lied. "Let him go." Steve tried to reason with the bike rider.

Tommy found his purpose again and started to edge Clarence to the open window. Clarence found renewed strength on seeing the police and struggled more but seemed to cry less.

Tommy, who was bigger than his prey, held Clarence by one arm and pulled his gun from inside his leather jerkin top. He pointed it at Steve and Peter. "Back off, coppers, I'll throw him out the window unless you back off and leave." He turned his gun towards Clarence's head.

Clarence stopped struggling and renewed his crying and pleaded, "Get me out of this, *please*, he's going to kill me."

Steve ignored Clarence. "Tommy, you know you won't get away with this. If you throw him out the window, you'll save the country a lot of money in legal bills, but you'll end up back inside on a murder charge, or else we'll shoot you and you'll both be dead. Now think about it. Is it really worth whatever you're getting for killing someone who's going to prison for the rest of his life?"

Clarence was screaming. "He's right, listen to him. Just let me go, please." The sobs were getting louder and Clarence's pleading more intense.

Peter said nothing but was ready to shoot if Tommy made any sort of move.

The room became quiet as everyone looked at each other. Only Clarence's whimpering broke the silence. Without warning, Tommy released Clarence and pushed him onto his sofa. He held his hands in the air and his automatic pistol by the trigger guard allowing it to dangle from his trigger finger.

"Let the gun drop to the floor." Peter Jones, as the firearms-trained officer, took control.

The black-clad figure dropped his gun. As soon as it hit the carpet, Peter rushed across and kicked the weapon out of reach. He placed his own gun in his waistband and immediately took Tommy Gunn's wrists. He forced his arms behind his back and handcuffed the bike rider.

"You're right, copper, the ten grand I'm getting for making this bloke have an accident ain't worth it with you lot looking on. Who'll collect my bike?"

Steve was amazed that the man could think about his motorbike when he stood in handcuffs.

"Don't worry Tommy. We'll take care of it."

"And as you said, I'll only get a police caution?"

"That was before you produced the gun. We'll be looking at more serious charges but at least it won't be murder."

Steve turned to The Cap and, out of Tommy's hearing, said, "Get him to central processing. Book him in on a charge of being in possession of a firearm and attempted murder. That'll do to hold him. He'll keep until we've finished with the Right Honourable."

The Cap nodded, took Tommy by the elbow and steered him from the flat.

"Right Mr Strum." Steve stood over a shaking Clarence. He signalled to one of the uniformed officers. "Go and get dressed. This officer will go with you. Take your time."

Clarence looked at the DCI as though he didn't understand. He was mumbling but Steve couldn't hear what he was saying. The uniform eased Clarence off the sofa. He looked a broken figure in his soiled pyjamas. He was bent over looking at the floor as he was led away still mumbling to himself.

"I don't suppose we need forensics in here Peter. This isn't a crime scene and Tommy Gunn's not going to cause a fuss. Get the boys to have a look around. The woman from the CPS wants proof the gun that killed our victims can be traced to Clarence. You never know, there might just be a receipt or something in his paperwork although I doubt it."

The officers spent fifteen minutes sifting through Clarence Strum's documents before their prisoner appeared in the company of the officer who had escorted him to his bedroom. They found nothing incriminating in Clarence's paperwork.

Peter read him his rights, told him the charge was triple murder and everything would be explained in detail at the station. Clarence was handcuffed and escorted by two uniformed officers to the waiting car and a journey to New Scotland Yard's holding cells.

Steve saw the young PC who'd seen Clarence to his bedroom waiting. "Yes, Constable, do you need me?"

"I'm not sure sir but the prisoner was mumbling all the time. At one point I think he said, "How did they find me, they're inferior beings? He seemed to repeat it like a chant." The constable shuffled his feet, slightly embarrassed. "I just thought you should know sir."

"Yes. Thanks, Constable, good spot."

As they left the flat of a triple murderer, the Right Honourable Clarence Strum, Steve had a sudden thought. "Peter, when we get back, have a doctor give him the once over. Your watchers reported he didn't get in until three or so this morning and he'd had a skinful. Check that he's sober enough to be questioned."

"Will do, sir." In the short time Peter had worked with the DCI he recognised that Steve had more to say. "Anything else?"

"No, not really. I'm just thinking about what that young constable told me. He said Clarence was repeating the same words like a chant. Something to do with, 'how did they find me', and 'they're inferior beings'. It sounds odd when you've just been arrested for murder." Steve saw Peter looking quizzically at him.

"Pay no attention. I'm just wondering if our murderer could be headed for Broadmoor rather than a secure prison cell. I'm wondering how sane he is."

Chapter Thirty-Two

Clarence Strum was examined by the police doctor and found to have excess alcohol in his blood, so he was left to sober up in one of the holding cells.

With several hours to wait before they could interview Clarence, Steve and The Cap decided to visit central booking and interview Tommy Gunn.

Tommy was an old hand and knew the procedure. He'd declined the services of a duty solicitor. Steve brought coffees into the interview room and Tommy gulped his down despite it being extremely hot. The Cap set up the recording machine and Steve started.

"OK, Tommy. You're not going to make us go all round the houses, are you? All we need to know is who hired you?"

"I'm no grass, Mr Burt. I took the job because I needed the money. I'm not long out after an eight stretch. I'm forty-nine and I've spent most of me life inside. I've had enough. If I didn't need the money, I swear I'd never have taken the job."

"I understand, Tommy. All I need to know is who paid you?"

"You know I can't say. I'd be a dead man."

Steve considered this. He'd heard it many times and most ex-cons of Tommy's age usually meant it.

"Tommy, you're looking at a very long stretch. We've got you on attempted murder and an unlicensed gun. With your record, the judge will give you the maximum term." Steve paused and let the silence fill the room. "Unless…"

Tommy's ears pricked up. "Yes, Mr Burt, unless what?"

Steve was making this up as he went along but as with all good stories it had a grain of truth.

"We're not really interested in what you did this morning. The guy you were sent to kill is wanted for three murders, so we'll take care of him. The problem is when he gets to court, he'll say someone tried to kill him and we can't stand up and deny it. Can we?"

Tommy was thoughtful. "No, I suppose not."

"But… if you told the judge at your trial that it was a mistake, then you might get a shorter sentence. After all, you didn't push him through the window. If you come clean with us and tell us what we need to know we can put it down to an incompetent and bungled job with no real harm done. You might not even get a stretch in a category three prison. There's nothing we can do about the gun. You'll have to stand up for that."

Steve knew he was on thin ice but took comfort in the fact he would only be reporting what he saw. A man wrestling with another man who thought he was going to be pushed through a window. The fact that the police arrived to stop the altercation meant no one would ever know if Clarence would have gone flying.

Tommy wasn't slow. He spent a few minutes thinking. "So, if I say I was hired to kill this geezer but had no intention of doing it, I was just frightening him like, then you'd back that up in court?"

"Well, Tommy, we can't testify to what you were thinking. As I said, you didn't push him out the window and you certainly put the fear of God up him. You've never killed anyone before so why start now?"

Tommy gave a sly grin. It said *you don't know what I've done in the past*.

Steve and The Cap waited in anticipation.

"OK Mr Burt, I'll tell you." Tommy explained he'd been approached by a friend of his who had a good job in a large City company. He refused to name the person. He'd been paid ten thousand to kill this Clarence Strum, but it had to be made to look like an accident. He'd followed Clarence a few times and decided a fall from a window would get the job done.

"Are we on the tape?"

Steve nodded.

"Of course, I'd never have gone through with it. I just wanted to frighten him. I'd been told he knew too much about bribes to government ministers that could hurt the company my pal worked for and that's why they wanted him dead. I was going to tell him to forget about these bribes otherwise I'd be back. You know, sort of frighten him so he'll forget, but I'd never have killed him."

Tommy sat back and nodded to Steve. A big grin appeared, and he looked like someone who'd just won the lottery.

"That's fine Tommy, but who did the person who hired you work for?"

"Oh, didn't I say? It's something called Colonial English something."

"Thanks, Tommy, now I'll get you a pen and paper and I want you to write everything you've just told us. I'm going to talk to someone about the charges against you and you can stay here until we get something sorted."

Steve and The Cap left to return to the Yard. "What's going on Steve? We have Clarence killing for this CEL company and now we have them trying to kill him."

"Mm. I hear you, but what about the allegation that Clarence had to die because he knew too much? We've got work to do when he sobers up."

As they entered the office, Poppy told Steve that Twiggy was desperate to talk with him.

"Call her up, Poppy. See if she can come down." The DCI walked into his inner office followed by The Cap. Steve called through to Poppy. "Any news from the doctor about Clarence?"

"Yes, he thinks any time after three you can interview him." Poppy was getting used to throwing her voice. "I suppose you'll want coffee?"

"Good idea and get one for Twiggy."

As Twiggy arrived, Steve noticed she had a glow about her that he hadn't noticed before.

Without being asked and while Steve and The Cap were standing, she sat down and nodded her heads towards the other chairs in a move that invited her two colleagues to sit.

"Steve, you're going to love me."

The DCI nodded but said nothing.

Twiggy was disappointed by his reaction. The Cap said nothing.

"OK, have it your way. I've been going through Clarence Strum's bank records and credit card purchases. I'd been through them before, but I couldn't believe he was so squeaky clean and a triple murderer. I found an account he closed down last week. It didn't show when I asked for his current accounts. There's a debit card payment for five hundred pounds the day before he closed the account."

Poppy arrived with the coffee. Twiggy didn't mind the interruption. She felt it added to the suspense.

When everyone had their coffee, she carried on. "I traced the payment, and it was to an account labelled 45. I tracked it through the black web and the financial intelligence unit. It's held by a bloke called Ross McKewn. He's got form for gun-running and selling weapons. He charges five hundred for Smith and Wesson 0.45 calibre pistols. The guys in Tactical Support told me he's a well-known supplier of weapons, no questions asked. I think it might be enough to link your man to the gun."

Steve put his coffee down. "How the hell did you get that? I only spoke with Ms Hancock this morning and she wanted a more direct link to the gun. This is great, Twiggy, but how did you know?"

"I didn't, I just went over his bank transactions and this popped up. I'd no idea." She giggled. "I must be psychic."

"Well, psychic or not, it's good police work. This is all we need to complete the jigsaw. Even Ms Hancock will be satisfied, thanks, Twiggy."

Steve looked at his watch. "Right, Cap let's go meet a killer. Oh Twiggy, can you run a check on Colonial and English Land Inc. We've picked up a story about bribery of government ministers. There may be nothing in it but as it's financial, I think you're best placed to look into it."

"You know Steve, one day you'll go too far away from your brief, and I won't be around." She smiled. "But not this time. I'll check it out. I suppose you need something yesterday?"

The DCI laughed. "No, but later today would be good."

As The Cap and Steve were leaving Twiggy called after them. "Oh, by the way. I thought you should know. Walter Bostrom is out of his coma. It seems he'll make a full recovery." From the other side of the wall, Twiggy heard a faint, "Thanks, Twiggy."

***

The Right Honourable Clarence Strum was seated in interview room four beside a well-dressed and no doubt expensive lawyer. Steve and The Cap introduced themselves, The Cap once again set the tape machine and Steve began.

"Mr Strum, you have been examined by a doctor and had your blood alcohol level tested. He has confirmed you are fit and sober enough for this interview to take place. Do you understand?"

Clarence seemed to have glazed over. He stared with bulging eyes at the far wall. He simply nodded.

"For the tape, please. Can you speak.?"

In a very weak voice, Clarence said, "Yes."

Steve was concerned his prisoner was in some form of shock. "You understand you have been charged with three counts of murder?"

Clarence didn't react at first. His solicitor touched his arm. Still staring at the wall Clarence spoke up almost in a whisper.

"Yes, but how did you find me? My brain is superior to all of yours put together. It was a perfect plan. How did you do it? It's not possible."

It was clear to everyone present that Clarence had suffered some kind of mental trauma. The Cap thought being threatened with being pushed from a window might do it.

The DCI noted Clarence was sweating and didn't seem to be connecting with his surroundings. He decided to carry on, expecting the solicitor to intervene and stop the interview.

Gently Steve said, "Yes Clarence, it was a brilliant plan, but can you explain it to us?"

The prisoner suddenly seemed to snap out of his dream. It was almost as though he needed to tell someone.

"Yes, it was a brilliant plan. Only someone with my intellect could have come up with it."

The high-priced suit sitting next to Clarence spoke up. "Clarence, I have advised you to say nothing. I need to examine what the police have before—"

Clarence became angry. "No, don't you see I have to tell them. I have to let them see how brilliant my plan was and how only I, Clarence Strum, could have devised such a thing."

Clarence's eyes were bulging. He had saliva dripping from the corners of his mouth and he sat proudly with his chest out.

"You see you plods aren't clever. If you were, you wouldn't be out there directing traffic and patrolling the streets. Real crimes planned by intelligent people are beyond you. My plan was brilliant, I knew you'd never work out my plan. I'd committed the most perfect murder."

"Tell us about your plan, Clarence," Steve spoke softly still trying not to upset his prisoner.

Clarence sat forward and took up what he thought was an impressive pose. In his mind, his voice was loud and imposing. He thought everyone should hear his tale of brilliance.

"I am a director of Colonial and English Land Inc. They really can't operate without my intelligence and IQ. A fool of a man called Rodney Glass overextended himself — against my advice might I add — on a project called Blackwood." Clarence pointed to himself. "You see, they rely on me for my advice and when they don't take it things go wrong. You do see that, don't you?"

Steve nodded and Clarence seemed satisfied. "Carry on Clarence."

"Blackwood was to be a new town in the north. There was an issue with planning so naturally, he turned to me to solve his problem." Clarence was now talking normally but Steve noted a faraway look in his eyes. "I reminded the board that I had advised against this thing." Clarence smiled and appeared to talk to himself. "They congratulated me, you know, once they saw I'd been right." After a few seconds, he seemed to return to his surroundings.

"Glass offered me a bonus of one million pounds if I secured government approval from my old chum Derek Layburn." Clarence digressed. He leant low over the table and spoke to Steve directly in a conspiratorially low voice. "Derek and I didn't really get on you know but for a million I was happy to make him my best friend." A funny gurgling sound came from Clarence. He was laughing.

"I offered Derek a handsome bribe to pass the project, but he turned me down, so then I had an idea. If he were dead, then he couldn't oppose the project and I'd get my money. That was my plan. Brilliant don't you think?"

Clarence now sounded like a schoolboy confessing to a misdemeanour he was proud of. "So, I shot him, and for good measure that horrible wife of his. But… you see I'm really smart. My original plan involved hiring a hitman. I found one and paid him to do the job, but he let me down."

Clarence again broke off his narrative. "You can't rely on anyone but yourself, especially me. My brain tells me what to do." Clarence wiped his mouth with the back of his hand before continuing. "People are unreliable, and the hitman double-crossed me." Clarence was laughing out loud as he recalled his exploits.

"I showed him. No one double-crosses Clarence Strum." His voice suddenly sounded aggressive as he said this. As he continued his voice took on a light, high-pitched sound.

The DCI didn't know what to think of Clarence's performance except it was obvious he was a nutter.

"He was the first one I killed. The next two were easy." Clarence stopped talking and went into what appeared to be a trance. No one spoke, waiting for him to recommence his narrative. After about five minutes, he started mumbling. "But how did you find me, my plan was brilliant." He repeated this over and over until eventually, he snapped back to reality. There were tears in his eyes.

"You see my plan worked and I did my job. By killing Derek, I got the company their approvals. I went to see that buffoon Glass yesterday morning to collect my money and he said he'd given it to some woman called Gloria Shaw. She was Derek Layburn's replacement as the Minister in charge. That idiot Glass said he'd offered her my million to get his project passed." Clarence suddenly became angry again. "That bitch stole my money." He was breathing heavily now and again took on a faraway look.

Clarence stared at Steve. He pointed his index finger at the DCI. "She stole my money and didn't even have a plan." There was silence as Clarence gathered his thoughts.

"I'm going to kill Glass you know. I'd have it planned by now but you lot stole my gun." Clarence was winding down. He looked tired. In a soft, almost exhausted voice, he said, "Then that thug turned up today. He said I knew too much."

To everyone's surprise, Clarence's voice rose in volume. "Of course, I know too much; I'm a genius! I know a lot more than any of you. He said I had to be disposed of to make sure I didn't tell anyone about the bribes." Clarence seemed on a roll. "Rodney Glass said this woman had had money from him before for helping with planning." He suddenly stopped, the volume of his voice dropped, and his chin rested on his chest.

Steve thought his performance was like turning a tap on and off.

"But she didn't have a plan. No, I'm the one with the plan, but you shouldn't have found me." Clarence again started to chant over and over in a low almost indistinguishable voice "How did you find me. You are all inferior."

Steve allowed this to continue for several minutes but it was clear Clarence had left the real world. The interview was over.

The DCI looked at the solicitor while Clarence continued with his chant. The solicitor shrugged his shoulders and started to pack away the file he had in front of him. A file he hadn't opened.

With Clarence sitting mumbling, Steve asked the officer standing by the door to escort Clarence back to his holding cell.

"Poor chap." The solicitor stood to leave. "I realised early on he needed help. I'll file a no-plea motion with the CPS on the grounds of insanity. From what we've witnessed I don't think it'll be an issue. I don't suppose you'll oppose it?"

"He's been charged with three counts of murder plus possession of an unlicenced firearm, but I don't imagine he'll ever see the inside of a courtroom." Steve and The Cap gathered up their papers, The Cap handed a copy of the tape to Clarence's solicitor and all three men walked out slowly.

***

Steve and The Cap were sitting in Steve's office talking about the interview with Clarence. The Cap looked at Steve and said, "I had a terrible job writing up my notes. How do you record a confession by a nutter?"

"With difficulty, but make sure you keep your notes. I hear Poppy typing away so you must have written something down." Steve was sitting back in his chair. He still felt tired but was pleased to have closed the double murder.

"You'd better get onto the Murder Squad handling the taxi driver case. Tell them we've got the culprit and have Poppy send the SIO a copy of Clarence's confession."

The DCI had another thought. "Oh, change the charge sheet on Tommy Gunn. We'll go with threatening behaviour and affray but strike out the attempted murder charge." The Cap didn't really agree but knew not to argue when Steve had made up his mind.

"Right Steve. What about the bribery allegations? You're not just going to leave it?"

"No. I'll have to go up and see Alfie now. He'll love it."

As Steve made to leave, Twiggy appeared in the doorway. She was carrying a file that looked very imposing.

"Are you going upstairs?" She directed her question to Steve.

"I was thinking about it but maybe you've got a reason I shouldn't?"

All three sat down. For a moment Steve thought back to the time all three were thrown together and formed the Special Resolutions Unit. Not only were all three still able to work together but the unit had prospered and done some good work. Surprisingly, he felt sentimental but proud. As Twiggy cleared her throat, he snapped out of his daydream.

"I've checked into CEL. They're clean on the surface but a lot of money seems to get converted to cash. They've got bank accounts all over Europe and in the Far East. On the surface, it looks OK. They file their accounts and annual returns on time, pay their taxes and generally are clean."

"Go on, Twiggy." The Cap was sitting well back in his chair balancing it on two legs. "You've got more."

"Yes. As I said, a lot of money is being turned into cash. Now that's not unusual in the building trade but the amounts are staggering. We're talking millions. I've gone back as far as I could in the time and found a transfer of one million yesterday. It went to an intermediary who specialises in turning paper into cash. Like I said, not unusual in that industry but when you gave me Gloria Shaw's name, I checked her accounts. Four lots of two hundred and fifty thousand were paid in cash into accounts controlled by her yesterday. She's set them up as nominee accounts, but I discovered she's the beneficiary. It's too much of a coincidence."

Steve entered one of his deep-thought modes. He sat back with his fingers steepled in front of his face. He made a decision and startled his colleagues by jumping out of his chair.

"Come on Twiggy, we'll both go upstairs."

***

Once they were seated in the Commander's office, they told him about Clarence's confession and Tommy Gunn's confirmation concerning Colonial and English Land Inc.'s involvement in his attack on Clarence. Twiggy explained what she'd found and after a good-natured discussion, the Commander agreed to pass everything on to the Fraud Squad.

"You know. It always amazes me how greedy people are when I hear things like this. I presume, Miss Rough, that you'll help out the Fraud Squad when they get the case?"

"Yes sir. I've told my superior at the Treasury, and he's cleared me to work on this."

The Commander looked satisfied. "Good. No doubt you'll put them away for a long time. I know the new Anti-Corruption Unit will be all over this. I don't suppose the Prime Minister will be too happy either. Bribery in high places." Alfie paused and looked at Steve and Twiggy.

"You'd better get started Miss Rough and put an end to this Colonial and English Land's illegal activities. They seem to be the only outstanding arrests."

Twiggy and Steve left with the Commander's 'well done' ringing in their ears.

The team agreed to celebrate the conclusion of the cases later in the week and the DCI went home to keep his promise to his wife of being home in good time for his evening meal. He bought a bottle of red from the off-licence knowing he'd drink most of it. Alison had reduced her alcohol intake because of the baby. He looked forward to a relaxing night and an early bed that he told himself he had truly earned. He'd no idea what tomorrow would bring.

Chapter Thirty-Three

Wednesday the 26th of October started normally for the DCI. Breakfast with his wife and a brisk walk to his office. He'd allowed himself to dally at home knowing his desk was clear except for some paperwork to tidy up. Because of his dalliance, he arrived later than usual, at 09.12 a.m.

As he arrived, he saw Poppy hard at work at her desk but there was no sign of The Cap. The DCI smiled to himself, *typical*.. Steve took an extra forty minutes of leisure time after wrapping up the caseload, but The Cap would take an hour.

Poppy looked up. "Good morning, sir. The Commander would like to see you at ten this morning."

"Thanks, Poppy. Anything else?"

"No sir. After the last few days, it's nice to have a bit of peace and quiet."

Steve agreed as he entered his office. He sat and looked at his desk. He opened various bits of mail, sighed at some of the rubbish that came through the internal system and had his desk cleared again by 09.27 a.m.

The Cap arrived bearing coffee and set to clearing his own desk.

"Cap, did you talk with the SIO on the Murder squad about the taxi driver?" Steve shouted through to the outer office.

"Not yet, I'll do it now." The DCI, although not pleased with The Cap's tardiness, said nothing. "What about changing Tommy Gunn's charge sheet?"

"I'm on it."

Steve sighed. He liked things done then and there and occasionally found The Cap's attitude to instructions frustrating. But he told himself, that was Abul.

***

297

At ten a.m. the DCI was ushered into the Commander's office by his dragon of a secretary, to be greeted by Commander Alfie Brooks and, surprisingly, Chief Superintendent Charles of Human Resources.

A full pot of coffee sat on Alfie's conference table plus three cups and surprise, surprise, a plate of biscuits. Steve was immediately suspicious. Coffee and biscuits plus Human Resources didn't feel right.

All three men paid lip service to the formalities before sitting down at Alfie's table. Steve sat facing his more senior officers. After Alfie had poured the coffee and offered the biscuits around, he leant back and crossed his arms looking at Steve.

"First of all, Steve, the Commissioner sends her heartfelt thanks. She was on TV last night announcing we had a result in the Layburn case. She didn't go into detail but was really pleased with your efforts. She has also asked me to tell you, well done for clearing up two very difficult cases in just ten days. I've made her aware that most officers couldn't have achieved what you have. Both these cases were difficult and to get results in such a short period was amazing. Everyone is delighted, so very well done."

Steve flushed up with embarrassment. He did however recall the arguments he'd had with the Commander over the past week and wondered where he would be now if he hadn't had the results he had.

Alfie carried on. "Chief Superintendent Charles here has already updated your file and we'll arrange a bit of a bash for next week." Alfie unfolded his arms and looked at Steve with a face that seemed to expect a response.

Steve was suspicious. Coffee and biscuits and now everything that had happened over the past week had been forgiven. As a detective, he smelt a rat.

"Thank you, sir," was all he said, leaving Alfie slightly lost.

The Commander recovered quickly. "Now Steve there's something else. Charles here has been receiving applications to join your unit from many very good junior officers." The Commander looked at the Chief Superintendent. "I think you said about three a week?"

"Yes."

"You've become a bit of a legend in your own lifetime, Steve, among ambitious junior ranks. That's why we were disappointed by DI

298

Ishmal at yesterday's briefing on the bullion job. It was clear he was out of his depth and that you were carrying him."

Steve opened his mouth to speak but Alfie cut him off.

"Your loyalty to your staff is one of the things that sets you apart from other heads of departments, but you can't go on shielding this officer. We feel he's not up to the standards you should be looking for, especially in light of our intention to expand the remit of Special Resolutions. I told you I knew he didn't have the mental agility to deal with the twists and turns of the bullion case. It was obvious to everyone at the meeting yesterday that it was you who solved the thing." Alfie paused and Steve remained silent. He knew The Cap was occasionally a bit below par, but he did have other qualities.

The Commander looked at Chief Superintendent Charles. "We've considered your DI's record and he will be transferred to Regional Liaison. We feel this area of policing is more suited to his approach to the job. His transfer will be effective from next Monday the 31st of October. He'll be notified in the usual way."

"And if I don't agree?"

"Steve, this is for your own good. You need people around you to take some of the load. You're a bloody good leader and a better detective but you can't carry every case by yourself. Let Abul go and move forward."

Steve knew Alfie spoke sense. He tried to defend The Cap but the weight of feeling against The Cap was overwhelming. In the end, the DCI agreed.

"Good. Now…" Alfie poured more coffee and helped himself to a biscuit. "I've had agreement that your unit will from now on have a mandate to cover every department in the Met that has issues with difficult cases. Also, you'll be first call on outside national operations, not just home counties and close by. I promised you I'd look at your manning levels and I have." Again, Alfie turned to the Chief Superintendent.

"As I said earlier, good quality ambitious officers are lining up to be transferred to your unit. We've had no difficulty in selecting the best." Charles started arranging files in front of him. Steve noticed, as he had at their previous meetings, how the Chief Superintendent managed to wear his uniform without creasing it. His high-pitched nasal voice hadn't changed either nor had his condescending attitude.

He produced a file with a flourish. "Number one, I think you know him, Detective Inspector Peter Jones. He's asked to join your unit on three separate occasions. I presume you have no problems with DI Jones. I understand he only finished his secondment to you yesterday."

In truth, Steve was delighted. "No sir, no problem."

Charles smiled and passed over Peter Jones' file. He was obviously pleased with himself.

"Second, Detective Sergeant Mathew Conway, another officer recently seconded to you. He has also requested to be attached to your unit several times. I presume you have no problems with this officer either?"

Steve felt all his Christmases had come at once. "No sir, no problem."

"Splendid." The Chief Superintendent now looked less sure. "As your unit is expanding both in manpower and responsibility, it is the Force's policy to nurture and encourage junior officers by assigning them a mentor. As the Commander has said, the junior ranks hold you in high regard. Therefore, we propose to assign Detective Constable Mary Dougan to you as the fourth member of your permanent team. She's a graduate entrant, very smart and needs exposure to the type of police work you excel at."

The Chief Superintendent passed Steve the file. From his expression, Steve guessed he was expecting a hard time persuading Steve to accept this DC.

"Fine. Thank you, sir, I've lost DI Ishmal but gained two officers plus a trainee. As a mentor, do I move up a pay grade?" This last remark was said without humour and sounded a sarcastic note.

Alfie stepped in. "You see, there you go again. You're admired by juniors but don't know how to respect your seniors. Over the last ten days, I could have seen you frogmarched down the road after all the crap and insubordination you've shovelled my way. You're lucky it was me in that chair." Alfie pointed to his desk. "I haven't long to go, and God help you, my successor won't take the crap that I have or put up with your lack of respect for the chain of command."

The Commander sat back and smiled at the DCI. "Still, you get results and make all of us on this floor look good. You also know how to pass the buck when you need to.

"I'm up to my armpits in paperwork with this African leader thing. The Home Office want to give him immunity but we're saying no. It's a real bugger's muddle and it's your doing, or rather your DI's. He shouldn't have charged right in. Anyway, water under the bridge. He'll still get his commendation for his work or rather your work on the case."

Alfie was back to his usual unflappable self. Steve didn't comment. "You've made the clear-up rate look good. A bullion robbery solved, a triple murder solved, a bribery case uncovered and a government scandal, all adds up to a good few days' work.

"I know the Prime Minister's not happy, and it looks like this Gloria Shaw will have to resign and is heading to the Courts."

Alfie laughed at his own words. "Now get off home to that wife of yours. Take a few days' leave. You deserve it. Get back in here Monday morning bright and fresh. Ready to take over your new team."

Alfie stood and warmly shook Steve's hand. "Good luck."

A slightly embarrassed DCI Steve Burt left Commander Alfie Brook's office on the twelfth floor of New Scotland Yard and headed straight for the exit. He thought about going to see The Cap but decided to let the wheels of the Force grind on. He'd call Abul later.

Once on the street, he found he had a spring in his step. Maybe the men from the twelfth floor were right. He needed freshening up. A new team and a bigger remit from Monday.

He stopped and bought flowers for Alison, together with a very expensive bottle of champagne and a plan for a few nights away in the country.

THE END

If you enjoyed reading *The Watchers* then look out for the next novel in the DCI Steve Burt Murder Mystery series. See how Steve's career progresses after he has cracked this case.

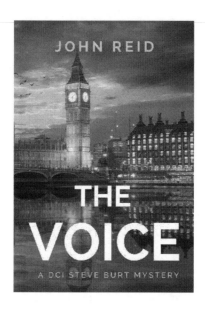

The world of warfare is changing, and a new weapons delivery system developed secretly in the UK is targeted by an international terrorist gang who set out to steal it on instructions from 'The Voice'. The Voice is a mysterious mastermind who uses an electronic device to disguise his voice and keep his identity hidden.

DCI Steve Burt is asked by his old Army Commander to search for his son, a serving Army officer who is missing. This unofficial inquiry becomes part of an official investigation and takes the DCI into a world of international intrigue, terrorism, murder and corruption at the highest level of government and the Metropolitan Police. The evidence always leads back to The Voice but who is he? Unearthing a phantom is a difficult task even for DCI Burt.

For further information go to www.steve-burt.com

Made in United States
Orlando, FL
13 April 2022